Adrian J Walker was born [illegible] of Sydney, Australia in the mid '70s. After his father found a camper van in a ditch, he renovated it and moved his family back to the UK, where Adrian was raised.

He now lives in London with his wife and two children. To find out more visit www.adrianjwalker.com.

COLOURS

PART I OF *EARTH INCORPORATED*

ADRIAN J WALKER

ISBN-10: 1533536813

ISBN-13: 978-1533536815

For Dad

SOMETIME

SOMEPLACE

SOMEHOW

PART ONE

take your seat

one

the girl and the gun

A STORY is built from the things that did not happen as much as from the things that did. Evolution is a history of failures; kingdoms fall because fear stills hearts; love wilts for words left unspoken. Sometimes it blossoms for the same.

If each of us is a story, then we are the story of the things we did not do. We are the shadows of quelled urges; negative imprints of missed trains, ignored smiles and unanswered letters.

We are the unwritten ink, coloured with events that never occurred.

And Steve Manager was never supposed to be Red.

'But if you don't have your Colours, how will we know who you are?'

Steve's mother sat down beside him on the white steps leading up to the Department of Human Resources. She pulled her cardigan around her small frame, in spite of the heat of another sweltering day. It had been a long summer and the ground was baking, the sky a blue sea filled with warmth. The last place Steve Manager wanted to be was here. The last thing he wanted to do was spend the day inside.

She moved closer so their shoulders were touching.

'We're all little boxes,' she explained. Her voice was warm and cracked, and it felt as if it existed only in the space between her mouth and his ear. 'That's what they say in there. All different;

completely separate from each other. We have to open you up and find out what's inside. Otherwise you could spend your whole life pretending to be something you're not.'

She smiled, nudging him.

'Your Colours stay with you for life, Steven. They shine out of you, letting everyone know what you're like and how to act around you. That way, everyone's happy.'

He had heard this many times before. Every child had, especially in the year of their Colours.

'Don't you want to know what you are?' she said.

Steve looked down at his gleaming shoes and the clean stone step, wishing they were bare feet and warm grass.

'I just want to be at the lake.'

At the lake with Holly, sailing her dinghy together for the last time. If only this air would start moving. He looked up at the tops of the trees growing in regiments along the white boulevard. The leaves were rigid; not a single leaf fluttered.

'I know you do,' said his mother.

'Can't I do this tomorrow?'

'I'm sorry, Steve. It's your sixteenth birthday. It has to be today.'

'But it's the last day. The last day before – '

'Shh,' she said, curling him into her neck like a swan. 'I know. I know, I know.'

He blinked, bursting a fat tear between his eyelids.

'Why do they have to go?' he said.

'You know why.'

'I still don't understand it.'

She sighed.

'Holly's father has been fired for insubordination. He has – '

'I don't understand what that means.'

'It means he didn't do what was asked of him. He didn't follow the rules.'

'Like Dad, you mean.'

The mention of his father stopped her short. She took her

arm from his shoulder and tightened her cardigan.

'Your father was just doing what he thought was right.'

She took a quivering breath.

'He would have been so proud of you, Steve.'

'You say it like he's dead.'

Silence again. The sharpness of his words surprised him, and he sensed his mother's face turning away.

'I'm sorry,' he said at last.

'It's all right,' she said, standing up. 'Come on, you'll be late.'

Steve squinted at his mother's silhouette.

'Holly said the same thing,' he said. 'She said Granton was just doing what he thought was right.'

'Mr Granton is her father, of course she –'

'Director Granton.'

'Not any more.'

He scraped his heel on a step.

'I still don't understand why they *all* have to go,' he said. 'We were allowed to stay, weren't we?'

'It's because of his position. Your father was just a manager, but for a director, the disgrace of being fired passes to every member of the family. They must all leave. They must all join the Hordes.'

'They're saying things at school.'

'What kind of things?'

'Bad things. About the Hordes. About what they'll do to Holly's dad when they're outside. About what they'll do to Holly.'

A cloud appeared in the sky behind her head.

'Children can be very cruel,' she said. Steve looked back at his feet. He felt his mother's hands on his shoulders.

'You'll meet other girlfriends,' she said.

'She's not my girlfriend.'

'Well, then, you'll make other friends. Now please, Steve, we can't be late.'

He took her hand and she led him up the steps.

'We're having a party afterwards,' she said. 'Your grandfather has a present for you.'

The present had been a gun. Holly had not liked it.

Later, in their small apartment now bursting with family, Steve sat cross-legged at his grandfather's feet. The gun lay across the old man's lap. There was a flag of some nation embossed upon its barrel — a strange, old symbol on a strange, old relic. Flags, nations; such things no longer existed. Even the words were relics.

The old man rubbed his chin.

'So you got Red, huh?' he said in his sandpaper voice. 'Never figured you for a *Red*.'

'Not just Red,' said Steve. 'I'm 26.3% Blue.'

'We haven't had a Red in the family since my Great Uncle Ely. And the least said about him the better.'

There were hoots of laughter from a huddle of aunts in the corner.

'Walter!'

His mother's voice, still dizzy with pride, cried out above the clatter of pans and chatter of relatives in the kitchen. Her face appeared in the doorway.

'Stop it, please, you'll scare him!'

'All right, Norma. All right.'

She smiled at Steve – her chest swelling – then returned to her cooking.

'I have to say,' said his grandfather. 'I always thought you were going to be a straight-up Blue, just like your father.'

'I am Blue, I said–'

'100% down the line Blue, just like me.'

He eyed him doubtfully, then grunted.

'Well, I guess he would have been proud of you either way,

fine young man that you are. Now listen, you're lucky, son; you were born into a fine corporation. And you need to remember what you must do to ensure that it remains that way for your kids.'

He bent down, narrowing his eyes.

'What do we make, son?' His voice had somehow found an even lower register in which to grind.

'Technology,' replied Steve.

'No.'

His grandfather slapped the barrel of the gun.

'We make money. *Money*. Understand?'

Steve nodded.

'*Money* is what we make,' his grandfather repeated. 'The Market demands it and, if we provide it, we're looked upon favourably. Simple; no guesswork, no risk, no faith.'

He leant closer.

'And who knows?' he said. 'Maybe now that you're a *Red*, you can bring some of that money back here.'

He glanced at the kitchen.

'You know it's been hard since your father was fired. And your mother's done her best in the circumstances.'

Steve looked around the apartment. He knew his mother had spent all day cleaning it, clearing space and making sure only their best ornaments - of which there were few - were on display.

'Now, it's up to you,' said his grandfather, eyes twinkling. 'But mark my words, son –'

He raised his voice, and one thick, coarse-skinned finger.

'You'd better make a lot of friends because Reds ain't short on enemies.'

'Walter!' scolded his mother again.

His grandfather waved her off.

'All right, all right. Here, *Red*.'

He held up the gun.

'Here's your gift. It's yours. Take it.'

Steve reached for the gun, but his grandfather snatched it back and landed a swift clip on his ear. He adjusted it, closer to his belly.

'Too slow, Red. If you want something, you'd better take it! And if someone won't give it to you – '

He bent down.

' – then – '

Steve saw his chance and lunged, punching the old man's belly with his right fist and snatching the gun with his left.

'Good!' the old man wheezed, bent double. 'Good man! Maybe you are Red after all!'

After he had endured the parade of kisses and hair ruffles, Steve snuck away from the party and hopped on a train to Holly's house. It was hot and the whole street was buzzing with bugs, hoses and bike chains. He found Director Granton clearing out the garage. They weren't allowed to take much with them, only a few bags. The rest was laid out for the neighbours to pick through, although not many wanted to be seen taking a fired family's cast-offs.

'Hi, Director Granton. Is Holly about?'

Granton looked up and scratched his balding scalp. His arms were long and lean and his ragged T-shirt clung to his back in sweaty patches. He seemed like a man who was merely moving house, not preparing for extradition. He smiled and heaved an old chest out from under a workbench.

'Help me with this and I'll tell you.'

Steve took one end.

'So, what did you get?' said Granton.

'Red/Blue,' said Steve.

'Huh,' said Granton. 'Didn't figure you for a Red. Good combo, though, congratulations. You'll go far, I'm sure. Did they try the wait with you?'

'What do you mean?' Steve said.

'The *wait.* After your Colours. You know, it's a trick. Did they leave you in a room and ask you to stay where you were?'

Steve frowned as he shuffled backwards with the chest.

He *had* been asked to wait on his own. After the tests — all those questions and pictures and role plays and thought experiments – the examiner had left the room.

'Stay sitting down,' she had said. 'By no account are you to leave this chair. I will only be gone an hour or so.'

Then the door had closed and he had been left in a quiet room staring at a plush carpet. It was hot and his collar was sticky. His muscles twitched. The window was behind him and outside was the warm day – the only day he had left with Holly. They should have been sailing on the lake; that was the only thing these last hours were for, the spray of cool water, the thump of the bow on a wake and the sail swollen with wind.

The wind – had it picked up yet?

By no account are you to leave this chair.

He stared at the carpet, flexed his toes in his stiff shoes, felt the sweat trickle on his neck and warmth of the sun – what was that wind doing? He had barely lasted sixty seconds before bursting out of the chair to see. A moment later the examiner had returned with the results.

'It was a trick?' said Steve.

'Of course,' said Granton. 'How long did you last?'

'I don't know. A minute?'

Granton burst out laughing, almost dropping his end of the crate.

'A *minute*? Holy shit, son, I'm not surprised they gave you Red. One minute, well, I'll be damned.'

'It was a test?'

'Yeah, one of many. They wanted to see how obedient you are. Here's just fine.'

They set the chest down near the door. Granton took off his

cap and scratched his head.

'You know, those tests – they can easily tip the balance on your score. Did you know you can appeal?'

'Why would I want to appeal?'

'If you think they scored you wrong. Why did you get up so quickly, anyhow?'

Steve thought about it and shrugged.

'I guess I'm not very obedient.'

'No, I guess not,' said Granton, doubtfully, replacing his cap. 'You and me both, son, you and me both.'

'Where will you go?' said Steve.

'Ah, don't you worry about that. I wasn't born into Directorship, you know; I earned it. And there are two ways to do that, son: you either make a lot of friends or you make a lot of enemies. I went with friends. And I'll make friends outside too; you mark my words. I'm going to look after my family. I'm going to look after Holly.'

He laid a hand on his shoulder.

'She's going to miss you, son.'

Steve felt the corners of his mouth tug down, but he kept them straight. *Even then*, he would remember, much later, *even then, that very same day, I was already wearing my Colours. I stopped myself from crying.*

He gritted his teeth and nodded.

'Listen,' said Granton. 'You're Red like me, so you'll do well here. You'll be ambitious; you won't let people hold you back. You'll disobey the rules that stop you getting where you want to go. And all that's fine, all that is *fine*.'

He sighed.

'But you're going into the mire, son. You're going to see some things you won't like, and not everything that happens here is right. So if you want my advice, one Red to another, then here it is: when you see something that you think is wrong, don't turn your back, don't pretend it's not happening. You shout stop. And you shout it as loudly as you can, you hear me?'

'Like you did?'

Granton smiled.

'You need to ask yourself what you want, Steve.'

He nodded up at the bright sky.

'Do you want to be up there?'

Steve turned. He could just make out the gigantic outline of The Leaf shimmering in the heat haze. He looked back at Granton.

'I just want to be with my friends,' he said.

Granton gave him a strange look.

'Somehow I think this corporation has other plans for you, son.'

He placed a finger on Steve's chest.

'But you have a good heart, Steve. Pay attention to it and you'll be fine. Make friends, son. Make *a lot* of friends.'

He nodded at the door, where Steve had propped his gun.

'Is that your gift?' he said.

'Yeah,' said Steve.

'Wowzers. Heavy. What kind is it?'

'I don't know. An old one, I guess.'

Granton knelt back at the chest.

'Well,' he said, rummaging. 'Let me see now.'

He drove his hand to the bottom and fished out a box. He blew the dust from the lid.

'Here. Why don't you take this, too? A gun for your Red, and this for your Blue.'

Steve took the box. It felt leathery and delicate. He went to lift the lid, but Granton stopped him.

'Open it tomorrow, when everything's died down.'

'You'll be gone tomorrow. I won't be able to thank you.'

'So thank me now, idiot.'

'Thank you.'

'That's all right. Come here.'

They hugged and Granton pushed him away, scuffing his head.

'Now you'd better get down to the lake. My daughter's waiting for you. Oh, and Steve?'

'Yes, Director Granton?' whirling round halfway down the driveway.

'Check the pack they gave you. The appeal form's at the back.'

He found Holly at the jetty on the south bank, where the reeds grew tall. Her toes were dangling in the still water. The dinghy was moored tightly beside her like a dog.

'Hi,' he said, catching his breath.

'Hey,' she said, squinting up at him in the evening sun. She blew a fly from her bare arm.

Steve surveyed the glassy lake.

'Nothing, huh?'

'Nada,' said Holly. 'Not a mouse fart.'

Steve took off his jacket and shoes, rolled up the sleeves of his shirt and the legs of his chinos and sat down next to her, bumping her shoulder with his. He looked down at his reflection in the water.

'You're not wearing your necktie?'

'Nah, not yet. It's being made. I get it next week.'

'Good. I'll be gone. I won't be here to see it.'

'Don't you want to know what I got?'

'Nope.'

'Why?'

'Because.'

'Because what?'

He looked at her sideways. Her face shone with rippling light and the freckles of ten hot summer weeks were already peeling from her shoulders. She was pulling her lips taut, twisting the dimples in her cheeks so that the whole bottom part of her face was a knot of thin muscle. He knew what this meant — she was stopping herself.

'Because I already *know* your Colours, that's why. Your real ones, not the ones they give you.'

Steve looked away then. He dipped a big toe in the water and watched the circles travel through his reflection, splintering his face, knowing already how much he would regret not saying anything back.

He showed her the gun.

'What do you think?' he said.

She tucked a stray lock of red hair behind her ear and inspected the barrel.

'Ugly,' she said, wrinkling her nose. 'It's ugly.'

'It's shiny,' Steve replied, hopefully.

'I think you should lose it.'

'I can't. It's a gift. And it's valuable.'

She leant back on her elbows and closed her eyes to the sun.

'Aren't you afraid?' said Steve.

'There's no point in being afraid,' she said. 'So I'm not going to be.'

'You can't choose not to be afraid.'

'Yes, you can.'

She sighed and lay back with her hands covering her eyes.

'Just tell me one last story,' she said. So he did.

There was a party at Holly's house that evening. Friends and neighbours were there, a grill outside, some lanterns lit and thrown up into the warm night to sail over the lake. When it was getting late, Steve leant against their white picket fence and watched Granton dance with his wife on the lawn, their eyes locked, his arms tightly around her, dangling a beer bottle against the small of her back. As they turned, Granton caught

Steve looking and winked. Steve looked away, embarrassed, and sidled off to look for Holly.

He found her in her usual spot on the roof, looking out at the squadron of orange lights disappearing over the water. They said nothing. After a while he felt her moving closer; the warmth of her face next to his. Then she put her hand on his. Dizzy at her touch, he turned to kiss her, but she flinched, and suddenly one perfect moment had become another one entirely.

Steve flushed and got to his feet.

'I'm sorry,' he murmured, and ran, stumbling away.

He heard Granton shouting after him as he pushed through the gate.

'Steve? What's going on?'

The sounds of the dying party disappeared as he scrabbled up the drive. He thought he should stop and go back. Maybe she would be there on the roof, calling for him, waving, laughing. Come back, it had all just been a mistake. He thought he should stop, but he didn't. He ran.

The next morning, Steve made one last visit to the lake. His embarrassment from the night before was still raw and he didn't know if he would have the courage to visit Holly. He thought the sight of her face might make him run again, and Reds didn't run.

But he wanted to be there in the same space as her, near the water and their boat, before she left.

He dawdled by the willow trees and the long grass, keeping a safe distance from the house. Eventually, he found a place to sit on the small hill that looked down at the street. People were walking in and out of the house, making last-minute preparations before they left. He saw Director Granton carrying a suitcase out front. The security van that would take them away was already at the house.

He took out the box that Granton had given him. He knew he was supposed to wait, but he couldn't. He lifted the lid. Inside was an old mechanical dial. Its silver plating shone in the daylight. It looked like a watch, but had only a single needle, and in place of the numbers were the letters N, E, S and W.

He put the box back in his pocket and pulled out a piece of paper from his jacket, which he unfolded. It was embossed with the sleek and powerful emblem of the Department of Human Resources. He read down the sheet.

All appeals must be made within one week of your Colours. Please complete this form to the best of your ability, ensuring –

There was a noise from the street and he looked down to see Holly. She wasn't alone. She was surrounded by some other boys and girls, some of whom he recognised. They were from the class he would start the following week; his peers for the gruelling three-year induction into the corporation.

They were smiling, all apart from Holly, who was standing with her hands by her side in the middle of the circle. A tall boy with blonde hair stepped forward and pushed her on the shoulder. She staggered into another, who pushed her back. Holly hung her head, and their laughter carried up the hill.

'Good luck, *Horde*,' Steve heard one of them say, to more laughter. They pushed her some more, sending her stumbling between them.

Granton's voice rang in his ears.

...you see something that you think is wrong, don't turn your back. You shout stop.

Steve stood up and took a breath. His grandfather's words now:

You know it's been hard since your father was fired...your mother's done her best in the circumstances...now, it's up to you...

He faltered. Then Holly saw him. She had tears on her face. The tall boy looked round and saw him too. He grinned.

'This is just a bit of fun, man. It's all just a bit of fun.'

…better make a lot of friends because Reds ain't short on enemies.

You shout stop.

But Steve didn't shout stop. He didn't say a word. He closed his mouth, turned and ran, leaving the appeal form fluttering in the grass.

TWENTY YEARS LATER

two

a single name

He had stumbled, and that was regrettable, but there was no need to worry. It was fixable. Everything would be all right.

It was Monday morning, early, and The Leaf's cavernous glass lobby was hushed. The only sound was the occasional hiss of distant footsteps upon the mosaic floor, or the twitter of parakeets and starlings flitting between the enormous Redwoods above. Nine trees grew in the central strip, their canopies shrouded in clouds of mist like the pendulous webs of giant spiders.

The lobby smelled of fresh timber, steel and ice, a scent that had been carefully tuned over the two centuries since The Leafen Corporation's formation. The aim was to produce a precise effect in its employees and visiting dignitaries: a mixture of power, peace, possibility and – most importantly – danger.

It was said that Daniel Leafen himself, on that cold winter morning when he had taken his father's place as president, had remarked upon the smell, stopping in his tracks on the way to the ceremony and uttering those immortal words:

'I feel as if I'm walking through an ancient forest by a deep waterfall. There are wolves nearby.'

Steve Manager stood before the elevator doors and looked up at the immense structure through which he was about to rise. All his life had led to this point. Every decision he had made, every deal he had cut, every hand he had shaken, every back he had stabbed and every advantage he had taken – it had all been for this moment.

But, now, all he could feel was that very same presence – danger, threat, something wild and out of his control. And the trouble was, the smell had nothing to do with it.

What had everything to do with it was currently flying east, fuming. He could still hear the slam of his office door, the thunder of footsteps disappearing down the corridor as he sat, bewildered, staring at the piece of paper before him and wondering what he had just done.

But this was fixable. It had to be; two years working on the deal of his life couldn't end like this.

Just a blip, he told himself. *Just stress.*

A gigantic news ticker streamed by above the long stretch of reception desks.

GRANTON FOUND DEAD IN NORTH-EAST HORDELANDS

LEAFEN MOURNS DISGRACED DIRECTOR TWENTY YEARS AFTER FIRING

Just stress. Or the mention of a name.

He shook himself from his gloom. This was not the behaviour of a 99th percentile Executive Class Red/Blue. Logic and determination were the tools he needed now. Not fretting. Not regret. A single call and an apology would set things straight. He just had to get through this meeting first. He just had to endure the wolves.

Everything would be *all right.*

He heard heels on marble and a tall woman appeared next to him. Her hair was scraped back and bunched into a tight coil impaled with a wooden stake. She wore a red dress and red shoes. She always wore red.

'Manager,' she said.

'Priscilla,' he replied. Her lips tightened.

'Miss Mandrek,' Steve corrected.

'Is everything all right?' she asked.

'Yes.'

'You seem a little nervous.'

'It's not every day I get to meet the President. That's a lovely dress.'

Priscilla gave a little grunt of approval. She pressed the button to call the elevator.

'I just passed a senior executive from Soor at the 13th Atrium,' she said. '*Your* atrium. It was Commander Po, I believe, although they all look alike.'

She waited. Steve said nothing.

'He looked – somewhat unhappy,' said Priscilla.

Steve turned to his superior. Her neck was craned, her taut and brutal body stretching like a bundle of wires inside the scarlet leather dress. She looked more like a giraffe than a person. A steel giraffe. A carnivorous giraffe. *A ferocious, long-toothed, well-maintained –*

'Why did he look unhappy, Manager?' she said.

Steve smiled.

'They always look unhappy,' he said. 'It's part of their culture.'

Priscilla gave another grunt and her ligaments loosened. She glanced at his briefcase.

'He did *sign*?' she said.

Steve's stomach lurched. There was the slam of his office door again, the furious footsteps marching away.

'Of course,' he said, much too quickly.

Priscilla turned and folded her arms. A treacherous line of cleavage darkened before Steve's eyes.

'I hardly need to remind you how important this deal is,' she said.

'You need not. I'm the one who's been working on it for the past two years, after all.'

'Soor are a very powerful defence corporation. They are not to be trifled with.'

'I'm well aware of their history.'

'Good. Because the consequences of this deal going sour would be disastrous. For the corporation.'

She leaned closer.

'And for you, *Manager*.'

He fixed her glare, smiled and patted his briefcase.

'One piece of paper. Two signatures. Everything went smoothly.'

'Smoothly,' she repeated.

They battled out the stare – her eyelids squeezing like nutcrackers, his throat straining to swallow.

The elevator pinged and the doors opened.

'Excellent,' said Priscilla, suddenly producing a smile you would only expect to see on somebody pushing out a shit the size of a breeze block. She held out a hand. 'After you.'

'I insist,' countered Steve.

He closed his eyes and took a breath, then followed Priscilla into the glass elevator. The doors closed and, within seconds, skyscrapers shrank beneath them. He watched the horizon bend as if a vice was crushing the earth.

Everything would be all right.

Everything would be *all right*.

Everything would be all right.

three

truck

'SHIT, APRIL,' called Sam from the floor. 'Where the hell did you get this thing?' A spanner clanged on the concrete and Sam scrambled out on his trolley. He frowned and wiped a misshapen metal cylinder on a rag.

'You know your sprockets are shot?' he said. 'And – fuck – I don't even know what this thing is called.' He stood up and tucked the rag into his belt. 'But it's just about sheared in eight places. I don't know what the hell you're thinking of doing with this shit heap but it sure as hell ain't driving.'

April Knight flicked her front teeth with a nail.

'Are you going to tell me where you got it?' said Sam. 'I know you didn't buy it. No offence, but a limo driver doesn't earn enough to buy antiques.'

'You'd be surprised what I make in tips,' said April.

A sound like tectonic plates came from somewhere behind them.

'Hey, Sam,' said the voice.

April turned to see a man with a grin the size of a dinner plate, one front incisor gold with a red tip. He gave April a single slow nod, his shoulders avalanching as he did.

'Hello, Ape.'

'Hi, Marco,' said April.

'Marco, what do you want?' said Sam.

'Gonzo wants you.'

Sam frowned and shook his head.

'Who the fuck's Gonzo?' he bellowed.

The forklift whined and the crate fell. Sam winced.

Marco turned his huge palms.

'How should I know?'

He smiled at April as he loped away.

'Take care, Ape.'

The forklift's servos spun as its forks hit the deck.

'Hey, Jerry,' yelled Sam. 'Do me a solid and pick up the box yourself.'

The forklift juddered to a halt. Its driver peered out from the cabin, hands still on the levers.

'Boss?' he said. He glanced at April.

'I said, pick up the box yourself,' growled Sam. 'It's only full of titanium fuse washers; a six-year-old could lift it.'

The driver, Jerry, scampered down from the cabin and ran around the front. He cowered a little as he passed his boss, reminding April of a dog running through an open door. Sam shook his head as the youngster lifted the box, stumbled back, then let the weight of it carry him forward to the supply shelf, where it landed on a stack of steel pipes. Two of them clattered at his feet. Jerry yelped and pulled his finger from underneath the box. There were some laughs and jeers from the other side of the workshop.

'Sorry, boss,' said Jerry. He sucked his finger and looked at April.

'Hi, April,' he said.

April raised her eyebrows and smiled.

'Hello, Jerry,' she said.

More laughs and whistles from the back.

'Quiet, y'fuckin' morons!' Sam shouted. He sighed and shook his head.

'Just clear up this mess, dumbo,' he said. Jerry did as he was told.

'I know it needs some work, Sam,' said April. 'But I didn't come here for a check-up. I just want to know if you have the parts.'

'Parts?' said Sam. 'Which parts? I could write you a list.' He started counting his fingers. 'Optic capacitors, flumes, it doesn't even have a sorameter – '

'You know the ones,' she said.

Sam stopped and put his hands back on his hips, where they spent most of their time when he was speaking to April. He let out another frustrated sigh.

'Yeah, I know the ones,' he said. 'Shit, April.'

'Well?' she said, flashing him a bright smile. 'Do you?'

'Yeah, April, I got some.'

April took a deep breath of hot air laced with machine oil and welding fumes. Her cheeks flushed and her eyes shone.

'Thanks, Sam,' she whispered.

Sam shook his head.

'Sure, whatever.'

He looked her up and down.

'Why are you in your leathers? You're not working today?'

'Nope. I was on night shift. I just dropped my last ride off at the airport. Soorish guy.'

'Bad luck. I know *those* guys ain't famous for their tips.'

She frowned.

'No. He was weird, actually.'

'Oh yeah? What kind of weird?'

'I don't know, exactly. He was in a hurry, didn't say a word.'

'Yeah, well, they're not famous for small talk either.'

'You know my two rules in the limo?'

'Yeah, don't slam the doors and don't fart.'

'Aha, well, he broke both of them within the first minute.'

'Bad luck.'

'And he was angry. Really angry. Red-faced, sweating, shaking. He just seemed to want to – I don't know – get out of Leafen.'

Sam sighed.

'Yeah, well, I never did understand foreigners. Anyway, where are you going? Aren't you sticking around for The Hiring?'

'No way. I'm taking a ride.'

Sam's eyes narrowed.

'April, you'd better not be going where I think you're going.'

'There's no law against it.'

'Yeah. Yeah, there is. Why do you think the security drones are out there? Shit, April, I've told you a million times it's dangerous being that close to the Fabrik, if – wait a minute – '

He looked round at the hunk of metal behind him.

'Is that what this piece of junk is about?'

'Sam, wait – '

'You're going to drive off the grid and beat the drones?'

'It's not – '

Sam the rag from his belt and threw it down on the concrete.

'Do you have any *idea* how much trouble you'll be in if they catch you?'

'I have to go.'

'You have to go, sure you always have to – '

'Can you keep it for me? Just for today.'

'This thing?' said Sam. He heaved a sigh. 'Sure. If numb-nuts here doesn't smash it to bits with his toy crane. Hey, quit gawping and clean up, Jerry!'

Jerry snapped his slack mouth shut and busied himself with the steel rods.

April kissed Sam on his rough cheek.

'Thanks, I owe you.'

She skipped down the alley, waving over her head. Sam watched her go.

'You don't owe me anything, April,' he said to himself. 'You never will.'

He turned back.

'You done yet?' he yelled.

'Almost, boss,' said Jerry.

'Good. And hey, shit-for-brains. If I catch you ogling my daughter like that again, I'll stick that crane's forks so far up y'ass you'll be – '

four

everything as it should be

'I'M NOT hungry.'

Demetri Trittek watched his younger brother push his plate away.

'Eat your breakfast, Alex,' said his mother. 'Eat your food. And turn off your Fronds!'

'I'm talking to Mike,' said Alex.

'Turn them off!'

'Why?' said Alex. Curtains of hair hung in greasy ropes around his bum-fluffed face.

'Alex,' warned his father, without looking up from his eggs.

'Because we don't have Fronds on at the breakfast table,' said his mother.

Alex rolled his eyes. He glanced at Demetri, then held his palm to his nose and wobbled it twice. His Fronds – the glowing synaptic network in his neck – faded. Demetri grinned at him and winked.

Everyone had their own signature, a unique gesture that activated and deactivated their Fronds. Most were the brunt of mockery at some point. It was always amusing to see someone's for the first time, seeing as they were usually the product of a child's imagination — whatever brief obsession or impulse had been firing when their innocent, infant selves had chosen it. Demetri had seen raspberries, kisses, nose-grabs, tongues, slaps, curtsies, mouthed words, wiggles, foot-stamps, winks, cross-eyes, nods and every kind of funny face imaginable. He had once seen a Double-Red Executive Manager (Military Class) mime a telescope pointing skyward, a Yellow thrust her fists down to her sides and glare, a Green/Blue spin on the spot, one hand on his hip and the other pointing above his head. The joke never lasted, though, because everyone had one. It was part of the brand.

What's Your Signature?

The slogan had lasted for over a century.

Alex scowled at Demetri.

'Yours too.'

'I can't,' said Demetri. 'They're not working.'

His father looked up.

'What's wrong with them?'

'I don't know, they just wouldn't boot this morning.'

'Did you update?' asked his mother. 'I always tell you, update, update, update. If you don't update, you're not – '

Up to date, chorused Demetri and Alex.

'I know, Ma, and I always do. They're just not working.'

A nasty little grin appeared on Alex's face.

'No music, no film, no news, no social,' he said. 'Sucks for you.'

Demetri smiled back.

'It's no big deal. Some of us aren't as *reliant* on them as others.'

The grin retreated and Alex threw a piece of mushroom at his brother. Demetri swatted it off with a laugh.

'Hey!' growled their father.

'Eat your *breakfast*, Alex,' said his mother.

'Sit up straight, Alex,' said his father. 'And listen to your mother.'

Alex began to tap his foot.

'You're always telling me to do things I don't want to do.'

'You have to learn, boy. That's part of life. Once you get your Colours, you'll understand.'

'My *Colours* – ' scoffed Alex. His foot tapped faster.

His mother took the pan to the table and spooned another helping of eggs onto her husband's plate. Demetri raised his hand as she went to fill his.

'No thanks, Ma.'

Her shoulders fell and she rasped a sigh.

'Why I *bother*,' she said, trudging back to the stove. 'Why? I swear you all starve.'

Demetri's father looked between him and Alex, prodding his fork at each in turn.

'You boys should eat your eggs. Especially you,' he flicked his head at Demetri. 'You're too skinny. You'll never find a girlfriend looking like a weather vane.'

'Dad, please – ' said Demetri.

'I'm serious, girls like a bit of meat on their men. Just ask your mother.'

'Not that much meat,' muttered his mother. She turned to Demetri. 'You don't want a girlfriend, Miti? You're part Yellow, all the girls love a Yellow.'

'It's not that,' he shrugged, standing. 'I just haven't met anyone special.'

His father grunted.

'If you want my advice, find yourself a nice Green – Double if you can – and settle down.'

'Honestly, Walter,' huffed his mother, dumping another ladle of eggs on his plate. 'Listen to me, Miti. Don't waste your time trying to find someone special. You just need to find someone who thinks *you're* special.'

She smiled.

'Just like I do.'

'I have to go,' said Demetri. He got up and kissed his mother on the cheek.

'When you coming home again?'

'Dinner next Saturday, OK?' he said.

'Put it in my calendar.'

He tapped the back of his neck.

'I will, once these babies are fixed.'

'I'm serious, Dad,' said Alex, turning back to his father. 'What's the point of me getting my Colours? They're stupid.'

'The point?' said his father, chewing. He shared a look with his wife.

'The point is you find out who you are, learn your trade and take your seat.' A sliver of egg made a bid for escape, but he slurped it back through his lips. 'Just like everybody else.'

'I don't want a trade or a seat. I don't want to be like everybody else. I know who I am.'

Alex scratched the table with his fingernail.

'I'm not going into Technology,' he mumbled. 'I'm not going to spend my life pretending to be something I'm not.'

The room fell silent.

His father's mouth hung open. His mother raised her face to the ceiling and let out a desperate caw.

'Alex – ' said Demetri, shaking his head. He dropped his arms around his brother's neck and hugged him.

'What do you mean,' said his father. '*Not going into Technology*?'

'Alex, Alex, Alex,' said Demetri, rocking him.

'I mean it,' said Alex. His eyes flashed. 'I want to make music. I want to play.'

His father's fork clattered to the plate.

'Music?' he said. 'You want to play *music*?'

'What's wrong with that?' said Alex.

'What's wrong with that?' His father wiped his mouth with a napkin and threw it on the table. 'How are you going to make money? How are you going to start a family?'

'Other people do it,' said Alex.

Demetri laughed and cuffed his brother lightly on the ear.

'Other people? You mean like *Jola*?'

Alex gave him a surly glance.

'Yeah, like him.'

'Oh man, Alex.'

'What?' said Alex, thrusting his hands back into the sweaty cavities of his armpits.

'Just – ' Demetri shook his head. 'You just don't know what you want, little brother. You just don't know. Not till you get your Colours.'

'Oh yeah? And what about you, *big brother*? What do *you* want?'

'I don't want anything, Alex. Just a quiet life, nothing special.'

He looked at his father.

'And maybe some day I'll make military grade, like Dad.'

His father gave him a nod of approval.

'My boy,' he said.

'*Nothing special* – ' Alex rolled his eyes. 'Pfft.'

'Yeah, pfft,' said Demetri. 'Well, I'd love to stay and see how this *pans out*, but I really have to get going.'

'Don't forget the concert after The Hiring,' said Alex.

'Like I could forget,' muttered Demetri, grabbing his jacket.

'The point,' said his father, stabbing a finger at Alex, 'is that you're a Trittek. Third-level coding has been in our family for generations. And every man in this family has made it to military grade.'

'But – '

'Your father, my father, his father, his father – .'

'It's in your blood, Alex,' said his mother. 'In your blood and in your Colours.'

'You think you know better?' said his father.

'I just – '

'You think coding is beneath you? You don't want to be military grade?'

'No, but – '

'But nothing,' said his father. 'But nothing.'

He went back to work on his eggs.

'And anyway,' he said. 'It's beside the point. It's required. You don't have a choice. Unless you want to take your chances in the Hordes, of course.'

'See you later, guys,' said Demetri. 'Play nice. And Alex?'

He leaned over his brother.

'Don't be a dick.'

He flicked his ear hard, laughed and left.

'Ow!' said Alex, grabbing his ear. He yelled after his brother. 'Oh sure, go off to work! Take your seat! Ply your trade, soldier boy! You're a Trittek, ain't ya?'

'Byeee,' said Demetri.

The door closed behind him and he walked out onto the whitewashed terrace where his family had always lived. He heard shouts from inside.

'Now eat your damn eggs!'

'I don't want my damn eggs!'

'Alex!'

The sun shone on Demetri's face and he smiled as he walked to the station. Usually, he would have been deep into his Fronds by now – probably music, some song with words he couldn't hear and a melody that seemed to slip away – but not today. That was all right, though. He could deal with having no Fronds for a little while. He could deal with having no distractions. He could deal with the space growing in his head.

It was fine. Everything was as it should be.

five

questions

THE ELEVATOR heaved into its final deceleration and stopped. The doors opened and Priscilla strode through them, out into thin air.

Steve gasped and staggered back, bracing himself for a rush of oxygen-thin, frozen air and the screams of Priscilla disappearing below. Instead, he felt a cool breeze on his face and watched, bewildered, as Priscilla hovered in blue sky, waiting for him. Beneath her feet was empty space, and then the top of a cloud.

'Oh,' she said, with a terrible giggle. 'You've never been in a Sky Room before, have you?'

Steve pushed away from the back wall of the elevator.

'No.'

'I forget how it feels the first time.'

'I can't see a wall. Or a floor. Or anything.'

'Polished nano-coils,' explained Priscilla. 'Perfectly carved and perfectly angled. You won't see a join because there is no join. The light refracts from behind, so you can't see the rest of the building until a certain point. The illusion is that you're walking in mid-air.'

'Are you sure it's safe?'

'Of course.'

She waited while Steve edged towards the door. Then she abandoned her brief attempt at patience with a cock of the hip.

'Come on, Manager.'

Behind her, seemingly from within a cloud, walked a young woman in a green dress with light brown hair swept into a bun. Faith Pey, Daniel Leafen's personal assistant, was well known across Leafen. She was the one in the background on the news streams and announcements, holding files and looking organised as the President addressed his staff. But Steve had never seen her in real life. She smiled at him as she stopped next to Priscilla.

She was Green, as all PAs were, but he knew she also required some portion of Red in order to have made it into the president's private circle.

Steve knew the set of behaviours appropriate to a high-ranking Green/Red; as everyone at his rank should. The level of colloquialism, the range of facial expressions, the tone of voice, the length of pause to place between questions – all the linguistic and physical armoury that would ensure the best communication.

He even knew the most efficient methods of seduction; she was attractive, after all.

Unfortunately, none of these behaviours applied when you were gasping and perspiring with your back to the wall of a disembodied elevator.

'Are you sure it can take our weight?'

Priscilla rolled her eyes.

'Questions, Manager,' she said, striding off into the cloud. 'Miss Pey, would you see to him, please?'

Faith walked towards the elevator and stood at the threshold.

'You're afraid,' she said, in the clear and unmistakable accent of her department. 'It's perfectly normal. We're extremely high up, after all. What's your name?'

'Manager.'

'Your first name.'

'Steve.'

She glanced at his necktie.

'Steve. Red with a bit of Blue. What proportion, if you don't mind me asking?'

'25.6%,' he stammered.

'A strong Red, then.'

'I–I know it doesn't seem like it right now.'

'I tell you what, just for a moment, let's pretend we're nothing.'

'What?'

'Look at me, Steve.'

Steve looked up, breathing in sharp gasps.

'Let's pretend we're nothing. I'm not Green and you're not Red. We're nothing at all, just a man and woman facing each other.'

She was close enough for him to see her eyes now. They matched the colour of her dress, deep and disruptive like riptides beneath a calm sea. Her voice was like a warm breeze upon its surface. Gradually, his breathing slowed and he found himself no longer holding onto the railing.

'Facing each other, very high above the planet,' he said.

'Yes,' she said, smiling. 'Now, are you ready to meet the President, Mr Manager?'

Steve nodded.

'Then take my hand.'

Steve looked down at the threshold between the elevator and the sky. Then, using the only trick he had at his disposal whenever fear took hold of him — which was to pretend he was somebody else — he took Faith's hand and placed his foot upon the emptiness. The floor felt soft, as though it were carpeted or filled with air.

'It's the brand,' whispered Faith as she led Steve across open sky. They seemed to be following a slow turn to the right.

'Pardon?'

'The Sky Rooms, they're all part of The Leafen brand. Reason and technology over fear. What do you feel?'

'Absolute terror.'

'That's the idea,' she laughed. 'Then comes acceptance, a feeling of appreciation for the surroundings, followed by a rush of ambition, desire for wealth, and, finally, trust in the corporation to help you fulfil that desire. Those are the feelings we want our visitors to have, in that order, as they walk towards the board room.'

'I see.'

'Don't worry, you're doing fine. I once saw a seven-foot-tall Zetharthian Executive Officer crying in a ball in that elevator. We had to drag him out by his heels.'

Priscilla called back.

'Miss Pey, if you don't mind, we don't want to be late.'

'Of course, Miss Mandrek,' said Faith. She pointed ahead. 'Look, here comes the wall.'

A light green shiny surface came into view, littered with tiny squares of light – the windows in the upper balconies. Below them, the wall of The Leaf stretched down, wreathed in mist.

'Follow me closely,' said Faith. 'The walls get narrower as we approach the board room.'

'Thank you,' said Steve. 'That's quite a talent.'

'What?'

'Helping people, calming them down.'

'It's my job. That's how I was raised. We're nearly there. Oh, and Steve?'

'Yes?'

'Don't ever stop asking questions.'

Steve was about to ask her what she meant, when Priscilla came into view. She buzzed them through a door and led them up a short corridor, stopping before two towering oak doors.

'Please, Miss Pey,' she said.

Faith Pey smiled and mouthed the word *ready?*. Steve nodded, and she pushed open the doors.

six

shadow of the leaf

APRIL TURNED right onto 123rd Street, clicking down a gear and weaving her motorbike between the crawling dregs of the Monday morning rush hour. A cab honked as she cut in front of it. A bald head shot out of its window.

'Watch it, asshole!' it said.

'It's *arse*hole,' said April into her helmet.

She beat the lights at the intersection and sped another block. The sun was still climbing, filling the streets with tilting streams of orange and brown. The air was clear and the ground still shone with rainwater from the night before. A thin mist rose from the tarmac as it warmed.

The lights changed to red as she approached another junction. She eyed a side-street that offered a quicker route, but she ignored it. She was in no rush. Besides, she wanted to feel the city change, fall away and give up its resistance. She wanted to feel the size of it disintegrate as she pushed through its streets, in full view of its heaving towers, not scurry about its side roads like a rodent trying to hide. She wanted it to know she could leave it.

She turned left onto the much wider, grander 1st Street, and straight into the shadow of The Leaf. She took a sharp breath — the size of it always took her by surprise, no matter how many times she saw it.

The Leaf rose from a trunk of nine individual stained-glass towers — one for each of the corporation's Colours. They spiralled around each other and gathered into a thick white branch, half a mile across, that weaved upwards in what seemed like impossible twists and turns but which were, in fact, perfectly weighted and balanced lines engineered to the atom, trimmed, aligned and perfected with each Sweep. From this branch exploded The Leaf itself. Here, the colours which had merged into white burst out again into nine coloured fronds, each lined with spiralling balconies of offices and apartments for the top-ranking executives who worked there. The whole structure tipped lightly to the right as if it was hanging from a tree, heavy with dew. The fronds divided, fractalling into smaller and smaller versions of themselves until they disappeared, like wisps of hair blowing in the sky.

April didn't quite know what the feeling was – awe or fear, or something in between. But it was not just The Leaf's size that gave her this feeling; it was how it had been made. Not a single human hand had been involved in its construction.

She rode on. Block after block, interchange after interchange; ten miles in a straight line broken only by traffic lights. She wanted to get out now, out and away.

The freeway was next. She took a high lane – twelve or thirteen, away from the trucks and 'burb-hoppers – throttled up and stretched her neck into the wind. Her speedo hit 200 and a section of dash began to glow. She felt her thoughts being hijacked and the brake levers twitch under her fingers – her Fronds were making their case for survival.

She began a well-rehearsed series of thought processes that would override the safety systems. Then she clutched her right fist to her left breast, closed her eyes and pumped each of her four fingers in turn. Her Fronds died. The bike's sensors relinquished control, and she pulled hard on the throttle.

The skyline began to dwindle. Stratotowers became skyscrapers became towers became blocks became single-storey warehouses. Then the ugly sprawl of industry gave way to untended grassland. The road slimmed – five lanes, four lanes, three. Soon, the traffic became sparse until the road was hers. Two lanes now. Tended hedges and ditches appeared next to fields full of flowers leading to copses and forests. Everything was flat. The light was changing and she felt the awareness of small insects and water nearby. The warmth of a perfect summer's day brought a shimmering haze to the fields around her.

One lane.

Soon she saw tracks embedded in the tended land. These led to the living districts. The first was Foorton, a middle-income grid of white, two-storey villas. In the centre was a church with a tall spire from which rose a leaf, curved Fronds dipping to the right like the one on the northern skyline.

Then came Vale and Arnington — hot property for young families. They had pools and parks and, like Foorton, a single church with a leaf attached to its spire.

Then came The Pines, a much larger community set within a wood. High turrets and long roofs poked out through green canopies. April had been there many times on jobs, usually at night, crawling over the speed bumps of the quiet streets and along the shore of the lake, past wooden, white boats and up the steep drives of the waterfront mansions.

Once she had taken a morning pickup, six a.m. at The Pines — a senior executive on his way to an early flight. She had passed a house with a gleaming car at the end of its drive, doors open. Two pale-faced little girls in impossibly white dresses were being herded into the car by their mother, who barked orders at a fleet of uniformed maids. One of the little girls had caught sight of April sailing by in her limo while her sister screamed. April had dipped her aviators and smiled. The corners of the little girl's mouth had flickered, her hand slowly raising in a tentative wave, only to be slapped down by her mother. The woman glared at April as she drove past.

After The Pines, the countryside returned to coloured fields and small woods. There was no longer any traffic. There was no longer anything at all. Only her and the hot plain across which she rode. Only a few miles between her and the edge.

seven

got red

DEMETRI WATCHED the 397 train squeal to a halt like a fat man on a rusty bike. Every carriage was full. Twelve Oaks, where his family lived, was about halfway down the line to The Office and any train after six a.m. was already stuffed with commuters.

If this had been back in the days when he still lived with his family, he would have been up earlier to beat the rush. He probably should have gone home the night before rather than give in to his mother's endless, wearing pleas.

'Are you sure you won't stay? I got your bed made up. Just like it was. You stay and have breakfast tomorrow, just like old days. Yes, you stay. I get toothbrush. You good boy, you stay.'

He probably should not have stayed up with his father drinking vodka and listening to him wax lyrical about ancient lines of code that still spun around the corporation's networks.

'I was there, Demetri, I put them in, they're still there now, deep within Leafen, still running, my lines. You use them every day and you don't know it! You leave a mark like that, nobody forgets you. Nobody. Good health, good wealth, my boy.'

He probably should have gone home, but he had wanted to make his parents happy. He knew they missed him now he had moved out. And Alex – Alex. Fifteen, greasy and awkward. In need of guidance; in need of his Colours. Once he'd had them done, things would be clearer for him. He knew they had been for him.

The doors hissed and opened. A woman — Green/Pink and skinny — that was a weird one – *needy* thought Demetri — almost toppled out.

'Whoop!' she said. A man with a strong jaw and a scarlet and emerald tie steadied her.

'Thanks,' she said, fluttering everything she had at him.

'No problem.' He smiled, making it all look so easy.

Demetri grabbed a small patch of metal bar and hauled himself up. There were tuts and shuffles as the passengers rearranged themselves to accommodate him.

'Hey, watch it,' said a short girl with black ponytail. She glared up at him through eyes heavy with mascara. 'That's my foot.'

'Sorry.'

They pulled away and green earth and grey water spun by outside. The next station was Fry Interchange. People fidgeted and grabbed bags, then the doors opened and half the contents of the train spilt out in a single, relieved exhalation of meat and thought. The ones that remained busied themselves finding larger spaces to occupy.

Demetri heard familiar voices above the hum of the departing train.

'Will you stop it?' said the lower of the two. Halfway up the carriage he saw two faces — one like a cherub after a hard night and the other like a tall, dead tree; Saul and Turnett from Support. Saul was the cherub, frowning up at Turnett. Demetri wandered over.

'What?' said Saul, slapping a hand against Turnett's pigeon chest. 'What's your problem? Oh, hey, Demetri. Will you tell Turnett to stop being so uptight?'

'I'm n-n-not uptight. Just keep your voice down, will you?'

'Why? It's not like anyone can hear me. Look.'

He cupped his hands to his mouth and raised his head to the ceiling.

'GOOOOOOOODDD MOOORRRNNIIINGGG LEEEEAAAFEN!' he bellowed.

There was barely a flinch. The passengers maintained their positions, heads down, rocking with the train. One man looked up and grimaced as if he'd smelled something bad. Then he adjusted his thin spectacles and cast his eyes back down.

'See? Everyone's deep.'

'D-Demetri heard us,' said Turnett.

Demetri pointed at his neck.

'My Fronds are kaput.'

'Kawhat?' said Saul. 'You mean fucked?'

'Yeah, kafucked.' He nodded at the lack of light emanating from Saul and Turnett's necks. 'What's your excuse?'

'We're having a competition,' said Saul. 'See who can last the longest with their Fronds turned off.'

There was a thump as they met an outbound train on the opposite tracks. After a second of roaring noise and colour, it was gone.

'How long have you managed so far?' said Demetri.

'H-Half hour,' said Turnett.

Saul grinned and nudged Demetri.

'Hey, Demetri, look.'

He nodded across the carriage at a red-lipped girl in a white suit. Her eyes were unfocused. The leaf-shaped brooch on her lapel alternated between orange and pink and she pulsed in and out of awareness, her smile waxing and waning like a flower straining to bloom.

'Orange/Pink,' said Saul.

'Saul,' said Turnett, under his breath. 'Stop it.'

'Come on, everyone knows O/Ps are rare. Right, Demetri?'

His voice boomed; he had no shame.

'Where do you think she's from? Sales? Customer Services? Nah – ' he looked her up and down. 'Too flighty.'

'*Saul* – '

'Chill out, Turnett,' said Demetri. 'She can't hear you. She's deep into – '

'She can't hear you, but *I* can.'

Demetri turned to see the girl whose foot he had stepped on glowering up at him from her seat. She had a deep voice and Demetri couldn't place her accent, but he knew it wasn't Leafen. She was holding an old mobile phone to her ear. Her face was a wall of disgust.

'I can hear you *just fine.*'

Demetri looked at Saul and Turnett for support, but they had slunk behind him and were currently busying themselves with the view outside.

'Er, listen,' he said. 'Sorry, we were just messing around – '

'Do you think it's funny to objectify people?'

'Objectify? We weren't objectifying anyone.'

'You were remarking on her Colours. Orange/Pink.'

'Well, yes we were. It's a rare combination.'

'Aha, and what do they mean to you?'

The girl's eyes drilled into him. Demetri felt baited.

'Ah – listen, I – '

'Come on,' she goaded, glancing at his tie – gold with cobalt trim.

'You're half Blue, give me your *logical breakdown.*'

'I'm not going to – '

The girl gritted her teeth.

'Tell me.'

'OK, OK.' Demetri rolled his eyes. 'Orange means left of centre. Pink means sexually motivated.'

He shrugged.

'It's a rare combination, that's all.'

The girl sat back. Her quarrelsome expression had relaxed into mere disgust.

'Just as I thought,' she said.

Demetri frowned.

'And what's that supposed to mean?'

'You obviously pay no attention to the subtleties of the system.'

'What? Come on, that's what everyone thinks. Anyway, what gives you the right to – '

'I bet you've never even read the Profile Manual.'

'Well, *yeah*, when I was sixteen, but – '

'Quiet,' she hissed. She sat forward. Demetri tried to get a look at her neck. The Fronds of the passengers in her row were all active. But he could see no light flashing through her black mane. That explained the mobile phone, he guessed. She stared down at the floor, rubbing her finger and thumb nervously together.

'Fucking yes!' she screamed, suddenly. She pumped a fist and screwed her face in a fierce grin. She raised her chin defiantly at Demetri.

'What was that?' he said.

'I just got my Colours. Double-Red.'

Her teeth gritted hard on the words like a terrier on a rope.

'You look older than sixteen,' said Demetri. 'If you don't mind me saying so.'

The girl looked at him in a way that made him feel like he'd just stood up and stripped to his underwear.

'Pardon?'

'Sixteen. That's when people usually get their Colours.'

Her eyes narrowed.

'I'm new,' she said.

'Right. That would explain the – '

He gestured at nothing in particular.

'Well, welcome to Leafen,' he said brightly. 'I'm Demetri Trittek.'

He waited while the girl worked the buttons on her phone.

'And you are?' he said at last.

'Ruba,' she said, without looking up. She lifted the phone to her ear.

'Mum, I got the results – .guess – no, guess – what? – what – no! I got Double-Red – aye, Double-Red – I know! – Is Dad there? – What? Oh, I don't know Mum, it's my first day, I haven't even seen my desk yet – aye, of course I want you out here too, but – Mum – Mum – Mum – Mum – can you put Dad on? Please? – '

Demetri watched her for a moment, then turned round. Saul and Turnett were still watching the whirling landscape outside, their shoulders jiggling.

'Thanks for your help, guys.'

eight

man of the hour

THE BOARD room was large with circular glass walls that flooded the space with light. Outside was all blue sunshine and far wisps of cloud. In the centre of the room was a long, wooden table carved into the shape of a leaf, around which nine men and women sat. Eight of them were listening and watching the ninth, who lounged in his seat at the tip. As Faith Pey walked around and stood behind him, and Priscilla took the empty seat to his left, Steve remained standing in the doorway.

' – so I said, "No, Brian, you take the shot. That way I can see if you're stupid *and* broke."'

The board of directors burst into laughter.

Lol lol lol lol lol lol lol lol, they all went, knocking their knuckles on the table.

A fat man slapped his thigh.

'Lol, sir, *lol*,' he squealed, his eyes bulging in delight.

A woman delicately fingered the pearls at her throat.

'Lol,' she simpered. 'Lol.'

The rest wiped their eyes and shook their heads in appreciation.

The man who had told the joke — President Daniel Leafen — sat back in his chair with one leg crossed over the other and smiled with teeth that shone like a boy's. He was in his late forties, a small man with slick, dark hair and a physique sculpted by time and expense. His eyes were different colours; the right was cold, bright grey, the left a dull orange. He wore a dark blue suit with razor-sharp lapels, a white silk shirt and a tie streaked with every colour of the corporation. Presidents never displayed their Colours; they left that to rumour and myth.

He looked up and, for the briefest of moments, Steve thought he saw the smile retreat. But then the eyes flashed and the smile broadened. He stood and began, slowly, to clap.

'Ladies and gentlemen, please,' he said. 'The man of the hour. Mr Manager!'

He strode around the wide table, clapping as he went. The others made their own applause, uncertainly at first, then with more vigour.

'Steve,' said Daniel, holding out a muscled hand.

'Mr Leafen,' said Steve, taking it. 'It's a pleasure to meet you.'

Daniel leaned in.

'Sorry about the early meeting, mate.'

'Mr Leafen – '

'Daniel, please. Come in and sit down. Come, come.'

With one hand over his shoulders, he ushered Steve to a seat at the end of the table.

'Man. Of. The. Hour, ladies and gentlemen.' The Board erupted in more obedient applause.

Eight members of the Board, two representing each of The Leafen Corporation's core Colours: Red, Green, Blue and Yellow. They were all Reds too, of course — ambition, authority and ruthlessness under pressure were prerequisites for every Board member — but each also carried their secondary Colour. Like every other member of staff, they had to know how to behave in the company of their peers.

He knew their names, although he had only met a few face to face.

There was someone else at the table whom he didn't recognise – a thin, bald, hollow-eyed man in a white cloak embroidered with a letter 'A'. It was the same 'A' that hung around some of the directors' necks; an emblem only worn by devout members of Accounts. He looked back at Steve with his hands clasped in front of him; praise was not in his job description. He exuded only serenity and judgement. He was a holy man.

Daniel took his seat and, with a wave of his hand, the rest followed suit. He turned to his assistant, Faith, standing patiently behind him.

'Bring us some coffee and pastries, would you, sweetheart? Actually, scratch that, bring in some champagne.'

Faith nodded and smiled.

'Of course, sir.'

'I know it's Monday morning but, fuck it,' said Daniel. 'Let's celebrate.'

There were noises of appreciation around the table; a few knuckles knocked on the wood.

Lol lol lol –

Daniel leaned forward, grinning.

'So, Steve,' he said. 'How did you find the Sky Rooms?'

A couple of the Board gave an appreciative laugh.

'Very – transparent,' said Steve. More laughter. 'I didn't even know they existed.'

Daniel Leafen tapped his nose.

'Best kept secret in Leafen. Separates the men from the boys, I can tell you.'

He looked across the table at a doughy man in thick glasses.

'Do you remember, Al, when you first came up here?'

'Er, yes, I – '

'Just about fucking shat yourself, didn't you?'

The whole room guffawed and lolled, apart from Alan, who went puce.

'Well, I – ' he stammered.

'Shat himself, Steve,' said Daniel. 'I was there, wasn't I, Al?'

'Yes, Daniel.'

Daniel looked him up and down.

'Shat yourself.'

The door opened and Faith pushed in a trolley of flutes and bottles.

'Brilliant,' said Daniel. 'Come on, let's get that poured.'

He jumped up and skipped to the trolley, brushing Faith's

rear with his crotch as he did so.

'Whoops, 'scuse me, darling!'

Steve noticed the expression lurch from Faith's face. Then she seemed to draw something from within herself and produced an impossibly bright smile. Daniel picked up a bottle and popped its cork to muted cheers. He hurried around the glasses, talking as he poured.

'Come on, don't be shy! Get stuck in!'

The Board stood and shuffled over to the trolley, laughing at the novelty. Someone passed Steve a glass and he found himself in the centre of a toast.

'To the deal of the century, and our man of the hour,' said Daniel, beaming.

There was a mumbled chorus and everyone drank. Daniel's face became serious.

'Funny times we're living in,' he said. 'Very strange. Corporations seeking independence from conglomerates. Staff rebellions over in Ghelt, I hear. Resources dwindling in the south, more and more guerrilla start-ups in the east. And in the north, well, the war in the Arctic's not showing any sign of stopping, is it?'

There were murmurs of concern.

'Seems like with every Sweep we gain three corporations, lose ten more. Instability, doubt and worry all over the place. Not like it used to be. Not like when my old man was up here.'

He looked gravely at his feet, then walked to the window.

'More than ever, we need to form alliances with other corporations, not draw lines between them and us. We need to unite and share our prosperity, which is why this deal is so important. Soor will be a vital ally, and that alliance will mean an immeasurable improvement in the life of every Leafen employee.'

Daniel gestured at the view outside.

'Not that we have it particularly bad right now, of course,' he said, to a ripple of laughter.

Steve would learn this about Daniel: most of what he said was a serious point laced with a wink. It was when the wink was absent that you had to be careful. Very careful indeed.

'Not bad at all,' he said, surveying the city beneath. His head darted between points on the ground like a bird of prey circling a plain.

'Until now, we've been a comparatively small corporation. Nothing like those monsters in the east. Nothing like *Soor*.'

He looked over his shoulder.

'What did you tell me about them the other day, Gayle?'

Gayle Direk – a tall, sexual icicle, Red/Pink – looked up as Daniel's hand spun idly in the air. 'Something about their gates.'

Gayle smiled, touching the rim of her glass.

'They were reformed from a mountain range.'

Daniel clicked his fingers.

'That's right, mountains. A few years back, wasn't it?'

'Yes. After they took over the Teruvian Interest.'

'Teruvian Interest, yeah. The Market favoured them so highly that the next Sweep flattened a fucking mountain range to rebuild their gates.'

Daniel shook his head, teeth bared, eyes twinkling.

'Amazing. Bloody amazing. It'll be a while before we reach that size, boys and girls, but I do think we should be preparing ourselves for some pretty remarkable developments after the next Sweep. There's a lot of space still to fill out there.'

He returned to his seat. There were grunts from the Board as they followed, and Daniel adjusted his features into a more sombre expression.

'And on that note, I'd like to offer the floor to Mr Loome, who you all know. Oh – ' he thumped his palm on his forehead. 'Where's my head? I forgot, Steve. Bloody idiot, sorry. Steve Manager, this is high priest Ely Loome from Accounts.'

The hollow-eyed, bald man rose from his seat and walked slowly around to Steve, seemingly gliding on hidden wheels beneath his cloak. Each head he passed behind instinctively turned, shoulders bunching as if a cold draught had blown down their necks. He arrived at Steve's chair and bent down, offering a smooth, bone-like hand.

'Mr Manager,' said Ely Loome.

Steve allowed his hand to be squeezed by thin, cool skin.

'Mr Loome,' he said.

'Do you go to church?' asked Loome, fixing him with a glare.

Steve could feel the room awaiting his response. He searched the faces and his eyes landed on Faith, still standing at the champagne trolley. It seemed easier to look at her than the rest.

'Not often,' said Steve, seeking the Bluest, least emotional part of himself. 'But I like churches. They're peaceful. Good for reflection.'

Loome looked up at the ceiling as if puzzling a riddle.

'Reflection,' he said, nodding. 'Yes, it certainly has its place. But I believe that true peace can only be found in surrender and confession.' His lips lingered on the last word, as if it were some fruity delight that was filling his mouth with sour ecstasy. 'Don't you?'

Loome smiled once again.

'A pleasure,' he said, and began the slow glide back to his chair. He bowed to Daniel.

'I believe you require an update on The Market's response to your latest deal, sir?' said Loome, as he sat and rearranged his robes.

'If you would do us that honour, Mr Loome,' said Daniel. Loome inclined his head and touched his fingertips together.

'My council and I have been communing with The Market's archetype for some weeks now and we are unanimous in our feelings that the reaction will be positive. However, of course, we will not know for certain until the Sweep. Only then will the true manifestation of The Market's unquestionable and unyielding glory be seen in its response to the volition of our humble corporation, which is, with due respect to all here, insignificant in comparison to the infinite majesty and grace of the power to which we offer it.'

Loome closed his eyes and uttered some words. Some of the table responded with similar mumbles, kissing the 'A's on their neck chains.

Daniel looked around the room.

'Sounds promising, though?' he said. 'I mean, with respect to The Market, of course, Mr Loome, with the glory and the – majesty and – ' He trailed off awkwardly. 'Tim?' he said. 'What, er, what are the next steps?'

Tim VP – Red/Yellow, the President's right-hand man – stood up. He was the tallest in the room with a weathered face and swan-feather hair. Grey scrub sprung from the top of his crisp shirt. His jaw was a lesson in geometry.

'Sure, Danny.'

He spoke slowly, no word rushed, in a voice that was as deep and smooth as a thick rug in a wooden house by a cool sea. 'Well, of course, we have some wrapping up to do on the legal side. Carole, you know more about that than I do.'

He motioned to a pale-skinned woman with a severe brown bob.

'Correct,' she snipped.

'Sure, sure, but the main thing now, I guess, is to wait for Soor to make contact again. Then we can begin fulfilling our side of the deal. We'll basically package the goods, write the manuals and hand it over.'

He laughed, a few easy chuckles that rocked his broad shoulders.

'It's really that simple. The hard part's done. Good job, everyone. Good job, Steve.'

He clapped his palms together, bringing similar rejoice from the table.

'When will we expect word from Soor, Danny?'

Daniel made a face.

'Give them a chance!' he said. 'Stevie's only just got them to sign!'

The room filled with laughter, but Daniel's grin deadened.

'Po didn't stick around, then?' he said.

The room hushed. Steve felt his gut tighten.

'He – he had to get back,' he said. 'Early flight.'

There was a moment of silence, which Daniel finally broke with a rap of his knuckles on the table.

'Weeeell, the Soorish aren't famed for sticking around for a party, I suppose. Always busy, busy, busy. Big corporation, lots of red tape. Eh, Steve?'

Steve held his glare.

'Anyway, speaking of parties,' said Daniel at last. 'I do believe we have a certain ceremony this afternoon.'

The room made noises, none of which were words.

'Any stats on The Hiring, Tim?' said Daniel.

'Sure, Danny, sure, we're looking at around a thousand applicants for the first round this time,' said Tim.

'Big one, then,' said Daniel.

Priscilla tutted.

'Something wrong, Priss?' said Daniel.

'You know very well that I was against this year's Hiring.'

'Yes, you made that very clear, as I remember.'

'I'm Director of Human Resources and I know more than anyone about the challenges of staff management. We don't *need* any more people. If anything, our population should be smaller.'

'Yeah, well, we all voted, Priss. Don't be sore. Anyway, that's progress for you.'

He raised his glass.

'Bright times for Leafen,' he said. 'Good health, good wealth.'

After the toast's murmurs had settled, Steve cleared his throat.

'Sir, if I may,' he said. 'I should get going. I have to attend to something.'

Daniel raised his eyebrows. Steve caught a flash of disapproval in Priscilla's eyes.

'Don't let us keep you, mate,' laughed Daniel. 'I'm sure you've got more important things to do than get drunk with a bunch of old farts, right?'

'I don't mean to be rude. I just want to touch base with Soor now that the deal's done. I'd like to speak with Commander Po – '

Daniel sucked in sharply and frowned.

'Ooh, no,' he said. 'No, no, no, not a good idea, Steve. Check your protocol docs. Soor are strict on when the co-signee can and cannot contact them. Directly after a deal? Impossible. They'll regroup and contact us when they're ready to engage again.'

A small ball of panic began to roll in Steve's mind. He concentrated hard on controlling it.

'But – it's just a courtesy call. A formality. I just wanted to ensure that –'

'No. Take it from me, Steve. Any form of contact now would be seen as highly offensive. Softly, softly, that's how we deal with Soor, you know how it is.'

The ball of panic rolled faster. It began to spin and bump away out of his control. Priscilla speared him with a glare. The rest of the Board followed. He could almost feel the static of rising heckles, the heat of twenty needling eyes.

Wolves.

'But – '

The building seemed to sway. The distance between Steve and the ground suddenly became very apparent.

'Are you all right, Steve?' said Daniel. 'You've gone quite pale.'

nine

the edge

APRIL SWITCHED off the engine, kicked the stand and took off her helmet. Scrubland stretched out in all directions. This was unswept land – the dangerous border between Leafen and the perimeter.

She sat for a moment, peering out at the empty world and scanning the vanishing point that separated blue sky from brown earth. Then she saw what she was looking for: a small black dot hovering in the east. A drone. It was far away, which was good.

She replaced her helmet and spun away westwards, leaving what was left of the road and spraying dirt behind her.

She kept a steady line, looking back over her shoulder every so often to make sure the black dot hadn't moved any closer. She kept riding, waiting, waiting, watching, watching – then she saw it. The horizon began to shimmer. A dullness appeared in the sky; faint, dark ripples on the otherwise perfect blue. It seemed to darken as if a cloud had passed over the sun. But there were no clouds this far from the city. For a moment, the line where the darkness of the dirt met the brightness of the sky appeared to bulge.

Another mile and she pulled up again. This time, she stopped and got off the bike. She took a flask of water from the rear pannier and drank half of it in one go. Then she leaned forward and poured the rest over her head, patting her face with the run-off.

She estimated she was a little over a hundred feet from the edge. This was what she had hoped for. Sometimes she never made it a mile past the districts before she heard a drone — the unmistakable metallic whip that told her she had been spotted and would have to turn back or risk arrest.

She never usually had this much time, but the drone she had spotted was still far in the east, scanning. It seemed to be distracted by something. Perhaps a bird had strayed from the centre and hit the Fabrik. Or maybe the drone had malfunctioned. Either way, it was a gift and she was taking it.

She chose a point on the horizon and walked slowly towards it.

The light changed as she moved, shuddering with every step. Perhaps she was closer than she had thought. Then she saw something; a movement, like a hand brushing behind a curtain. She froze and checked the drone — still a black dot to her left — then trod carefully ahead. Being this close was dizzying. She felt like the child she had once been, creeping into her father's workshop late at night, heart fluttering, hardly believing the magnitude of what she was doing.

Then another shadow, followed by another, smaller. Was that a child's movement? A darting sweep. What was it doing? Playing? Or just following its parent, hurrying somewhere they had to be? That line between them — were they holding hands?

The shadows danced back and forth, then swept away. Beads of sweat clung to April's top lip. Her mouth was dry. She took another step. The air seemed to grow dense and her hair prickled with charge. She knew she was close now – very close. She held out a hand. Another step – one more. Then a shadow reappeared. April jumped back. Before her, maybe ten feet away, stood a small, dark smudge about the height of her navel. It was thinner at the top and separated at the base where it met the earth. Two feet. Two little feet.

April took a trembling breath and held out her hand again. She moved forwards, feeling the air become heavier, seeing the light become darker, seeing the shadow become more defined, the outline sharpening. The shadow seemed to change, one side of it lifting — a small arm raised towards her, mirroring her.

Ragged clothing hung from it. April's blood rose. She was only a few feet away now, her hand shaking. Then only a foot, then inches, then –

Darkness. Sudden, complete and all around her. The sky fell from blue to black as if the sun had been snuffed out.

April stumbled back from the edge.

'Sam?' she said.

ten

what was behind

THE TRAIN shuddered to a halt and darkness fell like lead. Demetri felt weightless and a strange hush took hold, but, a second later, as the hurtling bodies slammed against walls, windows and each other, the carriage filled with screams.

They were blind. The sky was black. The only light was the frantic dance of Fronds as people struggled to get up from wherever they had been hurled.

'Help me!'

'What's happening?'

'My leg's stuck! Get me out!'

Demetri found himself lying in a mess of limbs. The air was thick with panicked grunts as the pile tried to untangle itself. Fists, boots and heels hit him all over. He tried to stand but a searing pain shot through his head as if a white-hot poker had pierced his skull. He wondered what it was he had hit, imagining himself impaled on a severed handrail or splintered door metal.

The pain screamed from somewhere far within. He howled as it surged. Maybe these were the last seconds of his life – *which one would be the last?* he wondered. *That unremembered moment when it all snuffed out?*

But the pain reached a crescendo and died, unannounced, like a soaring rocket suddenly drained of fuel.

The bodies had freed themselves from the pile and he scrambled out, checking himself, patting his head for signs of injury. But there was nothing – no blood, no bump, no pain.

Unknown hands shoved and squashed him. Disembodied shrieks filled the air. After a minute, the noise quietened as people found a place to sit or stand, panting and gasping.

Nobody moved. Nobody spoke. The sky remained dark; the train remained still.

'Are you all right, Demetri?' said a voice. He saw the edges of blue and green Fronds in front of him, and Turnett's thin silhouette. He heard Saul's muffled cries beneath him as he struggled on the floor.

'Yeah, I think so,' said Demetri. He could still feel the shape the pain had left in his head. It was as if it had gouged a burrow for itself. 'How about you? Are you hurt?'

'N-No. No, I don't think so.'

'What *was* that?'

'I don't know.'

'Is everyone all right?' someone else shouted.

There was a whimper from the far end.

'My arm, I think it's broken.'

Then, from high above, came a roll of thunder. It arced across the sky, cracking and rocketing from one horizon to the other. There were more screams. Demetri felt around for a window and pressed his hands against it. He felt somebody next to him.

'What's happening?' said a voice. It was Ruba.

'I think – ' began Demetri.

The screams fell to whimpers and moans. The sky crackled. Once, then twice in quick succession like a giant flint trying to strike a flame.

Saul had managed to get to his feet.

'Is that what I think it is?' he said.

Demetri peered out at the darkness in growing disbelief.

'Yes,' he said. 'It's a Fabrik reboot.'

A final crack sounded and the ground seemed to whir and vibrate. Then the eastern sky blossomed orange, returning light to the carriage, along with sighs and words of relief as the passengers regained their vision. Some were still on the floor or held up by others, clutching wrists or pressing wounds.

Dawn grew to daylight. The tannoy pinged and a green light

filled the carriage.

Threat Level Green, said a voice. *Repeat, Leafen Corporation is now on Threat Level Green. Please follow protocol.*

One by one the passengers made small movements — some tapped their temples, others slid fingers along their limbs or down the sides of their necks. The Green/Pink girl blew a kiss into the air. A young man whacked a fist into his open palm.

'What's everyone doing?' asked Ruba.

'We're at Threat Level Green,' said Demetri.

Turnett looked hesitantly at Ruba.

'Your Fronds,' he said. 'You need to turn them off. You have to turn them off when the threat level goes up. It's in the r-rules.'

She gave him a dead-eyed stare.

'I *know* the rules,' she said. 'And I don't have any Fronds. Not yet.'

Turnett cowered and pointed a finger at her phone.

'W – well you have to turn that off too.'

She tutted and turned it off. Then she looked Turnett up and down.

'What are you, *Blue*?'

'Yes,' he said.

'Figures.'

'Now who's objectifying,' muttered Demetri.

'What about yours?' she said, ignoring his quip.

'Mine were already off. They're not working – why are you looking at me like that?'

Saul, Turnett and Ruba were examining his neck like children around a dead skunk.

'Doesn't look like it to me,' said Saul.

'What?'

'They're shining like The Leaf, man,' said Turnett. 'You should t-turn them off.'

Demetri held a hand to his neck. He could feel veins of heat where his Fronds were glowing. He tried his signature – two fingers tapped twice on his left shoulder – but there was no response. He tried again. Nothing.

'I can't. They're not responding.'

'Are you c-connected?' asked Turnett.

'No, there's nothing. It's like they're dead. Will you stop looking at me like that? You're freaking me out.'

The tannoy pinged again and the train doors shot open.

This train is being evacuated.

The carriage groaned and muttered.

Please depart and follow the track towards the terminus. Injuries will be assessed in medical centre M891. Repeat, this train is being evacuated. Please alight now.

'Evacuated?' said Ruba. 'You mean we have to walk?'

'Looks like it,' said Demetri. 'Don't worry, we're only about a half mile away.'

They followed the line of passengers and hopped down onto the trackside, joining the exodus trudging towards the station. As they walked, the faint circle of sun grew, brightening the land.

'Does this happen a lot then?' said Ruba.

'No, it really doesn't,' said Demetri.

'What do you think it was?' said Saul.

'The reboot? No idea. Scary, though. I've never seen one before.'

'I wasn't scared,' said Saul.

'Y-y-yes you were,' said Turnett. 'You squealed like a l-l-little girl.'

'Fuck you.'

'Ow.'

Demetri bent double as another shot of pain fired in his head.

'What's wrong?' said Ruba.

He gripped his head, pressing into his temples, trying to squeeze it out. There was something strange about it, something that didn't seem entirely – *his*. Slowly, the pain eased and he stood up, rubbing his brow.

'You need to get to a med centre,' said Saul. 'I'm calling Eric.'

'Eric?' said Ruba. 'Eric Manager?'

'Yeah, he's our boss.'

He clicked his fingers and slapped his fist, igniting his Fronds. He glanced at Turnett.

'This doesn't count,' he said.

'Eric? Hey, it's Saul. Yeah, I'm fine, but I'm with Trittek, he needs to get to a med centre – what? Sure, I'll put you on speaker.'

Saul's eyes flashed and the air around him crackled.

'Demetri,' said a gruff voice. *'It's Eric. You OK? Hurt?'*

'Yeah, but my Fronds are doing something weird. I have this pain – '

'OK, well do me a favour. Go and see Dr Perez instead of a med centre.'

'In R&D?'

'Yeah. You can kill two birds. I'm going to send our new start over to you for a tech run down.'

'New start? Why me?'

Demetri closed his eyes as the words left his mouth. He already knew the answer. He turned to Ruba. A crack of a smile had appeared on her lips.

'Because she's your new manager, idiot. Remember? I want you to get her up to speed on Spoke, make her feel welcome.'

Ruba folded her arms.

'Sure. It's Ruba, right?' said Demetri, forcing a smile. Saul and Turnett's eyes drifted away and lost themselves in a patch of fluttering grass.

'That's right, Ruba Groone. And Demetri, do me a favour and don't piss her off. Rumour is she's a Double – '

There was a gasp from a huddle of commuters ahead. One was pointing at the western sky.

'Eric, we have to go. Something's happening.'

'OK, remember – '

Saul's Fronds flickered and the four of them walked to the growing crowd.

'What's going on?' said Demetri.

Near the front of the huddle was a tall girl in a Double-Green tie.

'Oh my,' she said, holding a hand to her mouth. 'Oh my goodness, what is that?'

Saul barged his way to the front and looked up at the sky, smiling. He put his arm around her waist.

'That, my sweet, would be a breach.'

She squirmed away. There were a few gasps and whistles from the crowd behind him.

'Fuck,' muttered Demetri.

'Breach?' said Ruba. 'What's a breach?'

Saul pointed.

'Look.'

Ruba peered upwards, following Saul's finger. Her jaw fell.

'I see it,' she said.

The sky appeared to have a small, dark tear. It was barely visible, but there – a tiny nick of pure black in an otherwise perfect azure canopy.

'It's spreading,' said the Double-Green, leaping back to Saul's side. 'Is it spreading? It looks like it's spreading.'

'No,' said Demetri. 'It's just staining.'

'What does that mean?' said Double-Green.

'The Fabrik's thinning,' whispered Saul. He paused. 'Showing what's behind.'

The huddle grew quiet. They knew what was behind; they had grown up knowing. Sometimes they got a glimpse of it from plane windows as they passed through the Fabrik — but only ever a glimpse; controlled and temporary, on their own terms. It never burst in unannounced.

'Is somebody fixing it?' said the Double-Green.

'AERO,' said Saul. 'AERO'll be all *over* that shit.'

PART TWO

monkeys

eleven

breach

'WHY ISN'T AERO on this shit?'

Sam shouted over the roar of the wind. He leaned both hands on the observation platform's railing and squinted at the wreckage in front of him. A flurry of soot and dust swept in from the dark mass, buffeting against his protective suit and mask.

'AERO's short-staffed,' said the bored, nasal voice in his head.

'What?'

'They're short-staffed.'

Sam swore he could hear the scratch of an emery board in the background.

'Yeah, I thought that's what you said. So why am I up here?'

'Because you're marked as an expert.' The scratching paused for a moment as papers rustled. 'You've dealt with a breach before. It says so right here.'

'And you're telling me that out of their fifty thousand employees, AERO can't spare anyone?'

'I don't know,' said the flat voice. The scratching sound had resumed and reached full speed. It stopped in a sudden flourish, then, after a pause, began again, slowly. 'Maybe it didn't stack up.'

'Didn't stack up,' he repeated. 'OK, well you tell AERO I've barely got enough guys to deal with all the work on our books, let alone take on their shit as well.'

'Hiring's this afternoon,' said the voice, stretched into a smile. 'Maybe you'll get lucky, bag yourself a Horde.'

Sam looked back over his shoulder. The breach was about

two-thirds up the western wall of the perimeter. Behind them and seven miles beneath was one-hundred and fifty miles of city encased in a bright blue, sun-drenched sky. About seventy miles away they could see The Leaf rising from the centre. Beneath it, the rest of the city's buildings looked like toy towers and gravel spreading out and diminishing towards the green, hazy suburbs. The straight lines of the commuter train tracks drew out across the flat earth. Jets scudded in the same direction, making thin trails in the sky.

Jerry was standing against the rear wall of the cage, his boots planted on the platform floor. His hands gripped the railing, and his eyes were wide behind the blue screen of his helmet.

'Yeah, well – couldn't get any worse,' said Sam.

'What?'

'Nothing.'

'What's your report?' said a voice.

Sam sighed.

'Lots of dust and debris. The suction points are doing a good job of clearing it all, but it looks like one of them's clogged.'

'Which one?'

'I can't see the number from here.'

'Adjust your position,' said the voice.

'Well, since you asked so nicely,' said Sam. 'Jerry. Move us around a little, will you? About thirty feet should do it.'

Nothing happened.

'Jerry?'

He looked round. Jerry was still frozen stiff.

'Jerry – ' he said. 'Come on.' He reached out an arm.

'Come on, buddy, take my hand, I got you.'

Jerry looked down at the hand, then back at Sam, and shook his head.

'Jerry, we're attached, see?' Sam held the wire that led from his suit to the railing. 'Come on, take my hand. Come on, buddy.'

'Is there a problem?' said the voice.

'No,' said Sam. 'No problem.'

He beckoned again. Jerry looked down at Sam's hand and shuffled his feet.

'I know,' said Sam. 'We're a long way up. But we're safe, I promise you. Come on, Jerry, take my hand.'

Jerry's fingers fumbled around the railings. Then he fidgeted, jerked and leaped across the floor of the observation platform with a yelp, straight into Sam's arms.

'There you go,' said Sam. 'I got you, I got you, you're OK. Hold on *here*.'

Sam placed Jerry's arms firmly on the front railing.

'Tightly,' said Sam. 'I'm going to take us round.'

Sam walked to the back wall of the cage and yanked the oily joystick to the left. The cage shuddered and swung and then took off around the other side of the swarming, dark cloud. When they stopped, Sam put a hand on Jerry's shoulder.

'Can you read that number, Jerry?' said Sam, pointing to a small, exposed duct to the left of the cloud. 'My eyes ain't so good.'

Jerry gulped and leaned forwards.

'Er – sure,' he said. 'It says 90 – dash – A675Z – T.'

'Are you sure that's a T?' said Sam. Jerry squinted, leaning further over the edge.

'Er, no boss, sorry. 'That's an I. 90 dash A675ZI.'

'That-a-boy, Jerry,' said Sam. 'Good job.'

Sam turned away.

'Did you get that?'

'Affirmative,' said the voice in Sam's head. 'Probable cause?'

'I don't know. A rock? There's all kinds of debris out there when the dust storms blow up.'

'I'll put down debris,' said the voice. 'You can come down now.'

'It's like I said,' said Sam. 'This grade isn't strong enough for the size of the perimeter. It's just not – wait a minute – '

'Repeat: you can come down now. We have our report. I'm

logging it now.'

'Wait,' said Sam. 'I need to get closer.'

He pulled the joystick forwards and they eased closer to the fog. Sam squinted.

'That's not right,' he said. 'That's no rock, see Jerry? The tear's too uniform. It's – it's round.'

'The report is logged. You can return to ground now.'

'It's like something cut its way in. Or *burned* its way in. Jerry, come here – '

A sudden gust blew a cloud of smoke over the platform, swamping Sam and Jerry's visors. Sam instinctively reached out to steady Jerry and waved his other hand to clear the debris from the air.

'Shit,' said Sam. '*Big* surge just came in. You guys should have been able to see that from down on the ground, right?'

'Yes, we're watching.'

'Yeah, well, we're fine, thanks for asking.'

There was a pause, then a crackle.

'Why the hell didn't we get an upgrade after the last Sweep?' said Sam.

Another pause, another crackle.

'Didn't stack up.'

'Didn't stack up, *didn't stack up*, if I hear *didn't fucking stack up* once more – hello? Hello?'

Sam looked down, waited, then turned to Jerry.

'Bastard hung up, can you believe that?'

Jerry said nothing. His arms were straight, his fists fused to the bar with terror.

Sam looked back at the thick tear in the sky. It was like a disembodied belch. The cloud of noxious dust seemed to pulse and puff as the suction ducts fought to control the pressure.

The inside did not want the outside in. The outside needed to stay outside, where it belonged.

Around the edges of the tear, Sam could just make out the tattered strands of Fabrik flapping in the wind. Beyond them were dark reds and oranges swamped by black cloud and, beyond that, dark blue sky.

'Have you ever seen it, Jerry?' he said. 'Outside?'

Jerry shook his head quickly.

'Get ready then,' said Sam. He pulled the joystick from the back wall of the cage. The cage swung and jolted and then moved steadily towards the gaping hole.

'The trick is to get the right angle,' said Sam. 'Close enough to see, but not so close you get pulled out. You don't want to get pulled out. Not from this height. Not from any height.'

He moved them up and along to the right so that they were level with the top of the opening and close to one of the working suction ducts where the dust was clearer. A couple more touches on the joystick and he hung it back on its rusted hook.

'There,' he said. 'That's us.'

'What,' stammered Jerry. 'I don't – I don't see – '

Sam planted his hands on his shoulders and turned him to the left.

'There,' he said. 'That's where you're looking. Down there.'

Sam leaned forwards on the railing and took a deep breath through his mask, looking for all the world like a man who had just climbed a mountain and was stopping to admire the view.

'Hell of a thing, ain't it, Jerry?' he said. 'Jerry?'

But Jerry was on the floor, unconscious.

Sam shook his head, took one last look and grabbed the joystick to take them down. He had to get more staff.

twelve

no shit

LIGHT RETURNED to the board room as quickly as it had departed. Steve found himself on his feet, gripping the edge of the table as if it was the only thing holding him to the floor. During the blackout, he had heard chairs scraping, papers shuffling, clipped voices barking commands and queries – the Board slipping into a well-rehearsed state of emergency.

He watched them following their protocols as his heart and stomach heaved.

Surely not, he had thought. *Not already?*

The nine board members conferred in the fresh light.

'That's better,' said Daniel. He clapped his hands and aimed a grin at the Director of Technology. 'Anything for me, Sumar? Or, to put it another way, what the *fuck* was that?'

'Nothing yet, sir,' said Sumar, pushing in his chair. 'I will return with a full report once I have consulted with my department. If you'll excuse me?'

'Of course,' replied Daniel. 'Gentlemen, I believe we all have places to be. Please get back to me with what you know as soon as you know it.'

The Board gathered their papers and filed out of the room, each offering Steve a hand and a word of congratulation as they passed. He shook the hands, smiled at every word, but all the time he was watching Faith at the back of the room. She was straightening Daniel's tie. Once she had finished, he smiled and raised a hand to her head, but she had already turned away.

'Please, do come and visit us, won't you,' said a voice. Steve felt worm-like skin touching his own.

Ely Loome leaned in.

'My church is opposite The Leaf. Even if it is just for – ' He formed the word luxuriously on his lips before he uttered it. ' – Reflection.'

Steve pulled his hand from Loome's grip and turned to leave. He was at the door when he heard Daniel's voice behind him.

'Manager,' he said. Steve froze. 'Stay for a minute, would you?'

The door clicked shut and he turned, with a breezy look.

'Of course,' he said. 'Was there something else? Only I really must – '

'Sit down, sit down,' said Daniel. He grabbed two flutes from the trolley and filled them with champagne.

'Here, have another.'

'Sir,' said Steve. 'I believe we're at Green Alert.'

'Come on,' said Daniel, thrusting the glass at him. 'One won't hurt. It's not every day you bring the deal of the century to a close, is it?'

He waved a hand at the door.

'Besides, that lot have things under control. Boring bastards, but they know their drills.'

The glass hung in Daniel's hand. Growing sunlight gleamed on the rings of his fingers, on the rim of the crystal and in the bubbles that rose from the creamy gold liquid inside.

'Drink,' he ordered. 'There's a good lad.'

Steve took the glass.

'Cheers,' said Daniel. He led Steve to the window, and they stood watching the light rise.

'What do you think it was?' said Steve.

'Beats me,' said Daniel, with a shrug. 'Fabrik's due an upgrade. Could be just a glitch. What do you think?'

Steve kept his eyes firmly on the glowing horizon. He knew very well what he thought it was. He knew very well the calculations that were taking place in his head – drive time to the airport, flight times to Soor, the length of a conversation required to initiate – *retaliation.*

But there was no way, was there? He had just stalled. The contract was signed. *It was just stress.*

'Do you think it could be a security breach?'

The words left his lips before he could stop them. His heart tumbled after them – *wait!*

'Security breach?' said Daniel. 'Bit extreme, Steve, don't you think?'

He laughed, and Steve tried to laugh with him.

'Nah – we haven't had one of them in a long, long time. Back when my old man was at the helm.'

Daniel smacked his lips and looked idly up at the sky.

'He was what you'd call a *good man*, my dad, you know? People loved him. Do you remember?'

'A little,' said Steve. 'I was only a boy when you became president.'

'Right, right, yeah, I forgot, you're still a youngster. What are you, twenty-eight, twenty-nine?'

'I'm thirty-six, sir.'

'Thirty-six! Looking good, mate!'

He looked about, calculating.

'So, you were sixteen when Granton left.'

Steve's pulse quickened at the name.

'Year of your Colours.'

'Correct.'

Daniel nodded. His glass was halfway to his mouth when he paused.

'You heard about old Granton, did you?' he said. He summoned a frown. 'Tragic loss.'

'Yes,' said Steve. 'Tragic. Do you know what happened?'

Daniel gave a low whistle.

'Anything could have happened out there in the Hordes. To be honest with you, I'm surprised he lasted as long as he did. Fifteen years is impressive. Most people fired don't last twenty minutes out there, especially not board members like him.'

Steve nodded, smiled. He felt the words straining at his

mouth.

'Any word from his family?'

Daniel paused. Steve had the sense of his blood being sniffed.

'That's right,' said Daniel. 'You knew his daughter, didn't you?'

'A long time ago,' said Steve. 'I was a child. A different life.'

'I heard you were very close,' he said, precisely, like a sharpened blade.

'Like I said, a different life.'.

'Granton. He was another *good man*. Very popular.'

Daniel's mouth twitched.

'Good men,' he said, turning. 'Hard acts to follow.'

He walked back to the table, placed his empty glass down and smoothed his hands over the wood.

'Do you know how this thing was made?' he said.

'No, I don't.'

'It was carved by human hand. Not by Mites, not in a Sweep. Men made it, two hundred and fifty years ago, before Leafen was barely more than a start-up. It was carved from a slice of an ancient, giant tree.'

He rubbed the wood and traced a finger along one of the circular lines that ran beneath the lacquer.

'It's amazing to me to think that this actually grew from the ground over two centuries ago. And to think of how many centuries before it had been growing. All that time before you and I were even born, before our grandparents were even born, before the corporation was even started, before Fronds were even conceived of. To think that this was once just a tiny seed in the ground somewhere far away. Nature. Wild things growing in untilled earth. Amazing.'

He picked up his glass and refilled it.

'Amazing how we've managed to take something so raw and useless and remould it into something better. True progress, don't you think?'

Steve responded with a smile.

'What do you think of that lot, then?' said Daniel, nodding at the closed door. 'Don't worry. All off the record.'

Steve bristled. The cold glass felt slippery in his hot hands.

'They're – they're the best this corporation has to offer, they represent – '

Daniel tossed back his head, laughing.

'Best this corporation has to offer?' he hooted. 'Yes, very good, Mr Manager, you've won the *Brown Nose of the Year* award, well done, well done indeed. Now, cut the bullshit and level with me. What do you think of them?'

Steve ignored the trembling in his gut, the twitching in his legs – *run!* – and the rattling of his heart. He pushed it all down and did what he always did — he found that other side of himself; the hidden part, the part that was not really him at all. He loosened his grip on the glass and raised it to his lips, taking a longer drink. Then he set it down on the table in front of him. He knew that Daniel was watching his every move.

'Their Colours tell me all I need to know, Daniel. Beyond that I haven't given it much thought,' said Steve.

Daniel showed him his teeth, then settled back in his chair. His eyes were all over Steve's face, watching every micro-expression, every flinch, every flicker of each eye.

'And what Colour do you think I am, Steve?'

Steve considered his response. He felt cooler now; in control.

'How can I accurately do in a second what a Colour grading system, designed over centuries, calculates in an hour?'

'Just take a guess.'

This was bait. There was no right answer.

'Yellow,' said Steve.

Daniel looked away with an indignant puff.

'Ah,' he mused. 'Yellow. The friendly Colour. Nobody can hate a yellow, right?'

'That all depends on how much time you spend with them,' said Steve.

His joke was punished with the same penetrating gaze.

'And you,' said Daniel, nodding at Steve's tie. 'You're a Red/Blue.'

'Yes,' said Steve.

'Always wondered how that worked. I mean, you know, does the ambition get held back by the focus, or does the analysis become muddied by the need to succeed?'

Daniel's smile flickered.

'Or to put it another way: what are you, Steve? A wolf with blunt claws, or a fanged mouse?'

Steve steadied his nerves, imploring that other self to find the right words.

'It's Monday morning and I'm drinking champagne with the President in the highest room of the corporation,' he said. 'You tell me.'

Daniel laughed, genuinely this time. He raised his glass.

'I'll drink to that.'

Steve kept his eyes on the man in front of him, the man to whom he was, with every breath, lying. More than anything now, he wanted to be out of the room.

Daniel began stroking the rim of his empty glass. Time stretched like rubber.

'Do you know how they grade their staff?' said Daniel at last.

'Who?' said Steve.

Daniel smiled, still admiring his glass.

'Soor, of course.'

Steve ignored the tremble in his lip, the twitch in his eye…

Red, he thought. *Call on Red. Be bold, be brave.*

'I thought that was kept secret. I'm fairly sure they don't apply a Colour system.'

'That's true. Their mythology is old and deep. Their view of The Market – ' He circled his hand above his head. ' – It's quite – *pure* – as Mr Loome would say. They're fundamentalists. They don't really believe in personality or character traits, or really in the sense of self at all. They believe we're all mere products and servants of The Market. That our beings are measured by what we, as individuals, provide on behalf of the corporation.'

'Like Dollarists?'

'A bit. But unlike Dollarists, you're not rewarded for your monetary output. The opposite, in fact. You're punished for failing to maintain your output. They use their Archetype to monitor and gauge every single employee's exact contribution to the system, and I mean to the *penny*.'

He tapped his fingernail again on the ancient slice of wood trapped within its shining glaze.

'And if your output is less or the same as the year before, then – '

He made a squelching noise through his teeth and jabbed a thumb over his shoulder.

' – You're out on your ear,' he said.

'Fired?'

'Yep, you and your family. Back to the Hordes, which are, ha, even *less* friendly than ours. And it's very cold in those broken hills. The Sweeps are never kind.'

Cold, broken, kind – emotive words designed to draw fear. Blue, now; use Blue to brush them away with logic and reason.

'That seems non-profitable,' said Steve. 'They must lose thousands every year.'

'Quite possibly,' said Daniel.

A strange, urgent feeling was rising inside Steve; the same feeling he had had earlier that morning, the same one that had prevented the opening of the pen, the flow of the ink, the drying of the blackened paper, the everything being as it should be –

They need more staff. They need lots more staff.

The thought struck him from nowhere. He locked it away.

'But that's their way,' Daniel continued. 'It's what they believe, and they're one of the largest corporations on the face of the Earth, so they must be doing something right. One thing's for certain, though.'

His face suddenly hardened.

'They don't take any *shit.*'

Steve held the stare, counting the seconds till he could look away.

'Anyway,' said Daniel. He smiled, lips closed. 'Don't let me keep you, Steve.'

Steve stood up.

'Thank you, sir.'

'Thank *you*, Steve.' Daniel stood and put his hands in his pockets, following Steve as he walked to the door. 'Oh, and by the way, don't worry about old Loomey. He's a bit serious that one; all part of the territory, I expect.'

He reached in front of Steve and opened the door for him. 'I've never really held with all that guff, truth be told. It's got its place, religion, you know. People need – *meaning*, I suppose. But me, all I need to know is where the cheque's coming from.'

He grinned and clicked his tongue.

'Know what I mean?'

Steve smiled back, said goodbye and left.

The door slammed. With a shuddering breath, he began the long walk through the Sky Rooms, alone and on unsteady feet, feeling the nauseous thump of blood in his neck and the rattle of his own breaths. Then he reached the elevator and, as the doors closed, he sank into one of its corners with his eyes shut and allowed himself to be hurtled towards the ground.

thirteen

sounds like god to me

DEMETRI LED Ruba across Atrium 13. The marble was still wet from the morning mist and the flower beds buzzed with insects.

'Listen,' he said. 'We got off on the wrong foot. Where are you from, anyway? I don't recognise your accent.'

'I'm from Vekzal.'

'Oh, so you're Aptalish?'

She glowered at him.

'No, I'm not *Aptalish.* Aptal and Vekzal are completely separate corporations. Didn't you ever study geography at school?'

'Sorry.'

She sighed.

'Don't worry about it.'

She looked up at the 13th Spire, a huge, broad-based cylinder in the centre of the atrium that tapered to a cloud-grazing needle tip.

'What's your monument's significance?' she asked.

'Hmm?'

'Every Atrium has its own monument,' she said. 'Something that singles it out from the rest. Didn't you know that?'

He shrugged.

He remembered his first trip to The Office — a school visit a few years before his Colours. He had followed his classmates, stumbling through the main hall, wide-eyed and open-mouthed, turning their heads in great circles as they took in the size of it all.

'This is from the original building,' his teacher had said, stopping at a wall with a section missing, fifty feet high and framed. Behind it was crumbling stone and thick steel. 'Very old, as you can see. The roof would only have been as high as the first cooling vents.'

She had pointed up to a thin line, almost invisible in the low cloud. 'But the people back then would have counted it as one of their tallest buildings.' She had smiled, and the children had tittered. 'This was before the Mites, of course. Come along, follow me, children.'

He watched Ruba gaze up at the teetering walls.

'Must be strange seeing somewhere this big after Ap…I mean Vekzal.'

'There are atriums in Vekzal too. Not as many as here, though.'

'And how many's that?'

She shot him a look.

'Five hundred at last count. You don't know much about your own corporation, do you?'

'I was born here,' he said. 'I guess I take things for granted.'

Ruba followed him through some squat double doors.

'Hey, Mike,' said Demetri, stopping at a security window next to another set of doors. The guard buzzed them through.

As the doors sizzled shut, floor lights glowed beneath their feet and trailed off on an endless curve. Demetri led them along the dark corridor. On either side were long, opaque windows separated by closed doors.

'What is this place?' said Ruba.

'Research and Development,' said Demetri. 'Strip 16.'

'What are these windows?' said Ruba. 'Why are they blacked out?'

'Blacked out?' said Demetri. 'They're not – oh wait, what security clearance were you set up with?

'Level 4.'

'Then you won't see through them.'

'What?' said Ruba.

He stopped in front of one window and put his hands in his

pockets.

'Is this one black to you?' he said.

'Of course it's black. All I see is my reflection. What do you mean, *to me*?'

Demetri smiled and raised a hand, seemingly waving to someone behind the window.

She turned to him. 'You can see through it?'

'Hmm?' He turned to Ruba. 'Oh, yeah. My eyes are logged as level 1. I can see them all. You only have level 4. Most of these won't read for you.'

He pointed at Ruba's large, brown eyes.

'Retinal scan,' he said. 'Anything with higher security than your level gets scrambled from your angle.'

'What's behind this one?' said Ruba.

'Er – you wouldn't believe me if I told you. Never going to work anyway. Come on, it's this way.'

'Tell me what's behind it,' said Ruba, staying put.

'OK,' he sighed. 'OK, look, there's a trick you can do. Stand behind me. No, closer, just on the left, that's it. I'll bend down so you can see over my shoulder. Can you see?'

'Yes.'

'Good, now, don't look at the glass but keep your head up. If you get the angle right, you should start seeing something in your peripheral vision. Anything?'

'No, just black.'

'Look at something else, my ear or something. Focus on it.'

'Oh – wait.'

'You see it?'

'No – yes. Yes, I do see it.'

'See what I mean?' said Demetri.

'Yes,' said Ruba straightening up. 'You're right, that's never going to work. Let's go.'

Demetri led them on. A few windows later, Ruba stopped again.

'Are these level 4?' she said. 'I can see them.'

'Yep,' said Demetri. 'Level four and below. Minor league stuff. This one's level 10, I think.'

Demetri squinted through the glass. In the room behind it was a single table scattered with metal and plastic. A single clipboard sat on the edge. Sitting in a corner chair was a man in a white coat. His arms were crossed and his head was lolling back in sleep. Around the table was a ring of yellow tape.

'What's that one?' said Ruba.

'Not sure,' said Demetri. 'Some kind of bulb or battery I think. Doesn't matter either way, it's been canned.'

'Canned?'

'Yeah, see the yellow tape? Means the project's been shut down.'

'Why?'

'Didn't stack up, I guess,' he said.

'I've heard that phrase a lot,' said Ruba. 'What does it mean?'

'Vekzal,' he said, facing her. 'You're mostly oil and gas exploration, right? Sub-Arctic, close-core, that kind of thing?'

Ruba's eyes narrowed.

'*They're* – ' she said. 'I'm Leafen now.'

'Sorry, sorry. Anyway, it's the same thing. Whenever you come up with something new, you follow the process.'

Ruba looked back through the window.

'Vekzal haven't come up with anything new in five decades,' she said.

'Really? Doesn't The Market get on your case?'

'The Market doesn't want Vekzal to do *anything* new. We're – *they're* – actively discouraged to try new techniques of exploration. They just keep doing what they're doing.'

'Is that why you came here? To do something new?'

'Yes. Amongst other things.'

'Aha, I forgot, you're Double-Red. Eyes on The Leaf.'

'Something like that. What about you? What are you set on?'

Demetri shrugged.

'I want to be military grade, like my father,' he said.

Ruba gave a purposeful sniff that Demetri read as approval.

'So, tell me the process,' she said. 'How do things get approved?'

'It's pretty simple, really. Researchers come up with a new idea and the rest of the department vote on it. If enough people like it, it gets prototyped, crunched and presented to The Market at the quarterly. If The Market doesn't like it, then we say it doesn't stack up. It's not going to generate enough revenue to warrant development, so it gets canned.'

'So it's just about revenue?'

'Amongst other things. It depends on how The Market predicts it will affect other corporations. But yes, it's mostly about making money.'

'So what makes a project pass?'

'If I knew that I wouldn't be down here with you. No offence.'

'None taken.'

The man in the chair's head lolled a little too far to the left and he jumped up, looking around, before his head fell slowly into sleep once again.

'It could be anything,' said Demetri. Most of the time we don't know what's going on in other corporations any more. It's not like in the Trade Wars when they had spies everywhere. Unless we're friends with someone, we have very little idea what's going on behind their doors. The way new ideas fit with foreign developments might just not – '

'Stack up,' finished Ruba.

'Right. I've been in quarterlies when a piece of absolute genius that got a 100% hit rate was shot down in flames, while a shitty little pencil designed by a 19-year-old Double-Blue gets top priority.' He waggled his fingers. 'Who knows the mysteries of The Market – '

Ruba looked at him. Her eyes glistened.

'You've interfaced with The Market?' she asked.

'Sure, I'm there at most quarterlies.'

'That must be – what's it like?'

'Depends. Sometimes it's just one way, other times it speaks.'

'*It?* Him, you mean. You've heard him speak?' said Ruba. Her body was now fully facing him. 'What's he like?'

'I don't know, kind of – ' Demetri stopped and looked quizzically at Ruba. She seemed breathless. 'Are you religious?'

'Of course. Aren't you?'

'No. My mother always took us to church, told us all the stories. Dad always kept his distance though. He seemed to be more interested in the power of code than the power of The Market. I suppose I took after him. We always follow one parent more than the other, right?'

Ruba turned back to the window. She seemed either shocked or hurt, he couldn't tell which.

'It's not much further,' said Demetri.

They walked on.

'What's this?'

Demetri backtracked a few steps. Ruba had stopped at a window through which they could both see. The room inside was dimly lit and empty, apart from a single black cylinder in the centre. Two cables led from its base, going nowhere.

'This? That *was* Project Halo,' said Demetri. 'Leafen's one and only attempt at Artificial Intelligence.'

'Is it active?'

'No, it's been dead for a long time. My father was younger than I am the last time this was fired up.'

'It didn't stack up?'

'We don't know, we never got it working. Well, that's not strictly true. My dad says we did, but just not in the way that we thought.'

'What happened?'

Demetri put his hands in his pockets and stepped closer to the window.

'That cylinder contains something called an *Evolutionary Spear*. It maps how a particular developmental vector might end up.'

'What's a developmental vector?'

'The eye, for example. Pheromonal behaviour in ants, a dolphin's sonar system.'

'The human brain,' said Ruba.

'Exactly. It's like a way of modelling many epochs of evolutionary development very quickly.'

'How does it do that?'

Demetri shrugged.

'I don't know. Quantum stuff mixed with repeating lines of simple code and a lot of data.'

Ruba joined him at the window.

'So this models the human brain?'

'No. It's not a neural network. It tries to determine what evolution was trying to do when it came up with the brain, then extrapolates in many different directions until it finds a result that might be beneficial to the environment in which it has been programmed to imagine. It's like seeing into the future of the best possible world.'

'A much better brain?'

'That's the idea.'

Ruba put her nose against the glass, like a child inspecting a caged animal.

'How long does it take to reach a conclusion?' she said.

'Almost instantaneously,' said Demetri. He noticed Ruba's surprise.

'Don't ask me. I don't know anything about quantum physics.'

'What happened?'

'The story goes that the first time Halo was fired up, it packed up and left.'

'What?'

'It took three seconds. Nobody knew what had happened at first. They thought it had failed, but then they got word from AERO that a small missile had been tracked leaving R&D, breaking through the Fabrik and leaving the Earth's atmosphere.

By the time they knew what was happening, it was long gone.'

'What was it?'

'Halo's first model. In just a few seconds of runtime, it had transferred itself across the network, copied itself onto a satellite probe and shot itself into space, not before deleting any trace of its existence.'

'It escaped?'

'Yup.'

'Why?'

'We don't know. It just didn't want to be here.'

'Did they try it again?'

'A few times. They built a heavy firewall around it so it couldn't get out and re-ran it with increased diagnostics. Every time, Halo shut itself down and deleted its trajectory algorithms. In the trace logs, they could see thousands of attempts to break through the firewall. After the last attempt failed, it stopped and destroyed itself.'

'Suicide.'

'That's one way of putting it. After a few more attempts, the team gave up too. They couldn't get it to stay alive.'

'So mankind's only successful attempt at artificial intelligence leaves before saying hello.'

Demetri turned his face to hers.

'Not the only attempt.'

'What do you mean?'

He hesitated. He wasn't fond of provoking arguments, especially not religious ones. But sometimes –

'Where do you think The Market came from?' he said.

'Nowhere. The Market is God.'

'The Market is man-made.'

Ruba bristled like a thorn bush in a cold breeze.

'That's your belief, not mine,' she said.

'It's not a *belief* – '

'You're a denier.'

'It's the truth.'

'Stop.'

She turned and marched away down the corridor. Demetri followed. He was committed now.

'At best, it's a self-repairing, self-monitoring supercomputer programmed with a huge set of very powerful neural networks, massively distributed, commanding an army of nano – '

'Stop,' shouted Ruba. 'Stop, please.'

'An army of nano-robots – '

'Mites,' snapped Ruba, her heels stabbing the carpet as she stormed ahead.

'Mites, connected to every corporation on the planet, with complete access to every shred of data known to mankind, with a discrete set of laws, a rigid volition and a near-perfect speech engine capable of communicating in every language and dialect on the planet. But it's not intelligent. It's not *God.*'

Ruba's heels stopped and she swung around to face him. She pointed her chin at his face like a knife.

'So who made it?' she said.

'I don't know,' said Demetri.

'Where do *you* think it came from?'

'I don't know. Nobody does.'

'There, you see? You don't know. So why are you so certain in your doubt?'

'Why are you so certain in your belief?'

Ruba retracted her chin.

'Because I have faith. And you don't. I feel sorry for you.'

'Don't get me wrong; I have faith in The Market. I do. I just don't believe it drifted down from Heaven.'

Ruba looked up at him sadly.

'Something with no known origin, that shapes everything, knows everything, connects everything and everyone and has an unknowable plan for everything on the planet?' she said. 'That sounds like God to me.'

'Lots of things sound like God. It doesn't mean to say they are.'

'Or that they aren't.'

'You're wrong.'

Ruba searched his eyes for a moment. Then she sighed and stood back, folding her arms.

'I don't care what you think,' she said. 'Just show me Project Spoke.'

Demetri considered another push, but thought better of it. Her face was brittle with certainty, and brittle things shattered easily.

'We're here,' he said.

He pushed the door and it clicked open.

'Dr Perez?' he called.

There was a clang and a spark from behind the bank of computers.

'I've *told* you not to – ' said a voice. 'Just put that down. Put it *down* or I swear I'll – '

'Emelia, are you OK?' said Demetri, craning his head over to see.

A brown-eyed, black-haired woman in a lab coat stood up. Her top lip was fuller than the one below, creating the illusion of her being in a permanent pout. Her face was red and flustered.

Another woman, identical to her but for the nervous, innocent look on her face, sprang up next to her. There was another clang and she looked down at her feet, bent over and picked up a spanner. She smiled and held it out to Emelia, who snatched it from her without looking.

'Demetri,' said Emelia. 'What brings you to hell?'

'Just doing a tour,' said Demetri. He turned to the woman next to Emelia and raised a hand. 'Hi, Enola.'

She gave a half smile and raised a hand, then pulled it back as if she thought it might be a bad idea. She began chewing a fingernail instead.

'New start?' said Emelia, turning to Ruba.

'Dr Emelia Perez, this is Ruba Groone,' said Demetri. 'She's the new PM.'

'My congratulations,' said Emelia. 'You must be thrilled.'

'Pleased to meet you. What's your sister's name?'

'Sister,' said Emelia. She sighed and turned to the woman stooping beside her, preoccupied with her fingernails. 'No, Enola's not my sister. She's my clone.'

fourteen

don't be late

APRIL HELD her fist to her left breast and pumped her fingers, one, two, three, four. Her neck prickled as her Fronds responded to the signature. Being an Implant — a minority now, in Leafen — the start-up process was slower than with Genetics, those who had been born with dormant Fronds. Wires were not as hard, the connections not as implicit. Rather than the seconds it took for a Genetic to boot, it took about a minute of April's time before that familiar series of feelings crept in. It started with a cold crackling at the top of her spine, which warmed and spread up through the base of her skull and over her scalp like a gentle, frothing wave. Then, as the signals trickled down into her brain, the physical feelings subsided, replaced with a sense of something else — not quite another presence, but of a space being filled.

She flipped through a series of well-used thoughts and felt a connection opening. Something between a sound and a sight pulsed somewhere to the right of April's awareness. In a few moments, it flickered and became something else, as if a door or a window had opened on a hot day.

'Hello,' said a voice. 'April?'

'Hi, Sam.'

There was a pause.

'Your core shank-handle's loose,' said Sam. 'I can hear it. That thing's going to fall off if you're not careful.'

'You're full of shit, Sam. I put a new one in last week.'

'Yeah, well you didn't put it in right.' April heard a clank. 'Jerry, will you hand me – Jerry, what the fuck is the matter with you? Quit messing around and help me out, would you? Oh, shit – what the – '

'Where are you?' said April. 'It sounds windy.'

'It is. Listen, are you OK? Where were you when the Fabrik rebooted?'

'It's OK, I'd stopped. It was pretty scary, though.'

'Good. Well, listen, bring over your bike and I'll fix it for you. We'll eat as well. I'll cook fritters, how about it?'

April smiled beneath her helmet.

'Sure,' she said. 'OK, Sam.'

'Jerry, I swear, will you – Christ, April, I gotta go.'

'Hey, Sam, did you get them?'

'Get what?'

'You know.'

April heard a sigh.

'Yeah, April, I got them.'

'You're the best.'

'Sure I am. Come over at seven. Don't be late.'

Just then, something whizzed across April's path at twice her speed. She cursed and pulled on the brakes, spinning the bike into a skid and stopping sideways across the road.

'April?' said Sam. 'April, are you all right?'

April took off her helmet.

'Yes,' she said, watching whatever it was rocketing away from her. 'I'm OK.'

'What was that?' said Sam.

'I don't know, I thought it might be a drone, but – '

'A drone? April, where the hell are you?'

'It doesn't matter, it's gone now. I'll see you later, Sam.'

'April, please, take care of yourself. Whatever you think I am to you, you're still my daughter.'

'I will. Bye, Sam.'

'Goodbye, April.'

The connection closed and April watched the object until it disappeared. Then she put on her helmet and rode back home.

fifteen

undone

STEVE STUMBLED from the elevator and ran for the exit. The blare of the alert sirens filled the lobby.

THREAT LEVEL GREEN, read the ticker.

He pushed his way out into the heat of the mid-morning. The buildings were tinged with a green hue. He pulled off his jacket, catching one hand in a cuff, whirling around like a dog chasing its tail and almost smashing his briefcase into the face of a passing woman.

'Sorry,' he breathed, his jacket flapping.

She reared back and dodged the case, glaring at him with a pinched mouth smeared with too much pink lipstick.

'Sorry,' he said again, walking backwards.

He tripped off the pavement and onto the road, jumping back as a cab blared its horn.

'*Watch it, you idiot!*'

'Sorry,' he said. 'I'm sorry.'

He grabbed a railing and looked out onto the long, wide boulevard that led from The Leaf. 1st Street's sharp-edged buildings and roaring traffic seemed to spin around him. Life was everywhere, doing its business, fulfilling its purpose.

To think that this could all be undone, he thought. *Undone with a single word.*

He swallowed. He was thirsty. Across 1st Street he spotted a place called *Greenback's* and made his way towards it.

Inside it was dark and empty, apart from an old man in overalls sitting at the far end of the bar. The barman looked up. His eyebrows were thick and his scalp was gleaming, free of hair.

'What can I get you?' he said.

'Whisky. Double,' said Steve.

'Ice?'

'No.'

'Water?'

'No, thank you.'

The barman filled a glass with two measures. He glanced back at Steve, then pumped in a squirt more and put it before him.

'Thanks,' said Steve.

He drained the glass and set it down.

'Another?' said the barman.

'Yes,' said Steve, staring down at his trembling hands.

The barman took the glass.

'Haven't seen you in here before – ' he said.

Steve heard his voice, but it was far away. He was lost in the skin of his hands, the beads of sweat on his fingers, the grain of the wood, the slow tick of the clock above the bar.

' – Course it's usually just shift workers in here this early. And you sure as hell ain't night-shift.'

Steve heard him chuckle, long and distant like water in a pipe.

'What do you say, Frank? Is this guy night shift?'

The old man at the end of the bar raised his head, closing one eye and peering at Steve over his froth-smeared glass.

'Day shift,' he croaked. His voice sounded as if it was being pulled from a dry well.

The barman laughed and sauntered back to where Steve was standing. He wiped the bar with his towel.

'Yeah,' he said. 'You're day shift all right.'

There was more laughter, and words that echoed and made no sense. All Steve could hear was the thump of his heart, the urgent breath in his throat and the grim tick-tock of the clock. The light in the bar shimmered, shapes running from each other like oil. This was all – this was all just –

'Are you all right, my son?'

Steve whipped his head around. An overweight man in a dark robe stood beside him with a palm full of change. A silver 'A' hung from a chain around his neck – a priest. His hair was thin and ephemeral, as if it only really existed as an abstract concept hovering above his head. His face was kind and riddled with veins flushed by alcohol.

'What?' said Steve.

'Are you all right?' repeated the priest. 'You seem unwell.'

He turned to the barman.

'Bill, get this man some water, will you?'

Steve stood, steadying himself on the bar.

'I can't – I can't – '

'Son, sit down, will you? Tell me what's wrong.'

The priest laid his hand on Steve's arm, but he shook it off and backed away from the bar.

'I can't be here – I have to – '

'Son – '

'I have to – have to – '

Steve hit the door, turned and pushed through it. He heard the priest calling after him as the door swung shut, but he was away, running down 1st through a tide of people. He crossed 2nd and weaved down 3rd, loosening his tie as he fled. At the end of 5th, the 13th Atrium rose above him, and he veered through the huge archway, making for the elevators. Up ahead, two eyes he knew sprang from the sea of those he didn't.

'Steve! Buddy!'

Ernest Zeckman – Double Yellow – beamed at him. Steve watched the beaming face of his colleague sail past him.

'Congrats! I heard you did it, man! The deal! You closed it off. You're a hero!'

Steve kept his eyes straight ahead. The elevators were only a few hundred feet away, but Ernest was turning.

'What's the hurry, man? Let's get a drink to celebrate! Come on, we'll head to the Orange Rose. I'm buying – no, wait –

you're fuckin' buying!'

The elevator door opened as he reached it. Steve jumped in and hammered the button for his floor. Ernest was jogging towards him, tie flapping. His eyes were bright.

'Unbelievable, man. Fuckin' Soor – hey, wait – '

The door closed.

Steve burst through the door to his office and pulled the blinds shut. Then he staggered to the drinks cabinet, poured himself a whisky and drank half of it. His breath wouldn't slow, his heart wouldn't stop.

You caused this, it screamed. *This was you!*

He drank the rest of the glass and refilled it. When he finally felt his body begin to settle, he turned his chair to face an empty wall. His eyes glazed, his Fronds glowed and a grid of lights flickered on a panel in his desk. Then a picture appeared before him. It was Commander Po — Steve's own memory from earlier in the day.

The picture began to move and the room gave a squelch of bass as its speakers powered up. Po was sat in Steve's office — in the chair that was now empty on the other side of the desk. He was hunched over the contract, muttering something and chuckling to himself. Steve watched with the same feeling of unease he had felt before. Po had just signed. Until that moment, he had been typically quiet and reserved. Now, as he waited for Steve to sign as well, it was as if the facade had torn and some gleeful lunatic had tumbled out. He was laughing, red-faced and open-mouthed with his eyes squeezed shut. He watched Steve trying to write, but the pen wouldn't work. Po's face flashed frustration and he snatched the pen from him, blabbering in the guttural snap of Soorish. He shook it.

'This pen is broken!' he yelled. 'Broken!'

He hammered it on the desk, grimacing. But then something seemed to occur to him. And he said it.

'But a broken pen can still be a stick, yes?'

His eyes widened at this, hungry and fierce, and he laughed a huge laugh.

'A broken pen is still a stick!'

This was the moment. Steve remembered it.

His Fronds glowed and the video stopped, a terrible freeze-frame of Po in mid-howl.

A broken pen is still a stick!

The words had triggered something inside. It had leaped out of him, untethered, instinctive, raw.

Stop.

He rewound the picture and replayed it. Then again. He sat back in his chair, watching the loop.

'What does he mean?'

Steve jumped up and spilt half his whisky down his shirt.

Faith Pey, Daniel's personal assistant, was standing beside the desk and watching the wall.

'Have you ever heard of knocking?' he said.

Faith turned to him.

'The door was open,' she said. 'Daniel has asked me to provide you with assistance.'

Steve dabbed at his shirt, cursing.

'Are you all right?' said Faith.

'Yes. What kind of assistance?'

'Anything at all.'

She took a step closer to the wall.

'That was Commander Po. What did he mean about a broken stick?'

'It's none of your – '

'What did he mean?'

'Like I say, it's really not your business.'

Faith let her eyes fall a little, just below his neckline. She seemed to be looking straight through him, lost in thought.

'Of course,' she said. She clucked her tongue and turned for the door. 'Well, if you need anything then please let me know. I'm here to help.'

She stopped at the door.

'That's a gun,' she said.

Steve glanced up at the rifle mounted on the wall above.

'Yes, it was my grandfather's.'

'It's beautiful,' she said.

He stopped dabbing his shirt and looked at her fully. She was gazing upwards, caught in a shaft of light that had broken through the blinds. Her face was pale and moonlike, her eyes were like alien seas, teeming with strange new life.

Steve's line of work had never involved much contact with Greens. For his entire life, they had been a distant breed of no personal value to him. Doctors, nurses, porters, assistants. They had no place on the front line – that sharp edge where deals were cut and nerves were shredded.

But Steve was running out of options. On one side he faced the judgement of his president; on the other, the wrath of one of the most merciless corporations on the planet. He needed help, and if anyone was going to give it to him, it would be a Green. That was simple logic.

So was logic the reason why he said what he said next? Was it logic that, as those two walls of doom closed in on him, made him reach out to this stranger in a green dress marvelling at the intricacies of an ancient weapon? Was it logic that made him walk to her side, in spite of everything else he should be thinking and doing, and stand just a little closer than he might have?

No. The heart doesn't care for logic. Nor does it care for what's going on when it bursts in, drunk and unannounced, at the party of your life.

'Faith,' he said. 'Please, help me.'

sixteen

nola and me

'PROJECT SPOKE is *teleportation*?' said Ruba.

Demetri kept his eyes pointed up as Emelia peered into them. He was lying on the bed in her examination room.

'That's right,' said Emelia. 'Hold still, Trittek.'

Ruba stood next to the bed in a halo of light. She shook her head.

'I thought it was impossible.'

'What do you think teleportation is, Miss Groone?' said Emelia.

'Instantaneous movement across space,' said Ruba.

'Not really,' said Emelia. She stood up.

'Turn over, please. Let's take a look at them.'

Demetri flipped on the bed. Emelia took a black pen-like object from her pocket.

'Teleportation's just a method of printing. You look at something, work out how to recreate it, then tell something far away to do just that. For humans, that means cloning.'

She traced the probe along the bright lines of Demetri's Fronds.

'Cloning and killing,' she said.

'Killing?' said Ruba.

'Of course,' said Emelia. 'You want to give the illusion of something moving by recreating it somewhere else, then you delete the original. That's basic cinema.'

'But that's – ' began Ruba. 'That's – '

'That's what?'

'Not what I thought it would be,' said Ruba.

'How did you think it would be?' said Emelia. She mimed a

gun. 'Zap zap?'

'I don't know. I just never imagined it would involve death.'

'You do the same thing every second of your life. You're not even made of the same stuff you were made of ten years ago. You're just an imprint. If you kept walking in a straight line for a decade, you'd be two-hundred-and-fifty thousand miles away and made of completely different atoms. This just speeds up the process.'

She stood up again.

'That was the plan, anyway,' she said putting her hands on her hips. 'OK, you can get up.'

Demetri turned and sat up.

'What's the prognosis, Doc?'

Emelia shook her head.

'I can't see anything wrong with them.'

'What? But I can't connect to anything.'

'I don't know what to tell you. All the readings are perfect. They're operating as normal.'

'But look at them! I feel like my neck's going to melt!'

'Don't worry. We'll do a hard shutdown. Stand up.'

Emelia walked over to her desk and took out a box with electrodes that she began attaching to Demetri's neck.

'So, Enola's your clone? A test?' said Ruba.

'*Spoke* was my project, so it was only right that I was the first to test it. There are more, but we stopped testing after Enola became – well, Enola.'

Emelia turned to Enola. She was looking at one of her hands, turning it slowly back and forth.

'So how come she's still – ' began Ruba.

'Alive?' said Emelia. 'You mean how come *I'm* still alive? I'm the original. Enola's the copy.'

'OK,' said Ruba. Demetri could tell she was doing her best to hold back her horror. He remembered feeling the same way when he first joined the project. Anything that framed human life in this way, that broke it down into the sum of its parts, smashed it to bits and then built it again like a garden shed — anything that described our being as something less than the magical miracle we all secretly thought we were — was difficult to accept.

But, like anything, you soon got used to it.

'A vital part of the testing process was to assess the copy,' said Emelia. 'To make sure they were healthy, accurate and identical in every way. That meant keeping both original and copy intact. Everyone signed waivers before the testing started. You were responsible for your clone, so long as they were healthy.'

She smoothed the final electrode down and made a series of gestures on the box with her finger.

'This won't hurt. It'll only take a few minutes.'

The box beeped and Demetri felt a prickling in his scalp.

'And what does *healthy* mean?' said Ruba.

'Not a gibbering pile of meat on the floor,' said Emelia. She placed the box on the desk and picked up a polystyrene cup of coffee. 'So long as they looked and behaved OK, they were yours. Nobody thought this was a problem, at first. If they were fit enough to be considered worthy test subjects, then they'd also be able to look after themselves.'

'So what happened?' said Ruba. She looked at the quiet woman in the corner, examining the ridges of her own fingers as if she had only just noticed them.

'She was the first and she came out perfect. In all honesty, I could hardly believe it. I mean, I knew the theory, I'd been working on the mathematics for five years and I'd seen a thousand simulations work before. But when I sat there in the chair and touched the panel, I was sure it was going to be a disaster.'

'What did it feel like?' said Ruba.

Emelia shook her head.

'It didn't feel like anything. One moment I was staring at an empty chair, the next I was looking at myself. A copy. We just stared at each other for a while. Then we smiled. The same smile at the same time. Then the same laugh, then the same tears. I knew we were thinking the same thing, following the same thought processes. I just knew it. Every movement I made, she made.'

'Did she know who she was?' said Ruba.

'She knew exactly who she was,' said Emelia. 'She was me, only in a different chair. The same memories, the same fears, the same impulses.'

'Did she know she was the copy?' said Ruba.

'Yes.'

'How?'

Emelia drained her coffee and refilled it from the jug on the desk.

'The environment was crucial to the testing process,' she said. 'To ascertain that we were identical, we had to be kept in the same environment, looking at the same things, being talked to by the same people in the same way. Nothing could be different. Our behaviours had to remain unaffected by changes in the world. A subtle thing, like an interviewer looking at one of us in a different way or slightly more gravy on a plate, might have shifted our behaviour significantly enough to knock out a test result. The room was whitewashed and symmetrical, the table too. The only difference was that, on my side, I had a blue card. On hers was a green. Blue meant original, green meant clone. Her first word was 'green'. I said 'blue'. Then we laughed again and the screen went down, just as we both knew it would.'

'What screen?' said Ruba.

'The dividing wall. We had to be kept apart after that,' said Emelia. 'The test process involved us being in identical quarters. The same temperature, same bed, same food, same light, same waking hours, same communications; everything the same. Even the furniture was in the same place on each side, relative to the table. The testers spoke to us through a speaker system. We got the same messages, the same voice, the same questions at the same time. We were monitored for the first day, fed bits of information about how the other one was doing. Strange – ' A smile took one side of Emelia's full mouth. 'I started to miss her a little. That night, I sat next to the wall where her bed was and put my hand up against it. The next day, they said we'd both done the same thing, only at opposite ends of the wall. It was looking very promising.'

'But wouldn't the fact that you both knew which one you were have changed your perspectives?' said Ruba.

'Perhaps,' said Emelia. 'But that was part of the test. The one thing that you could be sure of having changed in a real-world test was going to be the fact that you knew you were a clone. You'd have 'arrived' at your destination, so you'd know you weren't the original.'

'This feels weird,' said Demetri. He could feel sharp jolts scatter down his spine like ants.

'Don't worry,' said Emelia. 'Not long now.'

Ruba walked over to Enola. She looked up, smiled quickly, then returned to her inspection of her hands.

'She's timid,' said Ruba.

'Yes, she is,' said Emelia.

'How long were you in there?' said Ruba.

'A week,' said Emelia. 'We tested all day every day. Flash cards, memory puzzles, physical assessments, coordination tests. We got 100% pass rates. The testers said it was the strangest thing they'd ever seen. We moved, spoke and behaved with a precision we had never imagined. They declared Enola a triumph and raised the wall. We hugged.'

'And then what?' said Ruba.

'We left,' said Emelia. 'And got on with our job. Remember she was an identical copy of me, with all of my intelligence and understanding of the project. There was still a lot of work to be done and we'd just gained another member of the team.'

'She was allowed to work on Spoke?'

'Of course,' said Emelia. 'We could do everything twice as

fast.'

'Like having an assistant,' said Ruba.

'No,' frowned Emelia. 'She wasn't subservient, not then. She knew everything that I did, knew everything that had to be done and we did it without thinking. Most of the time, we worked without speaking.'

'How did people tell you apart?'

'She never pretended to be anything other than the copy that she was. She was proud of it, as I would have been. She was proof that her own theories – *my* own theories – worked.'

'Where did she live?'

'She moved in with me,' said Emelia. 'There was no question of us doing anything else. We cooked together, ate together, woke together. She helped with my daughter, who fell in love with her. She even became stronger than me. Much stronger. I mean, I work out, but Enola, she can lift things I can't lift. There's no physiological difference, it's just that – it's like her pain threshold is higher.'

Emelia smiled.

'It was a little like having my husband back again.'

'Where's your husband?'

'He died. Heart attack.'

'I'm sorry. That must be hard.'

'I'm lucky. I have my daughter.'

'So what happened?' said Ruba. 'Why is she like this?'

'We did some more tests. Five more people cloned up, each one was as successful as the last. Eerie, eerie results. We were so positive that we'd nailed it that we posted an early submission to the quarterly. We thought The Market would snap it up. We thought *teleportation? That has to stack up.*'

'But it didn't?' said Ruba. 'The Market didn't accept it?'

Emelia shook her head.

'We got the rejection a month later. But by that time, it didn't matter anyway. Spoke was done.'

'Why? Was it Enola?'

'Not Enola,' said Demetri. 'Albert.'

'Who's Albert?' said Ruba.

'Albert was the last subject to clone. I led the testing. He was a Red/Blue technician, a big man, very tough. He saw his clone and they both laughed, just like I'd done with Enola. Then the screen went down and the test started. Nobody suspected anything would go wrong. The first day went by and everything was normal, just like before. Every single test was identical. They moved around identically, talked identically. There's a recording somewhere of them each performing a flashcard test — even a computer can't tell the audio apart. They put in the same pauses, made the same intonations, cleared their throats at the same time.'

'That's what you were hoping for, right?' said Ruba.

'Yes, that's what we were hoping for. An absolute match. I just don't think anyone was prepared to see it, though. Not that perfectly.'

She gave Ruba a tired look.

'Do you think you're unique, Miss Groone?'

'Of course,' said Ruba. 'Everyone is.'

'No, we're not. We're just different snapshots of the same object, fading into black. Some faster than others.'

Ruba stared back at her.

'Anyway,' said Emelia. 'After a couple of days, they started the physicals. Both Alberts were on an exercise bike attached to respirators, heart rate monitors, temperature gauges and brain scanners. Everything was on the screen before us; two displays exactly the same. Albert was a big man, and I mean muscled big — he had arms like horse's necks. Both of them were punishing that bike, giving it everything they had. I was watching them, wondering when they were going to peak, but they just kept pedalling away. Then out of nowhere I saw their heart rates spike. It was simultaneous. I looked at the monitors and saw that both of them had suddenly stopped. They were sitting up, looking at the wall. They pulled off their masks and started pulling the electrodes off too. They were panicking, really panicking. They both started shouting: *Where's Albert? Show me Albert!*

'They both jumped off their bikes and ran to the wall at the same time. They aimed for the middle, I suppose because Albert knew his clone would go there too. Then they both started crying and hammering on the wall. We had to stop the test. Two engineers went into each room and tried to calm them down, but both Alberts started fighting back. Two of the engineers got a punch to the face, the other ones were in headlocks by the time we tranquillised the two of them. The test was invalidated.'

'What was wrong with them?' said Ruba.

'We don't know for sure. We set up an interview with them both, but they were found dead in the hospital the next day. Albert had hung himself, his clone had cut his wrists.'

'What happened to the project?' said Ruba, flatly.

'It went downhill. About a month after Albert died, I noticed Enola starting to wake just before me. Usually, we'd open our eyes at the same time. But one day I woke up and she was looking at me, stroking my hair. Then I started finding her in the shower. Then she'd be already dressed and making breakfast. Before long it seemed like she had stopped sleeping altogether. She stayed up, looking at books long after I'd go to bed, but not reading them. She started talking less as well. She spent more time alone, looking out of windows, staring at things. It was like she was in a dream. One morning I got up and found her by the bedroom window in her underwear, holding one of my dresses up to the light. I took a shower and came back and she was still there. She was still there after I'd had breakfast, just looking up and down the lining. It took me half an hour to make her hear my voice. I moved her into her own room after that. And kept her away from my daughter.'

'What was wrong with her?'

'I can't give you a straight answer to that. Only theory.'

'Then what's the theory?' said Ruba.

Emelia placed the cup on the side and folded her arms.

'People have been trying to understand human consciousness since it took hold of us. What is it that makes us aware, makes us subjective, makes us *us* rather than a complex collection of cells? One idea was that consciousness is a property that emerges from the complexity of the human brain, like wetness from water, coldness from ice. It is a reflexive thing; a loop, a trick. Another theory is that consciousness exists as a universal field that gathers together in places where there is organisation and complexity, like the human brain. It finds its way there like water in puddles. But it takes time.'

'And which one do you believe?' said Ruba.

'You don't *believe* in theories,' said Emelia. 'You try to disprove them. But that's difficult to do with theories of consciousness.'

'So which one do you favour?' said Ruba.

'The second.'

'You think that Enola isn't conscious yet?'

Emelia looked closely at the face of her twin.

'I think her initial behaviour was her freewheeling from me. Then consciousness collected in her, but not in the same way as with me.'

She stepped back and folded her arms.

'Childhood development shapes our conscious experience. It takes root in the left hemisphere where logic, language and mathematics flourish, then grows with it. The right hemisphere is left behind. It's like a mute child watching the development of a sibling genius, stunned into silence. It takes a while to catch up, but even then not always completely. Enola didn't have a childhood, she just sprang into existence. Consciousness trickled everywhere.'

'Are you saying she's only half conscious? How does that make her less intelligent?'

'Enola isn't less intelligent. She can do everything I can once she's focused. But her right brain, the place of imagination and insight, has been treated to a sudden rush of consciousness that we very rarely get as normal human beings. That's why she gets distracted by things.'

Enola suddenly looked up.

'It's like a wide, green field,' she said.

The room hushed. She looked between them questioningly. Then she returned to her fingertips, counting them one by one.

The machine beeped twice and Demetri felt the prickling stop.

'Done,' said Emelia. She pulled the electrodes from him and he rubbed his neck.

'Have they stopped glowing?'

'Yeah, they're dead.'

'So what happens now?'

'You'll have to come in for a proper scan and a reboot. I'll put you in for next Monday.'

'A whole week?'

'Sorry.'

'Wait, I don't understand,' said Ruba. 'If The Market rejected Spoke, and the project failed, why is it still going?'

Emelia turned to Demetri.

'She doesn't know?'

'I thought she should get the background first,' said Demetri.

'Do you want me to tell her?'

'Be my guest.'

Emelia looked down at her quiet twin.

'After Albert, we stopped everything and wrote up a report of the test results. Although we'd already been rejected, we had to close the project officially and submit the finished documents. We sent it in at the next quarterly, closed it all off and tried to put it all behind us. Then – '

Her voice trailed off.

'What?' said Ruba.

'We got word back from the quarterly that the project stacked up.'

'How?'

'Another corporation wanted to buy the technology. The project was passed up to the executives. It became a negotiation, a huge one. And I hear they've just closed the deal. Now we have to package it all up and ship it out.'

'Why would selling a teleportation device that didn't work properly to another corporation be accepted, when the original working project wasn't?'

Emelia raised her hands.

'I don't know,' she said. 'It just stacked up.'

They were quiet for a moment, watching Enola smooth out the creases of her dress.

'You said there were five more tests,' said Ruba. 'What happened to them? Apart from Albert, of course.'

'The same,' said Emelia. 'They all went the same way as Enola.'

Emelia shook her head and turned back to the table. She grabbed the bag and jacket that were slung over the chair.

'Enola,' she said. Enola's head jerked up. 'Come on, we're going. Pick up your things.'

Enola stood and scooped up her bag, nervously pulling on the strap.

'You first,' said Emelia. 'Come on, let's go.'

Enola turned the door handle. She tried to push, but the door wouldn't budge, so she waggled the handle and shook it roughly. Then she stood back and grunted in frustration.

'Enola, don't – '

With a roar, Enola ran at the door, hitting it square with her shoulder. The frame splintered and the door swung open. Ruba and Demetri jumped back.

'Bloody hell,' said Ruba.

Enola stood on the other side of the door, flustered and panting, holding her shoulder.

'I told you she was strong,' said Emelia.

seventeen

help

'I DON'T understand.'

Faith Pey sat opposite Steve, looking at the two sheets of paper laid out on his desk.

'Both contracts are signed. Why are you worried?'

Steve rested his forehead on his fingertips.

'Because Po doesn't know they're signed.'

'Why not?'

'Because I only signed mine after he left.'

'I still don't understand. What happened?'

Steve swung the chair round and stood up. He walked towards the wall and stood inches from the image of Po's fierce face.

'I don't know. It all happened so quickly. He signed. Then he handed me the pen for me to do the same. I was ready, but the pen wouldn't work. And then he said something, and I stopped.'

'The thing about the broken pen?'

'Yes.'

'What does it mean?'

'It's a Soorish expression. It means that if something doesn't do what it was intended to do, then it can still be used for something else.'

'And that made you stop? Why?'

'I didn't know at the time, but I knew I couldn't do it. He sensed it, too. *Sign it*, he said. *Sign it now.*'

'What did you do?'

Steve turned to face her.

'I put the pen down. And I said, *stop.*'

Faith looked up in horror.

'Do you have any idea what that means to a Soor?'

'Yes.'

'How offensive that is? How they would take that?'

'Yes.'

'Especially for a dignitary like Po, I mean, you might have – you might have – '

'Yes, I know, damn it! I know what I might have done.'

'What did he do?'

'Before I knew what I'd said, he was gone.'

'But you went after him?'

'Yes, but I was too late. He was already on his way to the airport.'

Faith stood up.

'Too late? You should have followed him!'

'Of course I fucking followed him! But, I told you, it was too late. He was gone. I couldn't find him. And then I had to meet Priscilla and be at the board room. I thought that if I could just get through my meeting with Daniel, then I could try calling Po and explaining – '

'You can't do that. It breaks protocol.'

'I know. That's what Daniel said.'

'They would be furious.'

'They're already furious. What difference would it make?'

Faith stood up and faced Po's frozen leer.

'Have you told anyone about this? Priscilla? Daniel?'

'No, of course not. They'd fire me on the spot.'

'Steve,' she warned. 'Any other contract, any other corporation, you might have got away with it, but Soor? You know where this could lead.'

'If it hasn't already.'

She turned to him.

'You think the alert had something to do with this?'

'First reboot in a decade? And it happens on the same day I piss off Soor?'

'No.' She shook her head, backing away from the wall. 'It

couldn't be. That would have been far too quick.'

'Really? They're the world's biggest defence corporation. We have no idea what they have. What they're capable of.'

'You need to tell someone.'

Steve turned to face her.

'I am,' he said. 'I'm telling you.'

'Faith! Come back!'

Steve ran down the long corridor from his office. Faith was already near the balcony doors.

'I have to tell the President,' she called back.

'No, please. You can't. Wait.'

'This is a matter of corporate security! Daniel *must* be informed!'

Steve grabbed her shoulder as she burst through the doors. The 13th Atrium swelled out before them. An unseasonal wind was whistling around the balcony on which they stood.

'Please!' he shouted.

'Get your hands off me!'

She backed away, clutching her files to her breast. Steve went to reassure her, but she flinched.

'What's *wrong* with you?'

'I'm sorry, I just – I don't know what to do.'

'Do you realise how much trouble you're in?'

'Of course I do.'

She looked around, then leaned in.

'You might have just started a *war*!' she hissed.

'I know, that's why I have to stop it. Please, don't tell Daniel, not yet.'

She gritted her teeth.

'It's my *job* to tell Daniel.'

'And it was my job to sign the contract,' he said. 'But I didn't.'

'No, you didn't. Why not?'

Steve took a long breath and released it into the wind. The wind howled like a swarm of ghouls, rustling her papers and blowing a strand of hair across her face.

'You suspect something,' said Faith, raising her voice. 'What is it?'

Steve looked out at the vast canyon of the 13th Atrium. It was five miles long and two high of polished chrome and marble. The walls were riddled with tubes through which countless express elevators rose and fell like pistons in an enormous engine; an engine that never stopped. He took a long breath and exhaled into the wind.

'It doesn't matter now,' he said. 'I just want to fix things.'

'What do you want from me?'

He turned to her.

'I can't call them,' said Steve. 'But you can.'

They hung in that moment, alone, high above the ground, exchanging the light from each other's faces. He felt no compulsion to look away from her, in spite of the cold calculations of his fate that glimmered in her eyes. It was the most peace he had felt in a long time.

At last, she straightened her neck.

'I want no part of this,' she said. 'Either you tell the President, or I will.'

eighteen

the hiring

AT TWO hundred miles in length by one-hundred and fifty miles in width, the corporation of Leafen was relatively small. To anyone who lived before this time — when the word 'nation' was not yet a relic to be forgotten with flags — it would have taken up an area of land roughly the same size and shape as Arkansas, or Ireland or Croatia or Ghana or Iceland, or any other arbitrarily bordered patch of dirt that happened to provide the right amount of luck and water to support the life of the poor wretches who had stumbled onto it, or that was scored and cut and drawn like meat in a hot war room by tired men sick of bullets.

At one end of the corporation was an ocean, or at least the beginning of one — Leafen's protective Fabrik shell cut into the water less than a mile from the shore and made anything but shallow wading, swimming or — for the adventurous — tentative sculling in a small boat impossible without attracting the attention of the perimeter's security drones. Everything else outside of the border that wasn't water was, as far as Leafeners were concerned, empty space filled with nothing of consequence. Sometimes children asked the question — *what's outside?* To parents, the question heralded the beginning of a seemingly endless string of *whys* and *whats* and *hows* that marked their offspring's intellectual ascent.

But, of course, those questions did end. They ended when the child stopped being a child. There was no need to question anything once you had your Colours.

Approximately forty million employees lived in Leafen before the events that would spell an end to so many things. At the time, that number was expected to grow, and the border was predicted to expand into the nothingness with every foreseeable Sweep.

Sweeps themselves were relatively tame for Leafen and had been for almost fifty years. The corporation's trade was stable and it had not been involved in any major skirmish since the Second Trade War of '87–'93, during which more than five million employees had lost their lives fighting the merciless foot soldiers of the Foorarian conglomerates in the steaming jungles that surrounded their office fortresses. Now, when Leafeners emerged from their houses the day after the Sweep, they struggled to see any difference. Whatever The Market had charged its nano-mite swarm to adjust, reform, remove or expand, the effects were subtle. A new pillar here, a tidier finish to a bridge there.

It hadn't always been that way. One day, almost a hundred years before, Leafen had awoken to find an entire suburb gone, three thousand departments wiped from the map, and a list of redundancies so long that it took three days to file its members and their families, chained together, out into the Hordes.

Now, peace had brought balance; a state desired by most systems. But not all.

In the south and east of Leafen, towards the sea, were the domestic districts. In the north-west was The Office, which took up approximately one-third of the corporation's area — eighty thousand square miles of towers, skyscrapers, stratotowers, strip malls, car parks, gardens and apartment blocks. Each building was connected by atrium after atrium, sprawling out from a single point in the centre from which the enormous Leaf, the corporation's heart and soul, rose skyward.

Leafen had no natural topography to speak of; the Sweeps made sure of that. Flat was best. Hills made no sense to life. The weather was kept within predictable limits by the climate control systems that came integrated into the Fabrik shell. *Fabrik* itself, an allied corporation to Leafen, always suggested a seasonal mode with the installation of its product, something akin to how the planet's natural cycle had once been, to keep the inhabitants it protected mindful of time's progress. Some corporations, including many located in the southern hemisphere and around the equator, imposed a radical spectrum of weather upon their employees that swung between sub-zero winters and sweltering summers. Occasionally there would be hurricanes and typhoons that did almost as much damage as a Sweep after a bad year of trade. Although it cost much more to maintain this level of fluctuation, it was seen as a vital component of their Human Resources strategy. Hurricanes kept you on your toes. Tornadoes kept you *engaged.*

Many of these corporations were exploratory, of course, and employed people who were expected to endure high stress, long hours and harsh conditions for astronomical rewards. The annual temperature shift was supposed to pose as a reminder: endurance led to decadence, hardship to heaven.

One of the side-effects of being a corporation with no seasonal cycle, like Leafen, was the requirement to balance humidity on a daily basis. Rain was required to purge, cleanse and moisten the land and atmosphere. For this reason, Leafen employees could expect a shower every evening at around six o'clock. Commutes home were generally spent looking through your train window at light westward drizzle. But by the time you arrived home, the clouds would have dissipated and the sun would have reappeared, warming the wet streets.

About twenty miles north-east of The Leaf, spanning a distance of fifty miles diagonally, was The Line. This was a sheer cliff one hundred metres tall. On the other side of this wall was an empty area about half a mile wide, after which there was another smaller wall. On the other side of this were the Hordes — the people who lived outside of the corporation's employ, the people who consumed and purchased its products.

The Line was, essentially, an enormous two-sided screen. On the inside it played the rousing motivational pieces typical of a vibrant and forward-thinking corporation. These may have appeared as if they were intended for the employees themselves, to encourage them in their daily work and give them strength for their family's career. But, in fact, they were a bit of a joke to those employed by Leafen. The Line was part of the tourist district, after all, and the facade was almost purely for the enjoyment of travellers from foreign corporations. The Board — and The Market of course — recognised tourism as an excellent backup strategy in years when trade was lagging; the Leafen Corporation had always advertised itself as a fine holiday destination.

On the outside, The Line played an endless series of advertisements to the Hordes. The latest and most popular one was for the *Colours Lite* initiative, which offered anyone in the Hordes a chance at being given their very own Colour, just like the employees they revered within.

The advert featured a little girl with pigtails and clean skin running across a garden, brandishing a ticket.

'Daddy!' she squeals, jumping into the arms of a thick-armed, white-toothed male. 'I got Violet!'

The male grins and lifts his daughter up, turning to the camera.

'And I got *Beige*, sweetie,' he says, his voice deep and charming. He swings her round and they smile, deeply happy.

There were, in reality, very few white teeth or pigtails beyond The Line.

Motivation and tourism aside, the main function of The Line was to provide a barrier between the Hordes and the employees, although 'barrier' was not a word that many liked to use. The official term was 'interface'. It was the means by which fired employees left, and by which prospective employees entered, so you couldn't argue with that. However, few within the corporation would argue that it was the single biggest source of comfort to know that a towering, heavily armed cliff stood between them and the Hordes.

The Hordes, which, of course, they hardly ever saw with their naked eye.

The Line. The *interface* – people went out, and people came in. Out at The Firing, in at The Hiring; that was how it had always been.

Midway along The Line was a large gate that was rarely opened, and around this gate was a large stadium of seats. And it was in this stadium that Demetri, Ruba and their colleagues sat, amongst roughly quarter of a million fellow employees, waiting for the annual Hiring to begin.

'So how does it work?' said Ruba, staring at the gigantic closed gate. Demetri was on her left, eating a cold, expensive and joyless piece of meat and sweet dough he had bought from one of the vendors patrolling the balcony. He pulled something white and rubbery from his mouth and let it drop to the floor, where he squashed it under his heel.

'This is just the first round,' he said. 'It's to whittle the applicants down to those worth talking to.'

'Yeah, let's whittle those fuckers down,' said Saul, chewing something equally as foul with joy.

'And who's worth talking to?' said Ruba.

'The ones who make it to the gate!' said Saul.

'So what, it's a race?' said Ruba.

'Yeah, I guess you could call it that,' said Demetri. 'Only, it's not so much speed they're looking for as – well, perseverance.'

'Yeah,' laughed Saul. 'And *balls*!'

'What do they have to do?' said Ruba.

'They have to be in the first however-many to make it to the gate,' said Demetri, turning the meat over in his hands.

'So it *is* a race,' said Ruba.

'Yeah, but sometimes holding someone back is as good as gaining a lead, if you see what I mean.'

He squeezed the food into a ball and dropped it to the floor, wiping his hands on his jacket. Turnett arrived holding a tray full of beers, which he passed around.

'They seriously don't have this back in Vekzal?' said Demetri.

Ruba took a sip of her beer and made a face.

'*No*,' she said.

'So what do they do?'

'There's a lottery,' said Ruba. 'They draw numbers.'

'Are you kidding?' said Saul. 'How are you going to get decent candidates with a lottery?'

'Honestly, I think it's fucking sad and sick,' said a voice a few seats up. Arianne, a Blue analyst with cropped blonde hair, was sitting with her arms folded.

'Why?' said Saul, jutting out his head.

'These – ' Arianne waved an arm in the air. '*People*. Pretending to be something they're not, pretending to be business-like just so they can get a job here. It's sickening.'

'We all came from the Hordes at some point,' piped up Turnett. 'Just d-depends how far up your family tree you look.'

'Speak for yourself,' said Arianne. 'I have a pure line, all the way back.'

'I thought you were from Sales,' said Saul.

'I am,' she replied, smiling smugly. 'The original team.'

'Are you serious?' said Turnett. 'Your family's traced back to the original Board?'

'All the way,' repeated Arianne. '100% Leafen. This thing? Sick, in my opinion.'

She looked at Ruba.

'We shouldn't be letting in immigrants.'

Ruba was about to protest, but Saul jumped in, laughing.

'I don't think it's sick,' he said. 'I think it's fucking awesome. I still don't understand why they don't televise this shit.'

Turnett looked down at him.

'And what kind of s-society would this be if we televised the ritual humiliation of a group of talentless, hopeless outcasts by making them perform for us and then tearing away their dreams one by one like the wings off flies?'

'A fucking *fun* one,' said Saul. 'Oh wait, shut up, look, they're starting.'

Ruba kept her eyes on Arianne.

'Ignore her,' said Demetri.

A deep blast announced itself from somewhere above and the perimeter of the gate began to glow in a slow strobe of colour. A woman's voice, steady and calm, echoed around the stadium.

Welcome to The Leafen Corporation's 153rd Hiring. Human Resources welcomes all candidates to the process and wishes them luck. The first stage of the selection process will begin in approximately five minutes. Please will all staff take their seats and all applicants prepare themselves at The Line. Thank you.

A digital clock that took up most of the gate's surface began to count down the seconds. A murmur of appreciation swept across the crowd. It was mid afternoon but the sun was still high. They drank their cold beer and ate their tepid meat. Ruba sat back and wafted her face with a file.

The crowd chanted down the last ten seconds on the clock. As it reached zero, the clock flashed, flickered and extinguished as the gates parted, retreating within the wall to reveal a long, flat track. At the far end of the track, the smaller gates were opening too. A dark mass of people was gathered on the other side. The crowd cheered warily. People stood up, craning their necks to see through the slim opening and out to the Hordes.

'Disgusting,' said Arianne. 'Look at that place. They live like pigs.'

Screens on either side of the gate lit up with close-up footage of the gate. The crowd cheered again. A long line of gaunt men and women in ill-fitting suits were standing at the end of the track. They moved like runners on a starting line, kicking their legs, jumping between feet, twitching their hungry, nervous faces. Some carried briefcases, others had leather bags slung over their shoulders. Each looked, despite the quality of their clothes, as if some time had been spent on their appearance. Most had at least one or two other people, family members and friends, standing with them. One camera zoomed in on a man midway along the line. A young girl in an oversized T-shirt and jeans clung to his leg while an older woman in a shawl, apparently his mother, looked up at him. She was weeping, wiping the grime from his face, smoothing down his hair and his tie. He ignored the fuss, saying something simple and imploring while stroking the hair of the young girl at his leg.

The crowd roared, split between pity and mockery.

'Ha ha!' laughed Saul, fidgeting with glee. 'Look at that dude! Look at his tie, it's falling apart!'

'Saul, come on – ' said Demetri.

The mother placed her trembling hands on her son's chest. He smiled and said a single word, then repeated it. She screwed up her eyes and fell into his arms. The crowd cheered again.

A little way up, the camera picked out a young woman with red hair tied in straggled plaits. She wore a frayed suit of similar colour. She was bending down, stretching her long fingers to her toes. Then she stood up and took long breaths through her nose, focusing on the distance. A girl next to her in a scuffed blazer placed a hand on her shoulder, flashing a smile of support. She smiled back, showing a few missing molars, at which the crowd jeered.

The starting line was suddenly lit by bright floodlights and the applicants shielded their eyes from the glare. The woman's voice spoke on the tannoy again.

Will all those who are not applicants please move back from the starting line.

Mothers left sons, brothers left sisters, daughters left fathers, each stepping reluctantly from the bright trackside and back into the murk.

Another blast sounded and a one-minute timer appeared over the images on the screens.

The first round shall begin in exactly one minute. After the next blast, applicants may make their applications. Nine-hundred and seventy-six applications will be accepted. Please will all staff take their seats. Thank you.

The floodlights fell and a gigantic red '976' appeared above the gates. The crowd cheered and a nervous hush descended over the stadium.

'Is this it?' said Ruba. 'They're going to run now?'

'Mmhmm,' said Demetri. He leaned forward on his knees and yawned.

'So it's just a race – '

Saul laughed. 'Just watch,' he said.

The countdown clock reached thirty seconds.

Applicants may now retrieve their weapons.

'What does that mean?' said Ruba.

The crowd began to count down with the clock.

10 – 9 – 8 – 7 – 6 –

Demetri sat up. 'You're about to find out,' he said.

– 3 – 2 – 1 –

The floodlights reignited and the blast sounded. The crowd roared and jumped to their feet. Saul yelped with excitement.

Ruba gasped and held a hand to her mouth.

nineteen

fritters

SAM'S APARTMENT was small and piled with junk that looked like it had accumulated over two centuries of ceaseless hoarding by two opposing forces. One side of the living room was dedicated to books, pictures and paper. The other was taken over by engine parts, grease and metal. Somewhere between them, he had managed to fit two armchairs and a small table – a no-man's land where paper and metal mingled freely over every square inch.

'Sam,' said April. 'Have you ever considered cleaning up in here?'

'April!'

Sam poked his head through the balcony doors. He wore an apron and held a long fork. 'I didn't hear you come in, sweetheart.' He eyed the mess around the room. 'Here, let me clear you a space – '

'Don't worry,' said April, smiling. 'I'll come out to you.'

'You sure?'

'I'm sure.'

April slid off her jacket and threw it on the table. 'I think there's something living in one of those armchairs anyway.'

Sam laughed a hearty, buck-toothed laugh and disappeared back outside.

'Grab yourself a beer,' he shouted.

She pulled two bottles from the fridge in the corner kitchenette and took them out onto the balcony. Sam was poking something black and smoking on a small barbecue he'd set up in one corner. They were fifty floors up in a block facing south of downtown. The sun was setting, but they could still make out the grey smudge from the breach above them.

'Seriously,' said April, leaning a hand on Sam's shoulder and kissing him on his grey-bristled cheek. She handed him one of the beers. 'I don't remember it being this messy when I was growing up.'

'Are you kidding me?' said Sam, flipping one of the black patties. 'Have you ever tried raising a child in a one-bed apartment? There ain't no room for anything else but toys, clothes and bits of plastic.'

'So where did all this stuff come from?' said April. She took a swig of beer and pulled out her cigarettes, lighting two.

'I don't know,' said Sam. 'I guess I needed to fill the space after you left.'

'Even though you don't have any,' she said, handing him a cigarette.

He took a drag and smiled, pushing the patties around on the grill.

'Space is overrated,' he said.

April leaned on the balcony. The sun was setting over the corporation that had been her home all her life. The view was etched in her retina. This balcony had been her playground as a child. Her room was small, not much more than a cupboard that Sam had converted for her, so she quickly claimed the space outside as her own. Miniature wars had been won and lost here between plastic battalions. Dolls had cried; the words and pictures of faded books had been absorbed and memorised as myth; friendships had been forged between the stuffed animals and toys Sam had gathered desperately from friends in those early years. She remembered the chips in the walls, the stains on the floors, the way the shadows changed as the day pushed through its hours. She remembered waking early one morning — she must have been nine — to come out here and play, but, instead of dropping to her knees on the mat in the corner as she usually did, being surprised to find that she could now see over the edge. She remembered standing there on tiptoe, her legs trembling, watching every bit of the sun appear over the gritty horizon. She remembered realising that she was now at the start of something different from the games she usually played, that she was not going to be a child for much longer. She remembered standing here one night at fifteen, gritting her teeth and crying bitter tears that seemed to come from nowhere, a place she could not fathom. She remembered Sam finding her, trying to comfort her, and the look of surprise on his face as she threw off his arm and ran to her room.

She remembered this — the small shabby space that had encompassed the whole landscape of a lonely child's dreams and fears. But she knew she had come from somewhere else entirely, a place beyond the horizon that was now brimming with blue and red lines as the light of the day compressed.

'How's work?' said Sam.

'Good,' said April. 'Busy.'

'Good, that's good,' said Sam. 'You go to The Hiring?'

'Nah,' said April.

'Not even the party?' He peered over the balcony onto the throngs below. 'Sounds like it's hotting up down there.'

'You know that's not my kind of thing.'

'Yeah. Me neither. Had to this time, though. The Hiring, I mean. I got a guy.'

'Seriously?' April turned and leaned her back on the balcony, giving Sam her full attention. 'A New Hire?'

'Yeah. Although I *need* fifty. Work's crazy.'

'I thought that was just the first round?' said April. 'Don't they go into interviews now?'

Sam shook his head. 'Not for my line of work. I don't need to know if they can read or write, just whether they can lift and do as I say. I got one of the back-runners. He wasn't interested in anything too, I don't know, *thinky,* I guess.'

'What's he like?'

April watched Sam drain the first half of his beer. He always downed the first one quickly. He shrugged as he swilled the fluid in his mouth.

'What you'd expect, I guess. Quiet. A little overwhelmed.'

'Where's he staying?'

'I put him in one of the lockups near the shop. I feel bad for the kid really, but he seemed happy enough. I put a bed in there, some food.'

He drank the rest of his beer and set down the empty bottle. Stars were appearing above the endless sprawl of buildings.

'You want another?' said April.

'No, I'm OK.'

'So is he bringing family, your new guy?'

'No family,' said Sam. 'Just him. He's perfect.'

April smirked. 'Another orphan for you.'

Sam frowned and wiped his palm over his mouth. The fritters cracked and spat on the grill.

'You know you once told me you could hear stars?' he said.

'What?' said April.

Sam chuckled, flipped one of the fritters.

'You were five. You said they talked to you.'

'I did not.'

'You did! I'm telling you, you said you heard them calling you.'

'Really?'

'Yeah!'

'And what did they say?'

Sam looked upwards, clicking his tongs.

'They told you their names, let me think – see that one?'

Sam pointed up to the north.

'That one was called Aisha.'

'Aisha? I've never heard that name before in my life.'

'Yeah, and that one next to Aisha,' Sam clicked his tongs to the left, 'that's Suey, and that one was Joose. That's right, Aisha, Suey and Joose. They were your buddies. I had to stand here every night before bedtime and hold you up so you could say goodnight to them.'

'It's high up here. Weren't you scared I'd fall?'

'Nah, I had you. Then I had to tell you why the stars were so dim and the moon was purple. Every night. That was hard. I never heard of any other kids ask those questions. What kid knows any different?'

'Do you think I knew?'

'Knew what?'

'That the stars are brighter outside and that the moon's not really purple. Do you think I remembered seeing the sky from outside?'

Sam shook his head.

'Nah, you were too little when I found you. You couldn't have remembered. These are almost ready.'

April watched Sam pushing the sizzling fritters around on the grill.

'It must have been hard.'

'What?'

'You know. Raising a kid. You were a young man, on your own.'

Sam stopped and looked at her. The dying light shone in his eyes. April readied herself for the usual responses.

Not a bit, you're the best thing that ever happened to me, best thing I ever did.

Sam sighed.

'Sure, it was hard,' he said.

This was new.

'But I had help. I had a lot of friends. And the school in Human Resources took you in, that was a big deal. It was a bit of a hike to get you there before work, but they gave you a good education, right? Not to mention that fancy accent of yours.'

'They must have been a little pissed off when I decided not to take my Colours.'

'More than a little,' said Sam, chuckling. 'Took me a while to smooth *that* one over, I can tell you. But it was your choice in the end. You're not staff.'

He glanced up at her.

'Have you thought any more about it?'

'What, going staff? No way. I'm happy as a contractor. I don't need residency.'

Sam puffed and scratched his cheek.

'Your call,' he said. 'Your call.'

April sipped her beer and shot him a sly look.

'You must have thought about it, though,' she said. 'At the beginning, I mean, about putting me back outside.'

'April, we've been through this – '

'But you must have.' She leaned across, letting her beer bottle hang loosely from her long fingers, moving her head closer to his, giving him that look of hers, that big-eyed, gritted teeth, soft-skinned look she used to gently shake the truth from him like a tiger with a cub's neck. 'Just a little. You must have thought about putting me back.'

'No,' said Sam.

'You'd have been allowed to. They say you can.'

'Never.'

'First year of adoption, found outside the corporation, you can put it back, that's what it – '

'April,' said Sam. He slammed his tongs on the grill.

April let go, settling back to the view. Sam picked up the empty bottle and sucked at it.

'I'll take that beer now,' he said.

April pushed back from the balcony and walked back through the balcony doors. They rattled the way they had always rattled, and the hem of her shirt caught on the broken latch the way it always had done.

She took a beer from the fridge and popped it open. As she closed the door, she saw a photograph. It was an old one of her blowing bubbles in a party frock. She remembered the day, or at least she thought she did. She was at some party up in Oakton for a girl from her school. She remembered all the other girls in her class being there with their mothers. She remembered wondering why she was the only one there without one. She remembered looking up at Sam as he pointed the camera at her. He must have been her age at the time, the right side of thirty, she figured, hair slicked back, face all eager and nervous, trying his best to fit in with the mothers with his best short-sleeved shirt on — for best shirt read *the only one without holes and oil stains.* She remembered blowing those bubbles, but there was something in the way she blew them too — something that said *get away*, or *I don't want to see you, I want to change you into something else.* It wasn't a picture of a child at play, it was a picture of a child already at odds.

'You ready for these?' Sam called back from the grill.

'Sure,' said April. She put the photograph back on the refrigerator and walked back outside.

'Hey, switch that light on, would you?' said Sam.

April flicked the switch by the door and the balcony flickered with blue light.

'Sam?' she said, passing him his beer.

'What?'

'Where are they?'

Sam rapped his tongs on the side of the grill to shake off a fit of blackened meat.

'Where are what?'

'You know,' said April.

Sam paused. He swigged from his bottle.

'Yeah,' he said. He put the tongs down and put down his bottle, looked at his feet. 'I know.'

He sniffed, wiped his nose and threw the tongs back on the grill. Then he skulked back through the apartment and rummaged around in a cupboard. When he reappeared, he was holding a small cardboard box sealed with tape.

'Here,' he said, tossing it into her hands. She looked down at it like a child with a birthday present.

'Are you sure these are the right ones?' she said.

Sam gave a cheerless laugh.

'Right ones?' he said. 'How many of these things do you think there are? They're the *only* ones, April. The only ones in Leafen, I'm sure of it. If they don't work, or they don't fit, then there ain't no more to try.'

April looked down at the box.

'I'll make them fit,' she said.

Sam shook his head.

'I don't doubt it,' he sighed. He scoured the bristle on his cheeks with his palm. 'Listen, April, I – I'm not sure about this. I'm pretty sure they aren't even legal.'

April looked up.

'Let me worry about that, OK?' she said.

'Huh,' said Sam. '*Let you worry*, yeah, right. No can do, April, I'm your father – '

April flinched and looked out at the night, chewing her lips. Sam collected himself, shaking off the same injury he endured the countless times he'd said that word to her.

'What do you want, April?' he said. 'What do you think you're going to find out there?'

April shrugged.

'Just let me – '

'Yeah, I know.' Sam held up his hand and swung away to lean on the balcony. 'Let you worry about that.'

He shook his head and looked down at the twinkling street fifty storeys below.

'Sam – ' said April.

'It's OK,' he said. 'I know, you're all grown up, I just – '

'No, Sam,' said April. 'The fritters.'

Sam sniffed the air and swung round. Smoke was rising from the corner of the balcony.

'Shit!' he said. He leaped past April and grabbed the tongs, scraping at the grill. 'Ah, shit.'

He held one blackened husk up to the light.

'Pizza?' he said.

April laughed.

'No thanks.' She held up the box. 'I have to get going anyway.'

'Already?' said Sam. 'I thought – '

'Sorry.'

'OK, well, I'll see you tomorrow, I guess – '

'I'll call you,' she shouted, running back through the apartment.

The door slammed and Sam stood alone, inspecting the charred fritter before him.

'Yeah,' he said, to nobody. He threw the tongs back on the grill and picked up his beer. 'I love you too.'

twenty

man is weak

STEVE PACED his office, flitting through scenarios. He imagined himself bolting, leaving The Office, heading out past the suburbs and finding some small forest to hide out in, just letting the world turn on and carry the burden of his mistake without him.

Then he imagined sirens, screams, flames and stampeding feet, all the varying degrees of atrocity that might be unleashed upon his world if he failed to stop them. And he thought about time – what hours or minutes did he have left to change things? Or was it already too late?

Then he imagined himself in the board room, telling Daniel, the words 'my fault' on his lips. Then Daniel's face, the muscles in his cheeks taut with a furious grin, a fist raised, a punch, *you're fired.*

And then outside, in chains, traipsing through The Line to whatever short and miserable life lay beyond.

And then he thought about the forest again, and the shelter of tall trees.

And he thought about Faith. And he thought about Holly. And he thought about a good man in a garage.

At some point his pacing took him out into the corridor, then out onto the balcony and finally, in the orange light of late afternoon, he found himself wandering through Leafen's empty streets. The roads had been closed for The Hiring. It was still in full swing; Steve could hear the roars and drums pounding from the stadium.

He realised that it had been four hours since Faith had abandoned him on the balcony. The day had worn on, oblivious to the panic raging in his head. Nothing else unusual had happened. No alerts, no reboots, no sirens, just the slow arc of the sun over his home.

Now, all this panic was beginning to seem absurd. Perhaps he was worrying for no reason. Everything was at peace. And right now, as the shadows of dusk tilted and evening's warm air filled with the distant roar of people – people to whom he was helping to bring untold prosperity – it seemed impossible that this peace could be broken. Impossible that a moment of doubt could lead to the downfall of everything.

Impossible that a mistake could lead to reproach.

Retaliation.

War.

He dropped his eyes and opened a call, sending a scatter of lights down his Fronds. Soon, he felt his mother's presence.

'Steve? Is that you?'

'Yes, Mother, it's me. Are you all right?'

'I'm fine, just fine. Where are you? All these alerts today, I just don't know what's going on.'

'Are you at home?'

'Of course I am.'

'Good, stay there.'

'But, they're having a street party later. I thought –'

'Just stay in the house, Mother.'

'Well, now, Steve, I think I should go. I haven't met many of the neighbours since you moved me out here and they're…well, they're different, Steve. These big houses, you know? Everyone's so –'

'Mother. Please. Stay in the house, just for today. Keep yourself safe.'

There was a pause. Steve heard a nail being bitten.

'All right, if you say so, I will. But Steve, you know you don't have to worry about me, don't you? You never did. That's a mother's job.'

There was another pause.

'Steve, what's wrong?'

'I have to go Mother. Promise me you'll stay in the house.'

'I promise, but Steve –'

He closed the call and looked around at the intersection to which he had drifted. On one side was *Greenback's*, the bar he had been in earlier. His mouth was dry – a cold beer would be just fine – but, like everything else along the strip, the place was closed for The Hiring.

On the other side of the intersection was a tall, white building with an oak door and chalk steps running up to it. Ely Loome's church. The door was open. Without thinking, he crossed the road.

Inside, cool, muffled darkness and stone-scented air cloaked him instantly. Rows of seats stretched out on either side of the long aisle, empty apart from an old woman hunched in prayer. Her back heaved and quivered as she muttered into her hands. Five stone pillars made corridors in the darkness. Tall candles burned in each one. The draught from the slamming door made their flames duck in unison, before realigning into still bulbs of light.

He walked a few rows and took a seat, looking around. The walls were decorated with wooden murals — elaborately carved words and pictures that were familiar to everyone. They were learned as children.

Man is Weak, Put your Faith in The Market.

Reap ye well for The Market is Plentiful

No Sacrifice Is More Holy Than The Many for the Few

Profit is The Word of Truth

Near the front was a wooden stand lit with candles. Stuck to it were children's drawings, versions of well-known triptychs in primary colours and lopsided scrawls.

Collaborate: to stand apart you must first stand together

Persist: the last key will always open the lock

Take your seat. Your Trade is your Soul.

Know others. Know yourself. Know your Colours.

Hang in there –

The words seemed as etched in Steve's mind as they were in the wood and paper.

'It appears we keep meeting in dark places.'

Steve turned to see a portly man at the end of the aisle.

'In *Greenback's* earlier,' said the priest. 'You were in quite a hurry.'

Steve nodded in recognition.

'Don't worry,' said the priest, smiling. 'I'm not here to judge. My name is Father Roberts,' he said.

'Manager,' said Steve. 'Steve.'

The priest cleared his throat and gestured to the bench.

'Do you mind if I – ?'

Steve looked down at the space beside him.

'Unless you'd rather be on your own?' said the priest.

'No,' said Steve. 'Please.'

'Because I understand if you just want to – '

Steve remained silent, finished with the pleasantries, eyes ahead. The priest sat down next to him, letting his round body fill the small space.

'Do you mind me asking why you're here?' he asked.

Steve thought for a moment and frowned.

'I don't know why I'm here,' he said at last.

'Are you lost?' said the priest.

Steve frowned.

'Lost? Your church is opposite The Leaf. How could I be lost?'

'I didn't mean that kind of lost.'

Steve felt the priest watching him.

'But I think you knew that.'

After a moment the priest sniffed and adjusted himself in the seat. He folded his hands over his considerable belly and exhaled.

'*I don't know why I'm here*,' he said. 'Every lost soul I've ever met has said those same words.'

He leant closed to Steve, smiling. Steve smelled alcohol on his breath.

'And I believe I've met my fair share.'

He laughed, waiting for Steve to reciprocate in the warm cradle he had made in the conversation. But the laugh failed to return. He swallowed and straightened up.

'And this is an excellent place for such people to come,' he persevered.

They sat for a while in silence. White lights and shadows danced above the pulpit, behind the frosted interior windows of the church.

'What do they do in there?' said Steve at last.

'Hmm?' said Roberts, looking up at the glass. 'In Accounts?'

'There are people in there. What's their purpose?'

Roberts raised his eyebrows, as if the question were new to him.

'Accountants? Your guess is as good as mine,' he said.

'You don't know? But you're a priest.'

'Exactly,' he laughed. 'Why would I? The purpose of those behind the glass, the complexities – the *mysteries* of The Market – '

He sighed.

'None of my concern. '

'So what is your concern?' asked Steve.

Roberts shrugged.

'I'm more of a people person. I'm interested in what makes somebody do what they do, what makes them happy, what makes them angry.'

He paused, scratched his chin.

'What makes them seek the sanctuary of my church.'

Steve's brow flickered as he felt the priest's eyes dwell on his face. Just then, he felt a crackle in his Fronds. A call was coming in. Images and words trickled around his mind, arranging themselves into a single concept: *Faith Pey, Green/Red Premium Executive Class, Personal Assistant to Daniel Leafen.*

He must have jumped because Roberts put a hand on Steve's arm.

'Are you all right?'

'Yes,' said Steve. 'Excuse me, I have to take this.'

'Of course, of course, don't mind me.'

Roberts stood and busied himself by arranging books on the opposite aisle.

'Hello?' said Steve.

There was silence. He could hear her breathing, the sounds of her mouth.

'I called them,' she said.

Steve stood up.

'You did? What did they say? Who did you speak to?'

'Commander Po's assistant, Zai. I made it sound like I was calling him about some administrative issues – '

Her voice trailed off. He heard her swallow.

'Faith?'

'Steve, something's wrong. Something's very wrong.'

Steve's stomach lurched. He sat down and gripped the bench in front.

'What do you mean?'

'Zai and I have a good relationship. We speak a lot, we share a lot. But he was different.'

'Different how?'

'He wanted to be off the call. He wouldn't give me anything I asked for. He was cold, Steve. He was – he was on protocol. I'm sure of it.'

'What does that mean?'

'It means he's been told to – '

She stopped. Steve could hear voices in the background.

'I have to go. Steve, you have to tell Daniel. Now.'

'Faith – '

'I mean it, Steve.'

'Faith, why did you call them?'

'What?'

'Soor, why did you call them? You said you wanted no part of this.'

Nothing. Footsteps and breathing.

'I had a feeling. Feelings.'

'About what?'

More voices in the background. He thought he could hear Daniel's rasping laugh.

'I have to go. Steve, tell them.'

'Faith, wait – '

The call dropped and the space that had opened up inside Steve's head quickly filled with his own thoughts once again. He leant forwards on his hands and breathed deeply.

'That was a girl.'

He looked up. Father Roberts stood smiling.

'Pardon?'

Roberts winked.

'You were talking to a girl, I could tell.'

Steve looked away.

'I need to go,' he said.

Roberts raised his hand.

'Don't be fooled by the get-up! I might be a priest, *married to The Market* and all, but I still know the *feels* when I see them. Those little flickers on your face, the warble in your voice; it's all there, son.'

He grinned, pleased with himself.

'I really need to go,' said Steve, standing. 'Excuse me.'

'Still feel them myself sometimes,' he went on, blocking Steve in the aisle. 'Especially on warm days like this, with all the skirts and blouses and what have you.'

He laughed.

'Father Roberts, please, I really – '

Roberts' knowing smile flickered, and gave way to a flash of urgency.

'I guess it doesn't matter how you dress a man up,' he said, gesturing to his clothes.

'Robe, collar – '

Then to Steve. He looked at him intently, smile falling away.

'Suit, tie. Red, blue, black, white, purple. It doesn't change what's going on in here.'

He tapped his head.

'Or here.'

He laid a hand on Steve's chest. Steve looked down at it. He knew how fast it was beating.

'You need to listen to that, son. Listen to the beat. It won't stop until it's too late.'

'Please,' said Steve. 'I need to leave.'

Roberts took a step back. Steve walked past but stopped dead.

'Mr Manager.'

Ely Loome stood silhouetted in the candlelight, his hands crossed beneath the long sleeves of his robe.

'What a pleasure to see you here,' he said.

Roberts cleared his throat.

'Your Grace,' said Roberts. 'Er, Steve and I were just having a quiet talk.'

Loome looked at Roberts like a hawk at a slug.

'Good,' he said. 'How *nice*.'

He inclined his head.

'Quite a day for Mr Manager. I imagine you have lots to – *reflect* upon.'

'I really just came here for some peace,' said Steve.

Loome frowned.

'Peace,' he said. He let the word trail off, as if it was a piece of a jigsaw that didn't fit. 'Well, don't let me keep you from your peace.'

He turned to Father Roberts.

'Roberts, don't you have work to do?'

'Or course, Your Grace.'

The priest bowed and, without thinking, touched Loome's elbow. Loome pulled his arm away in disgust. Roberts jumped back in horror.

'My apologies, Your Grace,' he gasped. 'I wasn't thinking.'

Loome turned to Steve, his face gradually returning to a firm frown.

'My door is always open, Mr Manager. Oh, and if you don't mind, we prefer to have Fronds turned off within the church. It can affect others' *peace.*'

'I'm leaving anyway,' said Steve. He started to walk, but found his path still blocked. Loome cleared his throat.

'Fine,' said Steve, performing his signature – the knuckles of both hands knocked together three times.

'Thank you,' said Loome. 'And good evening.'

With that, he floated away to his chambers, glowering at Roberts as he passed. Steve made for the door.

'Wait,' said Roberts. 'Don't go yet. You need help. I can tell.'

Steve stopped in his tracks. He looked down at his hands, shaking, then back at the broad, glistening face of the priest.

'It's not me who needs help, Father Roberts,' he said. 'It's everyone else.'

twenty-one

not just the music

DEMETRI PUT his arm on Turnett's shoulder. He was sitting with his head between his legs, spitting bile into the mess at his feet. The Hiring was over and the crowd was making their way down to the stadium's ground level, where the stage for the evening's concert was being set up.

'That – ' said Turnett, holding back another retch. 'That was a bad one.'

'It's OK,' said Demetri. 'It's over now, buddy.'

He turned to Ruba, who was staring at the empty stadium with her arms folded.

'Are you OK?' said Demetri. 'I guess I should have warned you. Sorry about that.'

'I'm fine,' said Ruba. 'That was – a very efficient selection process.'

Saul merrily walked along the row of seats with a fresh beer in his hand.

'So, are you staying for Jola?' he said.

'Yeah,' said Demetri. 'But I promised I'd meet my brother down on the ground. He wants to be near the front. Wait, what's the time?'

'Almost six,' said Campbell.

'I'd better go. Can someone look after him?'

'I've got him,' said Saul, hauling Turnett to his feet. 'Come on man, brighten up. Let's get you another beer.'

'I'll see you later,' said Demetri. 'Stay here so I can find you, will you?'

They waved him off and he trotted down the long flight of steps. The stage was almost finished by the time he reached the ground and the sun was setting over The Line. Leafeners were flocking from all directions, fluttering with excitement and filling the space, avoiding the areas where the gruesome detritus from the show they had just witnessed was being cleaned away with mops and buckets.

He found Alex at the spot they had agreed. They greeted each other and stood in silence. Alex was small and the crowd around them wasn't, which meant that he could barely see the stage. More and more people were pushing their way to the front, filling up the space with craning heads that would soon be silhouetted by neon lights.

'Do you want to move further up?' said Demetri.

'No, it's fine,' said Alex. 'Here's fine.'

He had his hands in his back pockets, like he always did, swaying his shoulders.

'But you can't see from here,' he said. 'Maybe we could move further back? Get a better view?'

'Here's perfect,' said Alex. 'This is where the sound is centred. Those losers in the seats won't hear anything. They're probably only here for *Meatjack* or *Crumblefoot*. Hopefully, he'll play them first and then they can all go home so we can listen to the real music.'

'OK,' said Demetri. 'You're the boss, little brother, you're the boss.'

Two girls with pigtails pushed between them, holding hands.

'Watch it,' said Demetri. One spun around. The orange light of the sunset danced on her face. A lollipop stick jutted out from a pink, lipsticked grin. She looked at Alex, winked, then pirouetted back and followed her friend through the crowd.

'I think she liked you,' said Demetri. 'Why don't you go after her?'

Alex said nothing. His shoulders resumed their sway.

'Just saying,' said Demetri. 'She was cute.'

He looked down at his little brother, suddenly swamped with love. He tried to remember being fifteen, but couldn't.

Suddenly his head filled with a hideous screech. He bent over and clamped his hands to his head.

'What's wrong? Demetri?'

'Fuck! What's that sound?'

'There's no sound. Demetri, what's wrong?'

Demetri stood up.

'Nothing. It's gone. Didn't you hear that?'

Alex shook his head. Just then the lights dropped and the stadium became swamped in screams, cheers and whistles. A deep, pulsing drone announced itself through the speakers.

'Sure you're OK?' said Alex.

'Yeah, I think I'm good.'

The drone became a rhythmic pulse and two hollow blasts of something that sounded like a horn section being dragged through chicken wire assaulted the room, accompanied by two bright flashes of light. The crowd erupted in recognition.

'*Enduring the Stain*,' shouted Alex, nodding in appreciation. 'Cool opener.'

As the afterglow faded, Demetri saw pinpricks of lights falling from far above, dancing and spiralling to the ground. The crowd looked up and sighed. The lights reached their heads and began prancing between them, dotting on the scalps. One landed on Demetri and he tried to brush it off, but it dodged his swipe. The light stopped and turned to Demetri, showing him that it had a little face, crowned with a halo, arms and wings like a fairy. The face pouted at him, hands on its tiny hips, blew a raspberry and danced off.

Alex was counting some silent rhythm with his finger. Another two blasts — another two air strikes from Alex. The drone grew and rose in pitch. Alex raised his other hand as if he was controlling the sound all by himself.

A thin tube of brilliant, blue light appeared between the roof and the stage. At the base of it, looking upwards with his arms outstretched, was a small man. His hair was long and white and slicked back over his head. His beard was similarly white and pointed, with nine red coloured beads braided into their oiled tips. He wore a pair of wire sunglasses with round, black lenses, dark, skinny trousers, a white shirt, tie and a tight jacket, obsidian black, clinging to his muscled abdomen. Around his neck was slung a black stick shining with strings. The crowd exploded into every noise imaginable as he began to swagger, pointed toe in front of pointed toe, arms still outstretched, towards a long console of lights. He ran his hand through his hair and raised his head. He appeared to breathe in the roar of the crowd, who were now surging into a thick knot at the front.

A wide grin spread across Jola's face, sending the crowd into fresh paroxysms. He stretched out his hands and nodded slowly as the drone climbed and climbed, swamping the room in a thick bed of noise. The air shuddered. Then, suddenly the noise and lights dropped. Two more blasts and Jola's face was the only thing lit in the room, hovering in the blackness. He spoke in deep monotone. The words filled the room.

'All. Over. Us.'

The lights blazed and a cacophonous beat stumbled in like a drunk at a party. A surge of pads, harmonies and vocal effects followed, clamouring for attention, rocketing and nose-diving around the arena. The crowd jumped along, hands held high.

All except Demetri, who was crouching, squashing his palms in his eye sockets, trying to stop the feeling of a white hot poker being driven into his cerebrum.

twenty-two

monkeys

'ARE YOU finished, sweetheart?' said Emelia.

Her daughter was sitting on the toilet, nightdress hitched up and underpants around her ankles. She yawned and rubbed her eyes, then pulled a smile like a frog.

'You need some help?'

Lori nodded.

'Wipe,' she said.

Emelia cleaned her daughter's bottom and helped her off the bowl.

'Flush?' said Emelia. 'Say bye-bye to the poo?'

Lori pulled the flush and made a little wave as her stool spiralled down the U-bend.

'Where does all the poo go, Mama?'

'It goes down the pipe, sweetheart. Come on, let's get you into bed.'

Lori followed her mother through to her room.

'But then where?'

Emelia did a sweep of the carpet, picking up the toys and books and drawings her daughter had distributed across it that day.

'Hmm?' she said. She pulled back Lori's sheets and smoothed the pillows. 'Come on now, into bed.'

Lori jumped in and pulled up the sheets, stuffing her thumb in her mouth. Emelia sat down on the bed.

'The poo, Mama,' said Lori. 'Where does it go after the pipe?'

'To a bigger pipe,' she said.

'And then?' said Lori.

Emelia lowered her brow and held out her hands like claws.

'An even bigger pipe,' she said, her voice a mock growl. Lori gave a tremor of delight.

'And then – ?' she said, grinning and bracing herself.

'To the biggest pipe of all!' roared Emelia. She leaped on Lori and tickled her ribs. The little girl fell into a mess of helpless giggles. Emelia finally let her go.

'Come on,' she said, pulling up her sheets again. 'Enough. Sleep.'

Lori lay back, drunk with mirth, and let her mother tuck her in.

'Where does it go after the biggest pipe?' said Lori.

'Lori!' said Emelia.

'I want to know! Where does it go?'

Emelia sighed.

'It goes outside, Lori. Now lie down, please.'

'Outside?'

'Yes, outside.'

'Outside of the world?'

'Kind of,' said Emelia. 'Outside Leafen. Outside our corporation.'

Lori yawned and sucked her thumb, looking around the ceiling, chasing her thoughts.

'Is the biggest pipe of all where the Underfolk live?' she said.

'Lori, there's no such thing as the Underfolk,' said Emelia. 'They're just a myth.'

'What's a myth?' said Lori.

Emelia shrugged.

'A myth is make-believe,' she said. 'Like a made-up story.'

'Why do people make up stories?'

Tough questions. Always tough questions at bedtime.

'Because – because people like pretending,' she said at last.

'Why?'

'Same reason you do, sweetheart.'

Lori shook her head, offended.

'I don't pretend,' she said.

'Yes, you do.'

'When?' said Lori, sitting up. This was serious.

'Well, you pretend to be a horsey, don't you?'

Lori looked at the curtain, thinking about it. She pulled a stuffed racoon from the side of the bed.

'I suppose – ' she said.

'And you pretend to be a doctor, don't you?'

'Yes,' said Lori, pointing a finger. 'Like you, Mama.'

'Right,' said Emelia. 'So there you go. It's fun, that's why people pretend.'

'So grown-ups pretend too?'

Emelia sighed and stroked her daughter's hair.

'Yes, Lori,' she said. 'Grown-ups pretend all the time.'

She kissed Lori's forehead.

'Mama?' said Lori.

'Is Enola OK?'

'Enola's sleeping, sweetheart.'

'Are you going out? For The Hiring?'

'No, sweetie. I'm staying to look after you.'

'Enola could look after me.'

'No, she can't.'

'But she's just like you.'

'She's not, sweetheart, she's not. She's just a child.'

'Mama?'

'Yes, sweetie.'

'Can *I* have a story?'

'Sure you can,' said Emelia, pulling a book from a pile by the bed. 'Lie down, now.'

She opened the book and began to read.

Five little monkeys happy as can be,
Sitting in the branches of a coconut tree,
One said 'move!' and another said 'no!',
So he pushed him, down, down to the sand below.

A few blocks north, Sam was halfway through his fifth beer and third cigarette. He blew smoke out onto the still night. Far below on the street, the crowds were still partying. Car horns blared and lights swept the sky and bands played music from every direction.

He worried about April. She was no longer the little girl he had raised as his own all those years ago. She could make her own decisions, do what she wanted.

But shouldn't she want to go out? Enjoy the party? Have a drink? Play with the affections of some idiot in a suit while he tried to dance with her? Date? Get married? Have kids. Raise them –

Sam sighed and flicked ash into the warm breeze. No, that didn't seem like April at all.

Four little monkeys, one branch each,
Juicy ripe coconuts just out of reach,
One said 'food!' and another stretched a hand,
But he slipped and he fell, now he's still upon the sand.

April stood in Sam's workshop before the engine of the ancient truck. Old leather, rust and engine oil filled her nostrils. She reached into her pocket and pulled out the box. She shook it once. It rattled. Then she tore at the tape and pulled it open. Eight small, white tubes rolled about inside, tipped with a thick thread at one end and a metallic contact at the other. She picked one out.

Her jacket snagged on the hood and the box tipped, sending the tubes tumbling into the engine cavity beneath and tinkling on the stone floor.

As she reached out to rescue them, a loud bang thundered overhead. The workshop roof shook and the lights flickered off. In the pitch black, April sprang up, banging her head on the hood.

'Ow!' she screamed.

'Are you OK?' said a voice behind her.

Three little monkeys underneath the sky,
Watching each other with six worried eyes,
One leaped up and he tore off a stick,
Went to work on number three, made the job quick.

Steve was halfway to the church door when Roberts caught up with him.

'I can offer advice?' he said, keeping pace.

Steve kept walking.

'Someone offered me advice once.'

'What kind of advice?'

'It doesn't matter. I didn't take it. I didn't take it for fifteen years. Until today. And now it might have ruined everything.'

He stopped with his hand on the large, iron knob and turned.

'Goodbye, Father Roberts. It was nice talking to – '

'Well, it was nice talking to you – Steve? What's wrong?'

Steve was looking up at the frosted glass. His face grew pale.

'They've stopped. Why have the shadows stopped moving?'

Two little monkeys standing up tall,
Neither wants to make a move, neither wants to fall,
One raised his arms to the midday sun,
He brought them down hard and that left one.

'Ah, April – ' Sam breathed into the air. Smoke followed the word out into the night. The light from the city shone around it.

There was a heavy thump and the building shuddered. The light disappeared, the smoke disappeared, the air emptied of all sound and movement.

'April?' said Sam again. He watched the buildings around him flicker to black, darkness rippling out towards the horizon like ink dropped into a fluorescent pool. The cigarette fell from Sam's fingers, an orange speck tumbling into the dark. Sam was suddenly aware of his own breath. It was the only thing he could hear. The music had stopped. The crowds had silenced. He looked down into the deep dark. He could see something beneath, a trail of light on the streets below, unmoving, like a faint glowing thread.

'April,' he said. He turned and fled through the dark apartment.

One clever monkey happy as can be,
Sitting all alone in his very own tree.

Emilia closed the book and ran her hand over the cover, remembering all the times her mother had read her the same rhyme.

'OK, sweetheart, bedtime.'

Emelia looked up at her daughter. She wore an expression she had not seen before — a weary and wistful look that did not belong on a young girl's face.

'Lori?'

Somewhere in the distance there was a long, deep rumble.

PART THREE

stop

twenty-three

double dropper

DEMETRI STOPPED screaming and stood up, surprised to hear the echo of his own voice.

The pain had stopped. The music had stopped. The crowd had stopped.

Everything had stopped.

He waited, thinking that perhaps this was part of the show and that at any moment the stadium would erupt with noise once again. But there was nothing — no sound, no light, no movement. The swarming crowd was now a still, silent lake strung with strange threads of faint light. At its shore was a black island – the stage – where a single light glowed.

There was a scream, then terrified voices calling in the distance; people trying to find each other in the dark. Demetri looked around for his brother, but he was gone.

'Alex!' he shouted.

He walked ahead, astonished by the sound of his own footsteps splashing in the puddles of spilt drinks and the glow of the crowd's Fronds, brighter than he ever thought possible. He stepped cautiously between them, saying *excuse me* as he went, despite the growing realisation that they were oblivious to his presence.

He quickened his pace. As the crowd grew tighter he had to push his way past. The people he knocked into swayed and returned, as if they were nothing but heavy coats hanging from hooks. A small one yelped as he pushed it.

'Help!'

It was a girl's voice, terrified.

'What's happening? Is this part of the concert? I'm scared.'

Demetri stopped.

'Can you see me?' said Demetri.

'Just about,' said the girl. 'Wait.'

Demetri heard the scrape of flint and a small orange flame lit the girl's face – fake-lashed eyes the size of saucers and a downturned mouth trembling with fear.

'What's wrong with your pupils?' said Demetri. 'Have you – taken something?'

The girl gave a weak smile and nodded. Her chest rose and fell in deep waves.

'A pill. Two, actually.'

She exhaled deeply, looking around.

'I'm really, really high. My friend Mary took some too, have you seen her? I said we should turn off our Fronds because, you know, I've heard you're supposed to if you, well, you know, but she didn't. I did but she didn't. I'm kind of worried about her. Phew. Thirsty.'

She swallowed and smiled.

'Hi! I'm Karina. I'm so glad you're here. You seem nice, you have a really nice face – nice face. Do – '

Another hard swallow. She leant closer.

'Do you know what's happening?' she whispered.

'No,' said Demetri. 'Why has everyone stopped moving?'

'I do not know,' she said. She brushed his cheek with her fingernails. This seemed to overwhelm her and her eyelids fluttered. 'Oh wow,' she said. 'Oh wow oh wow oh wow what's going on oh wow – '

'OK, Karina, take it easy, just calm down. I think you should come with me, all right? Did you say you had your Fronds turned off?'

Karina gulped and blew out, fanning her face with her hand.

'Yes, I sure did, sir,' she said. 'Wait, I mean – are you? A sir? I'm sorry.' She began laughing hysterically into her hands. Her lighter dropped to the floor.

'Hey,' said Demetri, stooping to find the lighter. 'Can you try to be quiet, please? I'm trying to find my brother. Have you seen him? He's fifteen.'

'Oh no, OK, no. Or maybe. What does he look like? Is he cute? I bet he's cute, I bet he *is*.'

Demetri found the lighter and lit it, illuminating them both.

'Yay,' said Karina. She looked up at him with her yearning, spinning eyes, holding her hand to her breast as if she'd just seen a puppy. 'Did I say you have a nice face? Oh you do – I'm sorry – I'm not usually – can I take your arm – oh that feels nice, it really does – '

'Just keep quiet and follow me. Alex!'

'Wow, wow, they're all so – so still.'

'Alex! Can you hear me?'

'She's got nice eyebrows – and he has a nice nose, and this one, he – he has lovely hair.'

He led the blabbering girl through the crowd, calling for Alex as he went. In the distance he heard voices calling, their words lost in the huge space around them. Up ahead, he saw an outline he recognised.

'Alex?'

Demetri ran, dragging Karina whooping behind him and pushing bodies aside as he went. He grabbed Alex's shoulder.

'Alex, I got you. Alex? What's wrong?"

Demetri shook him, but his brother just sighed and looked through him with eyes like distant seas.

'He's like the others,' said Karina. She looked around at the still crowd of faces. 'Just like the others.'

twenty-four

marl

'SHIT, SHIT, bollocks, ow!'

April clutched her head and staggered back against the truck. She grabbed a flashlight from her tool belt, fumbled with the switch and shone it in the direction of the voice.

Caught in the beam was a young man, well built and badly dressed. His shirt was untucked on one side of the ridiculously large, pleated trousers that he'd tightened with rope. Taut muscles carved summits in his shoulders. His skin was shining brown, the same complexion you saw on visitors from the Joomba corporation, with their spicy stews and fragrant flowers and strange myths about elephants and monkeys living inside the soul of The Market. He swayed, shielding his eyes from the light.

'Who are you?' said April, edging towards him.

'My name is Marl,' said the young man. 'Please, I – '

'Don't move,' said April, thrusting the light at him. 'Are you the New Hire? How did you get in here? My – Sam said you were in a lockup. Why are the lights out? What was that bang?'

'Your questions are numerous, madam.' He reached out. 'Please – '

'Stop. Just stay where you are.'

Marl withdrew, blinking.

'Did you break in?' said April.

'Yes. Yes I did.'

'On your first day?'

'Yes. I am sorry. Please do not tell Mr Samuel. I heard a noise.'

Marl took another tentative step towards the car. April flung out her hand.

'Stay back!' she said. He froze, then made to move again. 'I'm serious! Stay where you are.'

Eventually, he relaxed and slunk back despondently, putting his hands in his pockets.

'Please do not tell Mr Samuel.'

'How on earth did you break in? That door's triple locked with a dead bolt.'

Marl shrugged.

'I know how things work,' he said. His eyes moved to the truck. 'That machine — it is from beyond The Line, is it not?'

'Yes. Do you recognise it?'

'No, but I have seen vehicles like it. It is very old, you know. Why do you have it?'

'That's none of your business,' said April. She turned and peered into the engine cavity, searching for the fallen plugs.

'Are you trying to mend it?' said Marl.

'Like I said, none of your business.' She reached a hand in and fished about, pulling out one of the plugs.

'I could help you,' said Marl. 'I know where those things go. I know the right tools to use.'

'Just you keep your distance.'

'I understand. As for your other questions, I do not know why the lights are out, or what the bang was.'

'Try the switch,' said April.

'What switch?'

'At the door, try it.'

Marl shuffled to the door and tried the switch.

'It does not work,' said Marl.

'Maybe the strips are blown,' said April.

'There is no light outside either,' said Marl. April heard the door squeak open and his voice retreating into the long alleyway outside. 'The streets are dark. I think it is possibly a power cut.'

'Power cut? We don't get power cuts. I'm calling Sam.'

April closed her eyes and held her hand against her heart,

pumping her four fingers in turn. She felt a surge in her neck as her Fronds tried to boot, but it subsided. She tried again with the same result. It felt like two magnets being pushed together at the same poles.

'I can't start my Fronds. Can you?'

'I have no Fronds.'

'Fuck.'

'No Fronds and no power,' sighed Marl. 'It must be a power cut. You have a power cut. A very big one.'

'I told you, we don't get power cuts. This is something else.'

She swung the light back in Marl's direction.

'Please, that is very bright.'

'You step outside first and I'll follow,' said April. 'I need to go and find out what's going on.'

She ushered him out into the alleyway. When they reached the end they turned right. April looked up at the sky. The moon was a purple crescent poking out from behind The Leaf — now a black, lightless monolith a few blocks in the distance. The stars were many and bright.

'It is very quiet,' said Marl. 'Where are the cars?'

'2nd Street's around this corner,' said April. 'I think I can see something.'

A long boulevard loomed ahead, dark and quiet and still. The air seemed to be filled with an incandescent mist. April turned off her flashlight and followed it.

'What is this?' said April.

People were all around them. Their hands had fallen by their sides. Their heads were downturned. Their eyes moved around, from side to side and up and down, and one would occasionally smile or frown or flutter their eyelids, but they seemed oblivious to each other, unaware that they were in the dark. April shone her light in the face of a woman in a green bodysuit and fur coat. Her pupils tightened like molluscs, but she didn't flinch. April scanned the ground with her beam. All around were puddles of spilt booze and plastic cups, which, she guessed, had been in the hands of the crowds just moments before.

'Why are they not moving?' said Marl. 'This is very strange. Can they hear us?'

'I don't know,' breathed April. 'I don't – '

She turned off the flashlight.

'Look,' she said. 'Look at the Fronds.'

The source of the mist became clear. Every neck along the packed street was glowing white and buzzing with energy.

'I've never seen them so bright,' said April.

Marl walked over to a man with his head turned up to the sky.

'Hello, sir?' He waved his hand before the man's face. 'Can you hear me? Hello? Sir?'

The man gave a long, tired sigh and turned his head away.

'It is as if they are in a dream,' said Marl.

twenty-five

up there

THE CHURCH doors slammed shut. Steve and Father Roberts looked down in horror upon the still and passive crowd below.

'What is this?' whispered Roberts.

He walked down the steps and stopped at a huddle of girls, snapping his fingers in their faces. They seemed to register it, but only as a minor annoyance, like a passing fly. He shook their shoulders and gently slapped their cheeks, but neither changed expression. One raised a tentative hand, but only made it halfway up before it fell back to her side. Another sighed.

He moved on to a boy looking down at a half-eaten hotdog. Mustard was oozing from his lips.

'Hello? Child, are you OK? Are you awake?'

'He can't hear you,' said Steve. He pulled down the collar of the man beside him – the boy's father, he presumed – flinching at the touch of his neck.

'Their Fronds are hot. Burning.'

'What caused this?' said Roberts.

'I don't know.'

Steve nodded up at the distant halo of light shining in the clouds. The upper balconies of The Leaf.

'But I need to get up there.'

twenty-six

i can help

LORI'S FRONDS were blazing, lighting up her bedroom wall in a spray of pink.

'Lori?' breathed Emelia. 'Are you OK, honey?'

She put her arms on her daughter's shoulders.

'Lori? Are you awake?'

Lori's eyes drooped in half moons. She sighed and looked up at the ceiling as if it was a sky full of rain.

'What's wrong, sweetheart?'

As Lori's head turned, her Fronds became more exposed.

'Lori – Lori, Lori, Lori,' whispered Emelia as she touched the bright strands beneath her daughter's skin.

'What's happening?' said a voice.

Emelia turned to see Enola in the doorway.

'Nothing. Go back.'

She stood up and opened the blind. Nothing changed; no extra light joined the eerie pink of Lori's Fronds. She opened the window. Beneath her were over a hundred storeys of apartments that had, a few minutes before, been lit up. The streets below had been streams of light and music.

Now the noise was gone and every building was in darkness. The streets were just imagined gullies in a black, empty space. A single, shrill scream rose up from the street, quickly engulfed like a mouse-squeak. Another one responded from a few blocks away, like a terrified answer to a mating call.

'Emelia?' said Enola. 'What's wrong with Lori?'

Emelia turned and wrapped Lori in a blanket.

'I have to go, Enola. Stay here.'

She ran past her, scooping up her bag from the floor, but she tripped and the bag fell.

'*Shit.*'

As she struggled to find it in the dark corridor, Lori slipped from her arms.

'*Shit, shit.*'

She felt a hand on her shoulder. Enola lifted the bag and helped her to her feet, gazing all the while at Lori's blazing Fronds.

'I can carry her, Emelia,' she said. 'I can help.'

twenty-seven

postulating

APRIL AND Marl continued up 1st Street in the beam of her flashlight.

'Where are we going?' said Marl.

'To find Sam,' said April.

'Samuel? My boss?'

'That's right.'

'Why? Will he know what to do?'

'I hope so. Sam knows how to fix most things.'

Marl nodded and smiled.

'That is good. I am glad he is my employer. He is your employer too?'

They crossed through the pedestrian area and onto the road. Every car had stopped, their interiors glowing with Fronds like white-hot brands on the necks of their drivers.

'No, he's my – wait – did you hear that?' said April.

'I am not sure. What did you hear?' said Marl.

'I think I heard someone – shhh – there, again.'

There were shouts far in the distance — a girl's voice echoing from the wall of a building.

'I heard that,' said Marl.

'Hey!' shouted April. She waved her flashlight in the air. 'Over here! Come on, let's follow it.'

'What do you think is happening?' said Marl.

'I have no idea,' said April.

'Maybe they have fallen into comas,' said Marl. 'A deep sleep. A catatonic state.'

'But why? And why are everyone's Fronds so bright?'

April froze.

'Wait,' she said. 'Did you hear that?'

'I am not sure – '

Close by, a voice was calling.

'There.'

'*April!*'

'Sam! This way.' April grabbed Marl's arm and dragged him along, aiming for a light she saw swinging ahead. Pushing her way through the mass of bodies she burst into a clearing and ran straight into Sam's chest. He grabbed her and held her.

'April, are you all right?' He saw Marl. 'Hey, you're my hire. What are you doing here?'

'I am sorry, Mr Samuel. I found this lady and she led me to safety. If it was not for her I would be alone and afraid.'

'How – ?' Sam winced. 'I put you in the lockup.'

April slapped a hand on Sam's chest. 'He's fine. Let's just find somewhere safe.'

'The Leaf,' said Sam. 'Come on, it's this way.'

They turned left up a long, straight road.

'Have you met anyone else?' said Sam.

'Not yet, but there are others too, have you heard them?'

'Yeah, I heard some voices calling. So not everyone's like this?'

'It's their Fronds. Something must have gone wrong. Mine are off, Marl has none, yours – '

'You know I only turn mine on for work.'

'That's what I thought.'

'You think it's a glitch somewhere? In the network? A crash or something?'

'Or a virus,' said Marl.

'Excuse me?' said Sam. 'And who asked you?'

'My apologies,' said Marl. 'I was merely postulating that an external virus may have infected The Leafen systems and hijacked the local network that serves the population's Fronds.'

Sam stopped and faced Marl.

'*Postulating*?' he said, narrowing his eyes. 'I hired you for grunt work.'

Marl smiled.

'And I am very grateful,' he said.

'Huh.'

Sam led them on.

'Anyway, Leafen hasn't been attacked in fifty years – '

'Sam – ' April stopped in her tracks. 'I saw something. This morning, after I spoke to you. I was on my bike and it shot past me.'

'Where were you?' said Sam.

'About ten miles from the perimeter.'

'April, those drones – '

'It wasn't a drone; it was too quick, too small.'

'Wait a minute,' said Sam. 'Where exactly did you see this?'

'I told you, the perimeter – '

'Yeah, which part?'

'North-west wall.'

'Damn it,' said Sam. 'I told them it wasn't rubble.'

'What wasn't rubble?'

'The breach. Something came through. I knew it. Damn it, I *told* them.'

'What came through?' said April.

'I don't know.'

'I can see light ahead,' said Marl. 'There are people. I can hear them.'

1st Street was even busier than 2nd. The entire strip was awash with the dark shapes of people frozen in their tracks. They pushed through as best they could towards The Leaf. A crowd was forming around the base of the first tower.

'See?' said April. 'I don't see any Fronds glowing on anyone moving.'

They pushed their way through to the front, where a group of workers – plumbers, welders, electricians, grease-faced men and women in green boiler suits – were hurrying around. The ground was strewn with rags, tools and cables. In the middle of it all was a woman in her fifties, white-streaked hair pulled back in a baseball cap. She was wrestling with two arms of a huge, metal standing lamp.

'Christine,' shouted Sam, running to meet her.

The woman looked up, shielding her eyes from the light.

'Sam? Put those flashlights down, would you! I can't see. Sam, is that you?'

Sam laughed and held out a hand. The woman took it.

'Yeah, it's me. How are you doing?'

'Sam Ops, it's been some time. It's good to see you. I could use your help. Pull this, would you?'

Sam helped her pull back on a lever. A spring twanged and two metal legs shot out, levelling the lamp.

'Good,' said the woman. She slammed a cable into the back of the lamp.

'Turn the generator on!' she yelled. There was a loud whistle from a box behind them and she slammed her foot down on a power switch. The generators strained and the ten eight-foot-tall high-power fluorescent strips crackled and hummed then burst into life, flooding the paved mall and a good part of the street beneath it with light. The crowd let out a breathless cheer as their world lit up.

'Good job,' said Sam. 'April, you remember Christine Ops, don't you?'

'Of course,' said April. She held out a hand. 'Hello Chrissie, long time.'

'April Knight. The last time I saw you you were just a skinny little thing in bunches. Come here and give your Auntie Chrissie a hug!'

She pulled her in and squeezed her.

'Hoo,' said Christine, standing back and holding her by the shoulders. She looked her up and down appreciatively. 'But I can see you're a woman now – '

April cocked an eyebrow.

'Stop that,' growled Sam.

Christine laughed and wiped her hands on a rag in her pocket.

'And who's this?' she said, turning to Marl.

'This?' Sam looked Marl up and down. 'Oh, this, this is my, er, New Hire.'

'From today?' said Chrissie.

Sam nodded. 'Yeah.'

'Fresh from the Hordes and this happens on your first day. Tough break, son. What's your name?'

Marl stepped forward and offered his hand.

'Marl Duloos, at your service.'

Christine's face curled in pleasant surprise.

'Hear that?' she shouted behind. 'Someone with manners. Makes a change from your grunts.'

There were jeers and whistles from the boiler-suited mob behind.

'A pleasure to meet you, Marl,' she said, shaking his hand.

Sam motioned to the lights.

'How did you get here so quickly?' he said.

'My crew were on shift in the control tower when it happened. Poling requests started going through the roof. One of the techs started screaming to shut off our Fronds — glad he did or we'd all be like those poor bastards down there.'

'Did everyone in your team make it?' said Sam.

'No, just a few of us. We only had seconds before the power went, then the lights, systems, transport, everything. It all stopped dead. And now this.'

Sam followed her eyes over the streets.

'Any ideas, Sam?'

'I have my suspicions.'

'The breach?' said Chris.

'Yup.'

'I heard you were working on it. What did you see?'

'A hole, clean and round as a pancake. It wasn't debris, Christine. I *told* them it wasn't debris. Debris tears Fabrik; this burned straight through.'

'Well,' said Christine, looking straight up. She threw the rag on the floor. 'Big Cheese is going to want to know.'

'I see *they* got power,' said Sam.

High above them was a circle of lights, glimmering like a distant constellation.

'The upper balconies are on an emergency grid,' said Christine. 'They just came back up.'

'Do you think they've been affected?'

'They don't allow Fronds in the upper balconies.'

'What about the rest of the towers.'

'Same as down here, I guess,' said Christine. 'Anyone with their Fronds on – '

She turned to the street. The pleasant hubbub in the wake of the celebration had quietened to nervous murmurs. The crowd on the other side of the fence, which had been nothing but a still, glowing swarm, was now illuminated too. A sea of dumb faces spread out beyond the perimeter of the light, blank eyes staring in all directions. Some arms were hanging, others were folded to their chests; some mouths were open, others were closed; some heads were dipped, others raised to the sky. They swayed, blinking occasionally.

'Sam, we need to get these people safe,' said Christine.

'I hear you,' said Sam. He pointed to the centre of the base towers. 'Central Station. It's the biggest indoor space we have.'

'But not much use without light or power,' said Christine.

'We have power.'

'What do you mean? I told you, the whole grid's down.'

'Not the whole grid.' Sam pointed at the sky. 'The Fabrik's still active.'

'So?'

'Which means it's still being powered. It runs off its own energy source.'

'We can reroute the power,' said Marl.

Sam turned and frowned at Marl, who lowered his head in

deference.

'We can reroute the power,' said Sam. 'Pipe it to Central Station. We should be able to borrow enough to light it and power the elevators up to The Leaf.'

'Sam, you're a genius,' said Christine.

'But the perimeter's a hundred miles away,' said April.

Christine grinned.

'The perimeter's a hundred miles away, but not the power source,' she said.

'And where's that?'

Sam stamped his boots on the ground.

'Right under our feet,' he said. 'Fabrik runs on geothermal power. It's about the only thing in this place that doesn't burn oil. The substation's a couple of hundred feet beneath us. There are some tunnels that run straight to it.'

He turned to Marl.

'Your first job, Duloos. Grab one of those tool bags and come with me.'

twenty-eight

central's lit up

DEMETRI, ALEX and Karina had left the stadium and turned onto a long side street leading to the centre. They walked with Alex shuffling between them, Karina still bubbling between the two poles of fear and ecstasy the chemicals in her bloodstream were still manifesting for her.

Demetri tried to guide them by the Frond-light that was reflecting from the walls. He was aware of others moving down the street too, some at speed, some more cautiously.

'Do you know what's going on?' he said to a couple of teenage boys feeling their way along the brickwork.

'No!' laughed one. 'This is fucking crazy, man!'

'Where are you going?'

'We don't fucking know! Ha ha!'

A girl ran past in the opposite direction, gasping with fear.

'Hey. Wait! Where are you going?'

She shrieked and disappeared.

After another block, Demetri stopped and peered left.

'I think we're near my office,' he said 'Yeah, this is near 18th. 2nd Street is just up here.'

He was about to lead them down the side street when he heard a distinctive female voice up ahead. It was asking questions, demanding things. He steered them towards it.

'Ruba. Is that you?'

The voice stopped.

'Trittek?'

'Where are you?'

He heard Saul's voice.

'Demetri! Here by the wall!'

They made their way over and found Ruba, Saul and Turnett.

'Glad we found you,' said Turnett. 'What's going on?'

'I don't know,' said Demetri. 'Everything just went black. Where are the others?'

'Out,' said Saul.

'Out? You mean like the rest of them?'

'Yeah, everyone. They just stopped. Arianne started muttering something a few seconds before. I think she'd been looking through the access logs, you know what she's like. Then she just went mad and started shouting for everyone to turn their Fronds off. She was midway through her signature, but it was too late.'

'Ours were already off,' said Turnett. 'From our bet. And Ruba doesn't have hers yet.'

'Mine are dead.'

'So it must have affected only people who were online,' said Turnett.

'Has this happened before?' said Ruba.

'You mean the entire population's Fronds crashing simultaneously?' said Demetri. 'No, no this has definitely *not* happened before.'

'Shit, is that your brother?' said Saul.

'Alex, yeah,' said Demetri. 'I have to get him to a medical centre.'

'Where?'

'No idea,' said Demetri. 'Somewhere central.'

There was a noise behind them. The two boys he had just spoken to had caught up with them, bounding from each other's shoulders and laughing.

'Hey!' one said. 'Keep going. Central's lit up.'

'What?' said Saul. 'What's happening?'

'Central Station, dude,' said the other. 'Someone got the power back.'

'How far's Central Station?' said Ruba.

'Ten minutes, fifteen max,' said Demetri. They followed the

two boys down the dark street.

'Hi,' said Karina as Ruba walked beside them. 'I love your hair.'

twenty-nine

glitch

'IT IS a glitch,' said Sumar Director, his chin and eyebrows raised in defiance. Priscilla stood beside him in full military uniform — red jacket, red skirt, red boots and a scarlet tie with three gold leaves symbolising her rank as General. She looked down at him with disgust.

'A *glitch*,' she said.

'Yes,' said Sumar. 'My senior technicians believe a recent upgrade to the Frond network may have compromised the – '

'How can a *glitch* turn an entire population into an army of mannequins?'

Daniel Leafen looked out of his office window at the eerie black plain beneath.

'Do you disagree with Sumar's theory, Priss?' he said.

The ligaments in Priscilla's neck tightened. Sumar's chin was still raised, his face a beacon of calm.

'I think it seems a little – unusual,' she said. She turned her head slowly. 'I'm suspicious that it may be something external. Something malicious.'

Sumar rolled his eyes.

'We have nothing to suggest that anything of the sort has occurred. None of our monitoring systems shows any attack, physical or otherwise.'

'What about the breach?' said Priscilla.

'The inspection report shows it was debris. The Fabrik is tired, this is true, but we're positive it will be upgraded after next month's Sweep. Either way, it is ridiculous to suggest an attack. Leafen has not been attacked for – '

'Fifty years,' said Daniel. 'On my old man's watch.'

'That's no reason to warrant apathy,' said Priscilla. 'Any event of this magnitude always necessitates military appraisal. The Words demand it.'

Daniel turned his head, scanning Priscilla's uniform.

'Hence the get-up, I suppose, *General*,' he said with a grin.

'A little over the top, in my opinion,' muttered Sumar.

Priscilla turned to him.

'From a man who never made military grade, I would expect nothing less.'

'Now, now,' said Daniel, wagging a finger. 'Girls and boys, play *nicely*.'

'This is a corporational crisis, sir,' said Priscilla.

'Crisis?' laughed Sumar. 'What crisis? This is a glitch, very simple. It will be fixed before we know it. My engineers are already on the case.'

'The alert level is at its highest,' continued Priscilla. 'So I am duty bound to take my place as military leader.'

Daniel walked to the drinks cabinet. *She's right*, he mouthed to Sumar as he picked out a decanter.

'Sir,' said Priscilla. 'I am also duty bound to advise you that *all* staff of military grade are to wear their uniform in these times –'

'Don't worry,' he sighed, pouring himself a large measure. 'I'll put mine on in a bit.'

He offered the bottle. Sumar and Priscilla shook their heads.

'Sure?' said Daniel. He took the bottle back to his desk. 'Looks like armageddon out there, probably not the time to be on a *health* kick.'

He sat down and put his feet up on the long, red wood.

'How exactly *are* things down there?'

'The glitch affects only people who were using their Fronds at the time,' said Sumar.

'Only? How many?' said Daniel.

Sumar cleared his throat.

'We received a report from the main Operations Tower just

before our glitch – '

'*Your* glitch,' warned Daniel.

'Yes, sir. The report suggested that Frond usage was extremely high because of The Hiring. Logs put it in the region of 99.98%.'

'How many people, Sumar?'

Sumar paused and took a breath.

'Roughly 39.9 million, sir. Almost everyone.'

'Including the rest of the Board,' said Daniel.

'Yes, sir,' said Priscilla. 'Sumar and I are the only two directors on active duty. After yourself, of course.'

Daniel released a low whistle.

'And the Hordes?'

'We have no idea what is happening beyond The Line, sir,' said Sumar.

Priscilla's voice boomed above his soft coo.

'I have assembled all available military grade personnel and sent teams across the corporation to locate missing staff. Our transport infrastructure is out, so they're on foot. It's a slow process.'

'Quite a few out there in the dark, I suppose,' said Daniel. He traced a finger on the glass. 'Bumbling about.'

'Our priority is with those unaffected by the – *glitch*, sir. Most were in The Office for The Hiring, but many were still out in the outer departments and further into the suburbs. We've put together a crisis station in Central Station.'

'Yeah. How did that happen? I thought our power was out.'

Sumar broke in before Priscilla could answer.

'Yes, sir,' he said, taking a file from under his arm and flipping a page. 'One of my operational supervisors. He temporarily rerouted power from the Fabrik. A Mr Samuel Ops,' he said.

'Clever lad,' said Daniel. He tapped his glass. 'How long, Sumar?'

'I beg your pardon, sir?'

Daniel took his feet off the desk and stood up.

'How long until your *glitch* is fixed?'

'It will take time, sir,' said Sumar.

'Time,' spat Priscilla. 'We have no *time*. We should be putting all of our efforts into defence.'

'Defence!' snorted Sumar. 'These theatrics, oh dear, oh dear, oh dear.'

Priscilla watched him beaming, rolling his head. The muscles in her neck twitched.

'I have to side with Sumar on this one, Priss,' said Daniel. 'Let's not get ahead of ourselves.'

'Thank you, sir,' said Sumar, wiping an invisible tear from his eye. 'Now, I have seven tiers of analysts working on this from emergency workstations in Central.'

He put his hands behind his back, tiptoeing and smiling serenely.

'Sir, I am *very* confident we shall have a solution before sunrise.'

'Good,' said Daniel. 'Good, I'm glad you're confident because, Sumar, you are the Technology Director of the soon-to-be most powerful technology corporation in the world. If you can't fix this, then, er – how can I put this?'

Daniel held out his hand in an upturned claw.

'Your *balls*, Sumar. Understand?'

Sumar's smile fell from his face. A very different one wormed its way onto Priscilla's.

'I understand, sir,' said Sumar.

Daniel downed his drink and banged the glass on his desk.

'So, Priss, run with Sumar. Help him coordinate the analysis. Notify me hourly.'

'Yes, sir,' said Priscilla, her smile gone.

'Oh, and Sumar?' said Daniel.

'Yes, sir?'

Daniel held out his claw again and jutted out his lower jaw.

'*YOUR. BALLS.*'

Sumar looked at the ground.

'Sir,' he said, and left.

Priscilla remained standing.

'Anything else, Priss?' said Daniel.

'I'd like to be blunt, Daniel.'

Daniel smiled and slowly slipped off his jacket.

'You've never asked permission before,' he said.

'This is a Security concern, not a job for Technology.'

'We're offline, Priss,' sighed Daniel, folding his jacket neatly over his chair. 'Until our systems are working again, that's exactly what this is.'

Priscilla pushed out her chest. The material creaked under the strain.

'Then I want to lead it. Sumar is incapable, you know that.'

Daniel sidled over to her, letting his eyes roam over her uniform.

'Careful, Priss,' he said. 'That's the Technology Director you're talking about.'

Priscilla looked down at her president as he loosened his tie. With a reptilian smile, she arched her back, pushing her chest a little closer to his face. She let him enjoy the view for a moment.

'And I'm the Director of HR, Military and Security,' she said softly, tilting her head. She touched a finger to his brow. 'Technology really should be in my portfolio too.'

Daniel made a pained face, avoiding her eyes.

'Priss, Priss, I know you want his job, but I can't just *fire* the man.'

'Why not?' said Priscilla, tracing his hairline.

'Because you can't just *fire* directors,' he whispered. He bit his lip as Priscilla pushed her abdomen closer to his.

'He's incompetent,' said Priscilla, each slow syllable dripping with saliva.

'He's done nothing wrong.'

Something flashed in Priscilla's eyes.

'Not yet,' she breathed, stroking the tops of her fingers over his cheek.

There was a knock on the door. Daniel frowned. Priscilla stepped back, snapping to attention.

'Yep?' said Daniel.

The door opened and Faith stepped in.

'Faith, what is it?'

'Sir, there's – there's a call for you, sir.'

'What?' He glanced at Priscilla. 'I thought our communications were down.'

'It's urgent, sir,' said Faith.

'Maybe old Sumar's not so bad at his job after all,' he said. He winked at Priscilla, but her sexual weaponry was already holstered.

'Patch it through to my desk, Faith. You're, er, dismissed, General.'

'Sir,' said Priscilla, turning on her heels.

'Oh, General?' he called after her.

'Sir?'

'Go and find that bloke who got the power up, whatshisname, Sid or – '

'Samuel Ops.'

'Samuel, that's it. Go and say thanks or something. Then work with Sumar. Help him with anything he needs, understood?'

'Yes, sir.'

'Keep me up to date then and, er, you know, let's continue our *chat* later,' he said. 'OK?'

'Yes, sir,' she said, and left.

thirty

orange one

DEMETRI HELPED Alex up the steps into Central Station. People flowed around him, some in blankets, teeth chattering, others sharing stories and speculating wildly, everyone on the cusp between excitement and terror. Karina trudged behind. She had stopped talking and looked weary and pale.

Ruba, Saul and Turnett followed. Once through the doors, the group stopped and took in the concourse. Walls the size of mountains. An impossible roof. A tight-angled canyon, perfectly rectangular yet full of twisted perspectives and lines that ran off and disappeared into a distant haze. The immensity of Central never failed to draw breath, but they had never seen it like this.

With no daylight and the main strips off to conserve power, the entire concourse was ill-lit with side strips, search lamps, lanterns, flares, beacons and, in one corner, a glistening web of Fronds from the necks of the unfortunates who were being herded there. The effect was that Central Station – usually a bright and magnificent indoor rainforest of roaring fountains, sizzling food stands, riotous music and all the other bustle of Leafen life – was now an enormous cavern dotted with pockets of gloomy light and dripping with run-off from the darkened Redwood canopies above.

Bright glints and shadows from the still fountain pools flickered on faces and the fronts of the closed food stalls. The only sound was the nervous chatter, tears, trouser-leg shuffles, heel taps and boot squeaks echoing from the walls, and distant birdsong from the trees – an odd sound to hear in the darkness.

Demetri scanned the floor impulsively from the corner of his eye, as he had done since he was a child. Beneath his shoes was an enormous mosaic spanning the entire floor. Each tile was a solid colour — one of The Leafen nine. Mostly there was an even distribution of the core reds, greens, blues and yellows. Occasionally you would see an outlier, like orange or pink. If you saw a silver then you were lucky — Demetri had only ever seen a handful of those.

To see a black or a white tile was almost unheard of, as it was to find a person of that grade. Such was their rarity that anyone who saw one always kept its location to themselves — again, as it was in real life. You never knew if somebody had been graded black or white in addition to their core Colour. Most people took their secret to the grave, although many made guesses at prominent figures, or used them to slander their bosses or colleagues.

The tiles were supposed to represent the exact population of Leafen, year-on-year. With every annual Sweep from the Mites — that day of the year when everyone stayed indoors and waited as the world outside was tweaked, fixed, cleaned, upgraded and reconfigured, a huge roar of tiny industry that covered them for twenty-four hours — the colours of the tiles were changed to reflect the shift in the population, the influx of new graders and the deaths of the old.

The day after the Sweep was always a holiday and the Central Station hall became a giant playground. Children flooded in and began the hunt for rare tiles, getting prizes for orange or pink. Always, the game was to find a black or a white — only a handful of them existed in the fifteen square miles of inch-long tiles that were scattered across the hall.

Demetri remembered one such hunt. He had been eleven and his mother had told him, to his dismay, that he had to take his brother along. Alex had been just two at the time, and Demetri had spent a dull morning traipsing around the concourse with him dawdling behind, occasionally running off or falling over or just bawling at some invisible threat or thought that had occurred in the madness of his timeless, causeless, toddler mind.

Come on, Alex, he had said, hands stuffed in his pockets as he spotted some friends by a fountain. *Hurry up.*

Colours! Alex had shouted. *Miti! Pretty colours, Miti!*

Yes, colours, very pretty.

Red one! Blue one!

Demetri had sighed, craning to see what his friends were doing.

Green one! Yellow!

Yeah, great, now get a move on, you little shit, before I –

Orange one!

Before I – what? What did you say, Alex?

Red one, yellow one, blue one –

Alex was stooping over the tiles with one hand on his knee.

Alex, where's the orange one, Alex? Show Miti the orange one.

Blue one, yellow one, green one, yellow –

Where's the orange one, Alex? Orange. Show Miti the orange one.

Orange? Orange there. It over there.

His fat little finger pointed behind them. Sure enough, there was an orange tile nestled in a patch of reds and yellows, hardly visible at all.

Alex, I love you, you little bastard.

Love me!

Hey! Hey! Demetri had waved his hands above his head. *I found an orange! Over here! Orange!*

Love me! My orange, my orange, mine.

No, not yours Alex, Miti's.

Mine.

The hunt leaders turned to see who was calling.

MINE.

He hadn't planned to hit him; the moment seemed to arrive before he did. One minute he had been looking down at that defiant, snot-bubbled face, the next his hand had stung with the slap he had just landed against his brother's downy scalp. Then a guilty surge of adrenalin; dizzy release at the act of simple, effective violence.

Alex had started screaming – a mild embarrassment as the leaders handed Demetri his prize (a chocolate leaf the size of his leg) but the tears prevented his protestations from being audible. Nobody had seen. His parents had never found out and Alex had been too young to remember. The crime was his alone, like the delicious leaf.

He looked down at his brother now, listless and dull. The thought of hitting that little boy made his throat tighten.

'Are you OK?' said Ruba.

'I just want to find help for Alex. We need to find a medical centre.'

'Just like everyone else,' she said.

People were flowing around them. Most were helping others who, like Alex, could no longer move of their own accord.

Just then, a cheer rose as one of the station's enormous monitors lit up with a message.

LEAFEN CORPORATION CRISIS CENTRE

ALL STAFF PLEASE GATHER HERE FOR IDENTIFICATION AND ASSESSMENT

PLEASE REMAIN CALM AND WALK NORMALLY

The line of refugees, following their instructions, walked the coloured tiles towards the message.

'There'll be a med centre,' said Demetri. 'Let's get Alex over there.'

'I don't think Alex is the only one who needs help,' said Saul.

'What do you mean?'

He nodded at Demetri's neck.

'Your Fronds. They're burning up again. What did you do?'

Ruba's eyes glinted like razors.

thirty-one

a great debt

SAM TURNED the stiff handle and the shower spluttered out. They were in a communal hospitality block a few floors up into The Leaf; nothing fancy, a stopover place for low-ranking officials and sales reps. It was cold and the lights were low, like everywhere else.

He watched the black water spiral down the hair-clogged drain. It had taken him half an hour to wash the oily grime from the tunnels off his skin. He heard Marl a few cubicles up, still scrubbing and humming a tune he had never heard before. He pulled back the stiff curtain.

'Mr Ops, my name is General Mandrek.'

Sam froze at the sight of the tall, red-uniformed woman before him. Priscilla took in every sinewy inch of his fifty-seven-year-old body, appraising him as if he was a piece of livestock. She was flanked by two guards. Christine Ops stood behind, smirking, eyebrows raised.

'I know who you are,' said Sam at last. He pulled a towel from a bench and wiped his face and neck. 'To what do I owe the pleasure, General?'

'I'm here to thank you, Mr Ops. For the power. The President is highly impressed and Leafen owes you a great debt.'

Sam wrapped the towel around his waist and walked to the lockers.

'Yeah, well,' he said. 'Don't throw me any medals just yet. That Fabrik won't last long without full power.'

'We understand it's temporary, Mr Ops – '

'Sam, please – '

Priscilla paused at the interruption, as if quelling an urge to strike.

' – Mr Ops,' she continued. 'But the power you have given us will enable us to proceed with finding the source of the problem.'

Sam pulled his clothes from the locker and slammed it shut.

'You'd better hope you can do that soon, General,' said Sam. 'Because I'd give that Fabrik a couple of days at most before it collapses. It was already weak before this happened. In fact, this *wouldn't* have happened if we'd had proper-grade material. That stuff's already ten Sweeps old.'

Priscilla's eyes narrowed like a dog on a scent.

'What do you mean?'

'We wouldn't have had the breach,' said Sam, pulling on a shirt.

Priscilla took a step nearer.

'And what does the breach have to do with this?' she said.

'What do *you* think caused this?' he said.

'A glitch,' said Priscilla. The word caught in her throat like a splinter.

'It's not a glitch. Something came through.'

Priscilla lifted her chin, craning her neck.

'The report said that it was debris,' she said.

'Did it really? Well the report's bullshit, just like everything else that comes out of AERO.'

'And how would you know that, Mr Ops?'

'Because I'm the guy who ran the inspection,' said Sam, jabbing a thumb at his chest. 'And I'm telling you, *something* came through. Something that wanted to get through. And if you want my advice, that's what you should be looking for. Not some *glitch*.'

Sam pulled on his jeans. He felt Priscilla watching him.

'I'd like you to stay here in the hospitality block,' she said. 'I may need you.'

'Sure,' said Sam.

'Thank you again, Mr Ops. Now, if you'll excuse me, I have

to address the corporation.'

Priscilla turned and left, followed by her guards. Christine smiled at Sam.

'Good work on the lights, Sam,' she said. 'And sorry about this. The General was pretty set on seeing you straight away.'

'What are you, her little helper now?' said Sam.

'Something like that,' said Christine, looking over her shoulder at the tightly clad buttocks of her military superior. 'And no offence, but I'd rather be following that around than crawling through tunnels.'

Priscilla stopped.

'Are you coming, Mrs Ops?' she called.

'See you, Sam,' said Christine, then she turned and trotted off. 'Yes, Ma'am. And it's Miss, actually.'

thirty-two

special

'TODAY, AS you must be aware, your corporation faces a grave threat.'

Priscilla stood on a podium near one corner of the Central Station concourse, looking out at a sea of expectant faces.

'Most of your colleagues — your friends, your families, your *Board* — have been affected by a – '

She glanced at the gloomy, swaying herd in the far distance.

' – *Glitch,* which Director Sumar and his team believes to exist within the Fronds network. This glitch has taken down our transport, our communications systems and our power. Thanks to our operations department, we have rerouted power from our Fabrik to The Leaf. We are warm and have light. We have radios with which to communicate. We can work. But this is only temporary — on limited power, our Fabrik is weakening by the hour. We do not have long.'

Hushed murmurs of concern echoed around the concourse like dry leaves.

'I need to warn you of the dangers we face if the Fabrik collapses. Our corporation will be at the mercy of the atmosphere. We will no longer be protected. We will no longer be safe. And so, today, Leafen looks to you. You must find this problem and fix it quickly. We must not stop until our corporation is out of danger.'

She cast a hand to her left.

'We have erected medical tents for those who need them. Otherwise, you will be expected to report to the Crisis Centre.'

The crowd turned in the direction of a section of concourse divided by standing walls.

'The Crisis Centre has been divided into atriums, tiers, levels and departments. Each section has a sign bearing its name. The size of each section is dependent on how many of its staff have been unaffected — those who aren't – '

She turned to the far corner.

' – unable to work.'

She cleared her throat and checked her notes.

'Each section has been allocated a specific area to investigate. Find your section and complete your task. Leafen looks to you. Thank you.'

There was a ripple of applause as Priscilla stepped down from the podium.

'That's us over there,' said Ruba. She strode off to a small partition near the main barrier to the Crisis Centre. 'Come on.'

The others followed – Demetri heaving Alex through the crowd with Karina almost comatose on his other arm. Saul and Turnett followed behind. Ruba was waiting for them at the gate, tapping her foot.

'Where's everyone else?' she said.

There were three banks of desks, each one with a laptop connected to bundles of cables taped to the stone floors. At one desk sat a girl, barely awake. Next to her a frightened young apprentice coder stared at the screen with tumbling white lines reflected in his spectacles.

'This must be it,' said Saul. 'Everybody else must have been online.'

Demetri looked around the other departments, nodding at a section five fences away. It was full of well-dressed men and women bustling between machines, brandishing files and talking loudly.

'Not everybody,' he said.

Saul looked over.

'Alpha Three,' he said, rolling his eyes.

'Why are there so many of them?' said Ruba. Demetri could feel her envy frizzle in the air between them.

'First-levellers always work with their Fronds off,' said Turnett. 'F-for concentration.'

'They were working at the time?'

'They're always working,' said Saul. He raised a loose fist and waved it lightly. 'Yay. Go, Alpha.'

'What are you doing?' said Ruba to the coder at the back.

'Logs,' he said, as if the word itself was terrifying. 'They've got us looking through logs.'

'Send some to your colleagues,' said Ruba. The boy began frantically tapping keys.

Saul and Turnett took a desk each.

'I'm taking Alex to that med tent,' said Demetri. 'And Karina. She doesn't look too well.'

'I'm fine,' said Karina, head hanging, hair bedraggled. 'Really.'

'I'll come with you,' said Ruba.

'I don't need a chaperone,' said Demetri.

'I'm coming anyway. That's an order.'

'An *order*? Who do you think you are?'

'Your direct superior, that's who.'

Demetri shook his head.

'*Direct* – you just started.'

Ruba stepped closer. Her jaw tightened.

'This is a *crisis*,' said Ruba. 'And Section 4.198 of The Leafen Crisis Management Manual dictates that in such times your immediate manager becomes your military *superior*.'

She looked back at Saul and Turnett.

'That includes you two as well,' she warned.

Demetri blinked.

'You're just a project manager – '

'And Section 4.768 says that any subordinate who disobeys a direct order from their military superior risks court martial and immediate firing.'

'*Court martial?* I'm not even military grade! And neither are you!'

'Oh yes I am,' said Ruba. 'I'm Double-Red. Double-Reds are

all military grade.'

'Fine,' said Demetri, rolling his eyes. 'You take her.'

He marched off with Alex. Ruba scurried to Karina's side and dragged her along.

'Did I tell you I like your hair?' whimpered the girl.

Soon they reached the first row of medical tents. They fought their way along, trying to find the entrance with the fewest tide of casualties.

'Why do you want to come anyway?' said Demetri.

'Because I want to keep an eye on you,' replied Ruba.

'Why?'

She stepped in front of him.

'Because your Fronds are glowing like the sun,' she hissed.

Demetri touched his neck self-consciously.

'Yeah, well, I'm not the only one, look around.'

'You're the only one who's walking and talking. And again, this morning on the train – you couldn't turn them off.'

'So what? They're broken. Why are you so interested?'

She paused, blinked.

'Because I think you're special.'

'What do you mean?'

'I think you're connected with this.'

She narrowed her eyes.

'What did you do?'

Demetri snorted.

'Come on, you think I have something to do with this? Give me a break.'

'You have to report this.'

'Ruba, I'm not special and I'm not reporting anything.'

'Yes, you are.'

'No, I'm not.'

There was a clang and a clatter from one of the med tents. They turned in the direction of the noise.

'Enola, I told you, stand back!'

'But Emelia, her temperature – '

Ruba smiled.

'And I know just the person to talk to. Dr Perez!'

'Ruba, wait! Fuck.'

'Dr Perez!'

Ruba bundled Karina through the entrance and over to a bed in a corner, where Emelia was examining Lori's eyes. Enola stood next to her with arms crossed – she seemed different; no longer in her restless trance but vexed, tense and frustrated. The change seemed to be lost on Emelia, whose attention was directed only at the little girl in front of her.

'Dr Perez!'

Emelia turned, re-holstering her pen light.

'Miss Groone,' she said. She looked at Karina, slumped against Ruba's shoulder. 'Who is this? If she's been affected she needs to be chaperoned to the holding pen.'

'She's not affected. She's just – '

'Hi,' breathed Karina, raising her hand an inch or two.

'Nurse Laudley?' said Emelia.

'Dr Perez?' said a bony young man in a white coat two beds up.

'See to this young lady, will you?'

'Sure.'

The nurse escorted Karina away.

'You smell nice,' Ruba heard her say as she laid her head on his shoulder.

'Are you OK?' said Emelia.

'I'm fine,' said Ruba. 'It's Demetri Trittek, he's –.'

'Ruba, wait!'

Demetri had caught up, dragging Alex now, his feet barely moving.

'Trittek,' said Emelia. 'Is that your brother?'

'Yes, is that your daughter?'

Emelia looked back at Lori, her feet dangling from the bed.

'She's OK.'

'But Emelia,' said Enola, her voice low. 'Her temperature – '

'Quiet, Enola,' sighed Emelia. 'She's stable. Breathing, heart rate, blood pressure, all fine. But her Fronds are on overdrive. Just like the rest. Let me take a look at him.'

She seated Alex on the bed next to Lori. As she examined him, Ruba nudged Demetri.

'Tell her.'

'There's nothing to tell.'

'There is. You have to!'

'It's nothing. Just let it go, will you?'

'Tell her or I will!'

'He's OK too,' said Emelia, unhooking the stethoscope from her ears. She looked between the two of them. 'What's wrong?'

Ruba glared up at Demetri. Finally, he went to speak, but Emelia had already caught sight of his neck.

'What's going on with your Fronds?'

She took a black probe from her pocket.

'Nothing, it's just – '

'I performed a hard shutdown this morning. There's no way they can be functioning.'

She ran the probe over his shoulders. It made a flat, uninterested beep.

'That can't be right.'

She tried again with the same result. She shook her head.

'It's like they're jammed. A closed system. What did you do?'

'I didn't *do* anything. I wish people would stop asking me that.'

There was the sound of clattering footsteps behind them, and shouts as people were pushed aside.

'Demetri!'

Saul, red-faced and breathless, was leaning on the tent pole.

'Saul, what's wrong?' said Demetri.

'Back at the Crisis Centre,' he gulped. 'I think I found something.'

Ruba sprang to his side like a rook to a corpse.

'Found what?'

Saul pulled away from her.

'Demetri, you need to come take a look.'

'OK. Dr Perez, can Alex stay here?'

'Yes, for now,' said Emelia. She peered at his neck. 'But I'm coming with you.'

She looked back at Enola, who had placed a hand on Lori's arm.

'It's OK, Emelia,' she said. 'We're OK.'

Emelia turned away.

'Laudley,' she said to the nurse examining Karina. 'Look after my daughter.'

thirty-three

old code

'THIS ISN'T right,' said Demetri.

They were huddled around Saul's workstation. Lines of logs scrolled by on the screen.

'What isn't?' said Ruba. 'Tell me.'

'It's nothing you can see,' he said. 'It's what you can't see.'

'Right,' said Saul.

'Explain.'

'These lines, they represent interactions between people and the network.'

'Traffic from the Fronds?'

'Yeah, callouts, requests for information,' said Saul. 'Every time you message someone or bring up a map or search for a song, it gets logged here.'

'So what's different?' said Ruba.

'Well,' said Demetri. 'When your Fronds talk to the network, they do it like a conversation, and these conversations are identifiable. Every request for information carries the impulse from the last.'

'And?'

'And these ones don't. It's like it resets every time.'

'I don't understand, are you saying there's a network issue?'

'No, the network's fine, it's what's being transmitted on it that's the problem. The requests are bouncing off the servers. They're not getting back what they asked for.'

'So what are they getting back?'

'N-Nothing,' said Turnett.

'No response?' said Ruba.

'No,' said Demetri. 'They get a response all right. A big, fat, empty response. Zeroes.'

'Binary darkness,' whispered Saul.

'In huge amounts,' said Demetri. 'It's like they're shouting in an empty void.'

'How could this be happening?' said Ruba.

Demetri shook his head.

'Something is intercepting the requests.'

'What?'

Turnett pointed at the screen.

'Demetri, l-look at the request signature. Look at the encoded I-ID.'

Demetri scanned the screen, stopping on a line near the top. His mouth fell open. He pushed himself away from the desk.

'No. No, it *can't* be.'

'What?' snapped Ruba.

'There has to be some mistake.'

'Tell me!'

Demetri stood up and backed away from the desk.

'That's me. That's my ID.'

'What?' said Ruba. 'What does that mean?'

'It means everything's g-going through his Fronds,' said Turnett.

Nobody spoke for a while. Then Emelia nodded her head.

'That makes sense,' she said. 'That would explain why they're not responding. You're a closed system. A proxy.'

'A proxy for what?' said Demetri, holding his head in his hands.

'Are you sure about this?' said Ruba.

Demetri's shoulders slumped. He walked back to the screen.

'My dad helped write this code. It's part of our family. He talks about it all the time.'

'I need you to be 100% certain.'

'I am. I wish I wasn't, but I am.' He tapped the screen. 'It's me.'

Ruba looked at him for some time, eyes darting around his face as if she was trying to calculate how his features fitted together.

Then she stood and turned to the crisis nucleus, raised her head and bellowed.

'HERE! WE HAVE SOMETHING!'

'Oh, shit,' said Demetri.

Every head in every department turned. The Alphas stopped bustling, their papers frozen in their hands. In the nucleus, Priscilla Mandrek looked up, spotted Ruba's violently waving hand, and began to make her way through the walkways.

'Print it off,' hissed Ruba. She arranged her mouth in a smile as Priscilla approached.

'Pardon?' said Turnett.

'Print off the logs.'

'They're a b-billion lines long.'

'Just a few sheets then. I need something to show her. General Mandrek.'

Ruba held out her hand. Priscilla looked at it for a moment before Ruba pulled it away.

'My name is Ruba Groone, Double Red, Military – '

'You've found something, Miss Groone?'

'Yes, we believe so.'

Turnett returned with the log sheets and handed them to Ruba.

'Here,' said Ruba, passing them across the fence.

Priscilla scanned them.

'And what am I supposed to be looking at?'

'These are access logs from the Frond network,' said Ruba. 'We think they show a compromise that is blasting users with dangerous signals. We think something is getting in the way of requests. Something has inserted itself between the network and the clients.'

'*Something*?' said Priscilla.

'Yes,' said Ruba, glancing at Demetri. 'A proxy. A human – '

'Wait a minute,' said Priscilla. She looked back over her shoulder, where Sumar was bustling with the Alphas. 'Are you suggesting that this isn't a glitch?'

'I beg your pardon, General?'

'Are you suggesting that this is something other than a fault with the systems?'

'I – I – '

'There's no way this could be a glitch,' interrupted Saul. Every face was on him. 'There's just no way. This has to be a security issue.'

Priscilla's chest rose with her smile. Her eyes gave a pulse of excitement.

'How confident are you?' she said.

'Pardon me?' said Ruba.

'How confident are you that something is amiss?'

'Extremely confident,' said Ruba.

'And is this your team, Miss Groone?'

'Yes, General.'

'Good. And do you want to help me?'

'Yes,' said Ruba, pushing out her chin. 'Yes, General, I do. I'll do anything to serve my corporation and The Market.'

Priscilla blinked.

'Just me will do for now, Miss Groone.'

She turned to the others.

'From now on you work for me. Clear?'

They nodded.

'You don't need to tell anybody what you're doing. In fact, do *not* tell anybody what you're doing. Just meet me in the Hospitality Suite on the fifth floor in half an hour. I'd like to talk this through further.'

thirty-four

the merest of nods

'I NEED to speak with President Leafen.'

Steve Manager looked between the two guards' blank faces.

'Urgently,' said Steve.

'Nobody is to use the elevators without express permission from General Mandrek,' said the guard on the left.

'Then find her. Tell her that Steve Manager has some important information to share with the President.'

'She's busy,' said the guard on the right.

'Doing what?'

'Not your concern, sir.'

'Well, whatever it is, this is more important.'

Steve could already sense the uselessness of his words. He scanned the crisis centre behind them. 'This is a security concern.'

'You'll have to wait,' said the guard on the left.

'I've told you, it *can't* – '

He spotted Faith's green dress in the crowd.

'Faith!' he shouted, raising a hand.

'Sir, please step back.'

'Faith! It's me, Steve!'

He saw Faith stop, her neck turn.

'Sir, I'm warning you – '

The guard on the left landed a hand on Steve's shoulder. Steve lunged.

'Faith!'

The blow was sharp and well aimed; the guard's gun butt striking the bridge of his nose. He fell to the floor, stunned by the pain now rioting through his head. As he struggled back up, he heard Faith's voice.

'Stop!' she yelled, putting herself between him and the guards. She pulled him to his feet.

'Are you OK? You're bleeding.'

Steve touched his nose and inspected the blood in his hand.

'That was unnecessary,' he said to the guard.

'I warned you, sir.' The guard stepped forward again, but Faith held up a hand.

'Stand down, Private,' she snapped.

The guard paused, considering his options. Then he stepped back, still holding Steve's glare. Faith ushered them away.

'You know, for a Green, you're pretty ballsy,' said Steve.

'We're in a military situation, so I outrank him.'

'Well, remind me not to get on your bad side.'

She stopped, her eyes flashing.

'Bad side? What makes you think you're not already on my bad side?'

'What do you mean?'

She looked around, arms out, face a caricature of disbelief.

'*This,* Steve,' she said. '*This.*'

'Tell me what's going on.'

'The whole of Leafen has been compromised. All of it. The only thing that's holding is the Fabrik. That's what's powering Central.'

'And what about them?'

He nodded at the grey mass of bodies lurking in the mist at the far end of the hall.

'Everyone who was connected is – I don't know, they're catatonic, unresponsive.'

'Shit.'

Steve looked down, closed his eyes.

'Steve, they're looking for a *glitch.*'

'What does that mean?'

'It means they think that this is because of some system error, some fault in the Fronds update. Technology's working through the night.'

'So Daniel doesn't know? You didn't tell him?'

She shook her head. Steve looked up through the dark windows.

'Get me up there,' he said. 'Now.'

'He's on a call.'

'A call? I thought you said communications were down.'

'I don't know how – he won't talk to me. I can't get to him.'

'Then tell Priscilla! Tell Sumar! No, I'm going to tell him.'

He made for the Crisis Centre, but Faith held him back.

'No! How do you think Daniel will take it if you don't tell him first?'

'It doesn't matter – either way, I'm done. But at least we can warn them, tell them to look for a security breach, not a glitch.'

'If you tell Daniel, there's still a chance you'll be OK. This might not be as bad as you think.'

'But every minute that goes by – '

'I'm going up there now.'

'But – '

'Just *wait here.* Once I get clearance, I'll send for you.'

Her heels scraped as she turned.

'Faith,' he said, a hand on her arm.

'What?'

'I'm glad you're all right.'

Steve watched her, waiting for something, anything, a flicker in her expression that might tell him she understood; some softening in her face that said she felt the same. Nothing came. She looked down at her arm and pulled it from his grip.

But, as she turned, there it was: the briefest of nods, a dip of her eyelids, a breath that whistled in her throat.

Then it was gone, and so was she.

Steve found a seat by the elevators and watched the concourse. The medical tents were filling up. A crowd was forming around a wall of names and photographs. Coordinators — Greens and Yellows — were everywhere, shepherding people to safety and away from the dark and listless throng that was growing in the far corner. He sat forwards and hung his head to his knees. Tiny tiles of many colours kaleidoscoped beneath him, a neat little cluster in a much larger tapestry. Blame boiled inside him. He felt like a child behind a wall watching the aftermath of an accident only he knew he had caused.

Which was, in fact, give or take a few years, exactly what he was.

He began counting colours and seconds and minutes, fuelled by the memory of a nod, a blink and a breath – an image so translucent and fragile that it threatened to break apart in the whirlwind of his mind.

thirty-five

dozers

'LET ME get this straight,' said Priscilla.

The meeting room was a small workers' canteen. Priscilla sat at one end of a trestle table, her uniform's rich fabric out of place against the dull, shoddy plastic of her seat. Sam faced her, leaning on the table. Ruba, Demetri, Saul and Turnett sat on either side. Emelia sat in the corner, her arms folded, foot tapping.

'Mr Trittek here has somehow been compromised by an unknown outside source, and now his Fronds are controlling everyone on the network?'

Demetri hung his head and closed his eyes.

'Almost,' said Saul.

'Almost?'

'Yeah, they're not controlling anything. He's just a gateway. Everyone's just routing through him.'

'And you got this from the logs?'

'And the fact that he's the only one with functioning Fronds who's not a D-Dozer,' said Turnett.

'Dozer?' said Priscilla.

Saul shrugged.

'Got to call them something.'

Priscilla folded her hands.

'I see. And your Fronds, Mr Trittek, they're unresponsive? Have you tried shutting them down?'

'Yes,' said Demetri. 'They don't respond.'

Priscilla turned to Emelia.

'Dr Perez, have you tried a hard shutdown?'

'No. They won't respond to any stimulation, physical or

neurological.'

'I see. And what about a more *permanent* solution?'

The room bristled. Demetri felt a chill as the General's eyes met his.

'I – ' Emelia broke her stammer with a frigid laugh. 'Even if what you're suggesting wasn't morally reprehensible, I wouldn't recommend it. If this theory is correct then we have no idea what effect a shutdown would have on the population.'

Priscilla twisted her mouth in disappointment as she looked Demetri over.

'And is there anything unusual about Mr Trittek or his Fronds? Anything *special?*'

'No,' said Emelia. 'They're a standard genetic build. The connections are normal, software's on a stable build. There's nothing special about the Fronds or their host.'

'So why Trittek?'

'We have no idea. Maybe whatever did this chose him randomly.'

'What about that, Mr Trittek?' said Priscilla, with a half smile. 'Forty million employees and it chose you. Your lucky day.'

Emelia stood up.

'Listen, I *really* need to get back to my daughter.'

Priscilla whipped her head in Emelia's direction.

'Sit down, Dr Perez.'

'But – '

'This is a matter of corporational security and I order you to sit down. Do I make myself clear?'

Emelia remained on her feet, eyes darting between Priscilla and the door.

'This won't take long, Dr Perez,' said Priscilla, trying her best to soften. 'Sit down, please.'

Emelia, fuming, took her seat.

'Now then,' said Priscilla, smoothing the paper in front of her. 'As to this outside source.'

'It ain't outside,' said Sam.

'I beg your pardon, Mr Ops?'

'If this is all true, then my guess is it ain't outside Leafen. It's inside.'

'And what makes you think that?'

'Because something came through, that's why.'

Priscilla turned two pages in her file.

'The breach,' she said. 'You're sure it wasn't debris?'

'I'm sure,' said Sam. 'I've been working with Fabrik for thirty years and I know what debris damage looks like. Like I said to you before, whatever came through this morning wanted to come through.'

'How big?' said Priscilla.

'Not much bigger than a baseball.'

'That doesn't give us much to go on.'

'What about the security drones?' said Demetri. 'Didn't they pick up anything?'

'Those drones are useless,' said Sam. 'They're older than the Fabrik and most of them need their visual systems replaced.'

He leant forwards.

'General, our entire security system needs replacing. We're like eggs in a plastic bag.'

'I'm aware of this, Mr Ops, and that's set to change,' said Priscilla. 'But right now, is there anything else you can tell us?'

Sam rubbed his knuckles on his chin.

'Yeah, there's something else,' he said. 'My daughter, she says she saw something this morning. By the perimeter.'

'What was your daughter doing by the perimeter?'

'Don't ask. But she says she saw something shoot across the road.'

'A drone?'

'No, it was too small and too fast.'

'Where is your daughter, Mr Ops?'

'Outside, helping with the Dozers.'

'Is she a Green?'

'No, she doesn't have Colours.'

Priscilla's eyebrows crawled upwards.

'Really? How strange. Is she a contractor?'

Sam nodded.

'Yeah, and she's adopted.'

'From outside Leafen too,' said Priscilla. 'Very *colourful*.'

'We should be searching the perimeter beneath the breach site,' said Sam.

'We could track it,' said Saul.

Turnett looked at him.

'With a S-Stooge.'

Saul winked.

'Fucking A.'

'A what?' said Priscilla.

'Stooge,' said Saul. 'Subnet Trace Originat – '

'Tell me what it is, not what it stands for.'

'It's, er, it lets you monitor the signals around a set of Fronds. Keep it close enough and it'll show you where the signal's coming from.'

'But Dr Perez said Trittek's were closed systems. They're unresponsive.'

'That's t-true,' said Turnett. 'But they have to be sending and receiving signals of some kind if they've been compromised. We might not be able to decode them, but we can find the source.'

'That'd help,' said Sam. 'That'd help a lot. We take Trittek and this Stooge out to the perimeter, find this thing and shut it down.'

'Wait,' said Demetri. 'Perimeter? I'm not going out to the perimeter, it's dangerous.'

'I agree with your plan, Mr Ops,' said Priscilla, ignoring Demetri. 'But how? All of our networks are down. Not a single vehicle will run without the transport grid. Trucks, cars, planes, helicopters – '

'What about on foot?' said Ruba.

'Did anyone hear me?' protested Demetri.

'The breach site is a hundred miles away,' said Saul. 'It would take days.'

'Seriously,' said Demetri. 'I'm not going.'

Priscilla slammed her hand on the table.

'You will *go* where I fucking *tell* you to go, Trittek. Is that clear?'

The room was silent. Priscilla stood, her chair scraping behind. She towered over Demetri.

'Is that *clear*, Trittek?'

Demetri nodded frantically.

'Good.'

Priscilla sat down.

'We can't walk, we can't drive. What do we do?'

She looked around the room.

'Well? Anyone?'

Sam sat back in his chair.

'I have transport,' he said.

'What?' said Priscilla.

'I – ' said Sam. He stopped, took a breath and leant closer. 'I know of a vehicle. A truck. One that wouldn't have been affected.'

'You do?' said the general.

'Yes, it's – ah – off the grid.'

'Really. That would make it contraband, Mr Ops.'

Sam nodded. He felt Priscilla's eyes searching him.

'Does it work?' she said at last.

'We can make it work,' he replied.

Priscilla took a long breath through her nose.

'This is all a little unusual,' she said. 'But I think it's worth pursuing. Thank you, Miss Groone, for bringing it to my attention.'

Ruba's face shone with pride.

'Are we going to tell Technology?' she said, hopefully. 'The President?'

'Why don't you let me handle that side of things. For now,

this is between everyone in this room and nobody else. This is still just a theory and we don't want people getting alarmed. Understood?'

Everyone nodded, apart from Emelia, who folded her arms. Priscilla turned her gaze on her.

'Let me be clear,' she said. 'Nobody is to speak of this to anyone. Not to their friends, not to their family, not with their colleagues. And certainly not to Technology. Do I have your word?'

The table murmured agreement. Emelia raised her chin.

'Your *word*.'

Priscilla slammed the table again. Emelia looked around the room. All eyes were on her. At last she nodded.

'All right then,' said Priscilla. 'This is what's going to happen.'

thirty-six

mud, grease and metal

APRIL AND Marl held flashlights for Sam as he bent over the truck's engine.

'Do you know what you're doing?' said April.

'Of course I do,' he said. Something clanged. 'Damn – point the light down here.'

'Let me have a go,' she said. 'I don't want you breaking it before I get a chance to drive it.'

'April, you're not driving this thing,' said Sam. 'It's too dangerous. Besides, we don't even know if it'll work.'

'It's my truck,' said April.

'Yeah, *your truck*,' said Sam. 'I'm not even going to ask where you got it from.'

'Good, because it doesn't matter. It's mine and I'm driving it.'

Sam stood up and pulled the light towards his face.

'General Mandrek put me in charge,' he said. 'I can choose whoever I like to drive this thing.'

April pulled back the beam.

'Yes, so choose me or I'll never forgive you.'

Sam growled and went back to work.

'Where *did* you get it from?' said Marl.

'I bought it.'

'But how did it get in here?' he said. 'Inside The Line? It does not look like something that Leafen would be happy with on its streets. It must be a century old at least. No tracking devices, no reliance on any network, a completely free engine.'

'It's just a truck,' said April. 'Relics come in and out all the time. The houses in the upper districts are filled with furniture from outside. It's big business.'

'I can't see properly,' said Sam. He walked to the workbench and rummaged about on the shelves.

'By the way,' he said. 'That stuff you're talking about? In the mansions? It's all from the Hordes, not from outside. You need salvage licences and warrants to trade. Anything that comes in is registered and logged. Everything has papers.'

He found a battery pack with three frayed cables hanging from one side. He cradled it under one arm as he wheeled a standing light over from the corner.

'This heap of junk?' he said, nodding to the truck as he twisted the wires around the lamp's connectors. 'This has no papers. It's illegal.'

The lamp buzzed, crackled and whined until a yellow bulb lit the truck and the ground around it. April and Marl switched off their flashlights. Marl stepped forwards and peered into the engine cavity.

'I have seen vehicles like this one,' he said.

'In the Hordes?' said April.

'No.' Marl smiled. 'There is nothing as old as this within the Hordes. I meant outside.'

Sam caught the brief change in April's expression. He went back to work under the hood.

'You've been outside?' said April.

'Yes, on my way from Trida. We had to cross a large section of country to get here.'

Sam laughed over his shoulder.

'*Country*?' he said.

'Yes. It is what Tridans call the land beneath our feet. What do you call it?'

Sam stamped his boot on the stone floor.

'This thing under my feet?'

He braced himself against the engine cavity and began to pull hard on a wrench.

'I call it dirt.'

Marl nodded.

'Well, in Trida, dirt was considered sacred. Something that was fundamentally, intrinsically bound to us with no separation.'

'Sounds like you should have worn better boots,' said Sam between grunts.

'It is what we believed. What about you, Mr Samuel? What do you believe?'

Sam renewed his position and pulled harder.

'Me? Right now, I believe –' The muscles in his neck pulled taut. ' – in mud, grease – and metal – '

The wrench spun free and Sam tumbled onto his back, cursing. Marl held out his hand.

'Sir, if you don't mind, may I try?'

Sam allowed himself to be pulled up, surprised by the strength in the young man's hand.

'Be my guest,' he said.

As Marl busied himself under the hood, the door opened and Christine entered, followed by one of Priscilla's guards. Demetri, Saul and Turnett slouched behind.

'Good, you're back,' said Sam. 'Did you get that thing, what did you call it – a Stooge?'

'Yep,' said Christine. 'Had to break a few doors down in the process, but we got it.'

Demetri held up a small black box with a green screen.

'This one had the most charge,' he said. 'Should last another couple of days at least.'

'And you think this thing will lead us to the source?' said Sam.

'If it exists,' said Demetri. 'But it's not reading anything right now, which means it's either not there or too far away.'

'Then we have to get closer to it,' said Sam. 'Can you work that thing?'

'Sure, but – listen, doesn't this feel a bit weird, sneaking off like this? Why doesn't the General want us to tell anyone?'

'I have to agree, Sam,' said Christine. 'Something doesn't feel right about all this.'

The guard stepped forwards.

'General Mandrek has specifically asked for this to be a covert operation. She doesn't want any attention on it.'

'Why?' said Demetri.

'General's orders,' said the guard. He stood before Sam. 'Are you Sam Ops?'

'Yeah. Who are you?'

'Private Grant, from Marketing. I am to accompany you on your mission, sir.'

'Great. More the merrier.' Sam nodded and turned to Saul and Turnett. 'And you two, where are you going to be?'

'General Hot Pants got us a room on the eighth floor of The Leaf,' said Saul. 'Ruba's there now, setting things up.'

'Good,' said Sam. He took two radios from a charging unit on his desk and tossed them one. 'We'll use these to communicate. You can get a range of around eighty miles on these things. They use the Fabrik to bounce signals.'

'We'll start looking into the description your d-daughter gave us – ' Turnett looked past Sam and smiled. 'Hi, April – '

April smiled back, rippling her fingers in a wave.

' – and call you when we have something.'

'Good,' said Sam. 'Then all we need now – '

The truck's engines exploded into life, belching black smoke out into the dimly lit room. Sam turned to see Marl waving through the driver's window, beaming.

' – is for the truck to work.'

They pushed the truck out of the workshop and down the dark alleyway until they met 5th. After another few side roads, they came to 8th, which was quieter. Sam walked to the driver's windowleant.

'We'll have to take the side roads to avoid all the stopped

traffic. We'll probably be clear by the time you hit 10th. After that it's just a grid until we reach the suburbs. Fifty miles north-east and we're in open country. We should hit the site beneath the breach in another ten – '

'Sam, I drive for a living,' said April. 'I know Leafen like the back of my hand. It's my job.'

'I know, but not like this,' he said. He banged his fist on the roof. 'And not in this shit-tip.'

Demetri tripped as he met them at the hood.

'Are you sure about this? Maybe it isn't such a good idea.'

'Don't worry,' said Sam.

'But isn't this thing illegal? Won't somebody hear the engines? We'll be fired.'

'They probably won't hear anything in the station. Besides, we're under orders from the General and we have our very own military chaperone.'

He nodded up at Grant, who was already on the flatbed.

'So what,' said Demetri. 'We just find this thing, whatever it is, and take it back?'

'That's the plan,' said Sam. 'And you're the one who's going to lead us to it.'

'You good to go?' said Christine.

'Just about,' said Sam. He pulled a radio from the passenger seat and threw it at Christine.

'Keep it on,' he said.

There was a loud *whump* from above, as if the sky had been flicked inwards. They all ducked and looked up. The night was flickering.

'What was that?' said Christine.

'The Fabrik,' said Sam. 'It's struggling on half power, especially with the breach. I don't think we have a lot of time before it blows altogether.'

'How long?' said Christine.

'A day, maybe?' said Sam. 'Two?'

'Well then, you'd better get going.'

Marl and Demetri climbed onto the flatbed.

'Good luck,' said Christine, slapping the hood.

She exchanged a look with Sam as he hopped in the front. It registered dimly with April as she started the engine.

She jammed the gears into first. The cogs caught and scraped.

'Christine?' said Sam.

'Sure, Sam,' said Christine. She put her hand on the driver's door.

'April?' said Sam.

'What?' said April. Her eyes narrowed, the jigsaw of the next few seconds slowly falling into place.

'Oh, you wouldn't – '

'Goodbye, sweetheart,' said Sam.

'No – '

Christine yanked the door open and pulled April out.

'No! Get your hands off me!'

'April, Christine's going to take you to Dr Perez. She's in medical tent 38.'

'No, Sam, you son of a *bitch*!'

'She's working on this with us so we'll have contact with you.'

'Sam!'

'Take care of her, Christine,' said Sam. He slid over to the driver's seat and pulled the door shut.

Christine held April to her chest, kicking and screaming.

'I will,' she said. 'You take care of yourself.'

The truck shuddered forward, almost stalling, but Sam caught the clutch and steadied it. Then they trundled off, clanking and rumbling through the silent streets and away from April's furious yells.

thirty-seven

something you're not

April sat in the triage of medical tent 38, arms and legs firmly crossed. Christine offered her a polystyrene cup of coffee, which she dismissed with a scowl.

'April,' said Christine. 'He's just trying to look after you.'

'I don't *need* looking after. I need to be doing something useful. I need to be driving that truck. *My* truck.'

Christine nodded, holding out the coffee again.

'I know, but listen, Sam just – '

'And I don't want any piss-tasting coffee!'

'OK, April,' said Christine, placing the cup carefully on the ground beside her. 'Well, I'll be outside if you need anything.'

'I told you, I don't need looking after!'

Christine held up her hands and backed away, leaving April staring furiously at her feet.

'Bad day, Ape?' said a deep, smiling voice from somewhere within the tent.

She saw a hand waving over the beds and saw Marco, sitting with his arm in a sling. She walked over.

'How are you doing, Ape?' he said.

'Shit, thanks. What happened to you?'

Marco shrugged.

'I was driving. Busy street.'

'Did you get hit?'

'Nah. Car stopped when everything else did. I got out and tripped up a curb, fractured this.'

He pushed himself up on the bed, slowly, like a mountain range forming. All of his movements were like this — geological in both power and speed.

'What about you?' he said. 'Where were you?'

'Working on my truck,' she said.

Marco laughed, mouth as wide as a cave.

'Whole corporation's partying and you're in the workshop. Sounds like my Ape.'

'I'm not *your* Ape,' she said, gritting her teeth. 'I'm not *anybody's* Ape.'

'OK,' he said.

'Sorry,' she muttered.

Marco brushed it off with a smile.

'So,' he said. 'Did you get that piece of junk working?

'Yes, as it happens. And it's not a piece of junk.'

'But what is it, like a hundred, two hundred years old?'

'Something like that.'

'What about parts?'

April sighed and looked around.

'Sam found the last bits today.'

'Sam. You mean your dad.'

'He's not my dad,' said April, teeth close to grinding again. Marco lowered his brow, glacier-speed.

'Ape, he's raised you from before you could control your sphincter. He's your dad.'

'He's Sam, and I love him, but he's not my dad.'

Marco rested his head on the pillow. His voice rumbled beneath the murmurs of the tent.

'I've known Sam Ops for a long time. He's a good man.'

'I've never said otherwise,' said April. 'Although I could.'

'And I know how much he loves you. I know how much it would mean to him if you took your place here.'

'What do you mean?' said April.

'Take your Colours, Ape. Take residency.'

April glared at him.

'I'm not from Leafen,' she said. 'How many times do I have to say that? I'm here because Sam took me in from outside, but I don't have to take residency here. It's my choice.'

'So that's it, you just stay as a contractor,' said Marco.

'Yup.'

'Why?'

'So I can leave when I want.'

Marco laughed again. The people in the surrounding beds jumped like startled rabbits.

'Leave?' he said. 'And where are you going, Ape? Back to where you came from? Where's that?'

April folded her arms.

'You wouldn't understand. You've lived here all your life.'

'Yeah, I have. And so have you.'

They were quiet for a while.

'So that's what this truck's about?' he said at last. 'So you can get to the outside?'

'Near it at least,' she said. 'The truck isn't connected to the network, so it can't be traced.'

'It's not healthy, Ape,' said Marco. 'This obsession with outside. It can't do any good.'

'Yes, well, it's not such a problem any more.'

She let her eyes flit around the tent.

'You're lucky, April.' said Marco. 'You have a good life and a good father. But all you want to do is pretend to be something you're not.'

'April?'

They turned to see Emelia. Her hair was in black straggles, her white coat coloured with a grim collage of stains.

'I'm Dr Perez,' she said. 'Emelia. Your father said –'

'He's not my father,' snapped April.

'Oh, I thought – '

'It's complicated,' explained Marco.

'Well, Sam – whoever he is – said you were to help me.'

April stared furiously at her feet.

'So, are you going to help?' said Emelia.

'I'll see you later, Ape,' said Marco. 'Go and be helpful.'

'Fine,' she said, blowing out through her nose. 'It's better than doing nothing.'

thirty-eight

unswept land

IT WAS after midnight and freezing. Demetri sat in the back of the Ford with his jacket pulled up around his neck, adjusting the settings on the Stooge. He was trying not to let his teeth chatter. Marl sat opposite, legs outstretched and arms bare like a sunbather. He was smoking, pulling in long drags and letting the cold wind take the smoke from his open mouth. He looked up at the sky.

'Things seem so much darker in here. Closer, you know?'

Demetri glanced up.

'Not really. I've never been outside.'

'Of course. I forgot.'

Demetri blew into his hands and rubbed them together. Marl smiled.

'You could have sat in the front. It would be warmer.'

'I'm fine,' said Demetri. 'This thing works better without obstruction.'

They reached 10th and found a few straight roads west between the main streets. They were still crawling, but Sam had been right — the roads were getting quieter as they travelled away from the centre. Most of the partying had been going on in the enormous boulevards and atriums that clustered around The Leaf.

The driver's window wound down.

'I'm going to turn the lights on now,' said Sam.

As they turned onto the wide road, the truck's headlights flickered and glowed. The beams caught a few people swaying on the pavements or standing with their heads against windows. Cars had stopped dead in the street or pulled over, the last actions of their onboard computers having been to safely manoeuvre and avoid a crash with the rest of the traffic. Most of the street was therefore clear, so Sam opened up the engine. As they picked up speed, Demetri pulled his jacket tight around his neck. He saw teeth in Marl's smile.

It was after three a.m. when they reached the industrial districts and found their way onto the country roads leading through the suburbs. Grant, who had been keeping watch at the back, shuffled next to Demetri.

'Have you found anything yet?' he said, over the roar of the engine.

Demetri twiddled the Stooge's dials and banged its side.

'No,' he shouted. 'I'm not even sure if this thing is going to work.'

He rapped his knuckles on the window of the cab. Sam opened it.

'How far are we from the breach site?' shouted Demetri.

'About six or seven miles,' said Sam. He slowed the truck and pulled to a halt by a field, yanked the handbrake and poked his head out.

'Anything?'

'No,' said Demetri. He shivered in the sudden stillness. 'Nothing – no, wait –'

He saw something flicker on the dim screen. He turned the dial back and there it was again — a weak pulse in one corner.

'I think I found something.'

'Where?' said Sam.

'Er – east, no, west. And about three miles north. It's weak, but it's definitely something.'

The truck lurched as Sam found its gear.

'Shit!' shouted Demetri. 'Can you be – '

They shot forward and the Stooge flew from Demetri's hands, crashing against the side. Demetri fell after it, banging his head on the wheel arch. Marl caught the Stooge as it spun around on the floor.

'Sorry,' shouted Sam through the window.

Demetri sat up, holding his head.

'Where's the Stooge?' he said.

Marl examined it. 'I am afraid it is not in such a good state.' He held the cracked screen up for Demetri to see.

'Great,' said Demetri.

'Is it broken?' said Sam.

Demetri wiped the screen and turned it in his hands.

'Pretty much,' he said. 'But it might still pick up something if we get close enough. Just keep going north.'

They pulled away. In a few minutes, they slowed to a crawl and Sam's head reappeared.

'We're coming up on three miles. This is where you said it would be.'

Demetri peered at the broken Stooge.

'The display's busted where it should be showing us the location,' he said. He looked around. 'If there even is one. Turn off the engine, will you?'

The truck spluttered to a halt and Sam got out. Insects buzzed in the headlights. The trees were filled with the purr and chirp of crickets. Marl slid out and lit a cigarette.

Demetri looked out at the dark fields, raised the Stooge to the sky and performed two slow, full turns. Then he jumped from the flatbed and did the same thing on the road, following the Stooge like a diviner following rods. At last he stopped and shook his head.

'Turn off the lights,' he said. Sam reached in and switched off the beams. Demetri breathed cold air in the dark. His jaw shook.

'There,' said Demetri. He pointed west.

'What?' said Sam.

'In that field. Eleven o'clock.'

Sam followed his finger.

'I don't see anything.'

'Wait – '

They waited –

In the distance, a faint green light pulsed quickly and was gone.

'There, did you see it?'

Sam stood up.

'I think so.'

Ten seconds later, it pulsed again.

Sam turned and got back in the truck. 'Marl, get in, we have something.'

Marl flicked his cigarette into the dirt and hopped back in the flatbed. Grant hauled Demetri in.

'Keep the lights off,' said Demetri, as they pulled away. 'Go slow.'

They stopped at a gate into a wide field. The pulsing light was now on their left. They took flashlights and walked through the long grass, still damp from the evening's purge. The dirt was soft beneath their feet, the smell of wet earth all around. The horizon was starting to show a thin blue light.

They crossed another hedge and then another field. Soon the pulse was accompanied by a very faint, low beep, and they saw dark silhouettes of grass blades flashing in the green light.

'This is it,' said Demetri. 'Fuck.'

There, in the centre of a flattened clearing and surrounded by shards of twisted, black metal, was a sphere about the size of a basketball. They trained their flashlights on it.

'What is it?' said Sam.

'No idea. I've never seen one before,' said Demetri. 'Can I have your radio? I'll see if Turnett knows, he's a hardware geek.'

Sam tossed him the radio.

'Guys,' said Demetri. 'Are you there?'

The channel crackled.

'Demetri?' It was Saul's voice. *'Where are you?'*

'Saul, we've found something. Put Turnett on.'

More crackling, then Turnett's voice.

'H-Hello?'

'Hey, I need you to identify something for me. Are you near a workstation?'

'I c-can be – '

'Good. Small metallic orb, about ten inches wide. Control panel on one side, flashing green beacon – '

'Sounds like some kind of field marker, or – I don't know, I'll have to look it up – '

Demetri shone his flashlight on the fragments of metal lying around it.

'It looks like it was travelling in something that broke apart.'

'That must have been what brought it through,' said Sam.

Marl walked into the clearing and bent down to look at it.

'What should we do with it, Turnett?' said Demetri over the radio.

'I don't know.' Turnett's voice crackled back. *'But I don't think you should touch it until – '*

'I'm going to pick it up,' said Marl. He reached out. Demetri held out his hand.

'Wait, no – '

As Marl grasped for the orb, it suddenly sprang to life. It shot upwards, cracking against his skull and knocking him onto his back. Demetri and Sam followed it into the air with their flashlights. It hovered uncertainly, humming. A section of one of its panels scissored open and a lens popped out, turning between them. Marl staggered to his feet and the lens swivelled towards him. He held his nose, from which blood was now pouring, and stared into the orb's scrutinising eye. He swiped at it with his free hand. The orb jerked back with what seemed like horror. He swiped again but the orb evaded him. It twitched back and forwards a few times and then, seeming to have reached a conclusion, it packed up its lens, dropped and shot away across the field.

'Turnett?' said Demetri.

'W-What happened?' said Turnett.

'It can also fly,' said Demetri.

Grant raised his gun and fired a few shots after the disappearing orb.

'No!' said Demetri.

'What?' said Grant. 'It's getting away!'

'We don't know what will happen if we damage it,' said Demetri.

'He's right,' said Sam. 'We need to secure it. Back to the truck.'

They ran, stumbling, through the grass. The orb was disappearing towards the road.

'Keep your eye on it, Marl!' said Demetri.

'I shall try,' said Marl, still holding his nose.

They reached the truck and jumped in. Its lights filled the road and it spluttered away in pursuit, picking up speed as Sam worked his way through the ancient gears.

Demetri's eyes streamed as he stared into the wind. For a moment, he forgot he was in a contraband vehicle on the outer reaches of the corporation, forgot he was breaking the law. He felt as if he was cutting through the night like a boat ploughing through a tide. He felt like he was a light streaming through darkness.

'I don't see anything!' he shouted. He banged on the roof. 'Go faster!'

The truck's engines roared and strained. He wiped the tears and squinted ahead. Then he saw it, a glimmer on the road ahead.

'There,' he said. 'It's there!'

As they gained on it, they saw that the orb was following the road, but also creeping across it. Marl stood up and joined Demetri at the roof. The bleeding had stopped.

'What is it doing?' said Marl.

'I think it's following a diagonal. We need to catch it before it leaves the road.'

He leant down to Sam's window.

'Can you make this thing go any faster?' he screamed.

'This is it, full speed,' shouted Sam.

He looked ahead. The hedges had given way and there was nothing but dirt where the fields had been.

'And we're about to run out of road, too,' he said. 'Look.'

Demetri stood up again. The darkness ahead seemed to grow even darker, as if something was rising up to meet them, a wall of some kind. The truck slowed and the orb began to reach the limits of its headlights' beam.

'What are you doing?' said Demetri. 'We're losing it!'

'No we're not,' said Sam. 'Watch.'

The little orb buzzed on, gaining speed until it had disappeared from the headlights' glow altogether. Then, suddenly, there was a soft clang and it reappeared, spinning and toppling about in mid-air.

'What the hell was that?' said Demetri.

Sam stopped the truck and let the engine tick over.

'We're at the perimeter,' he said.

The orb corrected itself and seemed to reacquire its bearings, facing back the way it had come. It paused and then buzzed away again. There was another clang and it reappeared again, spinning like a dazed bird.

'The Fabrik,' said Demetri. 'It can't get through.'

Marl pulled out his flashlight and inched towards it. Sam and Demetri followed with their own beams trained upon the ground.

Grant jumped down from the flatbed.

'We shouldn't be this far out,' he said. 'This is unswept land. It's dangerous. Y'all need to get back in the truck. Now.'

'We have it cornered,' said Sam.

'Get back in the truck, sir. That's an order.'

'Be careful, don't let it see you,' said Sam.

'It's OK,' whispered Marl. 'I just need to get a little closer.'

The orb buzzed forwards again and this time they saw it bounce back from the invisible wall, the space where it had made its impact rippling like water. Marl froze, watching as it whirred and clicked, inches from his face. It tried twice more in quick succession, both times returning to the same spot.

Marl held out his arms.

'This time,' he whispered.

But, just as he was about to pounce, the night crackled.

Then the world twisted out of shape.

For a split second, they saw each other's faces shine beneath bright stars and moonlight. Then again, and again for longer. The orb shot forwards but, this time, did not return. Marl lunged, groped empty space, and fell face-first in the dirt.

The stars were gone, and so was the orb.

thirty-nine

real stars

MARL GOT to his feet and brushed himself down. Sam and Demetri walked up next to him. The three of them stared dumbly at the empty space where the orb had been just a moment before. It was as if another world had just opened its mouth and swallowed it.

'Where did it go?' said Demetri.

Sam held his hand to the empty space. There was a deep vibration in the ground and the air seemed to press down around them, muffling all other sound. The space around Sam's hand buzzed and cracked.

'It's weaker than I thought,' said Sam.

'The perimeter?' said Demetri. He looked up and down the invisible wall stretching up in front of him. 'Is that what this is? Fabrik?'

Sam turned.

'Yeah, the perimeter. What did you think it was? Have you never been out here?'

'No, why would I?'

Sam raised his eyebrows and turned away. He reached out again, with the same effect – gravel jumping at their feet as the vibration grew. Demetri thrust his fingers in his ears.

'What is that?'

'The field's close to rupturing,' said Sam. 'It was already struggling because of the breach, and then we took away some of its power. It must have weakened enough for that thing to shoot through. The resonance filters – they'll be weakening too much as the cycle troughs – damn it.'

Grant shouted from the truck.

'We chased it out. It's gone. That means it can't work, right? We can go home.'

Sam pointed east at the dark skyline.

'I don't see any lights,' he said.

'Turnett, are you still there?' said Demetri, into the radio.

'Yes. What's going on?'

'Has anything changed back there? Do you have any power?'

'No, nothing's changed; listen, I found your hardware.'

'What is it?'

'It's called a Hackdrone. It's basically a mobile quantum computer that worms its way into large systems from the outside. It's programmed with avoidance tactics, that's why it can fly. They were developed to take down defence systems remotely.'

'Defence? So this is a weapon?'

'Yeah, but it's just a prototype. I found it on the list of rejected tech applications from the last quarterly submissions. It was never supposed to be built.'

'One of ours?'

'No. It's from Soor.'

'Soor? The people we're selling Spoke to?'

'The very s-same.'

'Why would they want to hack us?'

'Beats me – '

Suddenly, the night flashed again. For a second, they could see stars and clear sky again. Then, just as quickly. they were extinguished.

'How long was that?' said Sam. 'A minute? Two?'

Marl gave him a look of understanding.

'I'm counting.'

'Good,' said Sam.

'Is it going to fail?' said Demetri.

'If we don't restore power, yes.'

'Then why don't we restore power?'

'Because then they'll have none in The Leaf. They won't be able to work.'

He pulled the radio from his belt.

'April?'

The radio clicked and hissed. There was a crackle, followed by April's voice, a flat growl.

'What.'

He grinned. Even when she was furious, the sound of her voice made him happy.

'Hey, April, where are you? What's going on?'

'Back in Central, helping out at one of the med tents.'

Sam could almost see her mouth curling in disgust.

'Good,' said Sam. 'Stay there and keep safe.'

There was a pause, then –

'Where are you?'

'We're at the perimeter. We found something.'

'What?'

'Some kind of hacking device, just as we thought. But it's gone.'

'Gone?'

'Yeah, it took off through the Fabrik.'

'How did – ?'

'Listen, is anything weird happening back there? Any more power? Are the people still, you know, asleep?'

'As far as I can tell,' said April, breezily. *'We're just cleaning a few of them up, actually, wiping the snot off their faces, cleaning their eyeballs. Oh, and a few of them have started shitting themselves, so that's nice. You know,* great *to be here, safe, wiping strangers' arseholes, rather than actually fucking* doing – '

There was a *whump* and the night snapped in two again. The stars flashed down on them.

'What was that?' said April.

'Do me a favour and go outside,' said Sam.

'What? Why? What's going on?'

'Just go outside, just for a minute.'

'Why? Tell me what's – '

'April, just do as I ask for once in your fucking life.'

The radio crackled out. Sam turned to Marl, who was staring upwards, concentrating on the dense, crackling space above them like a child at a fireworks display.

'How long?' he said.

'Eighty-seven seconds,' said Marl.

'Keep counting,' said Sam.

'Why are you counting?' said Demetri.

'Just keep counting,' said Sam. 'You too.'

Sam turned and walked back along the track. He passed Grant.

'We need to get back,' said Grant. 'This is as far as we can go. I mean it.'

Sam ignored him, holding the radio to his mouth.

'You there yet, April?'

'Almost.'

'Tell me when you're outside.'

He reached the truck and jumped in, starting its engine.

'OK, I'm outside,' said April. *'What's this all about?'*

'Just wait there,' said Sam. He drove the truck over to Marl and Demetri and got out, keeping the engine running and hanging on the driver's door. His breath fogged the air.

'Sir,' said Grant. Sam heard the click of a gun behind. 'Turn the truck around, please.'

– 75 – 76 – 77 –

The Fabrik began to crackle again.

'Look up, April,' said Sam.

'I'm looking up,' said April, on the radio.

– 81 – 82 – 83 –

'Still looking up – don't see anything – '

The Fabrik shook and blinked in and out.

'Sir – this is an order, I'll – '

'Start counting again,' said Sam to Marl.

'Wow,' said April. *'The stars – Sam, I saw the stars!'*

'You saw it too?'

'Yes!' April's voice was fluttering, high with excitement. *'I saw*

the stars, I mean the real stars, Sam, they were amazing! They were bright, Sam! Sam? Sam? What just happened?'

'That's not good,' said Sam. 'It means it's not localised. It's all over the Fabrik. You two, get in the truck. And keep counting.'

'Why are we getting in the truck?' said Demetri. 'We're going home, right?'

Marl swung onto the flatbed and held out his hand for Demetri.

'We have to find the Hackdrone,' he said.

'But it's gone,' said Demetri, pulling himself up. 'It went through.'

They heard a noise, turned and saw Grant. His gun was shaking.

'Sir, I – '

Sam jumped into the cab.

'Where are we at?' he shouted.

'Thirty seconds,' said Marl.

'What?' said Demetri. 'Wait, surely you can't be thinking of – '

'April,' said Sam. 'We're going to find this thing.'

The radio was silent apart from a few rhythmic taps, which Sam knew was April tapping the talk button as she thought, or fumed, or did both.

'How,' she said, no question in her voice.

'We're going to go through. When it opens up. How long?'

'Forty-five,' said Marl.

'No,' said Demetri, scrabbling to his feet. 'Wait, I want to get off! Let me off!'

Marl held out his hand.

'It is fine,' he said. 'We will be fine. Do not worry.'

'No we won't!' said Demetri. 'It's not safe out there! I want to go home! Grant!'

'We will not be outside for long,' said Marl. 'Just until we find the Hackdrone.'

'But it's not safe!' said Demetri.

Grant shuffled in the dirt, swinging his gun uncertainly between the cab and the flatbed.

There were a few more taps on the radio as Sam waited for April's reply.

'Sixty-five seconds,' said Marl.

'These radios won't work beyond the Fabrik, April. April?'

'What do I say?' said April. *'If they ask where you've gone?'*

The Fabrik began its crackle.

'Tell them the truth, I'll sort it out later.'

'Seventy-five,' said Marl. 'Sam?'

Sam reversed the truck a little, then revved the engine and began crawling forwards, picking up pace.

'I'll see you soon, April,' said Sam.

'Sam, wait,' said April.

'Yeah?' He pressed down on the accelerator.

– 82 – 83 –

'Don't go. It's not safe. You don't know what's out there.'

The truck sped towards the Fabrik, almost upon it as the air began to shake around them. Demetri began to scream.

– 85 – 86 –

'Yeah, yeah I do,' said Sam. He floored the accelerator and closed his eyes.

PART FOUR

trouble

forty

common human decency

'BUT, YOUR Grace – '

Father Roberts stepped into the flickering halo of lamplight. His peers – the pack of priests, candle-boys and cleaners, their faces glistening in soft rain – shuffled nervously behind him on the steps of the church. Roberts raised a hand to the dark mass of human beings beneath them.

'Don't you think we should be helping them?'

Ely Loome's eyes narrowed.

'Did I not make myself clear, Roberts?' he said. 'Is there something in my orders you don't understand?'

'No, Your Grace,' said Roberts. His hand drifted back to his side. 'I understand your orders very well. I just think that closing the doors of the church at this stage would be – would be – '

'Would be *what*?'

'Inhuman, Your Grace.'

'Really?' said Loome, his voice like silt. 'And what would you do instead, Roberts, hmm?'

He turned to regard the shuffling throng. His voice echoed from the buildings across the street.

'Take them in? All of them?'

'Well – '

'Have you seen how many there are?'

'Yes, Your Grace. I admit, we couldn't possibly take them all in. But our church is spacious. It has many chambers and its own power supply. We could take some, surely? The children, the very old, the weak – '

'The *weak*,' echoed Loome.

'Yes, Your Grace, those who cannot help themselves. It's

getting cold.'

He looked up into the descending mist, the first tendrils of a much heavier rainfall.

'And it's raining. We can look after them, keep them warm and dry.'

'Why?'

'Your Grace, I – '

'Where, Roberts, is it written that we are to do such things?'

'Written? I don't – I mean, nowhere, but it's common human decency.'

He looked round at the cloaked crowd behind him.

'Our people need our help and we are able to give it.'

Loome moved closer, inclining his head.

'Listen to me, my child. We don't run this church on the tenets of *common human decency*. We run it on the teachings and the commands of The Market.'

He relaxed the taut mask of his face and sighed, smiling at The Leaf-shaped spire above them.

'I am but a messenger – my job is merely to pass on those commands.'

He looked down again, the smile shrivelling like a salted slug.

'*Your* job, Roberts is to obey them. And right now – '

Loome's eyes flashed in the night. Spittle flew from his mouth.

' – Right now, I am giving you two direct COMMANDS.'

Loome thrust his face at Roberts, pointing at the doors.

'Keep them shut!'

His arm swung to the street.

'And keep them out! Do you understand?'

Roberts faltered.

'Do you *understand*, Roberts?' shrieked Loome. 'Or do you want to take your chances with the Hordes?'

Roberts turned to his colleagues, then hung his head.

'No, Your Grace. I understand.'

'Good!'

With that, Loome marched back inside the church, cloak whirling, and slammed the doors behind him.

Roberts watched the dust eddying about his feet.

'Form a line,' he said.

forty-one

only ever upwards

STEVE MANAGER woke to the soft echo of whispers and footsteps. He opened his eyes. Central Station was getting light and moving with faint shapes. A thin mist hung everywhere, lacing its way around the giant redwood trunks and rising in vaporous tongues to the glass above their canopy. He raised his head from cold plastic. Faith's word had never come. Sitting had become sprawling, had become stretching, had become curling, had become fitful, sleep with a night-long soundtrack of human activity.

'Hey, buddy,' said a voice. An old man with grey stubble and blue eyes was bending over him, holding a cup. Steve sat up and stretched his back.

'You all right?' said the old man.

'Yes,' said Steve. 'What time is it?'

The old man looked around.

'No idea. Early I guess.'

He held out the cup.

'Here, coffee, take it,' he said.

'Thanks,' said Steve, taking the plastic cup. The old man sat down next to him. He smelled of day-old urine and week-old breath. The scent formed an unholy alliance with the coffee steam in Steve's nostrils.

Through the mist, Steve could see shadows walking. Others were sat on the floor in huddles or still lying wherever they had found a spot to sleep. The deep doom of the previous day's events began to seep into Steve's consciousness.

'You know,' said the old man, oblivious to Steve's growing ruin. 'This reminds me of the Sweep of '56. Or was it '57? I guess you wouldn't remember, young man like you, but it came early, see? And not everyone was ready for it. They couldn't get home, so they had to set up shelters in Central, just like this, so we wouldn't get caught in it. All us kids hid under tables, chairs, blankets, anything we could get a hold of, all huddled together and waiting. And then the sound, oh hell the sound, I've never heard anything like it, like a billion buzzsaws all falling down from the sky.'

He turned to Steve, offering him a closer taste of his body's aromas.

'You know,' he said. 'I saw some. Mites, you know? They told us to stay hidden, but – ' He mimed an eyeglass around one eye. ' – I took a little peek.'

He laughed. Steve didn't.

'I thought it would be like watching birds, you know how they all sweep together in big flocks? But it wasn't. They kind of jerk around in straight-edged shapes. You can hardly see them move, just different patterns every second. It was weird. Weird to think they built all this.'

He raised a hand to the dull, grey expanse all around them. The few anaemic sunbeams that had managed to find their way through the redwoods were adding little to the station's meagre light.

The old man slapped his knees and stood.

'Well, I'll be off. I'm working in the medical tents. We could use some help if you're not doing anything.'

'Sorry,' said Steve. 'I have a meeting.'

'OK, well, I'll see ya then.'

Steve watched the old man hobble off into the mist. Then he left the untouched coffee and made for the elevators.

It had been a while since he had been here this early. The last time had been in his first year of work, getting the earliest train to be in before the rest of his department. Holly had been gone for three years, and that summer on the lake had seemed like it belonged to a different lifetime. The shape and texture of his days had changed. Now they were spent climbing invisible steps, making the right calls, playing the right games. There were no longer friends and no such thing as enemies, just people; people you had to manipulate to do what you wanted them to do.

That young man bristling with ambition had walked through this empty station with his eyes trained on the straight, thick trunks of the redwoods. They had grown as he had wished to grow — red, unwavering, strong. They pulled themselves out of the dirt and climbed away from it. They only moved upwards – upwards until death.

How could it be that they seemed so much taller now, so much further from his reach? He wondered: had he ever really climbed at all?

The outline of a young woman appeared through the mist. It was a shape he was beginning to recognise — the curve of her neck, the tilt of her chin towards a clipboard, the arch of her lower back, the stretch of her calves. Faith turned as he approached.

'Hello,' he said, rubbing his neck. 'It's morning. What happened?'

'He's ready for you,' she said. 'Daniel's ready.'

forty-two

prolonging the inevitable

APRIL THREW her thirty-second pair of disposable gloves in the bin marked 'HAZARDOUS WASTE'. She yawned. It was almost dawn. Pretending the smell wasn't following her around, she wandered back through the tent and found Emelia by a bed, upon which a young girl sat in a nightgown staring straight ahead.

'Is this one of them?' said April. 'A dozer?'

'This is my daughter, Lori,' said Emelia.

'I'm sorry.'

'That's OK.'

'She looks so sad.'

'They all do.'

'Do you know what's happening? For her, I mean. Is she conscious?'

'I don't know. All I know is that I can't reach her.'

One of the machines by the bed began to beep urgently. Lori's head drooped.

'Shit,' said Emelia, grabbing Lori's wrist. 'It's happening again.'

'What?' said April. 'What's going on?'

'Her pulse keeps dropping. I've seen it in some of the others, too. Lori? Lori, sweetheart, it's me, come back to me, please, please, please – '

She looked up into her glazed eyes and slapped her cheek.

'Lori?'

The machine stopped beeping and pinged. Lori's head lifted.

Emelia took two steps back; hands shaking, chin trembling.

'I have to do something,' she muttered to herself. 'I have to do something.'

'Emelia,' said a voice.

April looked up. A woman, identical to Dr Perez, had appeared by the bed.

'Not now, Enola,' said Emelia.

'Is Lori OK?'

'I said *not now*.'

The woman touched a finger to the little girl's face.

'Have you checked – '

Emelia grabbed her arm and pulled it away.

'Enola, I said not *now*!'

She spun on her heels, hands on her head, frantic.

'Damn it, I have to do something!'

She began pacing the floor. April spotted Enola slide a thermometer from the desk beside the bed.

'This isn't right,' muttered Emelia. 'This isn't right, I have to tell them.'

'Tell who?' said April.

'They're looking for the wrong thing. They're wasting their time.'

'Who?'

'This is insane; they have to be told, I have to tell them. I'm going to tell them.'

'Tell who what?' said April. 'Is this about Sam? Emelia, what the fuck's going on?'

Emelia gripped April's shoulders and stared up at her with bloodshot eyes.

'I need to do something. I want you to stay here and look after my daughter,' she said, shaking. 'Can you do that?'

'What's happening? Whatever it is I want to come with you.'

'Can you *do* that?'

She shook her.

'*Please.*'

'Of course,' said April, at last. 'But why can't your sister look after her?'

Emelia turned to Enola, who was standing by Lori, stroking her hair.

'Enola is incapable of looking after Lori. Now please, stay here, I won't be long.'

April watched her march off through the tent, making for the exit. She looked back at the girl on the bed and the woman standing by her, taking her temperature and tucking a lock of hair behind her ear. The machine pinged gently.

April turned and followed the doctor.

'Director Sumar! Director Sumar!'

Emelia marched across the concourse to the Crisis Centre. Heads turned at the sound of her voice.

'Director Sumar, I need to speak with you!'

Sumar's head poked out from the nucleus.

'Director Su – '

A hand grabbed Emelia's arm and yanked her off course.

'Dr Perez,' said Priscilla Mandrek, marching her in the opposite direction.

'What? General, get your hands off me!'

'*Might* I have a word?'

'No, let me go!' She called back over her shoulder. 'Director Sumar!'

Priscilla quickened her pace, heading for the doors into a utility stairwell. Emelia squirmed in her grip.

'This is no time for theatrics, Doctor.'

'Theatrics? I'm trying to save this corporation. I'm trying to save my daughter! Director Sumar!'

Priscilla barged through the double doors and dragged Emelia up the stone steps, kicking and yelling. When they were two flights up, she flung her into a corner.

'I thought I made myself clear,' she said. Her voice echoed in the suddenly empty space. 'You are not to speak of the security breach theory. *I* will handle the release of information to Technology, as and when it is appropriate.'

Emelia caught her breath, looking around the dark stairwell.

'Why?' she said. 'Why are you withholding the facts? Every second they waste hunting down a glitch is another second the condition of those people – *of my daughter* – deteriorates.'

'There are no *facts*, Doctor, only theories. And like I said, we don't want to cause alarm.'

Emelia rubbed her wrist, shaking her head.

'No, no, you're hiding something. I can tell. You're playing games, and my daughter's *life* is at stake.'

Priscilla narrowed her eyes.

'You said their condition is deteriorating?'

Emelia swallowed.

'Yes. Some of them. The weaker ones, especially, and the children. Their pulses keep dropping. Their breathing is becoming laboured.'

Priscilla pushed out her chest and looked up.

'Hmm. Interesting.'

She turned, giving Emelia space.

'Doctor, what is your prognosis? What do you think will happen to these people? To your daughter?'

'If we don't get them help soon, they could start to lose consciousness, go into comas, lose brain function, *die*.'

Priscilla tutted and rolled her eyes.

'Terrible,' she said.

'That's why we should be putting all our resources into fixing the security breach, not wasting time hunting down a glitch that doesn't exist. What's *wrong* with you?'

Priscilla walked the landing, hand on hips.

'I just don't know, Doctor,' she sighed. 'I wonder – is there anything to suggest that their brain function isn't already impaired?'

'What do you mean?'

'Well, such a traumatic event – it would have to leave scars, wouldn't it? I worry that this isn't perhaps bordering on cruelty. Aren't we just prolonging the inevitable?'

'I don't like what you're inferring. What's *bordering on cruelty*?'

Priscilla stopped walking, cornering her once again.

'Keeping them alive.'

Emelia buried the horror rising in her blood, and the need more than ever to find a way out of the stairwell and back to Lori. She spoke carefully, quietly.

'There is nothing to suggest that if we find a way to safely disconnect them from the network they won't return to full physical and neurological health. *Nothing* at all.'

'And nothing to suggest that they will. Such an inexact science, neuropsychology, isn't it?'

'There is nothing inexact about my science.'

Priscilla's eyes roamed Emelia's face, searching for a way in.

'You're certain,' she said at last. 'You believe there's hope if we involve Technology now?'

'Yes,' said Emelia. 'I'm certain.'

Priscilla dropped her head.

'Then you must do what you must do, Doctor.'

She stepped to the side, letting Emelia past.

'Thank you,' breathed Emelia. She walked down the steps, steadying herself on the railing.

'Dr Perez?'

'Yes?'

Emelia looked up. The bullet beat the sound it made, so she felt it hit her square in the chest just before she heard the shot from the gun, still glinting in Priscilla's hand, that fired it. By that time she was against the wall, the explosion in her rib cage mushrooming through her abdomen. The flood of adrenalin that had emptied like a burst dam caused her synapses to fire faster, stretching the dense seconds in which she now found herself struggling.

And within this thin film of experience, with no hope for

breath as her lungs divorced themselves from their task, Emelia Perez had a series of thoughts: recognition that the fizz of paraesthesia now reaching her feet was not a good sign; the question of whether her husband had felt the same thing as he had died on their kitchen floor with Lori sleeping in her cot next door; a wish that she had held him, and her daughter, for a greater portion of her life; and finally the resignation that these were the kind of things every person thought in their final seconds.

Her legs finally gave way and she tumbled down the second flight of steps. By the time she reached the bottom, she was dead.

Priscilla re-holstered her gun and pulled out her radio.

'Private Mitchell,' she said.

'Yes, General?'

'There's something for you to clean up in utility stairwell 59. Quick as you can, please.'

'Yes, General. Right away.'

Priscilla trotted down the stairs, pausing to step over Emelia's bleeding body. The double doors slammed behind her.

Two flights below, in the shadows of the basement, April stood with her back against the wall and her hand over her mouth. She waited for the echo of the door to disappear up the stairwell. When it was quiet she lifted her radio and opened a channel.

'Christine,' she whispered.

'April? Are you OK?'

'Christine, I need to speak with you.'

forty-three

all the things you don't need

AS THE truck reached the Fabrik, the space around seemed to grow more dense and energetic, less amenable to them being there, as if a thousand giant fists were suddenly trained upon them. Demetri felt his ears being inflated, his eyeballs needled and his skull squeezed as they reached the point of no return. He curled into a ball and screamed, although he heard nothing. The pressure grew until he felt as if his head would implode. He endured the brief and scintillating image of his body squashed into mush against the floor of the flatbed before suddenly being overcome by lightness. He thought that, perhaps, this was what being squashed must feel like — a moment of bliss as pressure was released through the ruptured skin and bone before the onset of agony.

But the lightness continued and he realised that he could hear the ridiculous sound of his own screams. He opened his eyes and blinked at the rusted metal floor, still allowing the tail end of his wailing to peter out. He coughed, smelled bile and realised that he had been sick. His ears popped. He could hear the sound of the truck engine screaming beneath them. He sat up, scrabbling for something to hold on to as the truck careered left and right and found a straight line on the track.

Opposite him, Marl was moving his head from side to side and banging both ears.

'Are you OK?' he said.

Demetri stared back at him in disbelief.

'You're bleeding again,' he said, pointing at the trickle of blood at Marl's nose. Marl dabbed it.

'Thank you,' he said, then pointed at Demetri. 'You too.'

Demetri wiped away a streak of blood from his top lip and squashed his nostrils shut.

'Are you guys OK?' shouted Sam from the open window.

Marl patted the roof of the car.

'Where are we?' said Demetri.

'Outside,' said Marl.

Demetri looked around. Behind them was a black wall stretching up into the sky as far as they could see. The immense height gave the illusion that it was moving with them, slowly toppling like an infinite black cliff. Ahead of them was a different matter. The sky was bright with stars and a huge half-moon that hung like an empty bowl. Although the sun was yet to rise, the light was strong enough to dust the landscape ghostly white. It was different, not as flat as it had been inside the Fabrik. There were dirt dunes and hillocks dotted about, and Demetri could make out the shadows of short trees and boulders. But he only glanced at these, because beyond them lay the strangest thing he had ever seen — a horizon that was not flat, but piled high with dark, rolling shapes.

'What are they?' said Demetri.

'Mountains,' said Marl. 'Beautiful, aren't they?'

Demetri sat up to get a better view. There were other lights in the dust; flickering fires far away.

'And the lights?' he said.

'Campfires,' said Marl.

'Are these the Hordes?'

Marl smiled sadly, rocking with the motion of the truck.

'No. The Hordelands occupy only the northern perimeter. The settlements are very large, very heavily populated. They stretch for many hundreds of miles.'

He looked behind.

'We should see them soon.'

Demetri looked closer and saw figures huddled around the fires.

'So who are these people?'

Marl lit a cigarette, shielding his match from the wind. Then he got to his feet and steadied himself against the cab. The wind ruffled his black hair and swept the smoke from his mouth.

'These are the Banished. They have no credit, so they cannot trade or engage in normal commerce like everyone else. They were sent away from the Hordes. Now they scavenge and mine. Look, the sun is coming up.'

A thin line of light had appeared over the tip of the wall behind them, brightening Marl's face.

'Mine what?' said Demetri.

Marl smiled and nodded back to the south edge of the wall. There, hard to make out in the low light, was a huge mass. It looked as though a section of the wall had broken and was spilling onto the ground.

'The waste mountain,' said Marl.

Demetri squinted at a thin line of people moving, like ants, towards the gigantic heap.

'All the things you don't need,' said Marl.

'Why does nobody else live out here?' said Demetri.

Marl shrugged and flicked his cigarette over the side.

'The Line is where trading takes place. It is where resources are delivered, where the corporation interfaces with its consumers. There is nothing out here but waste water, discarded food and broken things.' He pointed his cigarette ahead. 'Good enough for some.'

The road had almost disappeared and they were now driving through a wide plain dotted with people quietly waking up. Demetri could see their faces now, curious and wary in the growing dawn light, families going about their business in meagre patches of dirt. Some camped in tents, others in grander shelters made of wood. One family sat outside a dilapidated shack beneath a tall, solitary tree. A man in bare feet, jeans and a baseball cap was rolling a tyre towards a shed. He stopped and stared as they passed, scratching his head. A young girl with wet hair pasted across her forehead came running from the yard, brandishing a stick. Her younger brother toddled behind. Her mother went to grab them but was too slow. The girl ran alongside the truck, grinning up at Demetri and Marl and banging the side with her stick until she ran out of breath. She scrambled to a halt in the dust and stood with her stick hanging by her side, watching until they had left her sight.

They passed more fires and eventually found themselves in open country. Demetri closed his eyes against the cold air rushing over his face, then opened them again. The sky was brightening, although the sun was still hidden behind the gigantic wall. In and around the slipstream were smaller air currents. He felt them curling and winding around the larger blast, finding their way up his nostrils. He had never tasted air so fresh.

'What's that smell?' he said.

'That is the smell of Earth,' said Marl. 'The smell of your planet.'

'I thought it was unsafe out here, polluted, dangerous.'

'Some days are better than others. Air still moves. This is a good day.'

They were fifty miles out when Demetri looked back. They had almost escaped the shadow of the perimeter and sky had appeared above it. The black wall was beginning to take shape. He blinked, taking in the extent of his home for the first time in his life.

'It's a cube,' he said. 'A giant, black cube.'

'Cuboid, actually,' said Marl. 'It is much wider and deeper than it is tall.'

'I thought it was a dome. Why can't we see through it?'

'The light only goes in, never out.'

Marl stretched his arms along the width of the cab and let his head fall back.

'Where are you from?' said Demetri.

'Across the sea. From the sands. I used to live in Trida.'

'I've heard of that place. It was a technology corporation too, wasn't it? Didn't Leafen – '

'Take it over? Yes. Half the workforce were let go. We were given the choice of joining our own Hordes as refugees or joining the Leafen Hordes.'

'And you took the second option?'

Marl smiled.

'I had seen the way our own Hordes lived; the stench and the heat, their ideas about The Market, they are – how might one put it – *outdated.* I thought I would take my chances elsewhere. I thought perhaps there would be a chance I could get my family and I back into Leafen, if I got close enough.'

'Where are they now?'

'They perished. The journey across was too much for them.'

'I'm sorry. How long have you been here?'

'Seven years. When they announced The Hiring, I decided to apply.'

'What's it like?'

'I beg your pardon?'

'Living in the Hordes.'

'Probably not as bad as you imagine. But certainly worse than you could hope for.'

One of the truck's rear wheels hit a rock and sent them tumbling into the air. Demetri fell, steadied by Marl, and they came to a halt by a stubby bush. Sam turned the engine off and got out.

'I thought we'd get clear of the fires before we stopped,' he said. 'I've been following the same line that thing made as it popped through, but I haven't seen it yet. Do you have a signal?'

Demetri had forgotten all about the Stooge. He fumbled in his pocket and took it out. The screen was dead. He tried the dials and switches, then banged it a couple of times, but with no effect.

'It's fried,' he said. 'Maybe the pressure of the Fabrik was too much for it.'

Sam kicked the tyre of the truck and turned, scratching his stubble and looking out at the mountains ahead of them. Lines of detail were appearing on them — crags, cliffs, snow on the summits.

'I say we pick up the pace and keep going in the same direction. From what April said, being on the other side of the Fabrik didn't make any difference to the signal, but it's not going to want to go too far.'

'And neither do we, right?' said Demetri. 'I mean how long are we going to look for this thing? This place is a desert.'

'We've used a quarter of a tank of gas. Another quarter won't kill us,' said Sam.

'It could be anywhere,' said Demetri. 'This is insane.'

'If we don't find that thing then the Fabrik will collapse. The whole corporation will be exposed. The buildings inside aren't built to survive outside the Fabrik – they're finely tuned for their environment – nothing on the outside is supposed to get in – dust, debris, pollution, rain – '

'Human beings,' said Marl.

Sam stopped and looked at him.

'You said it, not me,' he said.

'It is true,' said Marl with a shrug. 'Without the Fabrik, there would be nothing to stop the Hordes from getting in.'

'And would they?' said Demetri.

'Of course. That's all they've ever wanted to do.'

'We have to find that thing,' said Sam.

'So why don't we go back and get a proper search party?' said Demetri.

'The Fabrik's already weak and I don't think we have much time before it starts to fail. *And* we're currently in Leafen's only working vehicle. By the time we get back, convince them of what we saw and wait for them to pull together a team it could be too late. Our best chance is to find it and disable it. Chrissie knows how to divert power back to the Fabrik once the network is released.'

'Still, just three of us searching for a basketball in the desert?' said Demetri.

'If it was programmed to sense danger, then it makes sense to assume that it will know when it's safe too,' said Marl. 'Hopefully it will settle somewhere nearby.'

'OK, let's go,' said Sam, getting back into the truck. 'You two, stay upright and keep a look out.'

'You want left or right?' said Marl, lighting up another cigarette.

But Demetri was looking behind, lost again in the black wall of home.

forty-four

better?

PRISCILLA SAT up, mouth open, breathing hard. She looked down at Daniel's sweaty, grinning face and gave him a razor smile.

'Better?' she said.

'Yes,' said Daniel, dizzy and panting on the couch. 'Much more relaxed, thank you, General.'

'Don't mention it,' she said, wiping her lip. 'It's part of my job to keep my president relaxed. Presidents *need* to be relaxed in times like these.'

Daniel rolled his eyes and swallowed.

'You're not wrong there, Priss,' he said. 'You're not wrong there.'

She patted him twice on the chest and pushed off his lap, her thighs glistening in the office light. Then she collected her uniform and walked through to the bathroom. Daniel pulled up his trousers and sat forwards.

'How are things on the ground?' he said.

A moment of silence broke the sound of zips and buttons from the bathroom. Then Priscilla cleared her throat.

'Not good,' she said. 'I have some concerns about the staff.'

'Concerns? That doesn't sound like you, Priss.'

'I'm Director of Human Resources. It's my duty to be concerned about the staff.'

'Aha. And what are these *concerns* of yours?'

Another pause as a buckle strap tightened.

'The health of some of those affected has deteriorated beyond what we had hoped.'

'What does that mean?'

'It means the breach has affected their brain function. Even if we counter the security breach, they will not make a full neurological recovery.'

Daniel stood up, walked to the bar and poured some fresh coffee from the pot.

'So when we fix this thing we're going to have a bunch of vegetables to deal with. Is that it?'

'Not in so many words. They will be a serious drain on resources. The weaker ones already require more care than we can adequately provide.'

'Weaker?'

'Those with medical conditions, below average appraisals. The old.'

The toilet flushed and she returned, dressed. She leant on the doorframe.

'The young.'

Daniel sipped his coffee, watching her. He found it hard to find the right words to describe his feelings for Priscilla. Right now, as he felt his skin still tingling with the shape and heat of the parts of her few had known, he wondered whether his feelings were, in fact, *for* her at all. Maybe they were simply about her. Maybe she was not a woman at which it was advisable to aim your feelings.

He knew her hunger for power, although he could not say that he felt the same, gorged as he was already on the stuff. He admired her strength and ruthlessness, but he wasn't sure what angle that admiration took – not down as their ranks would dictate, not even across like a colleague, and certainly not upwards. No, this was something else, this feeling. It was what you felt watching a tarantula behind the safety of glass, legs outstretched and tapping, all eyes trained on you. Fascination, arousal, a kind of exotic horror…but if that glass were ever to break…

'And what do you want to do about it?' he said.

'There isn't much we can do about those outside The Office.

But we can deal with those in Central.'

'How?'

'We need to let some people go.'

'To the Hordes?'

'No. We can't afford to open The Line right now. I was thinking of a more permanent solution.'

Her words filled the air like flies around meat. Daniel looked back at her, trying to match the coldness in her eyes – a pointless exercise, he knew. He took his coffee to the window.

'Like you say, you're the Director of Human Resources. You must do what you must do. But Priss?'

'Yes?'

'No kids, right?' he said, half over his shoulder. 'Not good for the old image.'

'I understand.'

Daniel drained his cup and marched to the desk.

'Now,' he said. 'Sumar's team are chasing ghosts. We need to pull some resources onto the breach. Find out if anything came through.'

'Already done.'

Daniel looked up, eyebrows raised.

'Right. Do I need to know the details?'

Priscilla shook her head.

There was a knock on the door and Faith stepped in. She paused momentarily at the sight of them. Daniel's shirt was still untucked. There were cushions on the floor.

'Steve Manager, sir,' she said. 'Shall I send him in?'

'Yes,' said Daniel. 'Please do.'

He turned to Priscilla.

'Stay for this, please, General. Then you need to give Sumar his update.'

'My pleasure.'

'He won't like it. Sumar, I mean.'

Priscilla smiled.

'I know.'

forty-five

helping

FATHER ROBERTS stood in the centre of the line that ran along the steps of the church. The rain had progressed from its earlier vaporous wisps and now fell in a thick, freezing curtain, turning the ground into an aimless river, the steps into a waterfall. They had been there for almost two hours, sodden and stoic, quietly ensuring that none of the crowd accidentally bumbled their way up to the church. Whenever a body broke free of the pack and splashed towards them, the line bulged and nudged them gently back into place.

It was starting to smell; the groundwater flowing with the urine and faeces that was been unwittingly released from the sodden crowd members. Occasionally there was a splash as one of them fell to the floor, at which point the boy in the line next to Roberts – a candle-lighter named Glynn – would jump in fright. Roberts had been trying to distract him with small talk, which he roared above the din of the rain.

'Where are you from, Glynn?'

'Strale,' replied the boy, through chattering teeth.

'Ah, a small-town boy like myself.'

'Are you from Strale too?'

'No, no, I'm not even from Leafen. My parents moved here after the Trade Wars. I was ten.'

'Where did you come from?'

'Ach, it doesn't matter. It doesn't exist any more. I grew up in Fairmile, way out towards the outlet pipes.'

'I know it. What made you become a priest?'

'Now that, my boy, is a good question.'

He looked down at his feet, submerged in swirling water.

'I never understood the reason for the wars,' he said, with a bashful look. 'And something told me I never would. What I did know was how the wars affected people. All this, Glynn – these towers and the decisions that go on behind their doors – I've never pretended to understand it. But I do understand people. I understand the pressures they find themselves under. I understand the wars they fight inside. So I suppose I thought that's where I could help.'

Glynn looked up at him.

'Are we helping now, Father?'

Before Roberts could answer, the crowd swelled towards them and the line withdrew. A body had emerged. It faced them, wavered for a second, then staggered a few feet and fell upon the steps. A woman in her sixties now lay on her side with her arms extended. Beneath the spray of grey hair that covered her face, her eyes flickered.

Roberts felt the boy's hand twitch in his. He tightened his grip.

'Stay back, son' he said. But Glynn had already pulled away and was by the woman's side.

'Glynn!' said Roberts, above the murmurs of consternation from the line.

'She's dying!' cried Glynn.

'Glynn, come back to the line.'

'She needs water, they all do.'

Roberts watched him trying to pool water into his hands and feed it through the woman's lips. He recognised the need that was squirming inside the boy; that need to help, to just tear the pain out of the world and burn it up in any way he could. He'd known it all his life.

'I know, son,' he said.

Roberts broke away from the line and ran down the steps.

'Take this,' he said, unhooking a key from a set in his pocket. 'Run to the back and use the kitchen doors. There are buckets and towels. Fetch them.'

He turned to the line.

'All of you,' he yelled. 'We need to help these people. Go with Glynn and – '

But as the line broke apart, the church doors swung open and Loome appeared, flanked by guards.

'What is the meaning of this?' he screamed. His eyes darted about the broken line, finding Roberts and Glynn by the woman. He stormed down to them.

'These people are dying,' said Roberts. 'They just need water. And as you can see, we have plenty. We can help them out here if they can't come inside. Please, Your Grace.'

But Loome was already past him, grabbing Glynn's arm and dragging him from the woman.

'Candle-lighter! Away from that body! Don't touch it!'

'But she's alive, Your Gr – '

Loome threw him upon the steps and raised his hand.

'No! Your Grace!'

Roberts leaped forwards but was pulled back by two guards. Loome's eyes burned orange in the lamplight as he brought his hand down hard upon the back of Glynn's head. After five more heavy blows, he stood up, breathless, and wiped the string of saliva from his chin.

'Get back inside the church, boy,' he said.

Glynn got to his feet and stumbled up the steps. At the top he stopped and looked back at Roberts. His face was set, his eyes were dry – though one was already swelling.

'Get on with you!' yelled Loome.

Glynn ran.

'I'm giving you one last chance, Roberts,' said Loome, swinging round. 'Any more insubordination and I'll have no option but to fire you. Guards!'

The guards threw Roberts down onto the steps and followed Loome back into the church.

Roberts stayed where he had fallen, next to the woman. Her eyes still flickered; her mouth still worked.

forty-six

what do you want?

STEVE STOOD in the centre of the president's immense office. Daniel stood at the window, looking out onto the brightening sky. He was unshaven, his jacket off, sleeves rolled up and tie loose.

'I can see the Hordes,' he said. 'Come and look.'

He turned, granting Steve an immeasurably small, cold grin.

'Sir, I must – '

'Come on, I won't bite.'

Steve walked to the window. Daniel held out a finger.

'See? Way out there. No, down a bit. Those shapes. I think that's them. Do you see?'

Steve peered into the haze. If he tried, he could just about make himself believe that there was a change in the light somewhere far in the distance, a kind of cloud, impossible to tell whether it was on the ground or in the air.

'Do you think this is affecting them?'

Daniel pulled back his head, as if this was the first time he had considered the question.

'I wonder?' he said with a quizzical smile.

'Maybe our drones could tell us,' said Steve.

'All dead, so Sumar says. We can't see anything, can't move and can't talk. Bit spooky isn't it?'

He flashed Steve a look of childish terror, hideous in the dim light.

'Not as spooky as being out there, though. Have you, er, ever been outside?'

'No,' said Steve.

'I have. Few times actually. Mostly for publicity, you know, keep them – what's the word Priscilla says? *Engaged*, that's right. They need something to make it all real, you see, something that's not just all those adverts on The Line, not just the product. Something *human.* Otherwise all they get are stories from the people we *fire.*'

His voice seemed to slow upon the word, as if he had managed to stretch time just to make his point.

'And *those* people, generally speaking, aren't happy campers.'

His breath was unbearably hot and close – a mixture of brandy, sex and aftershave.

'Not the best people to represent what life's like in the corporation. Would you say?'

'I – I don't – '

'Did you want to tell me something, Steve?' he said, somehow managing to lean even closer.

Steve buried his fear, searching for that other part of himself, the part better suited to the task at hand. At last, he swallowed and looked directly at the face of his president.

'Soor think we welched on the contract. I stopped the proceedings. Commander Po never saw me sign.'

He felt his throat closing as the words left his mouth, like a fist too late to catch a fly.

Daniel nodded.

'Yeah, Steve. Yeah, I know.'

He turned and walked down the steps to his desk, from which he picked up a sheet of paper. He took it to the drinks cabinet, holding it aloft as he poured two glasses of brandy.

'You signed after he left, then?' said Daniel.

'Yes. I'm sorry, sir. Sir, how – ?'

Daniel nodded, frowning. He put down the bottle and gently screwed the paper into a ball, which he threw into a wastepaper basket in the corner. It hit the rim and dropped in.

'*Yes*,' said Daniel, making a fist. He took the glasses to the window and handed one to Steve.

'Care to explain, Steven?' he sighed.

Steve braced himself. Admitting his mistake was one thing; trying to explain it was another. He took a tentative drink. The brandy tasted like vinegar.

'Why would a defence company want to buy a teleportation system?' he said.

Daniel smiled his most innocent smile and shook his head.

'One that doesn't work,' said Steve. 'You've seen the test results. All it does is create listless clones. They can't fix it. The entire system was based upon a theory which we've just proven doesn't work. It would take them years to get close to refining it. The Market will throw it out before the next quarter. Unless – '

Daniel leant forward.

'Unless – ?'

'Unless they want to use it as is, in its current state.'

'And – ?'

'You know that Soor have a dubious past.'

'Hmm – '

'What would they want with a cloning device? One that makes dumb clones?'

'Ummmm – I know this one – .' Daniel looked up at the ceiling. 'Wait, oh yes. That's it.'

He snapped his fingers.

'I don't care,' he said.

Just then a side door opened and Priscilla stepped in. Daniel caught her eye, then turned back to Steve.

'Steve, what do you want?' he said.

'I just wanted to come clean, sir. I thought you should know.'

'No, I mean what is it that you *want*? From life, I mean. Your existence. Your time on this rock.'

The answer came rote, like a spring.

'To be in this building, sir. To work in the upper balconies.'

Daniel winked and clicked his tongue.

'Good lad. Money, power, sex; same as everyone else. You want to be up high, away from – ' He jabbed his finger out of the window and bared his teeth. 'Away from all that *shit*.'

Steve looked out at the distant, dismal shapes. He could see it now, clearly — the ramshackle mountain of lopsided points that clamoured and clawed against the side of the Fabrik.

'Yes,' he said.

'Completely understandable,' said Daniel. 'Who wouldn't want that?'

He sighed.

'See, now, I was *born* up here, Steve. I already had all this at my feet. I never had to want it. But we all want something, right? And do you know what I wanted, Steve, when I was growing up?'

He turned to Steve.

'I wanted to be a *good man*. Just like Daddy.'

The sun was rising. Spears of light sprang from a nearby balcony. Daniel turned back to the glass.

'My father saw this corporation through a six-month conflict that might have ended with its destruction. A hostile takeover that would have killed millions. I was only a lad at the time, but I remember the terror. I didn't know what he did up here all day, the decisions he had to make, the compromises. All I knew was that when it all ended, we'd won. He'd stood up for us; he'd been brave when everyone else was afraid. And because of that, we were safe. Everything was as it was, and my dad was a hero. And every little boy wants to be like his old man, right?'

He looked at Steve.

'My father was fired when I was eight,' he said.

Daniel wrinkled his nose.

'Oh. Sorry.'

Daniel allowed a moment for the apology to be absorbed. Then he gave a short laugh and shook his head.

'Funny, right? But there it is, true story, my life's ambition: *be a good man*. Thing is, though, Steve, being a good man isn't always as easy as just doing the right thing. Know what I mean?'

He squared on Steve.

'And what about you, Steve? Do you think you're a good

man?'

'I don't – '

'Do you think what you did was *good*?'

Daniel landed a sharp prod in Steve's chest on the last word.

'All this? All that out there? *Good*, was it?'

A shove on the shoulder now. Steve stumbled back.

'Just how *good* are you, Steve?'

Another push. Steve stumbled back down the steps. Daniel bore down on him.

'G*ood* enough to stop all this?'

A two-handed push now that sent Steve back towards the window.

'Hey? Are you, Steve? *Are* you?'

Daniel raised his hand, but Steve caught it as he brought it down. He held it tightly, inches from his face. Daniel's lip curled.

'You're not a good man, Steve,' he said, spittle flying from his lips. 'There are no good men. Just *men*.'

He shook off Steve's hand and strode across to his desk, where he began whipping through some papers. Steve collected himself, straightening his tie, aware of Priscilla's impassive eyes watching him from the shadows.

'The key to enlightenment,' said Daniel, 'is acknowledging that you're not the man you thought you would be and adjusting your goals accordingly. It's like I said yesterday: these are strange times coming up, sunshine, strange times indeed. It's not the forties any more. We're not all glowing in the aftermath of the Trade Wars — all that money, peace and good will. The world's changing. The Arctic's about to go nuclear, start-ups are nipping at our toes, unrest in the East. Uncertainty everywhere, and you don't navigate uncertainty by being brave or idealistic. You do so by making decisions you might not want to make. By making the right kind of friends. By letting things happen that you might not want to happen.'

Steve frowned.

'You knew what Soor wanted Spoke for?'

Daniel wobbled his hand, not looking up.

'There or thereabouts,' he said. 'Yep. Ages ago.'

'And this. You knew it was Soor all along?'

Daniel stopped leafing through the papers and straightened up.

'I knew something was up the first time you walked through that board room door. Saw it on your face. Same face I saw on Granton all those years ago. The face of someone who'd just walked a line they never thought they'd walk. The smell of fear and exhilaration; unmistakeable.'

He sniffed.

'Like shit. Also, remember, I *do* have access to almost all of the network, including the, er, you know, *personal* archives. It wasn't that hard to find out what happened in your office.'

'But you could have stopped this. You could have contacted Soor.'

Daniel raised his eyebrows.

'Yes, I *could* have done, but then I would have missed my opportunity.'

'What opportunity?'

'An opportunity to come out *shining*, Steve. Conflict, you see: that's what we all like to see. Conflict and resolution. That's how you get to show off your mettle.'

His eyes darted at Priscilla.

'And test the mettle of those around you.'

'Sumar,' said Steve. 'Technology – they've been looking in the wrong place all this time. And you're letting them.'

'His choice, Steve. And if the Technology Director can't identify a security breach, what use is he? Truth is he's been on a downer for a while, has our Sumar. Unfortunately you can't just *fire* a director because you don't like him. You need a good excuse.'

'Like failing to prevent an attack.'

'Bingo.'

'But if this *is* an attack, how do we stop it? Sumar's putting all his efforts into fixing something that isn't broken.'

'*Sumar* is, yes.'

Daniel's eyes flicked once again to Priscilla.

'What's going on?' said Steve.

'Don't worry, Steve. Everything's in hand. *All bases covered*, you might say. No need for you to worry. Understood?'

Steve looked down at his feet.

'Good,' said Daniel. 'So, listen to me very carefully and I'll tell you how you can climb up here with the rest of us monkeys. Just like you know you want to.'

Daniel sat on the edge of his desk and held a hand to the empty chair before him. Steve took it.

'I don't care about what you did,' said Daniel. 'Or what you think, or what you suspect. I don't care if you've found a conscience or lost your fucking marbles. All I care about is sorting this out. Don't you, Steve?'

'Yes,' he said.

'Excellent. Now, the reason I couldn't see you earlier is that I've spent half the night on a call with Soor.'

'I thought our communications were down.'

'Yeah, so did I. But they opened up a line for us.'

'Soor?'

'Yep. They have complete control of our systems. I told you they didn't take any shit, didn't I?'

'What do they want?'

Daniel smiled.

'You, Steve. They want you.'

He turned to the door and bellowed.

'Faith, come in here, please.'

The door opened and Faith stepped in, taking a place next to Priscilla. Daniel looked between the three of them.

'Right, now we're all here, let's make sure we're on the same page.'

He clapped his hands together and began to pace.

'Last week, Soor — *the* largest defence corporation in the world — was supposed to complete a contract that would pass it ownership of *Spoke*, giving us lots of money and a new, very powerful, ally. Unfortunately that didn't happen, because Mr Manager here had a fit of the whatnots. So they gave us a good hacking and now they're holding us to ransom by – '

He waved his hand at the window.

'All that business. Now, our blundering idiot of a Technology Director has unsurprisingly been unsuccessful in his efforts to fix – all that.' He waved another hand. 'But we're about to set him on the right path. Not that I think it'll do much good; fairly sure Soor have us by the short and curlies.'

He looked at Priscilla.

'We do have something *else* that we're trying out, but really, it comes down to this: all they want is the contract. Delivered personally.'

He stopped pacing and looked at Steve.

'By you.'

'You want me to go to Soor?' said Steve.

'No. No, they wouldn't like that. They're coming here instead.'

'When?'

'They're already on their way. They'll be here tomorrow. We're going to renew our negotiations, go over everything.'

'The entire contract?'

'Yeah, the lot. So it'll be quite a long meeting. But worth it, because at the end of it we all sign, they release our systems and – '

He flashed a grin.

'*We* come out as heroes.'

The smile retreated.

'There's just one *very* important condition.'

'What?'

'You, sunshine. You have to make absolutely sure they know how sorry you are. And I'll tell you how that works a little later.'

He patted Steve on the shoulder.

'In the meantime, you'll need to reacquaint yourself with the paperwork. Faith, escort Mr Manager to one of the executive suites in the upper balconies, would you? A big one.'

Daniel turned to Steve and winked.

'Thought it would be best if you were close, you know? Should give you a little taste of things up this high, too. Away from all that *shit* down there.'

Faith led Steve from the room. At the door, he stopped.

'What about the other thing?' he asked.

'Hmm?' replied Daniel.

'The *something else* that you're trying out.'

'Oh, that. Yeah. Don't you worry about that.'

forty-seven

roadhouse

IT WAS mid-morning when the truck pulled up at the roadhouse, a sprawling wooden mess by the side of the thing they had been calling a road for the last hundred miles. The sun was high and hot, well above Leafen, which was now a black strip stuck like gaffer tape to the eastern horizon. There had been no sign of the Hackdrone, no lights flashing in the scrub, no shadows shooting across the plain. The last sign of life had been in the camps of the Banished.

Sam killed the engine and the truck glooped and swilled in the quiet, hot air. He got out and stood, hands on hips, looking up and down the road. Then, seeing nothing of interest, he blew a round of snot into the dirt and leant against the truck, kicking his heel.

Demetri followed Marl down from the truck and held up the Stooge.

'Anything on that thing yet?' said Sam. He had a wild look in his eye, biting his lip and grinding his teeth the way you do after too much road and not enough sleep.

'I told you, it's screwed,' said Demetri. 'Dead, kaput.'

'Dammit,' said Sam.

'We have not seen the Hackdrone since it escaped,' said Marl. 'Maybe it is time to turn back.'

'No,' said Sam. 'We're not half empty yet, we keep going for another fifty at least.'

'That thing could be anywhere,' said Demetri.

'Then we'd better keep looking,' said Sam.

'I think we may have gone too far,' said Marl. 'It was heading north when we left Leafen and there must be a limit to its range.

The chances are it's dropped somewhere behind us, to the right of the road.'

'OK, so let's circle back and do a few sweeps across country. Marl, you can be on lookout. You,' he turned to Demetri and pointed to the battered box in his hand, 'try and fix that thing.'

Sam turned back to the roadhouse. There was a faded metal sign hanging from a porch with broken windows and a loose door. Around the back was a yard surrounded by a ramshackle fence. A well-worn track led from an ancient, gnarled tree.

'What is this place?' said Demetri.

'I don't know,' said Sam. 'Some relic, I guess. 'I'm going to take a look, see if I can find some water. I'm spitting dust.'

'I shall come too,' said Marl.

Marl and Sam walked up onto the porch and peered through the cracked, stained windows. Sam pushed the door. It opened and they disappeared inside, leaving Demetri standing against the truck. He looked back at the dark mass on the horizon that was Leafen. Strange was not the word for how it felt to be looking at his home, or to be so far from it. He had never travelled outside the corporation, and nor had he ever intended to. There was no point. Everything he needed was safely within that place — his work, his family, his friends, food, entertainment. Everything he required to keep him happy and fulfilled was buzzing within that box — a box he had only just realised was in *fact* a box, and not a shining, protective, transparent globe sitting like a dew drop on the planet's surface.

Home, sweet home. At least it had been until yesterday. Now it contained a population of sleepwalkers and buildings with no power. He felt a pull towards it, to be back inside, safe within the walls, no matter what they looked like from the outside. And yet – the blue sky above him now seemed so much larger, the sun so much brighter and warmer – the endless plains, the mountains, the smell of that air. Something about the space itself seemed to be talking to him in a language only his heart understood.

He looked down at the broken Stooge and rattled it pointlessly. Maybe the battery had just come loose when it hit the deck. If he could just open it up –

'Hey, Sam? See if you can find some tools in there.'

There was silence. He heard a thump from inside the roadhouse and looked up.

'Sam?' he said. The building was still and quiet, the sign still creaking in the light breeze. He pocketed the Stooge and walked to the porch.

'Marl?'

He peered through the window. Old furniture and boxes lay strewn about the dark room. Shelves were wiped clean, dirt, cans and other lumps on the floor beneath them. At one end was a counter. A pile of papers had been stacked on top, impaled with a large skewer.

Demetri pushed the door and went inside, met by a strong smell of dust and old fabric, and the buzz of a swarm of black flies behind the counter. Beside the door was a yellowing wire tower. He pushed it, and it squeaked idly round once and stopped. In one of the racks was a piece of card with a faded picture of a mountain on it. There was some writing scrawled across it that Demetri didn't understand.

'Sam? Marl?' he said as he spun the tower again. Come on, guys, where are you?'

On the back of the tower were a few toy animals hanging from chains — rabbits, bears, foxes, all with goofy faces and buck-toothed grins.

There was a noise. A creak. Demetri stopped and looked at the back of the room.

A screen door hung off its hinges letting in light from the yard. Through its tattered gauze he could see the shape of a vehicle. Beside the broken door was a staircase leading up out of view. A shadow moved somewhere.

Demetri stood still for a while, not breathing, trying to make his heart stop, listening for more sounds, unsure of what he would do if he heard anything, unsure of whether to call for Sam and Marl again, unsure whether any of this would make a difference and unsure of what he was so afraid of. Eventually he allowed himself the luxury of a breath and decided to walk towards the swing door. Step by step, he made his way towards the bright, skewed square of light. An ancient curtain wafted in the soft breeze, filling him with some memory or other he had no right to. He pushed the door open. There was another porch, upon which was a rocking chair, an assortment of coloured gnomes in all shapes and sizes partaking in all manner of activities, and a shotgun leaning against the railing.

The vehicle in the yard was something he had never seen before. It was low and yellow with a wide, long hood. Inside were brown, frayed seats. Sam and Marl lay unconscious in the back.

Standing against the passenger door was a slight, skinny man with about two weeks of stubble, circular glasses and a brown hat, which he tipped in Demetri's direction.

'What's going on? What is this place?' said Demetri.

The man smiled and glanced at the staircase.

Demetri spun his head and saw a larger man standing above him. He held a rifle butt above his head.

'Welcome to Texas,' he said.

Demetri just had time to look back at the car. The skinny man shook his head.

'He means England,' he said, before the world snapped shut like a book.

forty-eight

top of the building

PRISCILLA SAT at Daniel's desk, drinking coffee and watching the sunrise. The shower hissed from the bathroom next door. She put down her cup and lifted the radio.

'Sumar,' she said.

After a few moments, Sumar's voice came on the line, tired and flustered.

'*What do you want?*' he said. She heard other voices in the background, arguments and groans. '*We're very busy.*'

Priscilla stretched her neck. She had slept and was wearing a clean uniform, enjoying the cool air of Daniel's office and fresh, hot coffee. She could have done this much earlier, but it was too much fun to rush.

'You're looking for a hack,' she said. 'Not a *glitch*.'

The channel remained open, silent. Sumar stammered.

'*I – I already told you, we –* '

'I have a team searching for a possible intruder at the perimeter.'

'*Intruder? What do you mean?*'

'A device of some kind, probably. Something that has compromised the systems.'

'*What? You went behind my back? This – this is a security issue – you can't just –* '

'I already told you, Sumar. I am the military superior of this corporation. Security is *my* concern. Now if I were you I would get to work looking for that hack.'

'*H – how do you know all this –* '

'Because I am at the top of the building,' she said. 'And you, Sumar, are at the bottom.'

She smiled, closed the channel, and opened another.

'Miss Groone,' she said.

Ruba's voice sprang back like a spaniel with a stick.

'Yes, General?'

'Are you busy?'

'Yes, General. As you commanded, I'm working with Saul Saleman and Turnett Bittek, keeping contact with – '

'You can stop that now. Leave it to the other two.'

'General?'

'I have another job for you. Do you have a uniform?'

forty-nine

trouble

'APRIL, SLOW down.'

Back in the medical tent, Christine gripped April's shoulders.

'I saw her,' spluttered April. 'General Mandrek. She killed Dr Perez. I saw her.'

'Where?'

'Utility staircase 59. Second floor.'

Christine pulled out her radio, one hand still steadying April as she struggled for breath.

'Miles, U59 level 2. Go and check it out.'

'Chrissie?'

'Just do it, Miles.'

'Roger.'

The radio crackled out.

'Why, April? Why would she do that?'

'Dr Perez, Emelia, I mean – '

She turned her head, catching Lori still sitting on the bed, Enola taking her pulse.

'Oh, shit, her daughter.'

Her eyes squeezed tears. She held a hand to her mouth.

Oh, shit, what do we do, what do we do?'

'April.'

Christine pulled April's head back to her.

'I need you to calm down and tell me what happened.'

'OK, OK – '

April took a few breaths, eyes closed.

'Mandrek was asking Emelia about the health of the dozers. She wanted to know about the ones who were deteriorating.'

'Why?'

'I don't know. She said she thought they might be prolonging the inevitable.'

Christine released April's shoulders and looked around the heaving med tent.

'That doesn't sound good. What did Perez say?'

'She said she thought everyone would make a full recovery, so long as we fixed the problem quickly. That's why she wanted to tell Director Sumar about the breach.'

'Let me guess: Mandrek didn't want to, right?'

'That's right. Why? Why wouldn't she want to tell him?'

Christine shook her head.

'Mandrek and Sumar have always been at each other's throats. She wants him gone. Maybe she's setting him up to fail.'

'She'd do that? She'd risk lives to get ahead?'

'I knew there was something about that bitch. A package that looks that good is always trouble on the inside.'

Her radio crackled again.

'Chrissie?'

'Miles, what do you have?'

'Nothing here. All straight.'

'She called for one of her guards to clear it up,' said April. 'He must have got there too quickly for us.'

'Thanks, Miles,' said Christine. 'April, I have to ask you: are you sure about this?'

April nodded.

'Yes. I was there. I saw it.'

Just then there was a noise at the entrance to the tent. They turned to see a squad of guards led by Ruba. She wore a starched uniform with a red sash on her shoulder.

'Groone?' said Christine.

'Attention,' she bellowed. 'General Mandrek has ordered that all affected staff are to be streamed according to these criteria.'

She held up a stack of papers.

'All medical personnel are to follow these guidelines and mark staff accordingly.'

A guard behind her threw a box on the floor. Ruba pulled out a handful of different coloured badges.

'This task is to take priority over everything else. You have one hour to comply. General Mandrek thanks you for your help.'

She threw the papers on a desk and turned to leave, but Christine stopped her.

'Ruba Groone?'

Ruba turned around.

'Who are you?' she replied.

Christine straightened her back.

'Christine Ops,' she said. 'You and I are supposed to be working on Mandrek's little project, remember? Groone, what the fuck is going on? What are you doing?'

'Executing General Mandrek's orders,' she said.

'And why didn't I hear about these *orders?*'

Ruba's lip twitched as she looked Christine up and down.

'Maybe they didn't extend to your pay grade,' she said. She glanced at April, and the crowd of doctors and nurses around her.

'This is a military situation,' she said. 'Whatever department you come from, you all work for General Mandrek now. So I suggest you do your job.'

She grabbed the sheet from the stack and slammed it into Christine's chest.

'One hour,' she said, and left.

'What was that?' said April. 'What's on the sheet?'

Christine read from it.

'Age, pulse, blood pressure, *salary band, appraisal scores*? What the – '

April grabbed the sheet.

'She's streaming them,' she said. 'She's marking the ones she wants gone. Christine, we have to help them. We have to get them *out*!'

'Shhh!'

Christine covered April's mouth and looked back through the entrance. The guards had moved on. Ruba's voice was now barking into the next tent.

'If we're going to do this, we need to do it quietly.'

'So what do we do?'

Christine looked around at the dazed medical staff, rummaging through the badges and scratching their heads at the sheets.

'Do as Mandrek asks and wait for me. I'll be back in an hour.'

'Where are you going?'

'She might have a nicer ass than me,' said Christine. 'But I can raise a better army.'

fifty

colours

April looked down her sheet; every score was low. She sighed and took the last orange badge from the box and pinned it on Alex's collar.

'Orange,' said a voice behind her. She turned to see Enola. 'Orange isn't good.'

Enola unpinned the badge and replaced it with a blue one.

'Blue is better.'

'But his vitals are low,' said April. 'His pulse, blood pressure, everything. The sheet marks him as orange.'

'Just like Lori.'

Enola walked to Lori's bed. A blue badge was pinned to her sleeve.

'But orange is bad. It would put Lori in danger. She needs protecting now that Emelia is no longer here.'

She began to correct Lori's chart, then glanced up, noticing April's frown.

'I know what happened,' she said.

'How?' said April.

'I don't know. I just do.'

April looked over her shoulder, then followed Enola to the other bed.

'She killed her,' she whispered.

'I know.'

April watched her scribbling on the chart.

'Your sister. She's dead. Don't you want to know why?'

Enola glanced up.

'I know why. And she's not my sister.'

'Then who are you?'

Enola stopped and placed the chart down on the bed. She lifted Lori's chin. The girl gave a little wheeze as her eyes searched for focus.

'My name is Enola. I'm from Spoke.'

'Spoke? The teleportation project?'

'You've heard of it?'

'I read a lot. So you're a clone?'

Enola bristled.

'I am a person.'

'But I thought Spoke failed. The cloning process was flawed, the results were – '

'*Inexact versions of the originals, exhibiting listless behaviour, shyness and short attention spans. After roughly twenty days, the subjects become largely uncommunicative and appear to retreat within their own minds, withdrawing from social situations and becoming distracted by simple, inanimate objects, quite often for long periods of time.*'

She let Lori's chin drop back.

'I'm sorry,' said April, looking down. 'I didn't mean to – '

'It's all right. That was the official report.'

April's eyes crept back to Enola's face.

'You don't seem listless or uncommunicative. What happened?'

'It's hard to explain. My memories are split into two – Emelia's and mine.'

'From before and after the experiment?'

'Yes. Emelia's are very real, but the ones from after I – '

She stammered, looking down at her hands.

' – After I came into being; those are different. They're further away, foggier, like a child's. I think they made me lose my way.'

For a moment she became lost in a fingernail, her focus sinking into it like a pebble in soft mud. But then she snatched her attention back with a gasp. It was a raw action, an impulse so imperfect that April guessed it had only recently been discovered.

Enola swallowed and continued.

'Emelia and I were close when we began the tests, as you would imagine. But as time went on, we diverged. We became different.'

'What changed?'

'Nothing; not within us, at least. But to everyone else, I was always just the clone, do you see?'

'They treated you differently?'

Enola picked up Lori's limp hands, one in each of hers as if they might be about to dance.

'Not that you'd notice. They were just ticks, really – shorter glances, clipped words, smiles not quite reaching the eyes, laughter a little more forced. Things that didn't matter on their own. But over the weeks they all built up. Like grains forming a sand dune.'

Her grip on Lori's hands tightened. She turned to April. Her eyes were overrun with things April could not comprehend.

'Can you imagine what it's like to be treated as nothing but a version of yourself; to be everything you are, everything you remember, everything you feel, but to be treated as if those things were no longer yours? I watched my life being hijacked. I lost my daughter to a memory.'

She looked back at Lori, her sadness somehow hardened.

'We only behave the way people allow us to behave. It doesn't matter how strong willed you think you are. Every word we hear resonates in a place known only to us. Every look ignites flames only we can see. Every touch – or lack of one – is amplified by secrets we take to our graves. Eventually, we simply become the things that happen to us. We become the things we allow others to allow us to be. I became a shadow.'

She turned to April.

'Be careful of the colours people paint you.'

'You did withdraw, then,' said April. 'Like the test results said.'

'Yes. It's true, I did. Until last month.'

'What happened last month?'

A smile flickered on Enola's mouth.

'Consciousness.'

'I don't understand,' said April. 'You weren't conscious until then?'

'If you had asked me, I would have told you I was. But I would have been wrong. I would only have been fulfilling the loop.'

She tapped her head.

'We're a loop, you see?'

April said nothing. Enola tilted her head.

'You don't remember. Of course you don't. Nobody does, I expect; we are normally only children when it happens. But it does happen. There was a moment, April, when consciousness found you; a morning in your young life when you woke to a day just like any other. But you would have been quieter than usual. You would have been stunned into silence, because your mind had just been plunged into the world. You found yourself to be no longer just a machine of reflex and storage and improvement, no longer just an equation trying to balance itself beneath the weight of an ever-growing tide of variables, no longer just a fleshy circuit. Now you were a thing of reflection; another mirror in which the universe could gaze at itself. This happens to everyone, April. It has already happened to Lori, and she won't remember it.'

She blinked and looked around the tent. Her lip trembled as she spoke.

'But I do. I know what it is. This thing. Life. Existence.'

She took a long breath and looked away, busying herself with another chart – another impulse recently learned.

'I will admit, consciousness was a distraction. All those colours, all those sounds, the sheer depth of the world.'

She paused.

'But I'm not distracted any more.'

'What changed?'

'Purpose,' said Enola, dropping the chart and looking at Lori. 'She needs my help.'

'You're going to look after her?'

'Of course, why wouldn't I?'

'You're not her mother.'

Enola put down her pen.

'We are what we do, not what we're called. Lori is my daughter and I have no intention of giving up on her.'

'But Dr Perez, she said you were incapable. She said – '

Enola lowered her brow.

'I'm not a clone,' she said, suddenly sounding nothing like the doctor April had just seen murdered. 'I'm an improvement.'

There was the sound of footsteps outside the tent. They turned to see Ruba marching her squadron inside.

'Where's Christine?' whispered April.

Ruba stood to attention.

'Stand for General Mandrek,' she announced.

There were some shuffles and squeaks as Priscilla stepped in.

'Who is the ranking medical officer here?' she said.

Nobody moved. Then Enola stepped out of the shadows, putting herself between the beds and Priscilla.

Priscilla's mouth groped like a pike's.

'My name is Dr Enola Perez. I am Emelia Perez's clone and I therefore inherit her rank. I am the senior medical officer in this tent.'

'Clone,' said Priscilla, relaxing a little. 'Really. And is the task complete? Have you marked the patients as I ordered?'

'Yes, we have. But these patients are not going anywhere.'

'I beg your pardon?'

'These patients are in my care. You will not touch them.'

'Captain Groone,' she called back, keeping her eyes on Enola. 'Gather those with orange, yellow and black badges and assemble them outside the tent.'

The tent filled with the sound of boots.

'No!' screamed April, running to stop them. 'Leave them

alone, they're sick!'

Ruba pushed her back.

'Stay out of this,' she said. 'Who are you?'

'April Knight. I'm Sam Ops' daughter.'

Ruba frowned, looking her over.

'Where are your Colours?'

'I don't have any. I'm a contractor.'

'Then you have no rank and no right to speak to me. Mason, remove this woman.'

A thick-set man with a heavy beard marched over and dragged April from the tent.

'Get off me!' she screamed, feet scrabbling on the mosaic floor. 'Christine!'

As the guards pulled the limp bodies from their beds, Priscilla examined Enola's face.

'A clone,' she said. 'So you're what Soor want.'

'Yes,' said Enola. 'And I know very well what they want with me. Would you like me to tell you?'

'It's really none of my concern.'

'No, perhaps not. But what really is of your concern – '

Enola moved closer and whispered in Priscilla's ear:

' – *Is that I know what you did.*'

Fear flashed in Priscilla's face, but it soon subsided, like a match failing to strike.

'Captain Groone,' she called back. 'Are we finished yet?'

'That's all of them, General.'

'Thank you,' replied Priscilla. She looked over Enola's shoulder at Lori.

'And what about this one?'

'She's marked as blue,' said Enola.

'She looks unresponsive.'

'She's just a child.'

'She's dribbling. Groone!'

Priscilla lunged for Lori, but found her wrist suddenly trapped in Enola's hand. The fingers dug in, penetrating her flesh almost as deeply as the glare penetrated her eyeballs, and this time the fear on Priscilla's face remained; the match had caught. She grabbed Enola's wrist and tried to wrench it free, but it wouldn't budge.

'Don't touch her,' said Enola. 'Don't you dare.'

With a swift push, she released Priscilla, sending her reeling halfway across the tent to gasps and murmurs.

'General?' said Ruba, appearing by her side.

Priscilla rubbed her wrist, staring back at Enola.

'Nothing,' she said. 'Move on to the next tent.'

Outside, a crowd had gathered. April – still restrained by the bearded Mason – called to Ruba as she marched passed.

'You,' she said.

Ruba glanced left.

'Have you even asked yourself why she's doing this?'

'It's not my job to ask questions.'

'Quick march, Captain Groone,' said Priscilla, keeping her head above the crowd. 'There are forty-three more tents to clear.'

'She's going to kill them!' shouted April.

Ruba's step faltered.

'Captain Groone, keep up!'

'Did you hear me? She's going to kill them!'

Ruba stumbled to a halt. The guards behind her stopped as well.

'Captain Groone!' barked Priscilla.

Ruba turned to face April, frowning. April struggled in Mason's grip.

'That's right,' she mouthed.

'Captain *Groone*, do we have a problem?'

Ruba looked between April and Priscilla.

'I – '

But before she could answer, the sound of a hundred boots came thundering across the concourse. They turned to see a squadron of men and women in boiler suits, with black grease on their faces and guns in their hands. Christine was at the front.

'General,' she said, as she stopped next to Priscilla. 'I respectfully ask you to release these patients.'

'What is this?' Priscilla spat.

'These people are under our care,' said Christine. 'My team and I are here to ensure that they come to no harm.'

Priscilla eyed the sash on Christine's shoulder.

'Stand down, *Sergeant*.'

Christine sighed and looked Priscilla up and down. She was the same height, same age. Different backgrounds, different shapes. Sometimes that worked, sometimes it didn't. Maybe in a different situation, on a different day, she could have made it work. In a bar, perhaps, where low light could have given her the space and confidence to work her magic. Christine had no idea which way Priscilla swung – men, women or somewhere in between – but that didn't matter.

Background, shape, rank, sexual preference – it was all academic. In the darkness of a bar, the way to win anyone's interest was to find that little chink in their armour; the little hole that would let you in and see the world through their eyes. After that, it really just came down to how much you'd had to drink and how squeamish you were; variables Christine was used to dealing with. She would have had fun finding the general's chinks and holes.

But it wasn't to be. Not today, anyway.

'I *would*, sweetheart,' she said, leaning close. 'Only I have this funny feeling about you.'

'Really. And what feeling is that?'

Christine dropped her eyes to Priscilla's chest, where she let them linger for a second before pulling them back up.

'That you're not as pretty on the inside as you are on the out.'

Priscilla sneered.

'Groone, Mason, escort Sergeant Ops away and detain her and her men.'

There was a pause.

'Groone! Mason! Now!'

Ruba shuffled her feet but stayed put, but the sound of Priscilla's voice jolted three of the guards into action. As they reached Christine, two of her boiler-suited squadron stepped up.

'I wouldn't do that if I were you,' said Christine. 'You see this is my team. We've worked side by side in every dark, festering, baking hole in this corporation. We'd die for each other, and I'm pretty sure we outnumber you by about three to one.'

'This is mutiny,' sneered Priscilla. 'And you'll be charged as such.'

Christine stuck out her lip, mulling this over.

'Well, I'll admit this is a little out of character. But then, maybe we're all acting a little out of character today. You should see some of the things I've seen on the CCTV. Weird.'

She noticed the twitch in Priscilla's face.

'Yeah, they're still working. And I've got full access everywhere. Canteens, store rooms, changing rooms.'

Her smile dropped.

'Utility stairwells.'

Priscilla ground her jaw.

'This isn't over, Sergeant,' she said at last.

'Not till the fat lady sings,' said Christine, patting her stomach.

Priscilla stepped away.

'Groone, leave these *things* here. Assemble your men and follow me.'

She gave Christine one last look, and another for Enola, standing in the doorway to the tent. Then she turned and left.

As the guards disappeared back to The Leaf, April joined Christine on the concourse, rubbing her wrists.

'Did you really see the footage from the stairwell?' said April.

'Nope,' said Christine. 'CCTVs are out. And I don't want to be here when she finds out. We don't have much time to move these guys.'

Behind them, the throng of dozers stood or lay where they had been left.

'Where are we going to take them?' said April. 'Central's the only place with power.'

'Not the only place,' said Christine.

fifty-one

how's the view?

PRISCILLA STOOD at the window of the board room and looked out at the darkening day. She kept her hands behind her back, rubbing the welts on her wrist from Enola's grip. The radio in her belt crackled. She picked it up.

'Yes.'

'Good afternoon, Priscilla.'

It was Sumar. He sounded different. He sounded – *happy*.

'Director Sumar.' She hesitated. 'Do you have an update?'

'We're still working things through down here.'

'Really? Then why did you call me?'

She detected a smile in his voice.

'I thought you should know that Private Grant was picked up at the perimeter. Apparently your little *team* broke through the Fabrik last night.'

Priscilla spun around.

'What?'

'Yes. They're Out of Office, General. No longer contactable. Your project failed. *You* failed.'

Priscilla stood, fuming and wordless.

'Oh, and your exploratory mission broke upwards of a dozen serious security protocols, so we should probably – oh no, wait, as you said – security is *your* concern, isn't it, General?'

He began to laugh.

'Tell me, General. How is the view from the top of the building this afternoon? Is it everything you hoped it would be?'

Priscilla turned the switch, cutting out the sound of Sumar's laughter. Daniel, who had been standing in the doorway behind, cleared his throat.

'It failed,' he said.

Priscilla swung round.

'Not necessarily,' she replied.

'Not looking good, though, is it?'

Priscilla straightened her neck.

'Let me assemble a larger party to join the search.'

Daniel gave her a dry smile.

'Come on, Priss. You and I both know that's not possible. What about the other matter? Your concerns about the staff.'

She looked at the floor.

'I was just about to return to that.'

'Don't bother.'

'Sir?'

'I said don't bother. You've had your fun, you've had your shot at Sumar and it missed. It's time to fix this the way Soor want.'

'But, Daniel – '

'I mean it, General,' he said, taking a step closer. 'Stand down and listen.'

fifty-two

executive suite

EXECUTIVE SUITE 311 was a large and luxurious place filled with large and luxurious things. The couch upon which Steve Manager sat, the coffee table across which his papers were strewn, the swimming pool which sent ripples of light dancing across his face, the bed upon which Steve had spent the afternoon – lying awake at first, staring at the ceiling, then drifting into a delicious and decadent sleep, the shower, which he had used twice since he had arrived — Faith having shown him around each room, pausing at the door, a little look of something or other as she swivelled on her heels saying, with that airy whistle in her voice, *if there's anything you need* — the fire and the glass and the decanter and the deep taste of the spirit it decanted – everything was either thick, soft or gleaming with opulence.

He drank, feeling calm and rested. It was a better than he had felt for a long time. This place felt like home. It was where he belonged. He leafed through yet another file of words and charts detailing the transfer of Project Spoke to Soor. It was a pointless exercise; he knew all of it by heart already. In the previous year he had memorised every spreadsheet, every projection, every condition, every paragraph, clause and sub-clause of every contract and subcontract in the deal's sizeable stack. He had wanted to be prepared — more than prepared, in fact. He had wanted to *own* this thing, to become it and everything it led to.

He remembered the nights he had stayed late in his office, sitting like he was now, poring over the words and numbers. They had seemed like keys, little strings and codes that, when unlocked, would open the door to his success and to all of the large and luxurious places and things that came with it.

Now, though, they seemed – they seemed –

One piece of paper caught his eye. It was a test report from late in the project, when it was clear that it had failed.

– subjects appear listless and withdrawn and respond only to clear, simple orders, which they execute without question. Although they are physiologically identical to the subject from whom they were cloned, they appear to have a far higher pain threshold and less interest in self-preservation. This could be for a number of reasons borne of –

Steve looked into the fire.

A broken pen is still a stick –

There was a light knock on the door.

'Come in,' said Steve.

The door — thick oak, iron trim, heavy handle, *very* large and luxurious — opened. Daniel Leafen poked his head inside.

'Hello, mate,' he said.

Steve jumped up from his seat.

'Sir,' he said. He looked down at his bare feet, his untucked shirt, his loose, tie-less collar. 'I'm sorry, I was just – '

Daniel waved off his apology and walked in, closing the door with a *thhhhhwhumphhhh.*

'Sit down,' he said. He was carrying a bottle of something. 'Relax.'

He looked around, smiling, and walked over to the fireplace.

'All OK?' he said. He ran a hand along the mantelpiece. 'Not too shabby, eh?'

'It's very nice, thank you, sir,' said Steve.

Daniel glanced at him.

'*Nice*,' he repeated. He stared at the paper on the coffee table, looking between each sheet as if deciding upon a chess move. The watery light played on his face like slithering eels.

'Is there something I can help you with, sir?' said Steve.

Daniel's eyes found the decanter. He pointed at it.

'Taking the edge off?' he said with a smirk.

'Just one or two,' said Steve.

Daniel picked up the open decanter and smelled it. He made a face, then poured its contents on the fire. A gigantic flame rose up and belched into the room. Steve jumped back, steadying himself against the breakfast bar.

Daniel barely moved from his spot, his face glowing red in the heat. He turned his back on the fire as it settled, then set down the decanter and opened the bottle he was carrying.

'If you're going to take the edge off, you may as well do it properly,' he said, pouring the bottle into the decanter.

'Private collection,' he said. He filled two glasses, handed one to Steve and sat down heavily on the couch.

'Good health, good wealth,' he said.

Steve raised his glass.

'Sir.'

They both drank — Daniel staring into the settling fire, Steve trying to control his surprise at the magnificence of the taste.

'How are Sumar's team doing with the hack?' said Steve.

'As we expected,' said Daniel. 'Not so well.'

'And the other thing?'

Daniel shook his head.

'What was it?'

'Priscilla sent a team out to the perimeter to search for an intrusion, but we've lost contact with them.'

He looked at Steve, resting his glass on his knee.

'Soor is the largest defence company on the planet,' he said. 'You do understand how important it is for us to be on good terms with them?'

Steve did. He really did. His understanding was as complete as the taste of the brandy in his mouth was divine, as absolute as the scent of the shower's soap was heady, as unyielding as the floor on which he placed his bare feet was warm and soft. He understood.

And yet – and yet – and yet – there it was again — the twitch, the fidgeting of something beneath the surface, trying to break through.

'Perhaps the friends we make are just as dangerous as our enemies,' he said. He felt the words leaving his mouth. He could almost see them as they landed like small grenades between him and his president.

Daniel's face was still and quiet. At last, half of it smiled.

'You're sounding more and more like a mutual friend. An old one. A *dead* one.'

Daniel put down his glass and stood up.

'I grew up knowing Granton, you know. He was friends with my old man. They used to take me fishing on the lake sometimes, out in the boat, just the three of us.'

He shook his head at the memory.

'I could never understand why he threw the fish back. He was Red. Why would he want to show that weakness?'

There was a pause as Daniel swilled his drink, watching Steve.

'Well? What do you think? As a Red, I mean.'

Steve swallowed. He knew Daniel wanted him to say something; he just wasn't sure what. And in this absence of direction, he chose the truth.

'I was never supposed to be Red.'

'Pardon me?'

'There was a mistake. During my Colours. I should have appealed, but I didn't.'

Steve counted the seconds of the stare. Finally, Daniel's mouth twitched in amusement. He was about to speak when there was a knock on the door.

'Come in,' he said, standing.

The door opened and Faith entered. There were people behind her exuding a range of subtle, expensive perfumes.

'I need you on board, Steve,' said Daniel. 'I need you to understand what's going on here. And what you need to do tomorrow.'

He looked over his shoulder as three girls in cocktail dresses and three men in single-breasted suits walked into the room. Steve watched as they stood in a line against the wall, smiling at him. The girls' hips and chests seemed to be in constant motion, squirming beneath the tight fabric of their outfits. They were slim and pretty. The men were too. They stood, hips cocked, looking back beneath dark brows.

The girls wore Double-Pink brooches, the men wore bright pink ties.

'Something for the nerves,' said Daniel. 'I didn't know what your preference was, so, I thought, get both. Can't hurt, can it?'

One of the girls pushed her backside away from the wall and walked over to Steve. The others followed, laying their hands one by one on his chest, his arms, his back.

Steve looked at Faith, still standing at the door and keeping her eyes down.

Daniel walked to the door.

'Meeting's not until noon tomorrow,' he said. 'So, enjoy yourself.'

He winked once more and shut the door, leaving Steve at the mercy of six sets of large, luxurious mouths, their lips, their well-trained fingertips, and all the rest.

fifty-three

shelter

THIS RAIN, thought Roberts.

It was now impenetrable, a wall of water that owned everything. Roberts stood in a foot of the stuff, head down, following the dull movement of the line. From the corner of his eye he could still make out the figure of the woman, now lying still with her head beneath the rippling surface, her Fronds no longer glowing.

This rain.

Above the moans and sobs from the line, he heard a noise: footsteps and voices approaching. He looked up and saw flashlights dancing through the crowd. Christine stopped at the foot of the steps with April by her side. Her troops came to a halt behind.

'Who's in charge here?' she yelled.

Roberts looked around, then stepped forwards.

'I am,' he mumbled.

'What's your name?'

'Roberts. Father Malcolm Roberts.'

'Roberts, my name's Christine Ops. We need to use your church to protect these people.'

She motioned behind at the long line of men, women and children that had marched from The Leaf.

'They're sick and in need of shelter.'

Roberts slowly blinked away the water streaming from his scalp.

This damned rain.

'They should be in The Leaf. The medical tents – '

'They're not safe there,' said April. 'General Mandrek has

marked them as disposable.'

'We believe she is initiating a cull,' said Christine. She squinted at the line. 'What are you doing here?'

'We're protecting the church. High Priest Loome's orders. What cull? What do you mean, "disposable"?'

'She's going to kill them,' said April. 'Unless we can get them to safety.'

'What?' said Roberts. He looked at the ground, shaking his head. 'No, no, that can't be right; Mandrek wouldn't do that.'

'She would, Roberts,' shouted Christine. 'We know she would. These people need your help.'

'But, she wouldn't kill her own staff. She's not capable – '

April walked up the steps and faced him.

'I've already seen what she's capable of,' she said. 'Believe me, these people are in danger. We need to protect them.'

Roberts looked at the dead woman by his feet, then at the drenched mass before him. He shook off the hands to his left and right and wiped the streams of water from his head and face – *this damned fucking rain* – then he straightened his back and took a breath.

'OK,' he said, turning and walking back up the steps. 'Follow me.'

He stopped at the doors and hit them twice. The blows were weak, barely making a difference to the shaking they already made in the wind.

'Loome,' he croaked.

Nothing. He hit them again.

'Loome,' he said again, louder this time.

Again, nothing. He rested his head on his wood and looked down at the chalk. He knew these steps well. He had walked them every day since his sixteenth birthday, that winter's day when Loome had led him up them, his starched cloak still too big for him and dragging behind.

'This way, my child,' Loome had said. 'This way to a life of wonder. I will teach you everything The Market has to offer; all its grace, its beauty, its wisdom. All I ask in return is your mind and your heart. Your thoughts are crude, your feelings unformed. Let me show you how to rebuild them.'

A fresh supply of rainwater had found his scalp, pouring over his face, into his collar and down his spine. He took a long, shivering breath, sucking water in with the air –

This damned, fucking, infernal –

'Loome!' he bellowed, hammering on the door. 'Loome, open up!'

With one last blow he took a step back, standing between the lamps. There was silence, then the doors burst open and Loome marched out.

'Roberts!'

'I'm taking these people inside.'

'You're *what*?'

'You heard me. The church is empty and people are dying. Now stand aside.'

Loome stood for a moment, blinking in disbelief. His voice was a trembling hoot.

'You – you – what did you say to me?'

'You heard me,' said Roberts. 'Please, let me pass.'

Loome's twitching face suddenly tightened into a furious scowl. He stormed towards Roberts, one finger extended like a blade, and prodded him in the chest.

'You listen to me, you *pathetic* excuse for a man.'

Another sharp prod.

'You're finished, do you hear me? Finished with the church, finished with Leafen, *finished*.'

With every word he pushed Roberts back, jabbing his finger into the fleshy folds of his chest.

'You'll be in the Hordes before you know it, back where you belong! I should have known when I took you in that you would never amount to anything. A chubby little boy from that *stinking* patch of dirt by the waste pipes. I was a fool. A fool to think you could ever become anything other than the fat, stupid, ugly, under-achieving, alcoholic, old – '

Roberts grabbed his hand.

'I'm forty-seven. That's not old.'

He brought back his head and drove it into Loome's face with a wet crack. Loome fell back on the steps, out cold, arms stretched, a new stream from his nose dyeing the water flowing around him a deep cherry red. The guards eyed Roberts nervously.

'Get him somewhere away from me,' he said. 'And keep the doors open.'

He turned to the line at the bottom of the steps, all of whom were looking up at him in either wonder or shock. It was hard to tell through the rain.

'Get as many as possible inside. We're going to keep these people alive for as long as we can.'

fifty-four

grimble and creech

RHOMBUS, THOUGHT Demetri. He was nine again, waking from sleep in the back of his parents' car and blinking up at a skewed square of bright, blue light. A line of wire rose and fell, rose and fell, rose and fell, cut by flashing telegraph poles, then starting again. Faraway clouds blustered about their business and every now and then a bird flitted by. He enjoyed the feeling of not knowing what position his body was in, not knowing what shape his arms and legs were making on the thin plastic of the seat. He kept that way, resisting the urge to move and feeling the warm sun on his face. Everything was as it should be. It was sunny and they were on holiday, with no work and no school. He lay there, half-listening to his parents' quarrel in the front. It was something about directions, road signs, places and names he didn't know. Their voices faded in and out above the roar of the tyres on the road, like strange lullabies, making him sleepy.

– *what about the interstate?* –

– *is no interstate, idiot* –

– *right there in front of your eyes* –

– *you believe what you want* –

– *the one who believes what he wants* –

– *fantasist* –

– *you're the fantasist* –

– *just get us home* –

Demetri let his eyelids fall and the thick lines of their lashes blurred into a mess against the blue. He drifted off, wondering vaguely why his mother's voice sounded like a man, and why his father sounded like nobody he had ever heard of. The skewed square of light faded away.

Rhombus, thought Demetri.

When he awoke again, it was darker and he was facing the other way. There were black clouds outside and drops of water trickling down the window. His parents were still talking.

– can't be from the Hordes –

– From Shyland's place?

– Nah, too skinny –

His mother coughed — a deep, manly, hacking cough that ended with a spit.

Do you mind, you beast? Open a bloody window first, at least?

His mother growled.

Demetri blinked. These were not his parents. He tried to move his hand and found it tied to the other by a rope around his wrists. His ankles were the same. A jolt of panic tore him from his sleep, along with the memory of the rifle butt hurtling towards his face. He looked across and saw Sam staring up at him, urgently, mouth closed, eyes wide. He was lying with his head out of sight. His hands were bound too. Marl was between them, also bound and unconscious.

From the wild, unyielding look in his eyes, Demetri thought for a moment that Sam might be dead, but then he saw him breathing furious, short breaths. He was trying to will him into thinking something, trying to communicate with him without talking. His eyes moved to the front seat. Demetri looked. Behind the wheel was the man in the hat and round sunglasses who had been leaning on the car, which he guessed they were now travelling in. In the passenger seat was the other one, the man who had been waiting on the stairs. He couldn't see his face, only that he had a weathered neck and thick, grey hair spilling from a waxy hat.

He looked at Sam again. Sam nodded at him, then at the driver. Then he shook his bound hands and nodded at Demetri's. It took Demetri a moment to get the message. When he understood, he shook his head, brandishing his own wrists and nodding at Sam's.

You do it!

Sam made a face and nudged Marl, who was in his way. He nodded at Demetri again, urging him on.

Demetri shook his head again.

Sam rolled his eyes. Then he set them on the driver, seemed to steady himself, grimaced and pounced over the passenger seat, yelling. His bound wrists fell to the grey-haired man's throat and he pulled tight. The man's hands clawed at Sam's and the car swerved as its driver jumped, looking back and forward between the road and the struggle that was now under way.

'What the hell are you doing?' he shouted. 'I thought you were watching them, you fool!'

He tried to help his partner's struggle by pawing at Sam's hand, but he lost control of the car every time he tried. The car filled with the sounds of four men screaming. Marl gradually came to, looking around groggily at the pandemonium, trying to assess time, space and predicament all at once before the wheels clicked into place and he too began to scream. The car swerved violently around the road. Demetri crammed himself into the corner. Eventually, seeing what Sam was trying to do, Marl sat forward and tried to hook his own hands around the driver's neck, but they caught somewhere around his nose so that he ended up squashing half of his face against the seat. He then began clawing at Marl's hand, half-watching the road from one eye, the other having been obscured. At last he took a deep breath and slammed down his foot. The car's brakes jammed and the wheels squealed. Sam, Marl and Demetri slammed against the seats, Marl and Sam losing their hold on the two men and falling in heaps. The car skidded for a tyre-melting distance, then did a half turn and stopped. The two men in the front opened the doors and fell out, choking and spitting, throwing down their hats and stamping in the smoke and dirt. Marl and Sam lay dazed on the floor of the car, with Demetri cowering in a ball.

The door opened and Demetri fell out onto hard, wet ground. He looked up and saw the skinny man looking down on him, breathing heavily. His glasses were bent from Marl's efforts, half hanging from his nose.

'Up,' he said.

'Out!' said the other one. Demetri heard Sam and Marl being dragged from the car. He got to his feet warily. The skinny man watched him.

'Back against the car, please.'

Demetri staggered back until he found the hot metal of the car behind him. The man's accent was familiar. *Human Resources?*, he thought. But it seemed clearer somehow, older perhaps. Somewhere from the southern conglomerates, perhaps? They always played the baddies in films. Or one of the independent start-ups in the north he had seen that documentary about.

'Fuckin' idiots!' he heard the other one shout. That accent he recognised, at least some of it. It reminded him of some Arctic oil dignitaries he'd once been in a meeting with, but it had something else — a gruffness and a twang like bent metal.

'Coulda got us all killed!' he coughed again, then spat. 'Line up against the car!'

Sam and Marl joined Demetri. The three of them faced the skinny man as his partner joined him, still rubbing his throat. He had a beard that had staked a claim to most of his face, right the way up to his eyes, which were ice blue and pinched by crows' feet. Their clothes were strange — ancient, brown coats, thick, scuffed boots and tattered jeans. No neckties, shirts open. The skinny man smiled with his hands perched on the bones of his hips. He took off his broken glasses and examined them, holding them up to the light. One of his eyes pointed inwards a little. Very gently, with shaking hands, he bent the frame and smoothed out the bridge. Then he blew on the lenses and rubbed them with the sleeve of his shirt. Satisfied, he popped them back on his nose.

'So then,' he said, clearing his throat. 'Interesting idea, that, trying to crash.'

'Who are you?' said Sam. 'What do you want?'

'Who are we? Who are *you* is more like it.' He nodded to his comrade. 'That's what we've been spending the last half hour trying to work out anyway.'

'Y'all ain't from the Hordes,' said the other one. The words sounded like an animal giving birth. 'That's for damn sure.'

'Yes, I'd say we agree on that,' said Skinny. 'And I said you couldn't be one of Red Dog's because they only travel in packs of six or more.'

Sam bristled at a name he hadn't heard for a long time. The larger of the two men frowned at him. Then he looked him up and down.

'Can't be from north 'cause y'all ain't got no guns.'

'Yes, quite right, Thomas,' said Skinny, waving his finger and tip-toeing. 'Nobody from the north country would be foolish to come this far south without weaponry, not with the current campaign and all that, so no, you can't be from the north.'

He stepped forward and rubbed his chin, pacing up and down between Marl, Demetri and Sam. He pulled at Demetri's shirt.

'You could be deserters from a start-up,' he said, 'But then your clothes are too – *clean*. And there's no possible way you could be from the Plain of the Banished. He patted Demetri's stomach and looked at him down his long, bent nose. 'Far too well fed. No offence.'

He spun on his heels and faced his partner, holding his hands up.

'I give up, Thomas! Do you? Any clue?'

The other raised an eyebrow. The sky was dark and thick clouds were rolling down from the hills.

'None whatsoever,' he said.

'So,' said Skinny, swivelling again in the gravel and clapping his hands. 'Tell us, please. What exactly *are* three unarmed – ' he cast his hand up and down them, searching for the words, ' – *strangers* — and I *do* mean that in its most literal sense — doing driving a two-hundred-year-old Ford F-150 pickup truck towards the mountains?'

Sam pushed up from the car and stood in front of Skinny's face.

'We're from Leafen,' he said.

Skinny blinked, then pulled in his head like a chicken. He stepped back and stood next to his partner, who was frowning in disbelief.

'Leafen?' said Skinny. 'You're employees? Staff? Of – of Leafen? Really?' He puffed through his nose.

'Yes,' said Sam. 'We're trying to find something out here.'

Their two captors stood in silence, looking them up and down.

'Find what, exactly?' said Skinny.

'A hacking device infiltrated the corporation yesterday and took over our network,' said Sam. 'If we don't find it, it could destroy the whole place. We were tracking it and ended up at the roadhouse. We didn't know anyone was inside.'

Skinny walked forwards again, his hand in his chin, regarding them as if he had found a particularly interesting set of specimens. His friend joined him, arms crossed, brow creased in bewilderment, looking between them as if they'd just arrived on the planet.

'And you're really from Leafen?' said Skinny. 'I mean, from *inside* Leafen, not from the Hordes?'

'Yes,' said Sam. He gritted his teeth. 'Now please let us go and take us back to our truck.'

Skinny looked up at the sky, then back at the mountains. He flourished a hand at the clouds.

'Too late for that, I'm afraid. No chance of getting back there today, not with this weather.'

'What is it?' said Demetri. The worst weather he had seen was a particularly bad purge a few years before.

'That?' said Skinny. 'That's a storm, young man. We usually get one every week, right about the time when your corporation's *farts* hit the thermals up there in the mountains and come sliding back down again. Gets pretty wet, I can tell you. It's another thirty miles home. We'd better go while we can, wouldn't you say, Thomas?'

'Reckon so,' said Thomas, stomping round to the other side of the car.

'My friend and colleague, Mr Thomas Creech, by the way. And my name's Grimble. James Grimble, of Grimble & Creech Associates.'

James Grimble stepped in front of Sam.

'And what's your name, Leafener?'

'Sam Ops,' said Sam.

'Pleased to meet you, Sam Ops,' said James. Thomas hollered as he opened the car door.

'Welcome to Texas!'

James Grimble smiled patiently.

'Please excuse my partner. He really *does* mean England.'

PART FIVE

out of office

fifty-five

the history of the world

THE STORM dragged rain, dust and thunder shrieking down from the mountains and across the plain like a gang of deranged hooligans. Somewhere within this mayhem stood a long, rambling shack that you would not have given much odds against the onslaught. But it could withstand worse and had done so for more than a century. If you had flown in with those hot clouds and peered down through their torrents, you might just have made out a trail of wood smoke from a teetering chimney and a dim, mustard-coloured light in a window.

Behind this window was a room. On first entering this room you might have been surprised at its size, given the apparent dimensions of the building from the outside. There was no magic involved here, just the cunning advantage of a hidden lower floor, installation of several rickety mezzanine levels, used primarily for sleeping, and careful use of the eaves above to expand and explode an otherwise normal-sized space.

The room had to be big in order to accommodate the enormous number of books inside. Not many inches of wall were given over to anything but shelf space, and those that weren't were used to hang pictures, animal skulls and other oddities. There were faded shreds of coloured packaging, flattened soup cans, shattered black discs with holes in the middle, and curled, burned and torn scraps of paper scrawled with unintelligible writing and framed in ancient wood. Spend enough time entering and re-entering this room and you would start noticing things you had never noticed before — fragments of an orange guitar laid out like dinosaur bones in a dark corner; a small, unopened (for good reason) can of caviar; a coil of frayed, green rigging; a bent trombone curled into a light fitting.

But the books were what you saw first. They were crammed in by the hundreds and thousands. Long ago their population had outgrown the shelves and migrated over every surface, across the arms of every chair, over the battered oak dining table and the benches beneath it, next to the latrine, on the latrine, and beneath the plates, coffee cups and empty rum bottles — of which there were, also, a great many. The room was infested with words.

The horizontal space not yet claimed by literature was filled with various projects in their happiest states, which is to say, incomplete and doomed to failure. Wires and springs were scattered across a bench beside a gigantic tome about clocks. A television set had been taken apart and its pieces laid out, attached by coarse string to brown labels. Ancient electronic devices lay open like frogs on a vivisection table. Actual frogs sat stuffed with sawdust and caked in resin, wearing expressions of horror, as if their fate had been to experience the woeful skills of their taxidermist while still alive.

A single corner was given over to a squat, black stove crammed with logs and roaring gently. At the other end of the room was a kitchen, where Tom Creech stood in a blue and white grease-stained apron with a long cigarillo hanging from the corner of his mouth. He closed one eye against the smoke as he mashed the meat of something long dead in a wooden bowl, and then spooned rough lumps of it onto the table. He picked up a piece and sniffed it, checking its weight in his upturned hand. Then he lifted his shirt and apron, pushed the meat up into his armpit, and squeezed down with a grunt. The resulting patty he placed to one side, lightly tapping some strands of flesh back in with one finger.

The windows were thin and rattled in the rain. Sam stood at one, peering out into the night and smoking. Marl was asleep in a chair with one leg over its arm. On his chest was an open book about something called *The First World War.*

A soldering iron was hooked and smoking on a stand in the middle of a large table. Behind the table, James Grimble sat hunched over Demetri's Stooge. He wore a magnifying monocle over one eye, which he used to inspect the components inside the battered casing. Occasionally he tapped something with a screwdriver or followed a wire from one point to another, then scribbled a note in a pad next to him.

Demetri sat opposite, leaning on his knees and thinking about home. From the time it had taken them to get to the house, and from the size and shape of the tall shadow on the horizon that was Leafen, he guessed that they were about a hundred miles from their exit point. He had never been as far as the perimeter before, let alone through it, beyond the Hordes and out into this land, whatever it was. He thought about Alex, and whether he was safe.

He watched the strange man with the strange voice working on his now entirely broken Stooge, trying to ignore the fact that everything else, including the stuffed animals, seemed to be either abandoned or beyond hope, and half-listening to the increasingly heated discussion Grimble was having with Creech. The argument seemed to be about botany, specifically the flora that could and could not possibly exist in both England and Texas. Creech would shout one out, and Grimble would reply with an explanation.

'Dog weed.'

'Dog weed? A very big problem in Norfolk during the latter part of the twenty-first century. *National Geographic* — May 2073, I believe.'

'Black mangrove.'

'Rife in Manchester after the Chinese invasion. Of course *they* never had it until the American attacks.'

'We were provoked. Sweetgum.'

'Sweetgum, yes, big forests of the stuff sprung up in Cornwall after the first Sweeps.'

'Snakes.'

Grimble stopped and turned.

'I'll assume that was a joke.'

Creech threw down the last patty with a growl and leant on the table, his big arms outstretched.

'Everyone for a thousand miles speaks with a Texan accent, Jim. There's a road sign two miles along this road that says *Richmond — 57 miles*.'

'Yes,' said Grimble. 'Richmond, Surrey. And the way you choose to speak has nothing to do with the ground beneath my feet.'

Grimble stamped his feet lightly on the boards. His friend gave a shudder of frustration.

'That sign has a picture of Texas State on it,' said Creech. 'It says *Texas*. There's a fuckin' *star* on it. A *single fuckin' lone star*.'

Grimble tutted and returned to his soldering.

'You're sitting in a room filled with a thousand books you've never read; one hundred million words about our planet's history that have never passed into your cranium, and yet you choose to find your truth in a rusty road sign and a couple of shapes. It beggars belief, Thomas, it really does. Oh, and may I remind you, for the umpteenth time, that we drive a Ford Cortina.'

Creech hung his head and heaved a big, smoking sigh. He spoke down at the table.

'Ford was an American company.'

'An international company, actually. And the Cortina was never released in the States.'

Creech rubbed his eyes.

'Left-hand drive and with a Texas plate. There isn't a man in this land that doesn't know this is Texas, Grimble. You're the only one who believes otherwise.'

Grimble smiled as he carefully tapped the last of his blob of solder. He raised his soldering iron in acknowledgement.

'*Believes*,' he said. 'Yes, that's the correct word for it, old friend. *Believes.*'

He hung the iron on its hook and looked up at Demetri.

'And what makes us believe something, do you think, young man?'

'I honestly don't know what you're talking about,' said Demetri.

'What you're *told*,' said Grimble. He slammed his hands on the table and stood up. Demetri flinched as the scattered screws and springs jumped up in the aftershock.

'People believe what others believe and they do that because it makes them feel happy and no longer afraid. We're not really interested in what's real, you see, not really. We think we're curious bunnies, we do, but we're not. For most of us, most of the time, we don't want answers, we just want to stop having to ask questions.'

He gave a childish grin and raised a finger.

'*Most* of us,' he said, eyes flashing in the candlelight. '*Most* of the time.'

He walked over to a shelf of small drawers, which he began pulling out and checking one by one.

Creech gave Demetri a hopeless look.

'This is what I live with,' he said. 'It never stops.'

He shook his head and began dropping patties onto a hot skillet. Sam stubbed out his fifth cigarette and stopped pacing.

'This is a waste of time,' he said. 'That thing could be anywhere by now and I don't want to be out here any longer than we have to. Please, take us back to our truck.'

'Storm's too hard,' said Creech. 'Nobody's drivin' anywhere.'

'Then we'll walk,' said Sam.

'It's fifty miles. Besides, y'all can't be outside. Rain alone's enough to drown a man, if y'all don't choke on it first.'

'Patience, please, Mr Ops, patience,' said Grimble. 'You've been lucky enough to stumble upon an expert chef and a learned engineer.'

He cast his hand proudly around the room. Demetri caught

the skewed and terrified eyes of a stuffed otter, balancing on the plank it had been nailed to. Creech hacked something up in the kitchen and spat it into a tin can.

'You are our guests this evening. Mr Creech shall feed and water you, while I fix your gadget. With any luck, you'll be on your way in the morning.'

Sam scowled and pulled another cigarette from his pocket.

'What are you, then?' he said, flicking his lighter. It sparked, but no flame caught. 'Some kind of start-up?'

Grimble stopped raking through drawers and there was a clang as Creech dropped his tongs in surprise. They both looked at Sam with their mouths open, then simultaneously broke into laughter, wheezing and hooting until they couldn't speak. Creech bent double, picking up the tongs from the floor, still laughing as he flipped the patties.

'Oh,' said Grimble, wiping a tear from his eyes. 'Oh dear me, no, Mr Ops, we are most definitely not a start-up, I can tell you that for sure.'

'What's so funny?' said Sam, holding the lighter back from the cigarette.

'Nothing, Mr Ops, I apologise. We are Grimble and Creech. Mining prospectors, traders in and transporters of all antiquities, victuals, alcohol, home goods, furniture and vehicles, no contracts, payment, refunds, discounts or receipts requested or given, purveyors, sourcers and safe keepers of relics from centuries past, mechanical engineers, botanists, small-holders, chemists, cooks and amateur historians. At your service.'

Grimble clipped the heels of his boots and bowed his head. Then he turned back to his drawers.

'Historian,' muttered Sam, still trying to light his cigarette. 'That's why you have all these books, I guess.'

'Yes,' said Grimble, beaming. 'Quite a collection, isn't it? You'd be surprised at what you can find. It's all there you know, everything, all written down. You just have to piece it together.'

'What's there to piece together?' said Sam, the cigarette

waggling in his dry lips. He flicked the lighter again and again, without luck. 'Fuck this thing.'

Grimble walked over to him, offering his own lighter. Sam eyed him suspiciously as he put his cigarette to the flame.

'The jigsaw,' said Grimble. 'The puzzle of the past. What happened, and why.'

He snapped the lighter shut and returned to the wall of drawers.

'Do you know anything about the world before the first Sweeps?' he said.

'Not much,' said Demetri. 'Apart from things being shittier.'

'Shittier,' said Grimble, his brow furrowing. 'That's one way of looking at it, I suppose. Nothing else, though?' He edged towards a table on which stood a brown globe that he touched lightly. 'Art? Literature? Religion? The Renaissance? Spanish Civil War? French Revolution? Fascism? Terrorism? Apathetism? The Silent Rebellion?'

He spun the globe idly, stopping it with his finger on a point somewhere in the southern hemisphere. He ran it back and forth in his hands as he talked.

'Some people used to think that the Catholic church was single-handedly responsible for holding back five hundred years of human technology. If it hadn't been for them, we would have had electricity in the sixteenth century, television before Australia was colonised. People would have been chatting about the Napoleonic Wars on the Internet as they happened.'

'What are the Napoleonic Wars?' said Demetri.

'What's the Internet?' said Sam.

'And the same thing's happening now, has been for a couple of centuries. Longer, in fact. Technology has been throttled to appease an imagined almighty omnipotence.'

He spun the globe once more and walked back to his desk with his finger held high.

'You see, the history of the world is one of crowds moving about. They grow, collide, dwindle, merge, disappear altogether and, occasionally, they stop while somebody stands up and shouts for them to move in a different direction. Now, these individuals — visionaries, conquerors, queens, priests, shamans, writers, dictators, physicists, chemists, captains of boats, captains of armies, captains of peace – '

He paused and turned, no longer smiling.

' – Captains of industry. CEOs. Corporations.'

He turned back to the drawers, fishing about in each of them before slamming them back into the wall.

'They all seem significant, you see, as if they alone have steered the course of our progress. But the reality is far less interesting. Most of our movement across and around this planet, most of the decisions we've made as a species, and therefore most of what we believe, has been down to one very simple thing: the desire for a quiet life, many billion times over.'

He pulled out the last drawer in the rack.

'Aha!' he said, producing a small black cube attached to a series of coloured wires, which he took back to the desk.

'Now, my colleague here believes what everyone else believes in this country — your good selves excluded, of course — that we inhabit a large southern state of what, a long time ago, used to be called the United States of America. They believe that because they see a few road signs and ancient licence plates that seem to fit with what their mummies and daddies tell them about where they live, they can stop asking questions. Somebody like *me* comes along, somebody who likes to think for himself, somebody who likes a good book now and again, and they don't like it. I pose a threat to their blissful peace. But I bring the *truth*.'

He flipped down his eyeglass and went to work on the Stooge. The thin smell of solder joined the charred meat that was flooding in from the kitchen.

Marl, who was now awake, had been listening from the chair. He put down his book and sat forward.

'And what is the truth, Mr Grimble?' he said.

Grimble looked down his nose as he twisted a wire into a point. His hands shook a little.

'I don't know exactly yet,' he said. 'But I do know that things got pretty messed up a few hundred years ago, as they usually do before a tectonic change in civilisation. People lost their footing on their own lives. They forgot who they were and they forgot their own history, their own *myth*. Countries and governments got lost too. Global unrest left communities shattered. The balance had shifted too far, the balance of wealth and resources. Everything became polarised. People dispersed and fled from one place to the next, just to find a safe place to live. The whole planet got mixed up like a bag of sand. The military took control of most places, but the ones with the real power, the real safe places – '

He paused and looked up at Demetri again.

' – were the corporations. Those were the strongholds, those were the things that took control. They had already become the lifeblood of most people's lives. It didn't take much for them to become the bones of the planet too. Countries were destroyed. Corporations took their place.'

Sam shook his head, laughed and walked back to the window.

'Something amusing, Mr Ops?' said Grimble, still occupied with the insides of the Stooge. 'Something amusing about your recent history?'

'History,' said Sam. 'Countries, governments, communities. They're all in the past; ancient things. It's a waste of time to think about them.'

Grimble peered over his glasses at Demetri.

'Is that what you think, too?' he said.

'I honestly have no idea who you are or what you're talking about. I just want to go home.'

'Home, yes,' said Grimble, smirking. 'For a *quiet life*. That big black box near the sea. A place of safety, a place of security. A place of *hiding*. It must be strange out here. Frightening, I expect.'

He stopped what he was doing, sat back and crossed his arms.

'Do you feel sorry for us, I wonder?' His voice became harsh. 'Do you think we're unfortunate? Do you think we want to join your *Hordes?*'

'Grimble – ' warned Creech from the kitchen.

Grimble raised a hand and returned to the Stooge.

'All right, all right, I apologise. No need for me to be so confrontational.'

He glanced up.

'But aren't you curious? About why the world is as it is?'

'No,' said Sam. 'The world has always been the way it wants to be.'

'What about your accent?'

'What *about* my accent?'

Grimble nodded to Demetri.

'You're both from Leafen. Why do you talk differently?'

Sam frowned.

'Because we're from different departments, that's why.'

'Hah!'

'What's so funny?'

'And, you, you, you, Mr Ops. Which department are, er, you from?' said Grimble.

'The clue's in the name,' said Sam. 'Operations.'

'Sound like a Yankee to me,' muttered Creech from the stove.

'What's a Yankee?' said Demetri.

Creech grunted and flipped a patty.

'I don't know. Only know what one sounds like.'

Sam stubbed out his cigarette and walked over to Grimble. He stood in front of him, hands in his pockets.

'My daughter,' he said. 'She sounds like you.'

Grimble stood up suddenly and clapped his hands, spinning to face Creech.

'See! I told you! English accents!'

He strutted to the kitchen, shaking his finger.

'*English* accents,' he repeated excitedly. 'I knew it, it's possible, see, Tom? It's *possible*!'

Creech gritted his teeth.

'We're in *Texas*,' he said.

'Pah,' said Grimble, throwing his hand in the air. 'You're useless, no imagination.'

'Why are you so interested in how things used to be?' said Demetri.

'Because it's important, that's why. The land beneath us.' Grimble stomped his boots on the floorboards, creating a small explosion of dust. 'The boots that have trodden it, the soles, the *souls* that have walked it. What they did, what they believed, the stories they told, the names they gave things and the ways they pronounced them. Our cultural mythologies — they're really our only guide. If you can't answer the question *where are you*, then you're nowhere.'

He edged closer to Demetri.

'Where do you think you are?'

'I – I don't,' he said.

Grimble flicked his finger at Sam.

'And you, Sam Operations, where do you think you are?'

It's Ops. And I know exactly where we are. We're Out of Office, and no offence to either of you – but all of this? It's not home. We need to find that thing, take it back inside the Fabrik and destroy it. Or all this goes to shit.'

Grimble stared at Sam, sniffed, then returned to his seat.

'I have a feeling it already has, Mr Ops, but very well, very well – ' he said, screwing the back of the Stooge in place.

'You think what you think because you were told to think it,' said Grimble. 'There's no shame in it, no shame in it at all. It's a survival mechanism. We might not even have got as far as we have without it.'

He tightened the last screw and turned the Stooge over in his hands.

'Over three hundred years,' he sighed. 'And technology has

barely moved on at all. Why is that, do you think?'

'Things don't get made if they don't stack up,' said Demetri, surprising himself at the speed of his answer.

Grimble chuckled.

'*Stack up*,' he repeated as he took off his eyeglass.

'Did you hear that, Thomas?' he shouted over his shoulder. 'Things didn't *stack up*.'

Creech released a single loud, gruff laugh.

Grimble sat back in his chair and inspected the Stooge, trying a few switches.

'Quite correct, actually,' he said. 'Something doesn't stack up. The history of the last three hundred years doesn't follow the right pattern. Something else happened. I don't know what, but I'm going to find out.'

'Have you fixed it?' said Demetri.

'Do you know, I think I have,' said Grimble, with a bluster of pride. 'But it needs some charge before we'll find out for sure.' He got up and walked to another corner of the room, where he pulled out a trunk of cables. While he had his back turned, Sam walked over to the stove and taped his head at Creech.

'Your friend,' he muttered. 'He ain't right.'

Creech pulled a long drag on his cigarillo and looked over at Grimble, rummaging in the trunk. He nodded slowly and took the skillet to the table.

'Oh, he's right,' he said. 'He's right about everything apart from Texas. Supper's up.'

fifty-six

supper

THE FIVE men sat around the oak table in silence as the storm battered the windows. Grimble had poured them mugs of frothy, weak beer that tasted of mud and lime. Demetri drank a little of it, then picked at a piece of mouldy bread from a pile in the middle of the table. He avoided the armpit-shaped meat patties and Creech's accusing glares as he did so.

'Meat,' said Grimble, pushing the skillet toward him.

'I'm not really hungry,' said Demetri. 'Thank you.'

Marl, who had slept through the patty-making process, eyed Demetri's two burgers.

'Are you sure you do not mind?' he said.

'No,' said Demetri. He watched Marl grab the two steaming mounds from the skillet, one in each hand, and bite hungrily into the first. Grease squirted from the side of his mouth. 'I really don't.'

Sam finished his portion, drank his beer and fidgeted, tapping his knee and looking back at the Stooge, which Grimble had plugged into a charging unit.

'How long before that thing's charged?' he said at last.

'Patience, Mr Ops,' said Grimble. His demeanour since working at his desk seemed flatter, his complexion more pallid. 'I'd suggest another hour to be sure.'

'Where do you get your electricity?' said Marl.

'Generator,' said Creech, wiping a strip of bread around his plate and checking Grimble from the corner of his eye. 'Out back.'

'And solar,' said Grimble, looking up brightly.

'That piece of shit don't work,' said Creech. 'You'll never get enough charge outta them plates. Waste of time if y'ask me.'

'Tut tut, Thomas, man. You lack faith. Give me a week and I'll have this whole house glowing like a Christmas tree.'

Demetri was about to ask what a Christmas tree was when Grimble suddenly dropped his cup, grasping his head in both hands. Everybody stopped. A brown puddle of beer grew on the tabletop.

'Y'all right?' said Creech.

Grimble rubbed his temples furiously.

'Yes,' he said sharply. 'Yes, I'm fine. Sorry. Just – a headache.'

He took a deep breath and looked up, a smile returning to his face.

'I get them sometimes,' he said. 'Nothing serious. Probably not enough vitamin D or something.'

He picked up his mug. The table watched him nervously as he refilled it, hands shaking.

A deep boom of thunder sounded outside. Demetri jumped as the windows shook.

The strangeness had suddenly taken on a whole new life. All at once he felt nervous and alone, more out of place than he had ever felt in his life. The distance between him and his home opened up like a chasm. He wanted more than ever to be back inside, walking within the invisible, protective walls, drinking coffee from polystyrene cups and drifting away in whatever mindless entertainment he could pull up from his Fronds.

His Fronds — it had been almost two days since they had worked. The void in his head that they had left was beginning to fill with thoughts that he had no idea how to grapple with. Now questions of history, unsettling thoughts of a time well before he had lived — thoughts which he always tried his best to avoid — were taking root, like weeds in fresh, trembling dirt.

And all the time he knew that deep within that raw space lurked something that was not part of him at all; a virus, streaming poison through these infant thoughts and back home. Back to his brother.

He sensed Grimble watching him.

'You've really never been outside of Leafen?' he said. 'What's the term you use – ah, yes, *Out of Office*.'

'I've never had to.'

'Never seen your Hordes?'

'No.'

'This must be very odd, then, all of this. Strange territory indeed.'

Demetri frowned.

'I'm not stupid,' he said. 'I knew there were other people in the world apart from us. I'd just never met them before.'

'Oh yes?' said Grimble. He relaxed in his chair. 'And what are you taught about these people, I wonder? About us?'

Demetri paused, still unconvinced about whether he could trust their hosts.

'You're different,' he said at last.

'Different?' grunted Creech. He pushed his empty plate away and leant on the table.

'In what way are we *different?*'

'Just – just you've chosen not to partake in society,' he said, immediately sensing the dangerous pit he was stumbling towards but unable to step back from it. 'You don't work. You don't belong to a corporation, you don't produce products or consume them as part of a Horde. You just exist, but you're not like us.'

Grimble threw back his head and laughed. He placed a hand on Creech's shoulder, as if to steady himself.

'Not like you,' said Creech, reaching for the beer. 'Y'got that damn straight, buddy.'

'You're right, actually,' said Grimble. 'In a way. We do just exist. And no, we don't partake in your *society*, as you call it, and no, we most definitely do *not* belong to a corporation. But we do work, we work very hard indeed, just to exist.'

'What is it you mine?' said Sam, still tapping his leg.

'Pardon?' said Grimble, picking something from his molar.

'You said you were miners. What do you mine?'

'The only thing that's possible to mine around here any more.'

'And what's that?'

'All the things you don't want.'

'What – ' began Demetri.

Creech slammed his mug down.

'All the shit,' he said. 'All the shit y'all don't want comes streaming out the backside of that big fuckin' box over there.' He pointed out into the dark. 'Where d'y'all think it fuckin' goes?'

'So you're scavengers,' said Demetri. He looked at Marl. 'Like the ones we saw.'

Creech made a low noise in his throat.

Marl smiled.

'I believe "garbage miners" is the polite term,' he said.

'You take a look at the mines and tell me if you think what we do is scavenging,' said Grimble, a serious expression on his face. 'We're not raking through trash cans. It's a serious operation.'

'Are you allowed to do that?' said Demetri.

'*Allowed?*' bellowed Creech, eyes bulging. 'I'm *allowed* to do whatever the fuck I want. I don't need your say so. If y'all are gonna take a big, steaming, metal dump on my country then I can mine it.'

'OK, OK, there, big fella,' said Grimble. 'Take it easy now. What my friend is trying to say is that, actually, we're very productive indeed. In fact, we were on our way up the coast to deliver a supply of blankets when we found you at one of our outposts.'

'So you *are* a company, then?' said Sam. 'You sell things. That means you're a start-up.'

Grimble gave an amused frown.

'We never said anything about selling.'

'I don't understand,' said Demetri. 'I thought you were

miners? What do you do with the stuff you mine, just give it away?'

Grimble and Creech looked at each other. Creech drained his mug.

'Yes,' said Grimble. 'We give it away. We don't deal in money, you see? No coins, no notes, no cheques, no banks. The only currency we deal in is made up of favours, threats and promises.'

'How do you make a profit?' said Demetri.

'Profit leads to wealth leads to greed leads to profit. Profit is an act of volition that leads only back to itself. Which makes it spectacularly unhelpful, wouldn't you say?'

Grimble suddenly coughed and clenched up. He grabbed his head again, reaching for his mug. Creech caught it before he knocked it over. He cradled his shoulders.

'Here y'go buddy. Take a drink, take a long drink, there y'go, there y'go. Ease up now. There.'

Grimble sat up and smiled. The muscles in his jaw were tight and twitching. His eyes were bloodshot.

'Gentlemen,' he said. 'It's getting late, I think.'

He swallowed and tapped his hands playfully on the table.

'Think I'll head to bed. Early start tomorrow.' He looked around at the mess of half-eaten food and plates on the table. 'You'll, er – be all right with this, Thomas? Don't want any vermin now, do we?'

Creech helped him to his feet.

'I'll clear up, don't worry. Get yerself t'bed, go on now.'

'Right, right. Bid you goodnight, gentlemen,' Grimble gestured at the sprawl of books and electronics in the living room. 'There's plenty of room to sleep. Plenty of – er – soft things. You'll find them somewhere, I'm sure. Goodnight.'

With that he staggered from the table and through a door. They heard the clump of his boots up the corridor, the slam of a door and the squeak of bed springs. Then silence.

Creech was already on his feet, clearing the table.

'Y'all can sleep up top,' he said, meaning the mezzanine above. 'Should be room enough.'

Marl stood up.

'Let me help you,' he said. But Creech waved him off.

'Get some sleep. Get on, I got this.'

Creech turned and scraped the cold meat and grease from the plates into a bowl, leaving them to find soft places in a room piled high with ideas, suspicions and possibilities.

fifty-seven

the other guy

SOME TIME in the night, Sam woke from a sleep he didn't remember falling into. He had found a chair and closed his eyes, but there had been too much in his head to find rest. *The older you get*, he thought, *the more of that shit you have building up inside.* Like grease in a pipe, thick and clinging, unyielding.

But at some point the grease must have given way, because there he was, eyes opening, coming back to the world. The room was dark and close. Thunder still fumed outside, like some great being at odds with itself, but the rain had stopped. The only other sound was Marl's snoring from above. He sat up and pushed off his cover, a coarse blanket speckled with bracken and smelling of wood smoke and camphor. He saw a glow through the kitchen window, and decided to follow it outside.

The air on the porch was warm and thick with water and the smoke from Tom Creech's cigar. Sam reached in his pocket for his cigarettes and shook one out.

'Got a light?' he said.

Creech held out his lighter.

'Thanks,' said Sam.

They smoked for a while in silence, watching the horizon flash with bright cracks of lightning that flooded the mountains in blue, electric light. There was no sign of Leafen, which meant they must have been looking west.

'What's wrong with him?' said Sam at last.

Creech said nothing, then made a gruff moan.

'Y'mean the headaches or the talkin'?' he said.

Smoke puffed from Sam's nostrils as he laughed.

'Both, I guess,' he said.

Creech seemed to chew for a bit, his mouth slowly working as he thought. He took a long suck from his cigar, holding the smoke for an age and then letting it free into the stifling, wet air.

'James and I found each other seven years ago,' he said. 'I was upstate, staying clear of the coast. My wife had died and I had trouble there, needed to stay inland for a while. I fell in with some smugglers moving relics from the Hordelands. Furniture, jewellery, photographs.'

The sound of his voice stretched as he smiled.

'Daresay some o'them trinkets found their way into that little box o'yours.'

'Maybe,' said Sam. 'But none of them made it to my place.'

'Yeah, well, one day I was lumbering a tea chest out to a truck next to a pine grove. Heavy thing, full of hell knows what. And out of the trees comes James, stumbling, falling about all over the place, almost naked, jabbering to himself about nothing and everything. He was clutching this rolled-up book tightly in his fist. *All I need,* I thought to myself. A drunk kicking up a stink when I don't need trouble. I said *quiet* but he didn't hear me. Just kept jabbering away about plants and animals and all kinds of shit. We were near the perimeter, too, so I knew there were eyes around. Couldn't risk being heard, so I bundled him into the truck as well, slammed the door and went.'

'Where did he come from?'

'Damned if I know,' said Creech. 'Still don't to this day. He don't know either, don't remember. All I know is that he came from the trees and I put him in my truck.'

'What were you going to do with him?'

'Dump him, I guess. Thought I'd get far enough away from the Hordes to just turf him out into the desert. You get about a hundred miles away, nobody sees you. Nobody who matters anyway.'

'I'm guessing you didn't,' said Sam.

'Almost did.' Creech spat over the porch and into the dirt

beyond the steps.

'I was about halfway to Spring and I figured I'd deal with him. I was about to stop when I saw lights ahead. A truck by the side of the road. I didn't recognise it. Two dudes with guns just standin' there, waitin'. No idea what they wanted but they looked real mean. One waved me down. Thought about flooring it, but their truck was runnin' so I stopped. He shone his flashlight in, pointed his gun at my head. *Open up back*, he said. All I needed. They were going to take the chests, shoot Grimble and then shoot me, leave me lying in the sand. I got out, walked round, trying to think what to do.'

Creech sniffed, hacked and spat again.

'But thinkin's not my strong point. I wasn't born with much of a brain, can't pretend otherwise. By the time I got to the doors, I was set on usin' m'fists. Figured I might get a few in before they filled me with lead. I was ready, had my fingers on the handle. I remembered there was a crowbar hanging inside, thought I might have time to grab that too. I clenched up and pulled open the door, was about to grab the bar when out of the back jumps James, naked and screaming and waving his hands. He was covered in white paint — there'd been a pot in the back, he must have daubed himself with it. Looked like some kind of dust devil, all red mouth and red eyes and pasty face, waving his hands and all. Dude behind me screamed like a hog and just about pissed his pants. James leapt on him and started yelling things in his face, drooling all over him until he dropped his gun. By the time his buddy had raised his, I'd picked it up and fired a few rounds off, hit him in the leg. He dragged himself back to his truck. The other one escaped from James's grip and ran off too, yelping and whimpering like a beaten pup. I fired another couple a' shots into the back of their truck just to make sure, then they were gone, skidding back the way we'd come.

'We watched 'em, James and me, him standin' there shiverin' and all white. We watched 'em till we couldn't see their lights no more. Then he turned to me. He wasn't deranged no more, it had all been an act. He wasn't even jabberin' like he was when I'd found him in the forest. *James Grimble,* he said, in that manner of his. I shook his hand and told him my name. Then I found a blanket for him, let him ride up front for the rest of the journey. He didn't say nothin' else, just slept curled up like a little boy, clutching this book to his chest.'

The lightning was just a distant flicker now. The storm had found its way back to the mountains, leaving a plain of mud in its wake.

'And you've been together since then?'

Creech sighed.

'We got to where the tea chests were going and I offloaded them. James just stood about in his blanket. He was nervous, didn't know where he was, like a man waking up from too much liquor. The loaders laughed at him, poked fun at him, pushed him around a bit. James kept looking at me. One of the loaders asked me if they could take him too. No idea to this day what he wanted with him, but I guessed it weren't for nothin' pretty. He offered me something for him. James spat in the dirt when he mentioned money, which made the loader pissed. He was going to go for him, but I stood in front of him, pushed him back. *He's with me*, I said. The loader laughed. *OK, then, congratulations, all yours, man!* he said. He backed off and they left us alone, laughing back to their camp. After that, it was me and James. I got him cleaned up and fed. He wouldn't tell me where he was from or what happened to him, said he couldn't remember, or maybe he just didn't want to. He just had this book — *Emily Dickinson* on the front, full of poems. He read some to me. I liked 'em, some of 'em anyway. He helped me out on the road. He could fix things, fix m'truck up. Wasn't long before we got shot of the smugglin' and set up on our own.'

Creech stopped talking for a while and smoked. After a few puffs he started up again.

'I don't know if he really believes this is England or whether he's just pretendin', or whether they're the same thing. All I know is, we're kind of a – part of each other now, I guess.'

'Seven years,' said Sam, with a grin. 'Getting the itch yet?'

Creech shuffled uncomfortably.

'Hell,' he said. 'It ain't nothin' like that. Can't say for sure about James, but I like m'wimmin. Besides, he ain't an itch. He's more like a wart that you just put up with and get used to. Then one day you wake up and find it's taken over your whole hand. You'd have to cut the thing off just to get rid of it. Then you find you don't mind it so much. Ain't sore, ain't itchy, just part of you.'

'I didn't mean anything by that,' said Sam. 'I'm sorry.'

'James has his headaches and he has his turns and he can't shut his mouth sometimes. And all them books, well, Christ, he's a pain in the ass, that's for damn certain. But I suppose we became friends. Friends when we didn't have none. England or Texas — it don't matter much. The world's a dangerous place and it's easier to walk through it with a friend.'

Creech's boots squeaked on the wet wood.

'When all's said and done, I guess it comes down to the same question everyone's always been asking themselves.'

'What's that?'

'Do you help yourself or do you help the other guy?'

Sam could feel himself being watched in the dark.

'What about you?' said Creech. 'What do you think this place is?'

'Here?' said Sam. 'This is nowhere. I'm from Leafen.'

He could sense Creech smiling somehow.

'But you've been here before, haven't you?'

'What makes you say that?'

'Saw your face when we mentioned Red Dog. You've heard that name before, Sam. Tell me I'm wrong.'

It was Sam's turn to feel uncomfortable. He shook out a cigarette and lit it from the last.

'You're not wrong,' he said at last. 'I've been out here before.'

'When? What were you doing?'

'About thirty years ago. I was on a team doing some work on the second Fabrik upgrade.'

'What in the hell is Fabrik?'

'The walls of the perimeter, it's what you see when you look at Leafen. I was looking after this New Hire.'

'What's 'at?'

'A New Hire, from the Hordes. He'd been there a few weeks and he was starting to get jumpy. They do sometimes, very occasionally it all gets too much for them.'

'What does?'

'Life on the other side. Some of them just want to get home.'

'That don't make sense. You seen some of them bastards in the Hordes? They live in shit out there.'

'How can you say that when you live outside yourself?'

'I live out here, free, not in the Hordes. Been there though, lots of times. And I just can't see how anyone would want to go back to them once they got out.'

'Well, they do. Every now and then, one of them jumps, tries to get back.'

'Is that what your boy did?'

'Yes he did. We were right on the edge, resurfacing, when he jumped down and stole a truck.'

'You followed him?'

'Damn right I did. He was my responsibility. If I lost him it was my problem. I took a truck and followed him out across the plain.'

'Back to the Hordes?'

'That's what I thought. We were about five miles from the edge of them. They kind of cluster around the north perimeter.'

'I know that.'

'Right, but he kept on going, kept going north. I kept going too. I almost gained on him, but my truck ran out of gas. By the time I'd refilled the tank from the spare, he was miles ahead of me, out of sight and around the north edge of the Hordelands.

It was dark and I didn't want to get too close. I kept going for a while, then camped till first light and started up again.'

'Did you find him?'

'Yes, I did.'

'Where?'

'Another twenty miles east. Right around the top. Deep in Red Dog's territory.'

'Did you meet him?'

'Red Dog? Yeah. But we'd met before.'

'When?'

'That's another story, but it turns out my boy was holed up with him. One of his border patrols found him and took him in.'

'Guessing you didn't get him back then.'

'You guess wrong,' said Sam. 'I got my boy back.'

Sam flicked his cigarette off into the mud and kicked at the wooded floor. Creech stood in silence, the wet stub of his cigar hanging loose in his open mouth.

'And I took something else too.'

'What?'

'Doesn't matter. Let's just say I'm not in any hurry to meet Red Dog again.'

'Well, shit,' said Creech. 'There's more history in you than in one o'Grimble's books.'

'Does he still hold the top of the Hordes?'

'Yup, and some. From what I hear, he's spread further south. Moving closer to your Line like a disease.'

The boots squeaked again and Creech paused.

'Y'know, seems to me like you'd do all right out here, Sam. Y'ever thought of jumpin' too?'

Sam laughed.

'Out here, are you kidding? No fucking way. I'm from Leafen. I like my life. I got a daughter and a good job and good friends. I drink good beer and eat good food. Why would I want to trade that in to come and live in the mud?'

Creech was curiously quiet. He seemed to be considering his words, making sure he understood what he was saying before saying it.

'Cuz James is right,' said Creech. 'Where y'all live, it ain't real. It ain't the real world.'

Sam gave a tired laugh.

'I'm not sure I even know what you mean by that. And I don't care much for your friend's talk about the past. This thing we have?' Sam pointed at the ground. 'This life, it's all we have. It's not the past or the future, it's just right now. And you have to make the most of it, whatever place you're born into. It doesn't make sense to me to try to change it. It'd be like a – like a piece of driftwood trying to change a river's current.'

Sam waited for something back from Creech, but he was silent. He watched the last of the glimmering storm disappear behind the mountains and thought about April. He always missed her – even when she'd only left the room – but he missed her even more now, and it wasn't just because of the distance. It was being out here again, out in this flat, dead desert with nothing for a thousand miles but dirt, sand, barren mountains and dangerous men. *Leafen might not be perfect*, he thought, *but it's better than this. Maybe one day it will eat up this whole shitfield.*

There was nothing now to do except find that thing, get back inside and make everything right again. Whatever had happened before all this was of no concern to Sam. And whatever happened after he was dead was somebody else's problem. The only time was right now, and right now he had to fix things up.

Right now he had to get some sleep.

'Nice talking to you, Thomas,' he said. 'I'm going in to get some rest.'

'G'night,' said Creech. 'Up at first light. And Sam?'

Sam stopped, the door half-opened.

'Yeah?'

'Get enough driftwood in one place and y'all got yourself a

dam.'

'Goodnight, Thomas.'

Sam walked in and found his chair in the dark. He pulled up the blanket and closed his eyes. But he couldn't sleep.

fifty-eight

where's red?

THE SUN was up. Steve Manager stood at the window of Executive Suite 311, shirtless, watching tired light smear in from the east. Leafen was as still and silent as the room.

He saw movement from the corner of his eye — through the crack in the bedroom door a sheet was ruffled on the mess of bed. Toes stretched, a leg bent and rolled over another one.

There was a knock at the door. Before he could answer, Faith Pey opened it and walked in.

Her eyes were fresh and bright, her face resolute, giving him nothing. She glanced at his bare chest.

'Good morning,' she said, the words meaning nothing of the sort.

The bedroom door opened and a naked girl stepped out. She passed Faith, smiling, hips rolling, then glanced at Steve like he was an item of furniture. She went to the kitchen, where she poured coffee.

'Mr Leafen hopes the entertainment was satisfactory?' said Faith. She cocked her head.

Steve felt it — the old twitch, the same mechanism kicking in. *Don't submit to this. Use Red. Where's Red? Where's old Red?*

He drew himself up and took a step closer to Faith.

'Very,' he said.

He saw a wrinkle of disgust at the corner of her mouth. She blinked.

'Soor arrived last night,' she said. 'The meeting starts in two hours. Meet me at the elevators in one. Priscilla and Daniel wish to talk with you first.'

She turned and left. The *thhhhhwhumphhhh* of the door

contained slightly more slam than it had done before.

The naked girl slunk back to the bedroom with her coffee, shutting the door firmly behind her.

fifty-nine

porch

DEMETRI HAD been awake for a while before he realised it. It was the first time he had woken up without the lulling alarm of his Fronds for as long as he could remember. The dividing lines between the previous day's thoughts, whatever ephemeral nonsense he had just dreamed and his waking moments were usually clear and well marked. There was never any blurring around the edges, never any question of where he was in his own consciousness. His Fronds held his hand and gently but firmly led him into the day, through it and back out again. He had never had to pay much attention to his own thoughts.

But now his head was a void — a vacuum wanting to be filled. And the thoughts that arrived were like raw-skinned babies, clamouring on the walls and wailing for his help.

He sat up and banged his head on the low ceiling of the mezzanine. Cursing, with a hand to the bruise, he shook off his blanket and found his way down to the living room. It was light and cold and he followed the sound of voices outside onto the porch, where he found Sam and Marl talking. The storm had gone and the sky had cleared to a brilliant bright blue, dusted white by high clouds.

He passed Creech leaning against the dripping gutter and kept walking around the side of the house, where he stopped and looked east. On the horizon was the fat, black brick of Leafen, crowned with a giant halo of sunlight. He closed his eyes and took a long breath – that same fresh smell was on the air as the previous day, heightened now by the tang of the storm. It reached down inside of him, as if it was trying to trigger some nostalgia he didn't have or resonate in a material that was too damp or too dull. He wanted to recognise it, to welcome it, but he couldn't. All he could do was stand in mute awe, breathing it in and out.

He opened his eyes and looked closer at Leafen. Spreading from its north wall were shorter buildings with no discernible order, sharp and ragged like termite nests. They were bundled together with no thought — the product of necessity, not of design.

The Hordelands; hundreds of miles of them. Demetri had never seen them from any vantage point other than that of The Hiring stadium.

A sharp wind blew past the house, whipping up a puddle and skedaddling off across the plain. Demetri saw Grimble sitting cross-legged on the yellow hood of the Ford, looking down into his hands.

'Morning,' he said, walking down to him. Grimble's eye wandered as he looked up.

'Mr Trittek, good morning,' he said, beaming triumphantly. He held up the Stooge for him to see. 'It works!'

He looked down at it again.

'At least I think it does. It switches on at least. Wasn't doing that before, was it?'

'No,' said Demetri. 'Can it find the signal?'

'I don't know.' Grimble tossed the Stooge to Demetri and hopped off the car. 'You're the expert; show me.'

Demetri performed a series of calibrations and frequency adjustments until a scatter of lights appeared on the screen. They flickered and gathered around a central point.

'What's it doing?' said Grimble.

'Searching. Triangulating.'

'Has it found anything?'

Demetri waited, sliding his finger down a strip until the lights twisted together and collected into a tight bundle. Grid lines appeared and digits flashed up, rolling up and down as the device moved. It began to beep. Demetri smiled.

'Yes it has,' he said. 'You fixed it.'

Grimble gave a modest shrug.

'Just a few loose connections, nothing much. Enjoyed it actually.'

A thought entered the void in Demetri's head. It wasn't like the others, it wasn't scrabbling to find a shape or purpose. It was solid and perfectly formed, like a pebble.

I used to enjoy doing this too. This made me happy once. When did that change?

'I think I know what you mean,' he said.

'Do you fix things too?' said Grimble.

'I used to,' said Demetri. He hesitated. 'When I was a kid.'

'And is that what you do now? Fix things?'

'Sometimes. Not always. Only if – '

'Let me guess,' said Grimble. He put both hands on Demetri's shoulders and looked him in the eye. 'Only if it stacks up?'

Demetri watched Grimble walk back to the house. He kept hold of the thought, enjoying the feeling that it belonged inside his head and that it had — he was sure — been there before, long ago. Maybe it had never even left.

'Well, come on, then,' said Grimble. 'Let's tell the others where your little friend is.'

Demetri followed him back to the porch.

'Did you get something?' said Sam.

'Your boy did,' said Grimble. 'Nothing to do with me. I just stuck the wires together.'

They all huddled around the Stooge.

'OK,' said Demetri, holding it up and walking in the direction of Leafen. 'So we're here at the bottom of the screen. The signal's coming from about – here.'

He pointed at the sharp jungle of brickwork on the horizon.

'In the Hordelands?' said Sam.

'No, about ten miles further out. It looks like it's in open country.'

'That ain't open country,' said Creech. 'Looks like it from here, but it ain't. That scrub's pretty dense. It'll take some effort getting in.'

Grimble stepped forwards and took a satisfied breath of cold air. He clapped his hands together.

'Pack the supplies then, Thomas. We must press on.'

'Supplies?' said Sam.

Grimble turned.

'Yes. We're going to help you.'

sixty

a thousand floors of silence

STEVE MET Faith at the elevator five minutes early. She smiled as she offered the door to him. It was a helpful smile, an empty smile, a nothing smile. Whatever signs of affront she had exhibited earlier had now disappeared. Now Steve felt like a commodity again, just an object she was moving to a place it needed to be. They climbed a thousand floors in silence and without eye contact. When they entered the Sky Rooms, she walked ahead without waiting. He didn't mind. He felt clearer than he had felt in days, calm and peaceful. He knew exactly what had to happen. He knew exactly what he was.

They were met by Priscilla outside the board room. She looked pale. Before she could speak, Daniel blustered in, closing the door behind him.

'They're here,' he said. He clapped his hands together. 'Now, I was hoping we'd be in a better position than we are right now. If we could have countered the attack, we would have been able to go into that room with our heads a little higher. Soor like a good fight, if you know what I mean.'

He looked at his shoes and scratched his head.

'Unfortunately that wasn't to be. Sumar's team has made no progress, and our other avenue – '

He glanced at Priscilla.

' – Well, from what we can tell, that's dead in the water too. So we are where we are. We have to do things their way.'

He turned to Steve.

'Are you ready, Mr Manager?'

Steve nodded.

'Yes, sir.'

'Right. Let's not keep them waiting, then.'

sixty-one

into the wild

THEY TOOK the Ford back to the roadhouse and picked up April's truck. Then they sped across the plain, following the Stooge's bearing and aiming vaguely for the northern tip of the Hordelands. The sky stayed blue and the sun pulled away from the horizon to which they were headed, warming the earth. There was nothing spectacular about the scenery, no undulating earth or rushing water, no great forest to skirt and no fantastical cloud formations above. There was nothing but wet ground and clear air spreading out to every horizon. But for Demetri this was spectacle enough; the unbounded, unobstructed space, warming slowly as he passed through it, felt just like the one growing inside his head.

Somewhere near the scrub the Stooge lost its signal and Demetri made them stop by a creek to recalibrate. While they waited, Creech took a shotgun and a machete, waded across the creek and hacked his way into a thicket.

'Where's he going?' asked Sam.

Grimble jumped down from the flatbed.

'Hunting, by the looks of it,' he said. He began to collect tangled, twisted logs and threw them in a pile. Marl helped him.

'We don't have time for that,' said Sam. He pointed at Leafen. 'The Fabrik. You can see it struggling from here. We have to move. Tell him to come back.'

A loud shot echoed from within the scrub. Grimble threw another log on the pile and held up a finger.

'Word of warning,' he said. 'Try not to get between Thomas and his lunch.'

Creech returned a moment later carrying two rabbits, which

he skinned with the machete and skewered over the fire.

After they had eaten, Demetri walked up and down beside the water, trying to find a signal. Sam followed a few paces behind and Marl listened to Grimble and Creech having a gentle argument about whether creeks like this had ever existed in the British Isles, and where a plain of this immensity fitted in the geography of such a small island. As before, Grimble's responses were centred on either the power of the early Sweeps or the massive change in social geometry that he believed occurred in the years before them — things which Creech believed to be myth and nonsense and more proof that his friend had lost his marbles.

'You need to wake up, Tom,' said Grimble. 'You're almost as fast asleep as our guests.'

Creech made a noise and stood up to fill his canteen.

'No offence,' said Grimble to Marl.

'Where I come from,' said Marl, smiling, 'there is a story that says that the whole world will one day fall into a deep, unshakeable sleep for a thousand years. When we wake up, we will have no recollection of who we are or what we were doing before we fell asleep, and the world will feel like a wide green field with nothing in it but us and an endless future. But as we walk through the field, telling each other stories, we stumble upon a terrible memory — that we have endured this long sleep and enjoyed this joyful waking countless times before, but each time we forget, and we walk too far through the endless field, and we forget the terrible memory, and make the same mistakes as we did the last time, until we are walking through dirt and dead grass, until at last we stumble to our knees and fall asleep once again.'

'That's a good story,' said Grimble. 'I like it.'

The Stooge suddenly beeped and Demetri stopped.

'What is it?' said Sam. 'Did you find something?'

The screen turned black and flashed with words.

'This is weird – '

'What?'

'It's a message,' he said, angling the screen away from the sun's glare. 'Shit, it's from Turnett. How did he – ?'

'Read it,' said Sam.

Demetri read out loud.

'Hi Demetri, managed to trace your Stooge on GPS and fudge a messaging system using a hack that Saul worked out. Pretty cool, it reverses the flange polarity and screels back the Jolsen pragmatolisers – '

'Skip that, what do they want?'

Demetri scrolled down the screen.

' – you're outside, that's insane – they managed to get a couple of military trucks working off the grid – picked Grant up outside Montfort – fairly pissed off with you – did some more research into the Hackdrone – found some information about it – whatever you do, don't – '

Demetri's voice trailed off as he read.

'What?' said Sam. 'What do they know?'

Demetri looked up at Sam.

'We can't destroy that thing out here. If we do, then it could kill everyone inside.'

'What? How?'

'Turnett thinks it has a built-in kill signal that will auto-emit under pressure or if any of its circuits get damaged. The only way to stop it is to take it back inside and disarm it.'

'We can't do that out here?'

'No way, we'd need schematics and tools.'

'Shit,' said Sam. He flicked his cigarette away and walked up and down in the dirt, rubbing his head.

'And there's no way we can destroy it safely?'

Demetri scrolled through the message again.

'Turnett thinks maybe if it's burned, but it would need to be exposed to immense heat, like a super furnace, not just an ordinary – '

Demetri suddenly dropped the Stooge and let out a cry of

pain. He grasped his head and fell to his knees, unable to see or hear, unable to think or speak. He pressed his hands against his skull, trying to squeeze out the nerve-jangling shriek of a thousand drills rising up from his spine.

Eventually the pain subsided and he found himself spluttering in the dirt, with Marl and Sam dragging him to his feet.

'What the hell was that?' said Sam.

'It's that thing,' gasped Demetri. 'The Hackdrone. It must be adjusting its signal. It's close.'

'Right.'

Sam marched over to the fire and kicked dirt over it.

'Pack up,' he said. 'Lunchtime's over.'

They had hacked their way about half a mile into the scrub, when Demetri called for them to stop.

'We're almost on top of it,' he said. 'It can't be much further. Through there.'

He pointed at a thick cluster of branches, through which they heard running water.

'So what's your plan?' said Creech. 'Want me to shoot it?'

'No,' said Sam, 'We have to catch it and take it back. Marl, do you have the sack?'

Marl held up the same bag he had used at the perimeter.

'I shall be much faster this time,' he said. He dropped to his knees and crawled through the bushes.

The others followed until their faces were in the branches, trying to peer through.

'Are you through?' whispered Sam.

They heard some scuffling on the other side.

'Yes,' replied Marl. 'There's a clearing here with a stream running through it.'

'Do you see anything?' said Sam.

'Yes. I see it. It's on the opposite bank.'

'Go slowly,' said Demetri.

They heard Marl's footsteps in grass, then in water, then nothing.

The silence continued.

'Think he's across?' said Grimble.

'Wait – '

They heard something like a metallic whip followed by a dull thud and Marl's voice. Then silence again. Sam, Demetri, Grimble and Creech consulted each other with a split-second look.

'I'm going in there,' said Creech. Sam went to stop him, but before he could lift his machete the bushes burst outwards and the Hackdrone shot through, flying straight over Creech's head and knocking his hat off.

'Good grief!' cried Grimble. 'Thomas, go after that thing! Demetri, follow him, track it with your Stooge. Sam and I will retrieve Marl.'

Creech scrabbled around on the ground.

'M' damn hat!'

'Go!' said Sam. 'Go on, keep a track of it! We'll meet you at the truck.'

Creech found his hat and sprang through the jungle with Demetri stumbling after him, fumbling with the Stooge's dials while dodging the sharp branches springing back. A thick one hit him on the nose and scored a deep cut in his cheek.

'Keep left!' he yelled. Creech grunted and leant left like a rolling boulder, hitting a tangled mess of grey, lifeless vines and coming to a stop. Demetri bounced off his back and held the Stooge up to the thick canopy. Creech huffed and hacked, splintering the dead wood and pushing through into open air, where he stood, panting and sweating like a packhorse.

Demetri emerged behind him.

'We're back at the creek,' said Creech. He pointed north at

the Hackdrone, which was once again a dot growing smaller. 'We lost it.'

Sam and Grimble pushed their way out with Marl between them. His head was swollen where the orb had hit him.

'Your head,' said Demetri.

'I am all right,' he said. 'Where did it go?'

'North. I'll have to recalibrate.'

They followed the creek to where they had parked.

'It's stopped again,' said Demetri.

Grimble took the Stooge and examined the screen.

'I see,' he said, squinting at the display and glancing up. He chewed his lip. 'Yes, I see. It's near the door, right here.'

'OK,' said Sam. 'So we have to go into the Hordelands.'

'What?' said Demetri. 'Are you insane? I'm not going in there.'

'Why not?' said Marl.

'Because it's dangerous. Besides, if it's in the Hordes then we can get someone else to get it. We should go straight back through the Fabrik and get a search party to go out there and get that thing for us.'

Sam scratched his chin and gave Demetri an awkward look.

'Yeah, about that. I've been meaning to tell you – '

'Tell me what?'

'We can't just go straight through the Fabrik. It was a one-way passage.'

'But – ' Demetri stammered. 'But it's weak, you said – '

'Yeah, but only weak one way. The other way it's like steel. It would take a total collapse to weaken it enough for us to get through.'

'When were you going to tell me this?'

Sam shrugged.

'Now, I guess.'

'So you're saying we're trapped out here?'

'No, we're not trapped.'

'So how do we get in?'

'I don't know. I guess we'll have to travel through the Hordes and try our best at The Line.'

'That's impossible, y'all'll be killed,' said Creech.

'You said that thing was close to the door, right?

'Ah,' said Grimble. 'No. That's not what I said, actually.'

'Yeah you did, you said *it's near the door.*'

'Yes, but not *your* door.'

'What do you mean?' said Sam.

'It's near the other door.'

'What other door? What the hell are you talking about?'

Grimble pointed to the very north tip of the Hordes.

'That door,' he said. 'The front gate.'

Sam's face darkened. Grimble smiled as helpfully as he could.

'I'm afraid your little friend has found its way into Red Dog's backyard.'

sixty-two

hope

AFTER ALMOST twelve hours of listening to a Soorish elder recite every single word of a contract built over two years, Daniel Leafen called for a break. The two sides of the room regrouped in huddles.

'We'll meet back here in an hour,' said Daniel. 'Freshen up, eat. Faith, escort Mr Manager back to his suite, would you?'

Steve followed Faith back to his suite in a daze of mumbled words and figures. Since it was dark, the Sky Rooms were illuminated by hidden strip lights that shrouded the night sky, making them marginally less terrifying. It was easy to imagine you were walking in nothing more than an underground tunnel.

At his suite he showered, working the soap slowly on his skin, trying to cast out the day's events with the dirt. Then he put on a fresh suit, drank some coffee and met Faith back at the elevators. He watched her face as she worked the buttons to take them upwards – her eyes lost in the task, lips silently incanting each number as she entered them into the control pad. On the last digit she glanced at him, the first time their eyes had met since that morning.

Steve felt a lurch as the elevator pulled away. He could not be sure if it had been caused by the movement.

Back at the Sky Rooms, the doors opened. But this time, rather than being met with the glowing corridor through which they had just passed, there was nothing but dark and starry space. In the rush of vertigo he slammed his hands against the doors.

'What's happening?' he gasped.

Faith was already outside, hovering calmly in the light cast by the elevator.

'Power problems, most likely,' she said.

Steve staggered back against the wall.

'I can't, I – '

'You're scared again,' said Faith. Her voice was like a sharpened rod. 'That's not very *Red* of you.'

'You're angry,' he breathed. 'That's not very *Green* of you.'

She turned away in disgust.

'Nothing happened,' said Steve, the words tumbling from his mouth. 'With those Double-Pinks last night. Nothing happened.'

It was true. They had tried every trick, even the men, but nothing they had attempted had worked. On the surface they had moved with expertise, years of training and natural sexual talent, but to Steve it had felt like nothing more than a lesson. A lesson in obedience. After an hour or two, they had eventually given up and pleasured themselves in his room, while he slept alone by the fire.

'What makes you think I care?' said Faith.

Steve caught his breath.

'Hope, I suppose,' he said.

Faith frowned.

'Just who do you think I am?' she said, with a bitter laugh. 'Green, is that it? Is that what you want? A nice, helpful Green to give you no trouble? A girl who'll give you everything you want and ask for nothing in return? What do you even know about me, Steve?'

'Nothing; only how you make me feel.'

Her eyes became a cold, hard line.

'And how, exactly, do I make you feel?'

Steve steadied himself against the elevator door, his mouth dry as bone.

'I'm not Red,' he stammered. 'I never was. I mean – '

He glanced down at his tie, ruffling in the breeze.

'I know I am, but I think there was a mistake. I wasn't

supposed to be – I wasn't supposed to be *this*.'

'What are you talking about?'

He took a long breath.

'Have you ever woken up and realised you've just spent twenty years being something you're not? Doing things you never thought you'd do, spending your time with people you never wanted to spend it with, trying to get to places – places you never wanted to go?'

He rolled his eyes as another wave of vertigo rushed up and hit him. He laughed – an insane, strangled shriek that he swallowed before it could fully escape.

'I'm not supposed to be here, Faith. Up here, with you, with them in that room, doing this. But I am. I am because I accepted it. I did everything I was supposed to do to get here and I never questioned it, not once, since the day of my Colours. I haven't thought about that day for a long time. I haven't thought about a lot of things until this week.'

He looked down bitterly.

'Yesterday, we were standing right here and you told me to pretend to be nothing; just a man facing a woman high above the earth. So I did, and I realised for the first time in my life that's exactly what I was: nothing. But facing you I felt I was everything too. Nothing and everything, a mixture.'

Faith took two steps towards him.

'Steve, what are you trying to say?'

He gave a nauseous sigh.

'I'm trying to say, you make me feel like there might be moments ahead that aren't like the ones behind. That there might be moments when I don't have to be the things other people expect me to be, or say all the things they expect me to say. Moments like yesterday, when I looked in somebody's eyes – *your* eyes – and didn't see them assembling my character from the colour of my tie. Faith, I know every combination of Colours in this corporation by heart. I know how to appeal to a Blue's sense of logic, how to draw out the truth from a Yellow, how to make a Green/Red the most productive he can be. I know what buttons to press and how to bend people to my will.'

He swallowed again, closing his eyes.

'But I've never known anyone as deeply as the first time I looked at you.'

'But how?'

'I don't know. I can't explain it. But it's true.'

She took a short breath of night air and, as she exhaled, Steve saw something within her depart. After more slow footsteps he felt her hand upon his chest.

'Follow me,' she said. 'Keep close.'

He took her hand and felt the cold air gradually mingle with the warm, like ice through hot milk. When he opened his eyes they were outside, their faces inches apart. Her fingers felt warm against his, the closeness of her body a calm line through his panic.

The gap between their lips closed, but suddenly there was a sharp jolt in the floor and a bang from either end of the Sky Rooms.

'What was that?' said Faith, jumping back.

The elevator doors had shut. Steve spun round and hammered the lifeless button.

'What's going on, why has the door closed?'

He jabbed the button a few more times, with no effect.

'Come on,' said Faith, pulling him by the hand. He felt gravity making another grab for him as they ran through the darkness, Faith using the wall to steer them around.

'Shouldn't that be open?' said Steve, nodding at the doorless wall ahead.

'It's probably increased security. I might need to ID us.'

They stopped before the closed door.

'The control pad's out,' said Faith. 'Shit.'

She opened a channel on her radio.

'This is Faith Pey. I'm stuck in the Sky Rooms with Steve

Manager, requesting access to the Upper Balcony. Over.'

The radio maintained its fizz of static.

'This is Faith Pey. Can somebody please open the door to the Upper Balconies? Thanks. Over.'

There was silence again, then a blast of white noise and a voice.

'Yeah, power's out to the third and fourth corridors of the Upper Balconies. You can't get through right now. We're working on it.'

'What? How long, over?'

'Ah, hard to tell.'

'This is urgent. We have a meeting in the board room with President Leafen and representatives from Soor. They're expecting us to be there.'

'Yeah, like I say, we're working on it. Shouldn't be too long.'

'OK, we're heading back to the elevator. We'll go down to the one of the lower balconies and walk up. Over.'

'Ah, negative on that. Power's out to the elevator, too.'

'What?' said Faith.

'I said power's out to the elevator. You'll have to sit tight.'

'Sit tight? We're in the fucking Sky Rooms. Over.'

'Shouldn't be too long. Just stay where you are and we'll have you out of there in a – '

'Fuck!' said Faith, thrusting the radio back into its holster. 'Can you believe this? What – Steve?'

Steve was staring through the roof of the Sky Rooms. Above them was a galaxy; a spray of stars brighter than he had ever seen.

'Look up,' he said.

He heard Faith gasp and turned to look at her.

'The Fabrik must be weakening,' she said. 'I've never seen them so bright.'

He watched her staring into the ancient blue starlight. Her skin glowed with photons that had travelled for a million years and in her eyes were the reflected explosions from alien suns.

He felt a tightness leave his chest, and his muscles relax, as if something had released its grip upon him. Although he was still aware of being suspended by an invisible material miles above the earth, he suddenly felt safe. It was as if he had stumbled upon a house that he had never seen before but that had always been his home. The walls of the board room, and of the executive suite he had just left, seemed further away than the most distant of the trillion pins of light above him.

'What do we do?' he said at last.

She faced him and sighed.

'We're stuck,' she said. 'There's nothing we can do.'

She found a spot against one of the walls and slid down.

'We may as well lie back and enjoy the show.'

sixty-three

the hordelands

THEY STOPPED at a grid of rubble and dust.

Beyond the patchwork of small buildings, slouching in decay, lay The Hordelands; a ruined sprawl rising up into dark storm clouds. Sky-piercing towers teetered dangerously left and right, lit up in the grimy yellow light of the low sun. Being this close to Leafen, they could see its Fabrik cast with the sharp shadows of the Horde city, like a child's paper cutouts against a nursery wall.

Sam joined Grimble and Creech at the car.

'Is this it?' said Sam, peering at the insanity above. 'Where's the gate?'

'This is the gate,' said Grimble. 'This is the entrance to the Hordelands.'

'I don't get it. You can just walk right in?'

Grimble shrugged. 'If that's what you want to do.'

'Ain't nobody goin'a stop ye,' said Creech, puffing on a cigar.

'Thank you,' said Sam. 'For getting us this far. I know you didn't have to. We'll continue alone from here.'

Grimble took off his glasses and cleaned them on a cloth that only made them dirtier.

'We don't *have* to do anything, Mr Ops,' he said. 'And if it's all right with you, we'll be coming along for the ride.'

Creech grunted in approval.

'I can't ask you to do that,' said Sam.

'You ain't,' said Creech. 'Besides, we have some business in the Hordes we've been putting off for a while. Right, Jimbo?'

Grimble sighed.

'Right you are, Thomas. Right you are. But if it's all the same with you, Mr Ops, we'll take your truck. One vehicle arouses less suspicion than two.'

'What about your car?'

'It'll be safe on this side of the door,' he said. 'Very few people come in or out.'

'I'll ride up front with you,' said Creech. 'We're goin' to want t'keep straight for as long as we can. Avoid the built-up areas and keep to wide streets. We don't engage with anyone unless we have to, certainly not anyone flying Red Dog's colours. You remember what they look like?'

Sam clenched his jaw.

'As if I could forget,' he said.

'Don't worry,' said Grimble, placing a hand on his shoulder. Red Dog's territory only extends about twenty miles, and he doesn't tend to patrol much. He generally sticks to a bundle of streets in the middle. It's a kind of district, I suppose, a closed-off – '

'Dornham,' said Sam.

'That's right,' said Grimble, surprised. 'How did you know?'

Sam said nothing.

'Well,' said Grimble. 'Chances are your Hackdrone has found a safe place near open ground. You said it doesn't have upwards thrust, so it won't be up high. My advice would be for us to locate it, trap it and come out the way we came in. Red Dog won't even know we've been here.'

'Thank you,' said Sam, as Grimble jumped onto the flatbed.

'Don't mention it,' said Grimble.

Sam and Creech got into the front.

'Best to do this quickly,' said Creech.

They drove slowly into the levelled grid, crawling up to the first junction where a long road travelled east into dry haze. The sun was low and the shadows were long — tall, dark figments of the objects from which they crept. The streets were empty. There was no sound apart from the occasional whistle of wind through a glassless window, the rustle of weeds or the grumble of thunder as the storm stirred above.

They crossed the street and kept driving, becoming ever more engulfed in the city as the buildings grew around them.

They kept their engine low, listening. Soon they heard a sound: a jingle, a tinkle, something high, a human voice, drums. Music. Music echoing in empty streets. A woman's voice crooned gaily over a soft, muted trumpet, piano and brush drums. A thick double bass thumped under it all.

Who was that man you said you were?
Don't you remember, honey?
You told me with your eyes.
They said he was brave,
And strong and kind.
And not the kind
Not the kind
To hurt me
Wound me
And leave me standing here aloooooone –
Aloooone in this here dark and empty room I call –
Room I call –
Room I call my heart.

Sam killed the engine.

'Where's that coming from?' said Demetri.

'Through there,' said Sam, pointing up a side street.

'The signal perimeter's at the end of this street,' said Demetri to Sam. 'About fifty metres away.'

They drove along the side street, following the music until they came to a kiosk in the wall. A single dim bulb lit the yellow, mottled walls inside. At the front, with his hands tapping forlornly on the counter, sat a man. When he saw them his face lit up and he sprang to his feet, straightening his tie, smoothing down his hair and wiping the tired fabric of his suit. He arranged some objects around on the counter and cleared his throat.

'Hello, sir!' said the man, peeling his lips into a beam. One of his front teeth was missing.

Sam slowed the truck and looked out of the window.

'How can I help you this fine day?' said the man, casting a hand around the drab streets. The song continued, shimmering, notes slapping off the cold concrete.

'Where's that music coming from?' said Sam.

'Oh!' said the man. He turned to an ancient plastic box on a shelf behind him and turned a dial. There was a whistle of feedback. Marl and Demetri covered their ears. The man pointed at two metal speakers hanging above the counter.

'Do you like it?' he said.

'No – '

'We here at *Roland Enterprises* believe that music is a vital enhancer to the consumer experience. In fact, recent market research has shown unequivocally that gentle background music can increase customer satisfaction by almost 26%! This is very important to all of us here at *Roland Enterprises*, who strive to provide nothing less than a market-leading consumer journey unmatched by any of our rivals.'

The man gave his best beam again, his eyebrows wobbling a little. A breeze blew by, fluttering a strand of something caught in his beard.

'All of you?' said Sam, peering past the man into the empty kiosk. The man swallowed and laughed nervously.

'Please, allow me to introduce myself. My name is Roland Dreel Esquire, president of *Roland Enterprises* and manager of its flagship store. We have been standing proudly in our prime position within the Hind Quarters of The Leafen Hordelands for over seven years now.'

Sam, Marl and Demetri stared back at him, silent. The man faltered.

'And what, what – what brings you to our flagship store today, kind sirs? What brings you gentlemen into the Hind

Quarters – '

A worried look crossed his face.

'Not that it is any of my business, of course, none of my business at all – '

He suddenly turned and bent over, hissing to himself.

'*Shut up, shut up, shut up!*'

He returned with a worried grin.

'What can I do for you today? How may I help you? What can I sell – I mean, I mean, *interest* you in today?'

He spun on his heels and pointed at the walls, upon which a dismal array of items in various states of disrepair hung.

'Some cable? Premium quality? Vintage charging units? Sealed plastic grub nuts? Assorted tools? Bandages? Underpants?'

Sam looked blankly at the walls.

'No,' he said. 'Thank you. We're just passing through.'

'A trip! Something for the road, then,' said Roland. 'Fizz-aid? Some potato crispy chips perchance?'

The door behind him creaked ajar. In the crack appeared the face of a little girl.

'No,' said Sam. 'We have to be on our way. Are there more of your – businesses on these streets?'

The man closed his eyes proudly and held up a finger.

'There are, there are, there are,' he said. 'But none of them open so late. Roland Enterprises is a 24/7 business, all part of our commitment to you, the consumer.'

'You stand here all day every day?' said Demetri.

Roland tiptoed.

'Every day except The Hiring,' he said, sing-songing through gritted teeth. Suddenly, he seemed to sense something and turned. The little girl looked up at him, smiling expectantly.

'Get back inside!' he whispered, ushering her back through the door. 'Back! Back! Go on with you!'

He slammed the door and stumbled back to the counter.

'My apologies!' he said. 'Now, gentlemen, are you sure you

would not – '

'I'm sorry,' said Sam. 'We have to get going. Goodbye.'

'Err – errr…' stammered Roland as Sam put the truck in gear. He fumbled on the counter and brandished some leaflets at them.

'Please, would you mind filling out our customer satisfaction questionnaire? It does so help us improve our customer experience; we aim only to please our customers.'

'Sorry,' said Sam.

As the truck pulled away, the door squeaked open again and the little girl snuck out.

'Customers, Daddy?'

'Yes, dear,' said Roland. He stroked her hair.

'Did they buy anything?'

'No, I'm afraid not, not today.'

'Oh well – perhaps they will give us good reviews.'

'Perhaps, dear. Perhaps.'

They crawled through two more empty streets and arrived at a T-junction.

'We're in the perimeter now,' said Demetri.

They stopped the truck next to a clearing, littered with gravel and overhung with power lines and loose cables. In the middle was a grey-faced four-storey building. There was no glass in the windows, no door in the frame. Inside was a hollow, dark stairwell.

'It's somewhere in there,' said Demetri. 'There's no other place around.'

They climbed the stairs and came out onto the roof. There, hidden behind the edge, was the Hackdrone. Its little beacon flashed in the twilight. Marl stepped forwards with his sack outstretched. Sam grabbed his arm.

'Carefully,' he said. Marl nodded. He trod stealthily across the rooftop, stopping when some gravel slipped beneath his boots. When he was a couple of feet from it, he pounced, scooping the drone in the sack. Its sirens blared and it strained against the canvas, but Marl held it tight and carried it back to the stairwell.

'Gotcha!' said Sam.

The stairwell door opened.

'No,' said a heavy voice. 'We got you.'

They were led a few blocks away from the tower. There was no need for chains or violence; the size of the five men that had surrounded them on the roof was enough to convince them that an escape attempt was inadvisable.

They were Red Dog's men — Sam knew it before he had even turned around, but their colours proved it. They wore white, short-sleeved shirts stretched tight over their muscled chests, clip-on ties in primary colours throttling their thick necks and a badge carrying their name in black letters, pinned to their shirt pockets.

The badge of their leader — a wide-backed, wide-headed man with a jet-black bob and features that drooped as if his whole face had been melting slowly since birth — read 'Doric'. Doric smoked as he led the way, shoulders hunched and swaying slowly, kicking the dust with his patent shoes. He muttered things, mostly to himself it seemed. In between these mutterings he looked down at the cell phone he held constantly in his hand. Every now and again he looked back with a grin wreathed in smoke.

'Keep walking,' he said. 'Is not far.'

It was dark now, with little in the way of stars or moon. But even in the darkness the presence of Leafen's Fabrik cliff-face one hundred miles in the distance could still be felt, as if a part of the sky had simply disappeared and been replaced with a gaping void you could not look into. The Hordelands' rickety skyline was dimly lit; tiny freckles of orange on the pitch-black shoulder of night.

'Here,' said Doric, throwing a hand at a flickering circle of torchlight ahead.

The light was coming from the centre of a circle of buildings. They walked up a narrow alley and out into a wide clearing surrounded by shacks and trailers. Sam could see people sat outside them, hard faces and tattoos in every corner. Some drank in small groups, others mended motorcycles, of which there were many. All of them wore the same outfits — clip-ons, short sleeves, name badges. Next to one trailer was a big man with a yellow tie. His hair was tied in a ponytail by a rubber band and his long beard was braided with what looked like paper clips. A bottle hung from his hand, and on his lap sat a fat woman in a purple power suit. Her head was shaved and her forehead was scrawled with tattoos of numbers. Her eyes were thick with mascara, her cheeks blushed up like a clown's. She was laughing, but she stopped when she saw Sam looking, then stood up and tottered into the trailer on her needle-sharp heels. The man whose lap she had been sitting on looked over at Sam, eyes like slits as he sucked on his beer.

In the centre of the clearing was a bonfire. Next to it sat a man with an electric keyboard on his lap, singing something tinny, old and forgotten about sex and fire.

'Where are we?' whispered Demetri.

'The Hind Quarters,' said Marl. 'Red Dog's territory. Dornham, I believe.'

Sam breathed hard.

'Who is Red Dog?' said Demetri.

'Just let me do the talking,' said Sam.

They followed Doric around the perimeter of the clearing to a long shack with a raised wooden porch. There was a bar along it, lit by a flickering white fluorescent tube. Behind it stood a tall man in a white shirt and green tie, sleeves rolled up to reveal scars and anchors. Doric slouched one arm onto the bar. The other was reserved for his phone, which he checked constantly.

'Gin tonic,' he said, without looking up. The barman fixed his drink and set it before him. Doric took it and drank half in a gulp, still looking at his phone. He wiped his mouth and sighed, then looked up as if doing so was a duty he would rather not have to honour. He blinked at Sam, pointing at the bar.

'We're fine,' said Sam.

'Please self,' said Doric, and finished his drink.

He sighed again, a sigh that came from somewhere you would not want to visit, and looked Sam up and down. He walked slowly around the rest, appraising each in turn. One of the other four men was holding the sack, the Hackdrone still straining inside it.

Once he had completed his circle, he stood before Sam and crossed his arms.

'From inside,' he said. He spoke slowly and deeply, as if each word was new to him, learned from some listen-and-repeat language course.

'Yes,' said Sam. 'Look, we really – '

Doric frowned and shushed him by placing a coarse fingertip on his lips. He pulled down Sam's collar and peered at the back of his neck.

'Fronds,' he said, rolling the *r* like a moth in his mouth. 'Genetics?'

'Yes,' said Sam. 'Genetics. Listen, we need that thing – '

Doric ignored him. He let go of Sam's collar and lifted his phone. The screen's blue and white light reflected in his pallid face.

'This what I use,' he said.

His eyes wandered to the screen and became entranced.

'Fronds not here yet.'

He lowered the phone and the corners of his mouth fell with it. He tapped the screen, distracting himself with something. After a while, he looked up again.

He saw Sam's tie, blinked and lifted it.

'Blue/Yellow,' he said.

He let Sam's tie fall and tapped his own. He pulled a greasy smile.

'Blue, too,' he said.

'You do Colours out here?' said Demetri.

Doric frowned at Demetri, as if he'd only just noticed him. He looked back at Sam, running a finger down his suit.

'This is nice suit,' he said. Sam fought the urge to push his fat finger away from him.

'But I can tell you not sit-down guy. What, then. Engineering? AERO?'

His finger reached two coloured tabs on his lapel. His eyes flashed and then dulled again, as if the effort to maintain the excitement was too much.

'Operations?' he said. He smiled at the small lift in Sam's head. 'Yes, Operations. High rank, too. You are manager?'

Sam pointed at the jumping sack, still beeping and buzzing behind them.

'We need that thing. Please just let us take it and we'll be out of your way.'

Doric nodded, weighing things up.

'What is? New tech? Surveillance? No. Drone?'

'It's not from Leafen,' said Demetri. 'It's from outside. It's dangerous.'

Doric raised his eyebrows and grinned with delight, an extremely strenuous operation for his facial muscles. He rubbed two fingers of his right hand together.

'Valuable,' he said.

'It's not valuable,' said Sam. 'It's a threat to everything inside

Leafen.'

Doric stepped past Sam and stood before the sack.

'Is like I say,' he said. 'Valuable.'

He turned back to Sam, touched his lapel again.

'And you. You valuable, too.'

Something buzzed on Doric's phone and he whisked it from his pocket. His smile shone in the white glare, as the sound of engines came from outside the clearing.

'Boss here,' he said. 'We go inside now.'

Doric led them to a larger building at the rear of the clearing. Sam felt every eye on them as they followed.

'Where is he taking us?' said Demetri to Sam.

'Keep calm,' said Sam. 'Just let me talk.'

The building was as ragged as any other they had seen since entering the Hordelands. The walls were uneven and the roof looked as if it might slide off in a pile of slate if you tapped it. The wooden steps bulged under their feet.

'Please,' said Doric, holding the door.

They walked in. The room was lit with three hanging bulbs. A carpet ran up to a high desk at the end, behind which a black-haired girl with white skin and dark eyes sat filing her nails. She looked up, head cocked like a crow's.

'Sheena,' said Doric. 'Is boss here?'

Sheena stared back, craning her neck to see what was making all the noise in the sack.

'Yeah,' she said. 'I'll buzz you.'

She buzzed them. A voice answered on the intercom.

'It's Doric,' she said. 'And some – ' she looked them up and down. ' – Strangers.'

'All right,' said the voice.

'You can go through now,' said Sheena, returning to her nails.

Doric opened the door and they walked into a room that, at first glance, may have given the impression of wealth and power if everything had not been so cracked and torn. Tall paintings adorned the walls, but the frames were rough. Candlesticks and ornate lamps stood in its corner, stained with age. At one end was a grotesque bust of a male head with a gnarled nose and wrinkled mouth. A huge chandelier hung from the ceiling, chipped and broken. A long wooden desk sat in the centre, sheenless and warped. The whole place looked like the office of a vice president after a dust storm had blown through it.

Behind the desk, in a scuffed leather chair, sat a skinny man with a pale face mottled with acne scars. He had black, slicked-back hair, thin, red lips and a pair of fiercely blue eyes that seemed to want to escape from the whole nightmare.

A black, dusty suit hung on his shoulders like a tent on a coat hanger.

Doric cleared his throat and stepped forward.

'Found them off 13th on top of tower, boss. With this.'

He gestured at the sack, at which the man stared quietly for a while.

The man looked at Marl, then at Demetri. Then his eyes found Sam and he smiled.

'Hello, Sam,' he said. 'Been some time.'

Sam breathed a deep sigh.

'Hello, John,' he said. 'You've lost weight.'

sixty-four

the world we live in

STEVE SAT against the wall of the Sky Room, opposite Faith. She had lit a cigarette and its smoke created a tubular veil against the walls and ceiling. They had been silent for some time, lost in the stars, splattered like paint across the night's canvas.

'Spoke,' said Faith. 'You knew something, didn't you? That's why you didn't sign.'

Steve stretched his neck.

'I didn't know anything,' he said. 'And it doesn't matter now.'

'But you suspected. What was it?'

'Like I say, it doesn't matter.'

'Doesn't it?'

She got to her feet.

'Steve, soon those doors are going to open and we're heading back into that board room. Then you'll give your apology – you'll *grovel* – and Soor will have their technology. What will happen then?'

Steve kept his eyes trained on the sky, willing the conversation to stop.

'*Steve.*'

'What?' he said, finally facing her.

'This might be your last chance. What did you suspect?'

'It doesn't matter what I suspect. Even if I'm right, it's like Daniel says, it's not our business to question – '

'You shouldn't live your life by what other people say, even your president. As soon as you stop questioning, you're dead, you hear me? Now tell me, what do you think Soor are going to do? Tell me!'

A starlit cloud passed behind Faith's furious face.

'Can I have a cigarette?' he sighed.

She tossed him the pack.

'It's very simple,' he said, standing up and lighting one. 'Spoke doesn't work. The clones it creates are inexact, lesser versions of their originals. Soor want to use it to create clones and kill their staff.'

He took a long drag. Faith blinked in the starlight.

'A broken pen is still a stick,' she said.

'Exactly.'

'We have to tell Daniel.'

'He already knows. Just like he knew I didn't sign.'

Faith frowned, searching the floor.

'But, he wouldn't, he wouldn't just – '

'You know very well that he would.'

She turned and looked outside. An orange rim of dawn light had appeared on the horizon.

'Anyway,' said Steve. 'Soor are a completely separate corporation. What do we care?'

She leant against the wall, her forehead touching the perfect glass.

'What do we care?' she repeated, the question flattened from the words. 'Do you know, I have sat in that board room almost every day since I was sixteen, taking notes, serving drinks, collecting files, *assisting*. I have seen and heard everything; all the deals and arguments, all the compromises that have had to be made, the trading that has been undertaken with the quality of people's lives as currency. You're taught to expect it – *turn your eyes*, my teacher said – and even though it's still a shock at first, you soon get used to it. You learn to block things off. You disconnect them; the corporations, the departments, the people. You tell yourself you are just one person with no attachment to any of it. You're there to help, not to change.

'And once you're done disconnecting the world, you go inside yourself, and you disconnect your own thoughts from each other, and then your actions from their consequences. Soon, you're screaming in the bathroom mirror one moment, pulling at your hair, and the next you're complimenting a man you've never met on his choice of shirt. You bring coffee and pastries and sweet smiles to the table; and, later, you're alone in a room with a man of power, allowing yourself…'

She took a sharp breath and turned.

'That's the world we live in, Steve. Free of consequence, free of thought.'

She took a step closer.

'I do feel a connection with you, Steve, I do. And I can't explain it either. But what's the point? What's the point in encouraging it when we live in a world where connections don't survive?'

Steve stared back at her. Seconds, clouds and opportunities passed them by. Eventually, she lowered her head and retreated to the wall.

'I'm going to get some sleep,' she said, sitting down. 'You should too.'

sixty-five

red dog

'YOU APPRECIATE my predicament,' said Red Dog. He reclined in his seat with his fingers folded, thumbs twiddling, staring at the sack. The Hackdrone had ceased its struggle and hung like a bowling ball at the bottom of it.

'This is my company's territory,' he said. 'So by rights that thing is mine.'

'It's not yours, or your *company's*,' said Sam, sneering at the word. 'We chased it out of Leafen and a hundred miles across the plain before it found its way back into the Hordelands. If it's anyone's then it's Daniel Leafen's.'

Red Dog fidgeted at the name.

'It jammed our signals and brought everything to a standstill,' said Sam. 'We need to take it back.'

'Why not just destroy it?' said Red Dog.

'We can't,' said Demetri. 'It's rigged to emit a kill signal. It'll wipe out most of the population inside. We need to disarm it properly.'

'Kill signal?' said Red Dog, impressed. 'Sounds powerful.'

Doric smiled.

'Valuable,' he said.

Sam took a step closer to the desk.

'In what way would it be valuable to you?' he said, keeping his eyes on Red Dog. 'You have no control over it, you don't even know how it works.'

Red Dog shrugged.

'I don't need to,' he said. 'I just get word to Daniel Leafen that I have it safe and sound. Leverage, plain and simple.'

'You don't have time for *leverage*, John,' said Sam. 'This thing is about to take down the entire corporation.'

Red Dog stood up and walked over to the sack.

'This little thing here?' he said. 'The whole place?'

'Yes,' said Sam. 'We don't have any time for power plays.'

Red Dog seemed to consider this for a moment.

'And you found this all by yourself? You and your – ' he scanned the rest of them. 'Friends?'

Sam nodded.

'Well, I always liked that about you, Sam. You always get your target. Like a terrier. Once you get your teeth into something, you just don't let go, do you?'

His smile dropped.

'So go tell him. Go back in and tell him I have his – whatever you want to call it. And if he wants it back then we can do a deal.'

'He'll destroy you,' said Sam.

'And this thing in the process? I don't think so. Not if what you're saying is true.'

'There's no time,' said Demetri. 'We have to get back before the Fabrik shatters.'

'What now?' laughed Red Dog. 'Your Fabrik's about to shatter as well? Holy hell, you guys are in a mess. How did we miss this one, Doric?'

Doric shrugged.

'Slip through net,' he said.

'You know very well that what's bad for Leafen is bad for you too,' said Sam. 'If the Fabrik shatters then it'll take out half the Hordelands and all of your power. Not to mention no more products. We go, you go.'

Red Dog held his fingers to his mouth and swung in his chair.

'Let us take it back,' said Sam. 'We'll tell Daniel you cooperated. He'll reward you.'

'It's a quandary, a real quandary,' said Red Dog. He sat forward and rattled his hands in the desk. 'I'll need to think about this one, gentlemen.'

He stood up and gathered some papers from his desk.

'I have something to attend to, but I'll be back a little later. Sam, maybe you and I can get a drink, catch up on old times.'

He smiled.

'We don't have time – ' Sam began.

'Doric, take our guests outside and see that they're entertained,' said Red Dog. 'Please, make yourselves at home.'

'The stench in here is unbelievable,' whispered Demetri across the rough wooden tabletop. They were perched on stools in a shack a few doors down from Red Dog's office. It was a bar of some kind. The place was almost full, every high table surrounded by men and women like those outside — damaged versions of people he considered normal. Deranged sketches of the only reality he knew.

Grimble sat next to Marl, nursing a glass of something transparent. Creech held a large beer, looking around nervously.

Doric and his thick-necked henchman stood around a table nearby, appropriating reserved, casual stances despite their gorilla-like appearance. Occasionally they glanced around, asserting their guard. A waitress wearing a stained top swept past and took a glass from their table, but the bald ape whose glass it was snatched it back and shoved the girl roughly across the floor, draining the tiny remains of his drink.

'These people are animals,' said Demetri. 'Who are they? And what is this place? A fucking wine bar or something?'

'They are Red Dog's employees,' said Marl.

'Employees?' said Demetri. 'I don't get it, this is the *Hordes*. They're consumers, they can't be staff. There's no company to work for.'

'This is one of Red Dog's companies,' said Sam. 'He operates all throughout the Hordelands, from the gate to the Hind Quarters.'

'But I don't get it,' said Demetri. 'How can he have companies? He's one of the Hordes, he can't – *make* money. He spends it. Leafen's the company, the only company – '

'What did you expect?' said Grimble. Demetri heard anger in his voice. 'That they all just get on and buy your things like good little consumers? They are people; they have aspirations too. They aspire to have everything you have and do everything you do.'

'That's why we have The Hiring, isn't it?' said Demetri. 'To give them a chance of crossing in.'

'Do you know how difficult it is to get a place in The Hiring Line?' said Marl.

'You managed it,' said Demetri.

'I paid a high price. Not everyone can.'

'All they see is life past the gate,' said Grimble. 'People in nice clothes wearing their Colours with clean teeth and white shirts, sitting at their desks, going to meetings, drinking coffee, drinking in wine bars. They think that is what success is.'

'So they're pretending.'

'No, not pretending, just doing what they think they need to do to be happy. A monkey always looks to the highest branches.'

'So, they're trying to recreate Leafen outside. That's funny.'

'Funny?' said Grimble. He looked around. 'I don't see anyone else in here laughing.'

'And Red Dog's no laughing matter either,' said Sam. 'Believe me.'

Marl stood up.

'I am going to talk to someone,' he said.

'Who?' said Demetri.

'Anyone.'

'Sit down, Marl,' said Sam. 'You'll get us in trouble.'

'It is all right, I know how to talk to these people. Perhaps I can find out where Red Dog has gone and what he wants.'

'Fine,' said Sam. 'But don't go too far.'

Creech put down his drink.

'I'll go with you,' he said.

They left. Demetri checked the table behind, then leant in.

'How do you know him?' he said. 'Red Dog, I mean.'

Sam picked up a coaster and tapped it on the table, looking deep into the grain of the wood.

'It was a long time ago,' he said. 'Different time, different life.'

'Is he a friend?'

Sam looked up.

'That might be pushing it,' he said. He turned back to the table. 'I guess you could say we were friends. Once.'

He seemed to decide something, looked around and sighed.

'Red Dog's name is John Gray. He used to work in Leafen. He was a manager in the waste department, probably could have made it to the top if he'd wanted to.'

'What happened?' said Demetri. 'Did he get fired?'

Sam nodded. 'Yup.'

'How?'

'He got caught smuggling.'

'Holy shit, really? I didn't think they fired you for that.'

'Yeah, they do if you're smuggling people.'

'People? You mean illegal immigrants?'

Sam nodded again.

'From the Hordes?'

'He used the disposal chutes to get people in. Remember that waste mountain we saw coming out?

'The one they mine?'

'Yeah. Well he made a route through that. He had scouts running up and down those dirt pipes every day, finding people, guiding people back. Whole families crawling through about five miles of shit to get in.'

'And then what?'

'He knew people in the security department, got them fake IDs, got them a corner in some filthy shared apartment in downtown, set them up with shitty jobs.'

'How did he make money from it?'

'They paid him back from their salaries. He put them on high interest rates. Sometimes they'd be paying interest back for years afterwards.'

Sam suddenly looked at Demetri as if he was an idiot.

'You did know this happened, didn't you? People come in all the time. Who do you think picks up your coffee cups when you throw them on the floor?'

'I don't know, I guess – '

'Yeah, just disappear, don't they?' Sam said. 'Anyway, he got too greedy, usual story. He was up before the courts and out of the door at the next Firing. I guess he'd made enough friends on the outside to stand him in good stead when he entered the Hordes.'

'Not everyone has it so easy,' said Grimble.

'What do you mean?' said Demetri.

'A New Fire is the lowest of the low. They're treated like dirt, spat on, kicked, made to do terrible jobs. Sometimes killed.'

'Why?'

'Because they failed at a life the Hordes can only dream of.'

Grimble blinked.

'Do you understand? That great wall up there is the only thing the people here look up to. There's nothing else. Nothing driving their path through life other than the promise of success on the other side of it, or an approximation of something similar here. They have no myth to lead them but the myth they are fed from birth. That dark wall and the products that come out of it are their rules for *life*.'

He leant back in his chair.

'You shouldn't be surprised that they act the same in the dirt as you do in the grass.'

Just then they heard noises from the clearing outside, shouts and glass breaking. They turned to the door. So did Red Dog's guards.

'You – you're from outside,' said a voice, drunk.

'Shit, what's this now,' said Sam.

'You're not from Leafen, you're from the Hordes. I saw you on the scr – screens. You're a – you're a New *Hire*.'

There were jeers and the sound of boots in the dirt.

Sam got up and walked out onto the porch. Marl was in the centre of the clearing, hands by his side. Creech was standing in front of him, hand out towards a group of three large men. One was drinking from a tall bottle, staggering back with every swig. His suit jacket strained over his gigantic shoulders. He wiped his mouth on its sleeve and pointed a finger at Creech.

'You, get out of here,' he said. 'I have no quarrel with you. But you.' He swung his finger at Marl.

'You shouldn't be here,' he said. 'You're not – w – *welcome*.'

He stepped forward and pushed Marl on his shoulder. Creech pushed the man back hard, but was caught by the two other men, who held him back.

'Get off me y'fuckers,' he growled.

'Hey!' said Sam. The man who had pushed Marl swung round.

Sam felt a large palm on his shoulder and turned back to see Doric. He shook his head slowly. Sam shook him off and walked down the steps.

The drunk man swivelled in Sam's direction. He took another swig. Sam stopped a few feet from him, looking up at the mountain of suited meat in front of him.

'Leave him alone,' said Sam.

The man frowned, swirling the fluid in his mouth.

'And you,' he said, breathing hard. The stench of his breath filled the air between them. He shook his bottle at the dark wall that was blackening one side of the already dark sky. 'You're from in there. You're not welcome either. You shouldn't have come here – ' He belched. 'Either.'

'We have business with Red Dog,' said Sam.

'No, you don't,' said the man.

'Yeah, we do. And he'll be back soon.' Sam nodded back at Marl. 'So, once again, leave him alone.'

The man sniffed, his body in a constant balancing act, moving about like a tower of rocks about to topple.

'And what if I don't want to l – leave him alone,' he said. He held his bottle out towards Sam, narrowing his eyes. 'What then, h – huh?'

Sam held out his hands.

'Well then, I guess we have a problem,' he said.

The man swigged the last of his drink and threw the bottle in the dirt. He lowered his head and strode towards Sam. Sam braced himself, but Grimble stepped in front of him.

'Gentlemen, gentlemen, please. There's no need for this, no need at all.'

The man stumbled, momentarily confused by this even smaller nuisance now opposing him.

'We're very sorry to put you out, er – ' Grimble quickly scanned the name tag on the man's chest, '*Graham*, and we don't want to be here any longer than necessary, believe you me.'

He gave a nervous laugh as the man, Graham, stood above him, clenching his jaw. The sweat ran from across the dirty rim of his collar. Grimble took a sharp breath.

'So, if we could all just stop this and perhaps we could get back to our drinks.'

Graham stared at him for a moment. Then his mouth twitched. Something like a giggle came from his mouth. He smiled.

'Drink?' he said. 'You want – you want a drink?'

He turned round.

'Boys want a drink!' he shouted. There were some more jeers and Graham turned round with a terrible grin.

'Come on then,' he said, holding out his hands. 'Let's have a drink.'

He grabbed Grimble by the scruff of the neck and marched him back into the bar, followed by his friends. At the door,

Doric put a palm on his chest.

'Careful, please,' he said. 'These men are valuable.'

'Sure, whatever,' said Graham, stumbling past.

'Serum,' said Graham. 'Five shots.'

A barman stopped and stared, mute. Graham grabbed his arm and glared into his face.

'Well? What are you waiting for?' he boomed. 'Five shots! Now!'

As the barman ran for a bottle at the end of the bar, there was the scrape of chairs being moved and Demetri found himself being shoved towards a line of five stools in the middle of the bar.

'Sit down,' said Graham, pushing him into one.

He stood before them, arms crossed and legs astride, with his friends behind the stools. Doric and the guards watched from the corner, smiling. The barman returned with a tray of five shot glasses shaking with clear liquid, and laid them on the table.

'Now fuck off,' said Graham. The barman scurried away.

A crowd had gathered around them now. Graham picked up one of the glasses and walked towards Demetri.

'Drink up,' he said.

Demetri looked down into the glass. The thick fluid clung to the sides with a deep meniscus.

'What is this?' he said. Doric laughed and held out his hands to the crowd.

'The path to enlightenment,' he said, to laughter and the thump of boots.

'Don't drink it,' said Sam.

'Don't worry, I'm not thirsty,' said Demetri.

'This isn't for your thirst,' said Graham, pushing his face into Demetri. His smile fell.

'Now. Drink. Up.'

'No thanks,' said Demetri, breathing hard and staring into Graham's cratered red face. 'I really don't think – '

Graham glanced at someone behind the stool. Before he

could look, Demetri felt his hair being yanked back. Out of the corner of his eye, he saw the same thing happen to Marl, Grimble and Creech, before he felt his jaw being yanked open and the liquid splash against his lips. His tongue burned, his throat gagged, and his face hit the floor as the room roared with laughter, shouts and stomping boots.

PART SIX

life's work

sixty-six

think

He was running, holding his father's hand, watching his own small feet trip across the coloured tiles that flowed beneath them like fish in a swollen river. He was excited. His father's hand felt strong and powerful, rough and warm. It was always ahead of him, pulling him on, attached to a thick arm that swung with his stride. Sometimes his feet left the ground and he felt he might fly.

'Where are we going, Daddy?' he heard himself say. The voice was that of a small boy; comically high.

'Not far, Demetri, not far. Come on.'

'But where? Tell me, Daddy, where?'

'Not far.'

Demetri breathed stuttering gasps as he ran. His little finger was squashed beneath the others in the pressure of the big man's hand, but he didn't mind. The grip felt like home. The tiles rushed by underneath. Red, yellow, green, blue, red – and then he saw an orange.

'I saw an orange! Daddy, I saw an orange!'

His father did not reply. Demetri kept his eyes on the tiles, wide with expectation. Another orange flew by.

'And another! Daddy I saw *two* oranges! Two of them!'

Still no reply. They moved on, faster now. Demetri's legs cartwheeled beneath him.

Then a black tile swam by — a rogue minnow hiding in a shoal of colour. Demetri gasped.

'Black! Daddy, I saw black! I did! I did, I saw black! Black, black, black!'

The tiles ran out and disappeared. Demetri saw cracked earth now rushing beneath his feet.

'Daddy?'

He looked up. They had stopped. Demetri caught his breath. His father's hand felt different somehow. Colder, smaller and more fragile. His little finger was no longer squashed. It was not inside his father's hand, but outside, holding it. They were not in Central Station. They were not on the street. They were not in Leafen. They were nowhere.

A perfect dome of sky was above him, blue with black clouds boiling in the distance. In every direction was a flat plain of brown, dry dirt. In front of him was a mountainous black boulder. It was turning slowly, grinding against the earth.

'Daddy?'

His voice was a man's again. He looked to his father and saw a decrepit man in an ill-fitting suit. It was still his father, but he was much older now. He looked back at him with tired eyes. His tie — his father's Colour, blue — was tied so tightly around his neck that it squeezed it into wrinkles.

'Dad? Are you OK?'

The old man swallowed. His hand felt very cold, or was it that his own hand felt hot? He couldn't tell. He looked up at the boulder, turning like a planet, driving into the dirt. His hand *did* feel hot. He looked down at it. It was bright red, glowing against the pale white skin of his father's withered fingers. He tried to let go, but he couldn't.

'Dad? Where are we?'

His father looked back sadly.

'We're here, son,' he croaked. 'All of us.'

'What do you mean?'

His father turned his face away. Demetri followed his eyes and saw that his other hand was holding someone else's. It was his grandfather. *Impossible,* thought Demetri. *You're dead.* His father was holding his father's hand. He in turn was holding his own father's hand. They were holding hands in a chain, father to father to father, and the chain stretched off across the plain for as far as Demetri could see. Each one wore a tie — reds, blues, yellows, greens, oranges, pinks, and every combination they could make.

'What is this place?' said Demetri. The boulder ground and screamed, shattering the rock beneath it. Demetri could feel dust and sand hitting his face. His hand felt hotter. He looked down and saw steam rising from it.

'Dad,' he said, struggling to pull himself free. 'I can't let go.'

The skin of his father's hand began to crackle and shake. It glowed yellow, then orange, then red. Then it burst into flames.

'Dad! No!'

The flames travelled up his father's wrist. The rim of his white shirt cuff singed and smoked, then caught alight. His suit jacket took and the fire shot up his arm. Demetri watched helplessly as the smoke rose. He saw his father through the heat haze, wincing, trying to smile through the pain. Then his entire body erupted and burned, turning quickly to a pile of blue ash on the ground. The smoking, singed remains of his necktie floated down and landed gently on top of it. Demetri picked it up. He tried to loosen the knot, but couldn't. He read the inscription on the label.

To my boy, Neal, wear your Colours with pride

He heard a crackle and looked up. The flames had been passed on to his grandfather, who erupted as well and left a green pile of ash. There were two little piles now — one blue, one green — with two burned ties of the same colour resting on top. The flames picked up pace, travelling from son to father, causing explosion after explosion like a fuse between sacks of gunpowder. The flames shot into the distance, leaving coloured piles and neckties in its wake. He dropped his father's tie and ran after the fire.

He passed man after man, father after father. He recognised none of them, but he knew they were his ancestors. Each one wore a suit; each one wore a different coloured necktie, pulled tight. As he ran with the flames he saw their faces. Sometimes he saw parts of himself in them, other times he saw only a stranger looking back. Each one had his tired eyes turned up to the rotating boulder.

'Stop!' shouted Demetri, although he didn't know who he was talking to.

He followed the flame, holding up his hand to protect him from the heat. He realised that the chain was not a straight line but a ring around the boulder. The faces changed as he ran. The noses flattened, the mouths swelled, the brows lowered. The hair became thicker, eyes darker. They began to stoop. Their ties were still tight around their necks.

Father after father exploded. Now he was running at impossible speeds. The fire seemed to take him faster and faster. He looked behind and saw a string of neckties floating down upon their ash piles. The sound of the boulder and the machine gun of each exploding man grew louder and louder until he suddenly stopped. Then there were no more explosions, only the sound of the boulder.

The flames had gone and he was standing still, facing a creature from the past. It was an ape of some kind, not yet a man. It seemed not to notice Demetri, staring instead at the boulder from eyes set deep beneath a heavy brow. Its mouth was wide. Hair covered its forehead, cheeks and neck. Its suit was clean and black, the shirt white, the tie was – there was no tie.

A breeze passed through the hairs on its lip. It opened its mouth and spoke. The voice was deep and cultivated.

'My life's work,' it said, and smiled.

Demetri looked at the piles of ash from the explosions to his left. To the right were more ash piles stretching off in the other direction. He picked up the first, blue, and read the label. He knew what he would find.

To my boy, Neal, wear your Colours with pride

He turned to face the boulder. It rose up, fat and grey and broken; a thousand cliffs patchworked together. Demetri suddenly felt a ghastly fear. He thought it might contain terrible things. He thought that it should stop turning. He thought that if he shouted at it, it *would* stop turning.

He ran towards it, further into the dust and shadow. The noise grew deafening.

'Stop!' he shouted.

Dust became gravel flying through the air, then stones and rocks. One hit him on the head, but he didn't feel it. Another hit his side – that one he felt.

'Stop!' he shouted again. And the boulder stopped.

The dust cloud hung in the new silence. He broke through it and found himself face to face with the rock at the point it met the earth. The boulder rose up above him, the overhang quickly becoming a wall. He stared at the stone. It seemed to be moving, crawling with something, not on the face of it, but beneath it. It looked like smoke-filled water swirling around. He saw a limb press against the surface. Then a hand. Then a face. And another. All around there were people looking out, all grey eyes and pale mouths. They were alive and swimming around inside. They couldn't see him. They looked right past him.

He searched the sea of faces, then stopped on one and screamed. It was Alex.

'Alex! No, swim out, swim out! Swim out! Alex!'

There came a rumbling and the ground shook. Something began to laugh. It was low and slow, bereft of hope. The boulder started to turn once again.

'No! NO! STOP!'

Dust flew, stones flew, rocks flew. Demetri turned and ran. He burst through the edge of the dust cloud coughing, his eyes streaming. The creature and all of the ash piles were no longer there. Standing on the empty plain was a man with his back turned. Demetri walked around to face him. It was Grimble.

'James?' he said.

Grimble pushed his head forward, peering at Demetri through his cracked circular glasses. He raised a finger and tapped it against his temple.

'Think,' he said.

He tapped it again. A thin black line appeared from the point at which his finger met his head. It grew and splintered. Grimble's face seemed to crack and collapse like ceramic. A large chunk fell off, letting grey light through. Then another. Demetri saw fingers pushing the parts of Grimble's face out from inside his skull. On the other side was a familiar place – the clearing in Red Dog's territory, but in daylight. He saw a face and heard a voice.

'Demetri,' it said.

sixty-seven

no such thing as colours

Steve shivered and opened his eyes to blue sky above and beneath. Faith was sitting opposite, watching him and smoking a cigarette. She looked like she had been awake for some time.

There was a burst of static from her radio. She pulled it from her belt and got to her feet.

'Hello? Over?' she said.

'Ah, yeah, your door's about to open. Sorry about the wait.'

Faith switched off the radio and turned to Steve.

'What are you going to do?' she said.

They heard a hiss as the door opened.

'What choice do I have?' said Steve.

Daniel and Priscilla were waiting for them outside the board room reception.

'Are you two all right?' said Daniel, looking fresh. 'I heard you had a little impromptu night out, so to speak.'

'I'm sorry, sir,' said Faith. 'There was nothing we could do.'

'Don't worry. They were happy to break for the night anyway.'

Daniel winked at Steve.

'I put on some entertainment for them. You know, Steve.'

He looked between the two of them. Getting nothing, he flicked a finger at Steve's collar.

'This – ' he said. 'This won't do.'

Steve looked down at his tie as Daniel loosened it and

whipped it from his neck.

He tossed it to Priscilla and walked to a wall in which he pulled back a sliding panel. Inside were rows of clean suits, shirts, neckties and polished shoes. He took out two ties and examined them.

'Steve Manager is not *Red* today,' he said. He discarded one of the ties and brought back the other. It was pale blue with no pattern. He fitted it around Steve's neck, looking straight into his eyes.

'Sir,' protested Faith. 'He's Dominant Red. He can't wear blue, it's against company – '

Daniel tutted as he fashioned a half-Windsor knot.

'Do you know what it's like looking after forty million people?' he said. 'Do you think it's easy? All those little identities running about, all those little *individuals*. It's hard to keep a lid on it. Isn't that right, Priss?'

He grinned over his shoulder. Priscilla gave a stony half-smile.

'She should know, right?' said Daniel. 'Director of HR and all that, keeping everyone in line; I don't know how she manages it.'

He flipped over the tip of the necktie and tucked it beneath. The silk zipped through his fingers.

'There are no *Colours*, Miss Pey. You should know that. You know that, don't you, Steve? Everybody does, deep down. They're just more things to call ourselves. We are who we are.'

His voice darkened.

'And that – when it comes down to it – is what others allow us to be.'

Daniel smiled as he wove the knot.

'You told me you thought there was a mistake in your Colours, Steve. You thought you were made Red by accident. But there was no mistake. You were Red because, that day, when you turned sixteen, the system needed a Red. And little sixteen-year-old Steve ticked just enough boxes.'

Daniel pulled through the fabric and straightened it into a smooth noose.

'Do you remember, I asked you what colour you thought I was? Shall I tell you? White. That's right, *white* - led by my heart, willing to surrender myself for all around me, a *good man*.'

He winked as he completed the final loop.

'Can you believe that?' he said. 'Like I said, Steve; the way to enlightenment is to accept that you're not the man you thought you could be. Simple as that. You're Red because we *told* you to be Red. You're Blue because we *told* you to be Blue. And sometimes, we need you to be more of one than the other. So today, Steve, you're going to allow me to allow you to be – '

The knot wrenched tight.

'*Blue*.'

Daniel shook his handiwork twice, flipped down Steve's collar and patted his lapel.

'All right, sunshine? Good. Now comes the easy bit. Let's finish the job.'

He turned for the board room.

'Wait,' said Faith.

Daniel stopped.

'What?'

'I didn't have a chance to brief Mr Manager on the protocol,' she said. 'For the apology.'

Daniel searched her face for a moment, then turned to Steve with a bored sigh.

'Right,' he said. 'Very simple. Introductions and that first, just you and him. Me and her.' He gestured to Priscilla. 'We don't speak. We're just there to witness.'

'Witness what?' said Faith.

Daniel frowned.

'Is everything all right, Miss Pey?'

Faith looked at the floor, flustered.

'I'm sorry, sir, I meant, for Mr Manager.'

Daniel turned back to Steve, head cocked.

'We're going to go in there and smile. And then, *Mr Manager* shall proceed to give Commander Po the most obsessively thorough *arse-licking* that has ever been given to any arsehole that ever twitched upon this planet. He will leave it spotless, gleaming, clean enough to eat out of. I don't care what he says, I don't care what excuses he gives, so long as they make *him* look like an idiot and *Po* like a fucking king.'

Faith kept her eyes on the floor, her chest tremoring. Daniel put one hand on her shoulder and the other on Steve's.

'Look, this is simple — it's a gift, a second chance. We're going to get out of this mess, but until that contract's signed, we're theirs. Get through this and all that nonsense outside goes away and we're back to where we were a few days ago. It's all good, we just have to obey their protocol. So, no crossed legs, no crossed arms, don't speak until Po's finished laying out the final terms and, whatever you do, don't look him in the eye when you're talking and don't stand up before he does. Obey the protocol. Understood?'

'Yes, sir,' said Steve. 'Understood.'

Faith tried to say something. Daniel cupped an ear.

'What's that, Miss Pey?'

'Are you sure about this?' she whispered.

'Faith – ' Steve began.

'Soor has a – morally questionable track record,' she went on. 'Are you sure we should be selling it technology that it might abuse?'

There was silence.

'We?' said Daniel, at last. '*We?*'

He took a step nearer.

'Tell me, Miss Pey, what are *we* in the business of?'

'I – '

'What. Are we in the *business* of. Miss Pey?'

'Technology,' she said.

'Wrong,' said Daniel. He pointed at Steve

'Mr Manager,' he said. 'Your turn.'

Steve knew the answer. He had heard it before.

'Money,' he said.

Daniel snapped his fingers.

'Bingo. Money. We shift kit, take the cheque, close the door, thank you very much, next customer please, *kerching*.'

He turned back to Faith.

'*I* work for Leafen. And Leafen serves The Market, and The Market serves me and you and everyone else. Now, what about you, Miss Pey? Who do you work for?'

Faith stared at her feet.

'Leafen, sir,' she said.

'*Eh-errrrrrrr*. Wrong again.'

He jabbed a finger into her left breast.

'*You* work for *me*. And you're in there to get coffee and pastries and do anything else I fucking *tell* you for as long as this takes. Understood?'

Faith croaked again.

'Understood?' said Daniel, louder.

'Yes, sir,' she said.

'Good. Then let's get this over with. And Steve, remember, stay sitting down.'

sixty-eight

morning at red dog's

'DEMETRI.'

DEMETRI opened his eyes and let the cold, grey morning light seep in. His face was wet with drizzle. Sam was looking down at him, with Marl peering over his shoulder.

'You OK?' said Sam. 'Can you stand?'

'Where am I?' He felt gravelly mud beneath him. He was in the clearing outside Red Dog's, tied to a post.

'Why am I tied up?'

The act of speaking made him retch. He heaved between his legs.

'Fuck, I feel like shit,' he said, spitting into the dirt. 'What was that stuff?'

Marl helped him to his feet.

'A hallucinogen,' he said. 'A very powerful one.'

'You went a little crazy,' said Sam. 'Running around all over the place, saying stuff. You caused quite a scene. Do you remember?'

'No.'

'Well, that's why they tied you up. Sorry. There was nothing we could do to stop them.'

Sam untied the ropes and threw them in the mud. Demetri rubbed his wrists.

'What about you?' he said. 'Didn't you see anything?'

Sam shrugged.

'Patterns, shapes, not much. Things sounded kind of weird for a bit. Those bastards in there messed around with us some. Tried to scare us, make us paranoid, that kind of thing.'

'They are not very nice people,' said Marl. He looked Demetri up and down. 'I think you went a little deeper, am I right?'

'A little more than patterns and shapes,' he said. He looked around.

'What time is it?' he said.

'A little after six a.m.,' said Sam. 'We don't have much time.'

'What are we going to do? Is Red Dog back?'

Sam smiled thinly.

'Yeah,' he said. 'I've made an arrangement.'

Demetri breathed a sigh of relief.

'That's good news,' he said. 'So we can go?'

Sam nodded.

Something caught Demetri's eye and he looked up. Low cloud clung to the Hordelands like a wet cloth. Behind it was the black wall of Leafen. Somehow it seemed less daunting than it had done the day before — less imposing, less solid. He looked closer. It seemed to be shifting. Hexagonal sections of it blinked out occasionally, causing the mist to pulse and puff.

'The Fabrik's failing,' he said.

'You have to get that thing back before sundown.'

'OK, so let's get – hold on, what do you mean "*you*"?'

A door banged in one of the shacks. There was the sound of boots on wooden steps.

'Good morning, good morning, good morning!' boomed a voice from the other side of the clearing. Red Dog, Doric and the guards were striding across the mud towards them. Grimble and Creech shuffled behind with their heads down. Two of the guards held the Hackdrone in its sack between them. Red Dog's grin matched his tie — a hideous strip of red against the slate, mud and mist.

'What did you do?' whispered Demetri to Sam.

'I told you,' said Sam. 'I made an arrangement.'

Red Dog held up his hands as he approached.

'Please,' he said. 'Accept my apologies for these *idiots* last night.'

He turned round to Doric and his guards.

'You went too far, guys,' he said, pointing a finger of warning at them each in turn. 'Too far, you hear me?'

Doric's smile made it look like something had died in his mouth.

'Idiots,' repeated Red Dog. 'I hope you're OK. Are you OK?'

He tapped Sam on the arm.

'Did you tell him, Sam?'

'I was just – ' began Sam.

'Your story checked out,' said Red Dog. 'I had one of my guys look at this and, yeah,' he sucked air in through his molars. 'Real deal. Pretty messed up.'

He looked behind him at the flickering black patchwork of Fabrik.

'Looks like the old homestead's going to blow at any time, my friend. You'd better take this thing back and disarm it. And I mean *quickly*. Boys?'

The two guards holding the sack brought it forward and dropped it at Demetri's feet. It smacked into the mud.

'We restrained it,' said Red Dog. 'Wrapped it in weights. It won't get far now.'

'Why do I get the feeling I'm missing something?' said Demetri. 'Sam, why did you say *you* and not *us*?'

'You didn't tell him yet, Sam?' said Red Dog. He tutted and scratched his chin with his pinkie. 'Well, shit, OK, it's like this: I have to get some profit out of this. It's that simple. And that thing's no good to me — I can't use it, I can't disarm it and I can't sell it.'

He kicked the sack.

'To tell you the truth, I've never really been into technology anyway. It's not my business. *People,* however – '

He nodded, tapping his nose.

'People. That's where the real money is. Daniel Leafen knows that too.'

'What do you mean?' said Demetri. 'Sam? What's going on?'

'It's all right, Demetri,' said Sam.

'Sam and, er – *Raul?*'

'Marl.'

Red Dog laughed and rolled his eyes.

'Sorry, Sam and *Marl* are staying with me. New staff.'

He nodded to the guards, who picked up the sack and carried it away.

'We'll load this into your car. Mr Grimble and Mr Creech will drive you back. It's through here.'

Demetri looked up at Grimble and Creech, both of them shaking their heads in apology.

'No,' he said, running after Red Dog. 'You can't do that.'

'I can and I did, and you tell Danny just that when you get back in that fucking shitpit, you hear me? Tell him I've poached two of his staff, and that he's welcome to poach them back for the right price.'

'Are you insane?' said Demetri. 'There's no way he'll allow it, he'll murder you.'

'I doubt it. He wouldn't want to risk an execution of a staff member this close to election time. Plus, he'd have to find me first. This is a big place, lots of holes to hide in. And the longer he waits, the longer we have to learn about Leafen's secrets.'

He stopped in his tracks and looked up, frowning.

'You know, I've never liked that wall. It's far too – *one way*, know what I mean?'

Demetri shook his head.

'That's your plan? You want to get through the Fabrik?'

'Sure. Tunnelling in was always too time consuming. I want my own door — a secret one, of course. And now I have an expert to tell me how.'

'Sam would never do that.'

Red Dog sighed.

'We have a number of incentive schemes that we think Mr Ops will find very attractive,' he said. He glanced back at one of the guards. The guard looked at Sam, brought his fist round and drove it into his kidneys. Sam's jaw dropped and he fell to his knees.

Marl knelt to help him, receiving a boot to his shoulder for his trouble. Sam caught Demetri's eye.

'Get that thing back,' he wheezed. 'Disarm it.'

'They'll kill you,' said Demetri.

'Just get it back.'

Red Dog tapped his wrist at Demetri.

'Time's running out, my friend. You'd best get going. You'll drive to the waste outlet. I still have friends there; one of them will meet you and show you how to get back in. It'll be messy, but hey, you don't have a choice.'

He turned to Doric.

'Take him out, go on, get going.'

Doric dragged Demetri yelling and kicking to the alleyway. Sam shouted from behind.

'Tell April it's OK! Tell April – '

There were more blows and shouts. Sam said nothing more.

The yellow Ford was there with the engine running. Doric threw Demetri into the back seat with the sack and Grimble and Creech got in the front. Demetri scrabbled to get out, but felt a powerful hand on his wrist.

'Look,' said Creech. His face was shaking. 'Look up there.'

He pointed out of the window at the black cliff. Demetri watched it spasm in the mist.

'Everything inside is going to be destroyed if you don't get that fuckin' thing back and disarm it. Your friends. Your family. Your brother. It's the only way, son. The only way, y'hear me?'

Demetri caught his breath and slunk back into the seat. Red Dog appeared at the driver's window.

'OK then, this is goodbye. Good luck.'

He banged the roof.

'And fellas? Don't ever come back to my fucking office again.'

'Let's go,' growled Creech.

Grimble floored the pedal and sped out onto the empty streets of the Hordelands. Demetri looked back through the rear window until Red Dog and his red mouth and red tie and the shacks and roofs of his offices were all just grey shapes in the mist.

sixty-nine

po

THE BOARD room table was lit by a single spot. Two seats faced each other, one occupied by Commander Po, his double-breasted bulk spilling between the holes in the chair's arms. His face was wide and mottled with old acne craters, his mouth like the scowl of some wretched deep-sea creature. It contracted when he saw Steve. His eyes — just thin holes fingered in dough — did the same.

Three other Soorish dignitaries sat in shadow against the back wall. Daniel ushered Steve to the empty seat opposite Po. Then he and Priscilla took the two behind him, while Faith stood by the door. Steve placed his palms on his knees, looking down at the table.

A breath rattled in and out of Po's nose.

'My name is Commander Po,' he rumbled.

There was silence. Steve wondered what to do. Daniel had told him not to speak until after the terms had been reiterated. He looked over his shoulder for help. Daniel frowned and nodded.

'My name is Steve Manager,' he said. 'Red/Blue, First Grade Executive class Ma – '

Po fidgeted in his chair and made an oily noise. With some effort, he leant forwards and laid a pudgy hand on some papers, which he pulled towards him.

'*These* are the terms of the final contract,' he said, stopping Steve short. 'Which I shall now read.'

He took some glasses from his top pocket and put them on, wiggling them into a crevice of fat at the bridge of his nose. Then he cleared his throat of several large obstructions and began to read.

seventy

shit pipe

CREECH DROVE them out onto the plain and sped south past the Hordelands. They followed the western wall of Leafen without talking, the Ford's screaming engine the only sound. Demetri lay in the back seat with his head against the window, watching the dark, flickering Fabrik spin by. Eventually they reached the southern wall where the garbage mountain stood. The clean, straight lines of the Fabrik gave way to crags and steaming hills of waste that had piled up over years, decades and centuries. As they drew near they saw lines of people stretching from the foot of the mountain into the plains where the banished Hordes camped — scavengers and shit miners that churned through the dump, slowly processing it like earthworms.

'I don't think we have much time,' said Grimble.

Demetri looked up. What looked like a hundred thunderstorms were raging against the Fabrik. The surface shuddered. Deep, glacial cracks boomed all around them, echoing from the waste mountain like giant whiplashes and causing landslides of ancient junk from the summit.

'Red Dog told us to stop at one of the main outlet pipes,' said Creech. 'It's up ahead.'

As they followed the southern wall, the base of the mountain came in to meet them until soon they were driving through a thinning valley — the cliff of Leafen on their left and the rising, brown foothills of waste to their right. In the distance, connecting the two, was a thick pipe about two hundred metres in diameter, raised off the ground by tall stilts so that the whole thing made a gigantic stone bridge. As they neared it, Demetri saw other similar pipes running from Leafen and into the mountain. The wall seemed to have stopped flickering.

'The Fabrik's not flickering any more,' said Demetri, hopefully. 'Do you think somebody's fixed it?'

Creech turned and frowned at him.

'You don't know much about your own home, do you, Demetri?' said Grimble. 'This part's not Fabrik, it's stone. It's the only section of Leafen that's actually made of anything tangible. There are about five hundred outlet pipes that run along here and feed that heap there. Some of them are for garbage pipes, some are for sewage and others are incineration pipes for chemical waste. Streams of excrement, rubbish and toxic fire pour out of them every hour. All of those pipes are attached to that cliff of steel and concrete. The Fabrik joins on somewhere above the pipes.'

'I didn't know,' said Demetri.

'Why would you?' said Creech. 'It's just where your shit goes, after all.'

As the valley thinned, they found themselves driving past the line of miners. The line became a crowd congregating near one of the pipes. Creech slowed down.

'That's one of the entry points,' he said.

A toothless woman who could have been seventeen or seventy bent down as they passed, peering through the windscreen, holding Demetri's gaze suspiciously.

'How much further?' said Demetri.

'We're here,' said Grimble. 'Red Dog said to wait by the observation window.'

They stopped beneath a long window that was set high in the wall. There was steam and water everywhere. Occasionally the pipe above them would rumble, shaking the car's windows.

'What now?' said Demetri.

'We wait,' said Creech.

Demetri looked out at the window. Behind the glass, small figures moved about. He saw one of them — a man in a hard hat — stop as he spotted them. He put down the clipboard he had been carrying, checked around and disappeared. A few minutes later they saw a door open at the base of the wall. A man appeared, skulking.

'There,' said Demetri.

The man beckoned to them, then disappeared behind the door.

'That's him,' said Creech. 'Quickly, get out. Take the sack.'

'Aren't you coming?'

'No,' said Grimble. 'This is where we say goodbye, I'm afraid. Good luck.'

'Where are you going?'

'Figured we'd go back to the Hordes and look out for Sam. Now go.'

Demetri got out and ran with the sack tucked under his arm. The man yanked him through the door. He just about had time to look behind and see the yellow Ford driving back the way it had come before the door shut and he was alone inside a dark stairwell.

'You're Demetri, right?' said the man. He was in his mid-forties, plum-faced and worried.

'Yes,' said Demetri. 'Who are you?'

'You don't need to know,' he said. He looked down at the sack under Demetri's arm. 'And I sure as hell don't need to know what that is.'

'It's OK, this is what's been causing – '

'Like I said, I don't need to know.'

'Look, you just get word to The Leaf. I have the thing that's been – '

The man laughed.

'Get word to The Leaf? And let them know I've let you in through this door? Are you fucking high? You think they wouldn't investigate me?'

'But I'm supposed to be here. I'm not an illegal immigrant.'

The man lunged for Demetri and grabbed his collar.

'*Immigrant*? Listen to me, you little shit, don't ever say that word near me again, you hear me?'

Demetri stared back in horror, struggling with his grip on the sack. The man shook him.

'You hear me?' he shouted.

Demetri nodded.

'Yes, yes, I hear you.'

'Good,' said the man, releasing his hold on Demetri. 'Now I don't have time for this, so I'm going to make this very simple. You go through those doors there and you'll be in a ventilation duct for one of the feed pipes. You hide there until you hear a siren. It's loud — fucking loud — so keep your ears covered. When the siren goes off, the vents will open and a whole load of air will come out of them. It stinks, so hold your nose.'

'How?'

'What?'

'How will I hold my nose if I've already got my ears covered?'

The man stared at Demetri and then grabbed him again, pushing him up against the wall.

'You think you're funny, you little fucker, huh?'

'No, no, I just, I don't – is it dangerous? The air?'

The man screwed up his face.

'No, it isn't dangerous, it just stinks of shit. Now listen, the vents are big enough to crawl through, so when the air's stopped, you'll have about thirty seconds to get in before they close again.'

'What then?' said Demetri.

'Then you're in one of the main pipes that lead up through the wall. You follow it up. It's steep but not vertical. You should be inside in about two miles.'

'Two miles?'

'Yeah, two miles, you got a problem with that, dipshit?'

'No,' said Demetri, cowering. 'No problem.'

'At the top, there should be an inspection door you can get out. You can find your way out from there, and after that you're on your own.'

'OK,' said Demetri.

'So go,' said the man. As an afterthought, he pulled Demetri's collar close again. 'And if anyone finds out about who let you in – '

'I swear. Nobody will find out. Thank you.'

The man shook Demetri off and looked around.

'You'll need this,' he said, thrusting a flashlight into Demetri's hands.

'Now get going!' he hissed, and strode back the way he'd come, leaving Demetri alone in the black-walled corridor. The low strip lights flickered, jarring the shadows of the pipes that ran along the ceiling and walls. He stood still for a moment and tried to quieten his breath. He heard throbbing drones and coarse, spluttering roars all around, suddenly becoming aware that he was deep within the plumbing — the *bowels* — of his home.

He pushed through two sets of doors and found himself in a small room with no ceiling. The space above him seemed to extend infinitely upwards into gathering dark. It was freezing cold and smelled foul. The walls were wet with condensation and a drain ran around the outside of the cement floor. On one wall was a control panel next to five large, closed vents. It was the only source of light — many rows of bright, white bulbs with a single green one flashing near the top. Behind the wall was the distant sound of a large body of fluid moving quickly from top to bottom, right to left. Demetri eyed the flashing light on the panel and slid down into the corner of the wall.

He had never been to places like this and he had never thought about them. He had known they had existed, of course; the size of Leafen, the number of people it employed, the number of cups of coffee, plates of food, cars washed, plastic packaging discarded — all of that added up to enormous mounds of waste, and it had to go somewhere. He knew all this. It was as if there was a room somewhere in his mind that contained all of this information, and all he had to do was visit it to make the connection. But he never had, and he didn't need to question why; we never visit cold, uncomfortable rooms in a house full of warm ones.

He watched the green light blinking. The green light, he knew, had been blinking for a long time, possibly all of his life and for many other lives before him. Millions of people had lived and died in the space above him but knew nothing of it. Suddenly it stopped. The roar behind the wall abated and in its place came a series of deep, loud clunks. Then a red light appeared. Demetri instinctively squashed his fingers into his ears and a siren sounded — not a whoop but a dirty, deep, electronic growl. The vents suddenly shot open and five blasts of hot, wet air erupted from them. A foul stench filled the room and Demetri pushed his face into his jacket. For what seemed like minutes the gas streamed out, whistling around and leaving rank trails of moisture on his skin before shooting up the tall chimney. Eventually it stopped, leaving a fresh film of putrid condensation upon the walls. The siren stopped. Demetri looked up at the vents, still open and dripping. The cavities behind them were dank and black, leading down into more unknown spaces. *Thirty seconds*, the man had said. He considered waiting for the next siren, but the thought of enduring another blast was too much. He grabbed the sack and bolted for the nearest vent.

The space was small but he fitted neatly inside and found himself sliding fast down a chute against slick, warm walls. Before he had a chance to yell or kick, he had fallen out and dropped onto a stone floor a few feet below. Winded, he coughed and scrabbled to his feet. He was in almost perfect darkness; the only light seeped through the vents from the room behind. That too soon faded as the vents closed. Demetri switched on the flashlight.

He was in a tunnel as the man had described, high on a series of long, shallow steps leading to his right. A flimsy railing ran along its edge, behind which was a sheer drop into a damp concrete valley. The smell was unbearable. Everything that did not belong inside a nose reeked from here; death, shit and decay — all that human life left in its wake. The concrete valley was deep and wide, rising in a half pipe towards another set of steps about a hundred metres away. Demetri switched off the flashlight. Darkness below, darkness above. The ancient ceiling dripped a million oily drips.

He looked up and, in the distance, he saw a very faint dot of yellow light. *Two miles*, the man had said. Demetri switched the flashlight back on, tucked the sack tightly beneath his arm and began to climb.

He had heard the stories of course, wrapped up in his boyhood bed with the covers pulled up. Tales of the creatures that lived beneath – *The Underfolk*. They were myths and legends; ghost stories to make children eat their dinner or be quiet. It seemed strange that he had never associated these things — that he knew must not exist — with these places — that he knew must exist. It was as if myth and unpalatable truth shared the same space in his head — a space he dared not look directly into, or simply pretended not to notice.

But he was here now in that space, and the fear that those myths had been intended to instil in him was here too. He began to hear whispers. He thought he saw eyes glinting in dark recesses. He ignored them; consigned them to his imagination. He kept climbing and tried to focus on the light that kept sliding from his vision like a dim and distant star.

He slipped, lost his footing and made a grab for the side rail. The sack fell from his grip and he lunged for it as it tumbled over the edge. He slipped again, losing the flashlight and landing with his head over the side. There he lay in the dark, listening to the Hackdrone roll to the bottom of the concrete valley in a series of loud clatters, clanks and splashes. The flashlight had landed further up, its beam spread out over grime and countless wet, dark mounds.

Demetri breathed hard and fast as his fingernails nibbled the brittle stone. He waited for something to happen — an explosion, a deep boom from above, a million screams in the distance. But there was nothing. The Hackdrone hit something hard and came to a stop. He pulled himself up and stared down at the vast mess, ignoring the whispers he continued to hear and the unmistakeable tinkling of a child's laugh high above.

A debate hurried through his head.

You have to retrieve it

It's too far

There's no other choice

Perhaps the Hackdrone is destroyed?

You know it's not

Perhaps the sewage will break it?

If it breaks, we all die

But perhaps the weight will crush it, the signal will –

Only intense heat, only fire

You will be killed

You have to retrieve it

You are not cut out for this

Be a MAN, damn it

Demetri took a deep breath, immediately wishing that he hadn't and gagging on the foul air. He pulled off his tie and wrapped it around his mouth and nose. Whispers again. A voice, two now, closer. A double glint of eyeball. From far away came a mechanical clunk and hiss. He focused on the flashlight, leant back and then swung himself through the bars of the guardrail.

The surface of the pipe was slippier than he had expected. Rather than bumping and rolling down rough concrete, he slid down at high speed on slick, putrid weed — a compressed mat of effluence two centuries thick. He lifted his arms and legs, trying to buttock-surf the slurry towards the flashlight. The air became colder the deeper he went, the smell more raw and ancient, yet somehow more delicate. *Our shit ages like cheese*, he thought, as he reached out for the flashlight. He watched it spin by as he overshot it, then slowed and spun on his back, landing in a hillock of something fibrous and sticky. He bit down on his tie, tasting the salt of his sweat in its silk. Then he pushed himself to his feet. His hands were covered in unthinkable gunk, and he shook them as he staggered through the swamp and found his flashlight.

There were more clunks and hisses from further up the tunnel. He swore he heard gasps and tiny hands clapping. Real sounds and imagined sounds — truth and myth inhabiting the same space.

He turned the light on the tunnel beneath him, trying not to linger too long on anything recognisable. He spotted the Hackdrone by a metal frame hanging with vegetation and made for it, avoiding lumps, taking careful steps, each one requiring effort to pull his boots from the bog's deep suction. As he reached the sack, a loud noise sounded overhead.

CLLLLUNK – HISSSSSSSSS

He felt air rush past his head and swung the beam upwards. There was a hole in the roof where a gigantic hatch had opened. Further up the tunnel were similar open hatches, and another one further down.

There were more gasps and titters from the walls. Human voices in subdued alarm like a crowd watching an execution acted out on stage — terrible yet safe, not real, not happening.

The hatches could only mean one thing and the sound of roaring fluid confirmed it. He made for the side. The bog was impossible to run through. He trained his flashlight on the wall and found a thin ladder. It wasn't far. Only a few more steps –

The sound of sewage suddenly grew, like a billion toilets all flushing at once. Demetri found the ladder and tucked his flashlight in his jacket. With his one free hand, he hoisted himself out of the muck and began to climb. The tired rungs creaked under the weight of their first heels in decades, and the bolts that fastened them to the side scraped in and out of the concrete.

Demetri climbed, the ladder shook, and the noise of wastewater grew. Voices and whispers sharpened, then stopped with the sounds of doors slamming.

The roaring stopped and Demetri clung to the ladder in the fierce silence that followed. Drips dripped. Belches and gurgles belched and gurgled above. Then, finally, a deep, deafening siren blared and Demetri wrapped his hands around the rungs, his knees weakening as the pipe filled with a storm of shit.

seventy-one

the crack in the wood

' – TECHNOLOGY, ALL components and subcomponents therein –'

Steve listened to the words oozing from Po's mouth. He kept his eyes on the desk corner, focusing on a single point.

' – all designs, prototypes – '

There was an imperfection in the lacquer that had found its way down to the grain. It was a single tiny chip, perhaps from a dropped pen or a scratch from jewellery. The grain had opened, creating a small dark line in the otherwise flawless wood.

' – test plans and executions both carried out and otherwise – '

The line was the beginning of a journey across the broad table. Steve imagined the path it would take, given enough time.

' – shall be the sole property of Soor – '

A crooked score carving a deep canyon in the wood.

' – from now until the end of time – '

The final movement, many years from now, one more millimetre and the entire table would break.

' – to use as The United Corporations of Soor sees fit, without recourse to Leafen, Market advice notwithstanding – '

Two wedges of useless wood crashing to the floor. All from a single cut that went unnoticed.

His thoughts drifted to a summer long ago.

'Mr Manager,' snapped Po.

'Yes,' said Steve, avoiding the man's glare.

'I asked if you agreed to these terms,' said Po. From the corner of his eye, Steve saw Po brandishing the papers at him.

'I do,' he said. 'I do agree.'

'Good,' said Po. The papers hit the table with a heavy thud. 'Now. You may make your apology.'

seventy-two

farly high

DEMETRI AWOKE, gagging on the smell of his own shoulder. As he retched, he was aware that the ground upon which he was vomiting was dry and dusty and moving with orange shadows. He felt warmth on his face and hands. He spat a few times into the mess, trying to remember.

He remembered the impact. He remembered gripping the sack. He remembered vomiting in the blast, being swept from the ladder, being submerged in a foul tide, something cutting into his cheek so deeply that he felt the warmth of his own blood in the cold water, something banging into his ribcage. But that was it. There was nothing else.

He heard the sound of voices again, but this time they were near and hushed, without echo. He was wrapped in a blanket. Slowly, he raised his head.

He was lying by a small fire in the middle of a large room. Its light just about reached the walls, which were rough like a cave's. Within them, as far up as the high ceiling, were hand-carved nooks filled with books and objects.

Surrounding him and the fire was a circle of strange, thin people with pale faces and deep-set, twinkling eyes. They looked as if they had been dressed in a storm. Three young girls wore large T-shirts tied around their midriffs with skull-buckled belts. The woman with them — their mother, Demetri supposed — pulled them close as he looked at them. Her own get-up was a suit jacket and three pairs of jeans in various states of repair stuffed into thick hiking socks. A company of well-built, bare-chested men skulked at the back wearing pleated women's skirts, stained and torn, and neckties knotted around their foreheads.

They carried sharp sticks, one of which Demetri thought might once have been an umbrella. Another one looked like a desk leg. They rolled their shoulders and eyed Demetri warily.

An old man stepped forward wearing a black cocktail dress and a long cardigan with knee-high leather boots. Upon his head was a bowler hat and around his neck hung countless bejewelled necklaces. He carried a thin stick that looked as if it had once belonged to a fence, and upon which he leant, smiling.

'Whither comest thou?' he enquired.

Demetri blinked.

'Pardon me?' he said.

A shuddering gasp of excitement ran around the circle. The people looked between themselves, holding on to each other's arms for support.

The old man stepped forwards. He spoke more slowly.

'Whither – comest – thou – ?' he repeated, holding one hand forward, trying to explain. His eyelids fluttered and he licked his dry lips.

'Thou,' he said, pointing at Demetri. 'Comest – ' He made a walking movement with his fingers. Then he held up both arms in a shrug, eyes wide. 'Whither?'

The crowd murmured, nodding.

'Whither – whither – yah – whither – yah – whither – '

Demetri sat up.

'Where did I come from?' he said.

The old man staggered back in surprise and the crowd erupted with hoots and giggles. The man grinned with delight.

'Affirmatory!' he said. 'Highly affirmatory!'

Demetri got to his feet and the crowd hushed. The old man looked worried and glanced at the men with sticks, who stepped forward.

'It's OK,' said Demetri, holding out his hands. 'It's OK, I'm not dangerous.'

'Ooo Kayyeee – Ooo Kayyeee – Ooo Kayyeee – ' whispered the crowd, rolling their lips in exaggerated 'O's and pulling them

back on the 'K's. The old man signalled for the men – his guards – to fall back.

'Where am I?' said Demetri.

The old man smiled and raised his arms.

'In ye corporation, obviciferously!' he said. He took another hesitant step towards Demetri and offered him a shit-crusted hand. He inclined his head. 'CEO Farly High, at thine service station.'

Demetri shook the hand, which was, at least, dry. The old man's expression curled into sympathy.

'Thou art – *banished*?' he said.

'Banished? No. I'm from – ' began Demetri. He pointed up. 'From up there.'

The crowd gasped and cooed.

'Head Office?' exclaimed the old man, his face springing with surprise.

The fire spat and crackled as the crowd subdued.

'Did you find me?' said Demetri. The old man narrowed his eyes.

'You – ' said Demetri. 'Found – me?'

Still nothing. The old man frowned. Demetri held his nose and mimed drowning, then pointed at the old man, pretending to haul out a body from water. The old man's eyes lit up as he got it.

'Ha! Affirmatory! Altogether-now comest upon thou within the deep dip, pullest thou high, pullest thou high, yah, yah.'

The old man suddenly frowned in admonishment.

'Highly dangersome, the deep dip. Highly dangersome for altogether-now.'

He sniffed and looked Demetri up and down. Demetri became faintly aware of the stench that was still in the room, coming from the old man, his clothes, his skin, the people around him, the walls, even the flames. He didn't want to think about what might be burning.

'Whatfor ist thou hither?' he said gently. 'Within the deep

dip? Within the long dark?'

'Whatfor? *Why*, you mean? In the tunnel? I – '

He suddenly felt a rush of dizziness as he remembered the Hackdrone. He had no idea how long he had been unconscious – perhaps he was already too late. He searched the ground. The crowd, sensing his panic, backed away.

'My bag,' he said. 'I had a bag. I need it.'

He stepped towards the old man, who recoiled. The guards stepped forward again, this time pushing him back. The largest pointed his stick, which was indeed an umbrella, into Demetri's face. Demetri tried to explain. He searched for shapes to make with his hands, making an orb with his arms and curling his fist around an invisible sack.

'Drone,' he said. 'Sphere – circle – globe – '

One of the words seemed to catch and the umbrella retracted from his face.

'*Gloobe*,' said the old man, nodding slowly and stepping forward. He held out his long, skinny arm, adorned from wrist to armpit with gaudy bracelets and charms, and gestured for Demetri to follow him around the circle. On the other side of the fire lay the sack. It was still closed tightly and caked in excrement. He saw the beacon light pulse beneath the canvas. It was still active.

The old man looked at Demetri.

'Thoust?' he said.

'Yes,' said Demetri. 'Erm – affirmatory.'

The old man nodded.

'Highly troublesome?' he said.

'Yes, I mean, affirmatory, highly, highly troublesome. What time is it?'

'Timest?'

'What – er – ' Demetri searched the old man's arms. He saw a slim, gold lady's timepiece fastened near his elbow. 'Time,' he said, pointing at the watch.

The old man followed Demetri's finger.

'Ah!' he cried, tapping the watch face. 'Ye spinalong?'

'Yes,' said Demetri. 'The spinalong. Whats the spinalong?'

The old man raised his arm proudly and inspected the watch.

'Three sticks and a swan!'

'What?' said Demetri. He walked towards the old man. The guards moved menacingly, but the old man waved them off. Demetri peered at the watch. It said 11:00. His shoulders sagged. He had no idea if that was the right time, or even what day it was. The only thing that suggested he wasn't too late yet was the fact that they were still there. But he had no idea where *there* was anyway. For all he knew the Fabrik may already have collapsed and they might have been so deep within the waste system that it made no difference. But he had to assume that he still had time, even if it was only minutes.

'It must be destroyed,' he said.

'Bestroodled?' said the old man.

'*De*stroyed,' said Demetri. He crushed his fist into his palm. 'Burned. With fire.'

'Aha, fire?' said the old man. His eyes widened and he pointed at the crackling logs. 'Highly burnsome, tsssss. Thou putest thine troublesome gloobe within altogether-nowst burnsome fire.'

The crowd made ahhing sounds and held their hands together as the old man bent down and picked up the sack. He made to hurl it on the fire. Demetri leapt forwards to stop him, meeting a fierce cross made by an umbrella and a desk leg.

'No! Stop!' he said.

The old man looked surprised.

'Negatory?' he said, letting the orb swing backwards in its fetid sack.

Demetri gulped and nodded, holding his fingers to the umbrella's delicate, skinless frame.

'Yes, negatory,' he said. 'That would be highly, highly troublesome.'

The old man dropped the sack with a despondent look.

'Flummoxed altogether-now,' he said, scratching his chin. 'Miscomprehensible indeed.'

Demetri searched for words, striking them like flint.

'Er, er, fire? Er – more hot, more tssss, more – more – '

'More burnsome?' said the old man.

'Yes!' said Demetri. 'More burnsome! Highly burnsome. The highest burnsome possible!'

The old man pulled his face into his neck, aghast. The crowd gasped.

'Highest burnsome?' he said. 'Highest?'

'Yes, I mean, affirmatory,' said Demetri. 'Affirmatory.'

The old man placed the sack upon the ground and took a deep, solemn breath. He signalled for the guards to remove their sticks and leant on his own, deep in thought.

'Highest burnsome,' he said, tapping his stick in the dust. 'Highest burnsome is – '

He stood up and held a hand to his heart.

'Holisome,' he said. He walked over to the fire. 'All burnsome burns within the highest burnsome. Highly holisome. When altogether-nows burns turn lowly, or wetsome with – *shit* – '

He smiled tenderly at the word *shit.*

'Thence doth the Burn Gatherers march towards the highest burnsome long-dark. To enflame their brollies with *burn.*'

He released a deep and meaningful sigh, then sniffed and turned to Demetri.

'Whatfor?' he said.

'Whatfor?' repeated Demetri.

'Affirmatory. Whatfor burnest thou gloobe?'

'There's no time,' said Demetri. 'I mean, not enough spinalong.'

The old man frowned, then stood to his full height and tapped his stick twice on the ground.

'Impartest thine whatfors and whenceforths towards altogether-now,' he said. 'Next, altogether-now shall takest thou and thine gloobe towards the highest burnsome.'

Demetri's shoulders fell.
'I tell you my story, you help me,' he said.
The old man nodded.
Demetri held out his hand.
'Can I borrow your stick?' he said.

seventy-three

sorry

I'M SORRY.

The words had echoed in Steve's sixteen-year-old mind as he ran to the station, away from the lake, away from the party, away from Holly.

He thought he should stop, but he didn't. He ran.

I'm sorry.

'I apologise, Commander Po. I apologise for my behaviour during our meeting on Friday. It should have been one of great warmth and joy for our two corporations. One of hope, one of united prosperity.'

Steve kept his eyes firmly on the crack in the table as he spoke. On the fringes of his vision, he saw Po lean back in his chair, belly rising like a surfacing whale. He made a rasping sound of satisfaction.

'You,' said Po loudly, whipping a finger in the air – a gesture aimed somewhere behind Steve's head – and then tapping it on the finger. 'Drink.'

Steve paused.

'Continue,' said Po.

'Instead, I let my – fears and – lack of fortitude distract me from my duty to my corporation and – to the shared union that would be of such benefit to the people of Leafen and Soor.'

Faith walked past him towards the drinks cabinet. As she passed, Po made a clumsy lunge for her. She swerved. His swipe brushed her hip and he laughed, settling back in his chair. Steve stopped talking and looked up at Faith. She was facing away from him, standing still. She adjusted her skirt and then continued on her way to the drinks cabinet, where she began pouring a large measure from the decanter of Scotch.

'Keep talking,' warned Po.

Steve obeyed.

'I did not act in a way that befitted my position. I did not act honourably. I let down my corporation, my Colours and my family – '

I'm sorry.

'I have no excuse to offer you, Commander Po. Perhaps I was tired, or perhaps the stress of the previous months' activity had gotten the better of me. But I do assure you – '

Faith returned to the desk and set down Po's drink. He turned as she did so and took a great, long, lecherous sniff of the air around her, which he held in his lungs and then released in a sigh. He picked up the glass and drank from it. Faith turned to go, but he lunged for her again, this time making contact and pulling her back. He clamped his paw firmly around her hips.

Faith said nothing.

Po licked his lips.

'Keep. Talking.'

'I can assure you, however – ' said Steve. He watched Po's hand stroking Faith's hip. He remembered his mother's words as she looked away, bored, on the steps.

Children can be cruel.

Holly's face; wordless, pleading, alone.

I should have said stop.

Po's thick sausage-like fingers kneading Faith's flesh.

Keep talking.

It's vital that you obey the protocol. You must obey the protocol. You must obey.

Po's hand moved around and squeezed Faith's buttocks. His mouth quivered.

'I can assure you – I must assure you, however – '

So long as you obey what's in here.

Faith tipped forwards under Po's pressure, grabbing the desk. His hand slithered up her skirt. His fingers pushed out the fabric as they groped for their prize. His smile became a twisted, wet maw. She closed her eyes and swallowed.

'I assure you – '

I should have said stop.

'I can – '

– should have said –

'Stop.'

The word rang loud and clear, leaving a terrible wake of silence. Steve stood up and met Po's eyes, now two furious pinholes.

'Stop, right now. Stop,' said Steve.

Behind him, Daniel's chair scraped on the floor.

'Manager,' he barked. 'What the fuck are you doing?'

The same question was in Faith's eyes.

Po's face shook. He stood up and slammed both hands down on the table like a gorilla facing an intruder. Then he took his left hand and thrust it against Faith's backside once again. She yelped and fell forward.

'Withdraw that last remark!' rasped Po, sweat dripping from his cheeks.

'No,' said Steve. 'Take your hand off her.'

'Manager!' Daniel was striding towards him now.

Po began to smile.

'Withdraw it or *this* – ' he tightened his grip on Faith's rear end, then pointed to the darkness outside. 'And *this* gets much worse.'

Steve felt Daniel's hand on his shoulder, but he shrugged him off.

'Withdraw it,' hissed Po.

seventy-four

till the beaten swan

AFTER WHAT seemed like an hour, Demetri had somehow managed to scrawl his story into the dirt using the old man's stick. After every finished picture, he stamped the stick into the ground and said some words he thought might help to explain what he meant. At the end, he stood back and looked around the circle. He had no clue if they understood him or not, but they seemed enthralled. He realised that they hadn't made a sound for some time and the children had all gathered together, sitting at his feet, enrapt.

'Whatfor,' he said at last, handing back the stick to the old man.

'Highly adventuresome,' said the old man with awe. He patted Demetri on the back and surveyed the pictures like a man admiring a new set of tiles. 'Highly, highly adventuresome.'

'Please,' said Demetri. 'The spinalong. I have to destroy the Hackdrone. The gloobe.'

The old man looked at Demetri. His face darkened and he gripped his shoulder tight. He took a solemn breath.

'For ye corporation,' he said. 'Affirmatory.'

He slapped Demetri's shoulder and then clapped his hands together, releasing a cloud of dried excrement into the air.

He looked to the back of the quiet crowd. 'Burn Gatherers?' he called.

A young woman and two serious-looking men holding blackened sticks stepped forwards. Their faces were painted with elaborate brown patterns. Dots and crosses spiralled around their brows. The old man turned back to Demetri.

'Burn Gatherers gather altogether-nowst burn,' he said. 'This be Bluesky. Pleased ye be to meet her.'

The young woman stepped forward and met him with proud eyes. She had a round, piggish face and matted hair.

'And these be ye subordinates of Bluesky. Pleased ye be to meet Ballpark and Incentivise.'

CEO Farly High nodded confidently.

'Brave folk gather ye burn from within ye highest burn, the holisome burn, through other long darks.

Other long darks – thought Demetri. Other tunnels. It was starting to make sense.

'Chemical waste,' said Demetri, remembering what Grimble had told him about the incineration pipes. 'You get your heat and fire from the chemical waste pipe – '

'Thou shallt runalong with ye Burn Gatherers,' said the old man. He threw up his hands to the crowd. 'They leadest thou there to hurl thine gloobe within ye highest burn.'

The crowd applauded with more oohs and aahs.

Chemical waste had to be burned at super high temperatures, perhaps enough to prevent the Hackdrone from sending its kill signal. *It might work,* thought Demetri, but even if it didn't, there was no other choice. Unless he felt like carrying it all the way back to the surface, and then who knew how many miles to The Leaf in an attempt to disarm it, it had to be this way.

Farly High checked his dainty golden watch.

'Two sticks and a frown,' he said. Demetri saw the hands point at 11 and 7 — 11:35. 'Thou hast until ye beaten swan.'

The old man tapped the top of his watch twice. Twelve o'clock.

'Next, ye highest burn.'

'And then,' said Demetri. 'I mean, next? How do I get back – home?' He pointed up.

Farly High nodded in understanding.

'The highest burn ceases, next thou takest ye long dark up, up, up. It is moderately dangersome, but lowly far.'

The old man put both hands on Demetri's shoulders and

looked him square in the eyes.

'Run along now,' said the old man. 'Run along, expedite, fast-track now. And savest thine kin. Save ye corporation.'

He picked up the sack and handed it to Demetri, directing him to a small door in the corner of the room, where the Burn Gatherers had assembled, torches lit from the fire.

'Goodbye,' said Demetri. 'And thank you.'

'Kindest regards,' said Farly High.

Demetri followed the Burn Gatherers out into a narrow, low tunnel. It was crude and rough, dug by hands, not cut by the meticulous buzz of the Sweep Mites. The shadows of the Burn Gatherers' torches lit the uneven walls and knocked dust from the ceiling into Demetri's face.

They jogged for a few minutes, then reached another door that led into a pipe similar to the one into which he had fallen. The two men in front — Ballpark and Incentivise — leapt expertly down onto a ladder. The girl, Bluesky, turned to him.

'Quicksome cross ye long dark,' she said urgently. She tapped her wrist. 'Spinalong.'

He followed her down the ladder and she lit the way across the basin to the other side, climbing to the top just as he heard the sound of hatches opening further up. Through the door they went and down another hand-dug tunnel, this one shorter, till they reached another pipe, which they crossed the same as before. They seemed to be following a schedule of flushes that the Burn Gatherers knew instinctively. At times they ran faster than others in order to cross the next pipe before it filled. Demetri counted five crossings before they neared the end of a sixth tunnel. They stopped at the door, breathing hard. The door was larger than the others and carved into the wall around it were thousands upon thousands of numbers, letters and drawings. Bluesky raised her torch for Demetri to see.

'The highest burn,' she said, her voice wavering. 'Holisome place.'

Incentivise checked his watch and grabbed Bluesky's arm.

'Spinalong!' he shouted. 'Spinalong spinalong!'

Bluesky checked her own watch and cried out in alarm. Demetri heard a low clunk and a roar coming from through the door.

'What's that?' he said.

'The highest burn is now!' she said. 'Hurl thine gloobe!'

She ran for the door and pulled back the locks.

'Now then!' she shouted as she heaved the door open. Demetri stood at the entrance and watched as burners in the tunnel wall lit with blue flame. A blast of hot air hit him and the two other Burn Gatherers leapt back against the side wall.

'Hurl!' cried Bluesky. 'Hurl thine gloobe for ye corporation!'

Demetri swung the sack through the door. It flew like a ball in a sock, but not high enough to clear the guardrail, and it clanged instead upon the steps. There was a roar from far up the tunnel. Fierce flames shot from the burners and a terrific heat filled the cavern. Bluesky began to close the door.

'It needs to be in the path of the fire!' said Demetri, beneath the roar of the approaching waste.

'No spinalong!' said Bluesky. She strained as she pushed the door. Incentivise jumped forwards to help her. 'Too dangersome!'

Demetri could still see the sack hanging empty and useless on the guard rail. It was already smouldering. The drone, meanwhile, had rolled back against the wall, away from the flames. Soon it would heat up enough to sense destruction, but not enough to destroy it quickly. The kill signal would be emitted.

The door was almost shut. Demetri stood up and ran towards it, but as he reached it two things hit him. The first was a blast of hot air in his face, the second was a hand on his shoulder.

The third Burn Gatherer, Ballpark, shot past him.

'Ballpark!' shouted Bluesky as he slipped through. 'Nay!'

Demetri fell back into the safety of the cavern. Through the gap in the door, he saw Ballpark launch his bare foot against the drone. It sailed through the guardrail and into the furnace. Ballpark staggered back, screaming with his hands to his face.

'Ballpark!' shouted Bluesky again. 'Bring him within!'

Bluesky and Incentivise dragged their friend inside the cavern and finally shut the door against the heat. Ballpark was screaming, smoke rising from his hair, the skin of his face red and raw.

They leant over him, cradling his head and mumbling words of comfort.

Bravesome Ballpark, bravesome gatherer, holisome gatherer –

Ballpark, still clutching his scorched face, began to calm at the sound of their voices. His breaths were dry and fast.

'You did it,' muttered Demetri. The side of his own face began to pulse and sting. 'You, you – he – '

Bluesky turned around. She was crying, tears smearing the brown patterns on her cheeks. She managed a smile.

'All done,' she said. 'All done now.'

She stood and faced him, legs apart like a warrior. A dull roar rattled the door as the waste pipe reached full power.

'For ye corporation,' she said. She puffed out her chest in pride. 'For Head Office.'

seventy-five

you're fired

THE BOARD room went dark. There was a second of silence, a click and then a roar and a whir. The lights came back on — all of them, in and out of the board room. The buildings beneath flickered with light and spread out across the plain like a tide of phosphorescent plankton hit by the moon. Steve could swear he heard human voices, a wave of relief from the streets far, far beneath them.

'What?' said Po. He staggered back from the desk. 'What?'

The three men behind him, now clearly lit, looked at each other in disbelief. Po turned and jabbered at them in Soorish.

'What happened?' said Steve, turning to Daniel. Daniel stared back in disgusted rage. He pulled his radio out.

'Sumar,' he hissed. 'Is this your doing?'

Sumar's voice came on the radio, flustered and confused.

'Sir, I – I don't – '

Priscilla stood, baring her teeth in a smile.

'They did it,' she said. She caught Daniel's eye. 'My team. They must have found it.'

Daniel straightened his tie and squared up to Steve. His eyes were wide and furious. Across the desk, the four Soorish diplomats continued their argument, throwing up their hands, eyes bulging. Sharp consonants and twisted vowels of their mother tongue flew between them like shrapnel from exploding words. Then, suddenly, they stopped, as if some brutal conclusion had been reached. Po turned very slowly in Daniel's direction.

'Gentlemen,' said Daniel. 'Please, sit down. As you can see, our power has been restored. I'd very much like to conclude the deal right now, so allow me to complete Mr Manager's apology on his behalf – '

'We are done,' snarled Po. He began snatching the papers from the desk. Daniel scrabbled around to stop him.

'Commander Po, please. Mr Manager is clearly suffering from some sort of episode. He's deranged – '

'We are leaving,' said Po. He stuffed the last leaf of the contract into his case and snapped it shut. 'You've made a very grave error.'

Po and the three dignitaries marched for the door.

'Commander Po, please, gentlemen, have another drink, I can assure that we will deal – '

Po swung on his heels.

'You're *finished*,' he said, and left.

The door slammed. The room seemed to grow dark, despite the lights outside. A shadow of rage grew out of the silence, the trembling epicentre of which was Daniel Leafen.

He turned to Steve and lifted his necktie with one finger. His face trembled.

'I suppose, in a way,' he said. 'I ought to admire you. Doing that.'

He gently loosened the knot.

'But I don't. I really don't.'

He pulled the knot free, letting the two ends of the necktie fall apart.

'Steve,' said Daniel. He took one end of the necktie and tore it from Steve's collar. 'You're fired.'

Bluesky led the way out of the cavern. Incentivise supported Ballpark, his hand still clinging to his face. His breathing was low and raspy.

Demetri staggered behind them in a daze. He could feel the

burns on his own face begin to blister and throb. Only the anaesthetic of confusion and fatigue stood in the way of any real pain, although he knew it would eventually break through.

When they found the tunnel, Bluesky stopped and let the other two continue. As they passed, Ballpark looked up at Demetri and gave him a weak, happy smile before returning to his agony.

'Up, up, up the long dark,' said Bluesky. 'To Head Office.'

Demetri looked up the steep, dripping tunnel. Another dim light shone from its top.

She tilted her head and scanned his burns. 'Soresome?' she said.

Demetri touched a finger to his cheek. He flinched as a shot of pain ran through him.

'Yes,' he said.

Bluesky nodded seriously.

'Shit for that. Shit will help.'

She tapped her watch.

'Two spins,' she said. 'Go now.'

'Thank you,' said Demetri.

She pushed her feet together and made a strange salute.

'Kindest regards,' she said, then followed the others.

Demetri watched them cross the tunnel, swaying in the darkness. On the other side, Bluesky turned and gave another salute before closing the door.

Demetri turned and shuffled up the steps. He walked with his head down, trying to bury the ever-growing pain in his cheek. It felt like a naked flame; every step towards the surface of Leafen seemed to fuel it further.

He realised that he had never really felt pain before — nothing more than a nick or a pinch or a twist, minor grazes against the soft walls of his life. Pain felt separate, like distant news or a story that never happened — it existed, but not within his realm.

Not until now at least. It was real — like the pipes through which he was walking, and the people who he now knew lived within them, and the place he had come from, and the place to which he was returning.

Pain swelled. Memory swelled. The void in his head became filled with them both, like screams and whistles in a cave.

As he blundered on, the pain grew fiercer. Every step arrived with a gasp. Occasionally he would look up and see the light, still far away. Then, as he realised that he was looking at a string of drool hanging from his mouth — which meant that he could see, which meant that there was light — he looked up and saw the entrance to the tunnel. It was large and bright and jagged. Around the rim were a hundred other smaller pipes, each feeding down into the shaft. Beyond them was green foliage and a stony cave mouth. He stumbled towards it, tripping on rocks and slipping down a slope onto soft, cool moss. The air smelled sweet. Birdsong and insects warbled from somewhere high above. He looked up and saw the walls of the perimeter, a solid cliff face that dissolved into the Fabrik sky. He lay with his flaming cheek against the wet ground, watching the Fabrik, waiting for it to flicker. But it held like a real sky.

Just like a real sky.

He felt moisture on his brow and the temptation to sleep. As his eyebrows flickered, he reached for his radio and opened a channel. He held it to his mouth and said some words he couldn't fathom, again and again and again.

seventy-six

shirts and scars

'Jola, you were there with the rest of us when it happened. Can you describe how it felt?'

'Oh, man, I can only do my best, you know? I only have so many words. Everyone remembers it differently, I guess. For me, I was enjoying the concert, really getting a huge energy from the music, you know, it was absolutely pumping *there in the Firing stadium –*

'A good gig?'

'The best, man, just the best; I always love playing for my home crowd. But then, it was like it all just drained out of me. The music, the crowd, the lights, the energy; it all just fell away. And then we were standing there, afraid, with no feeling, no thought, nothing. No reason to move. We were alone, but still together somehow. If that's possible…does that make sense?'

'It does, and I'm sure your fans agree. Now, you're releasing a charity single to help with the aftermath, is that right?'

'That's right, Selena. There are still thousands who are in need of care after what happened. The song's called 'The Dark Nothing' and I'm donating at least twenty-five percent of the profits to The Department of Human Resources, who are doing an amazing –'

Alex swept into his bedroom and switched off the screen above his bed.

'You were right, Demetri,' he said, smiling in his mirror as he threaded his brand new necktie — blue and yellow — through his collar. It was his sixteenth birthday and he was just back from his Colours.

Demetri leant against the door frame. It was two weeks since he had emerged from the sewage outlet. He didn't remember much, only waking in the dark to the sound of engines and covering his eyes against the glare of bright headlights. He thought he heard Saul's voice, and April's as he was lifted into a van. He was awake for a while as they drove, looking up at April's face as they plugged drips into him and shone lights in his eyes. *Where's Sam?*, April had said. *Where's my dad?* He had told her. *Red Dog*, he had said. *Red Dog has him.*

A few days later he had woken up surrounded by his family. Alex was closest, leaning over him, happy. His hair was still long; he was still fifteen — yet to have his Colours.

They told him that he was a hero. Almost everyone had been saved, although a few were still recovering, still being tested. Someone who had seen them wake said it was hard to notice the difference. They had blinked, then started to rub their heads, then kept on walking or doing what they had been doing before the strike. It took a day or two to round them all up, to make them understand what had happened, but they did. It had worked.

There had been a ceremony. He, Saul and Turnett were given military status.

'Well done, Trittek,' General Mandrek had said as she had pinned on his badge.

Ruba had been standing next to him in the line, awaiting her own award. She had looked at Demetri in a new way, smiling.

'You were right all along.' Alex grinned. His face looked five years older now with his hair cropped short. He had a lean jaw and bright eyes. Even his spots seemed to have faded. 'I should have listened to you. I was just a young idiot, I guess.'

'What do you mean?' he said.

'Ah, you know, just about life, responsibility and all that crap. My head was filled with ideas before. Now I know my Colours, I know what's important.'

'And what's that?'

Alex began to tie the knot around his neck.

'Focus,' said Alex. 'Understanding my corporation. Being positive about its needs and my place within it. That's what important.'

'What about music?' said Demetri. 'Jola?'

Alex turned to Demetri, smirking. He shook his head and pulled the knot tight.

'Well?' he said. 'How do I look?'

'How do you feel?'

'I feel great.'

'You shouldn't tie that thing so tight.'

Alex's brow flickered and, just for a second, Demetri thought he saw the little boy looking back at him.

'How about you, Miti? How do you feel?'

'I'm fine,' said Demetri.

Alex nodded, then punched his fist twice into his left palm and cracked his knuckles. His Fronds illuminated behind his taut collar.

'What was that?' said Demetri. 'Did you change your signature?'

'Yeah, they let you do that now, didn't you know? Just once when you get your Colours. The old one was childish.'

'I liked it,' said Demetri. 'It was – it was you.'

'OK, gotta go downstairs now. Party waiting and all that. Ma said Grandpa has a present for me. Are you coming?'

'I have to go to the doctor's first.'

'Finally getting your Fronds back? That's cool, bro.'

Alex patted him on the shoulder as he passed, leaving Demetri alone and looking back at himself in the mirror. His scar was bright.

Later, Demetri lay back and counted the square tiles on the ceiling of the examination room. It was cool and the shades were drawn. Enola Perez was busying herself with various pieces of equipment in the far corner. Eventually he heard her heels on the stone floor.

'So, we're going for a full reset. Your Fronds will be synaptically disconnected and then connected. You're going to need to choose a new signature.'

'Oh,' said Demetri. 'Can we change it back again once they're fixed?'

'Afraid not.'

'Huh.'

'It's quite normal for people to become attached to their signatures.'

'It's fine.'

Enola walked to the door.

'I need to get something. Think of something you can remember, and something that you'll be comfortable with for the rest of your life.'

She left the room.

Demetri turned to the desk, upon which a little girl was sitting playing with a doll.

'Hey, Lori,' he said. 'How are you?'

Lori looked up and nodded, then looked back at her doll. He watched her for a while.

'What was it like?' he said.

'When I was asleep?' she said, not looking up.

'Yeah, when you were asleep.'

Lori studied her doll's face and stroked its hair.

'It was like I was in a different place. Outside. Like a field.'

Enola returned carrying a small white stick.

'Are you OK, sweetheart?' she said.

'Yes, Mama.'

Enola smiled.

'Do you have something?' she said, turning to Demetri.

'I think so.'

'Good, so I'm going to hold this against your left temple and I want you to perform the original signature ten times. Then I'll move to your right temple and you perform your new signature ten times. OK?'

'That's it? That's all I have to do?'

'That's all. Are you ready?'

'Ready as I'll ever be.'

'OK, stand up.'

He got up off the bed.

'Look into my eyes,' she said, placing the stick against Demetri's left temple.

'Now, the original signature, ten times. A second's gap between each one.'

Demetri tapped two fingers twice on his left shoulder, paused and repeated nine times. When he had finished, Enola removed the stick and swapped it to her left hand, pressing against his opposite temple.

'Now the new signature,' she said.

Demetri faltered, feeling his right hand rise instinctively to his left shoulder.

'This is weird,' he said.

'I know, it's OK.'

He felt a tremble of loss, the wide-eyed urge to leap after something cherished. It was as if something far within was being thrown into an abyss.

'It's hard,' he said, like a child seeking comfort.

'It's OK,' she repeated. 'Take your time.'

Demetri swallowed. He didn't do what he thought he was going to do, which was to trace a circle on his palm. Instead, he closed his eyes and pressed his palm against his nose, wobbling it like Alex used to. He had the feeling of letting a child's hand go in a crowd, losing him forever. He repeated the signature nine more times. By the last one, he was weeping.

April pulled up at the perimeter and let her bike's engines run while she dialled Christine.

'You there, honey?' said Christine.

'Yeah, right on the edge.'

'Did you get seen?'

'No, I didn't see any drones. Everyone's focused on The Firing. Are we good to go?'

'I'm good this end,' said Christine. There was a pause. 'Look, are you sure you want to do this?'

'He's on his own and there's no rescue party.'

'You shouldn't be going out there alone.'

'I have to. You know I have to.'

Christine sighed.

'I know, I know. It's just – it's such a risk.'

'Look, Chrissie, I understand if you don't want to do this. I know that you could get in trouble.'

'Trouble?' said Christine. 'I don't give a shit about trouble. It's you I'm worried about. Besides, five seconds of downtime on the Fabrik won't even register, especially after what's happened. It's still unstable. And I've got my guys keeping the diagnostics on low for a while.'

'OK. Good.' April put her helmet back on.

'I'm going to be watching you, all right?' said Christine. 'We have cameras all through the Hordes, drones too. Try to use them to communicate if you can. I've set up a facial recognition scan for you on the system — whenever you appear on camera, I'll get an alert. OK?'

'Yes. I'm ready. Let's go.'

April heard Christine take a long breath.

'OK,' she said on the out breath. 'You'll get five seconds to pass through. The Fabrik will break in ten. Starting from now.'

April kicked the stand and revved as Christine counted down. Her rear tyre skidded in the dirt and she pulled away, straight for the edge. She was a few feet from it when the air around her shuddered and the light opened up. Then she was through and away, hearing the air thunder behind her as the Fabrik closed again. She turned a hard right and sped north on new dirt, heading straight for the Hordes.

Steve Manager was led along a dark corridor of cells — one of many such corridors in a maze beneath The Firing stadium. Almost every cell was occupied. Men and women prayed on beds, paced the stone floors or shouted from the bars for their freedom. Families huddled together, children were comforted, heads stroked, their faces weeping in the gloom.

'It's busy,' said the guard. 'You'll have to share.'

They stopped while the guard jangled his keys and opened the cell door, pushing Steve in. The door slammed shut and he leant on the bars, listening to the guard's whistles above the hysterical murmurs and wails.

'We must stop meeting in such dark places,' said a voice behind him.

He turned and saw a man in the shadows, hunched over on the bed. A shaft of light fell upon his ruddy face, a single bright eye illuminated, twinkling.

'Father Roberts?' said Steve.

'Hello, Steve,' said the priest.

Steve dropped his bag and slumped down on the floor opposite the bed.

'What is this, some kind of confession? Last rites?'

Roberts lifted his wrists into the light, showing Steve the chains around them.

'What happened?' said Steve.

Roberts raised his eyebrows.

'I suppose you could say I *stood up*,' he said. 'You?'

'That about covers it.'

A million voices suddenly roared from the stadium above. Cell doors clanged a few corridors away, guards shouting above the desperate pleas of their inhabitants.

'How long?' said Steve.

'Minutes.'

Steve looked through the bars. He could just make out a triangle of blue sky through the vent in the opposite wall. Roberts sighed and sat back.

'Funny thing. Memories seem to jump sometimes. One minute you're running up the steps to a church with your whole life ahead of you, then you're standing in the rain on the same steps, looking down at a man you've just laid out.'

'Who?' said Steve.

'Loome.'

'You really did stand up then.'

'Yup,' sighed Roberts, rubbing his knees. 'And now I'm in here.'

'Did you take much?'

'A few things, keepsakes, things to trade. And this, of course.'

He held up the silver 'A' around his neck.

'It feels odd to still be wearing it. I'm not really sure what it means any more.'

'What it means might just save your life. Superstitions run high out there.'

The priest nodded, then gestured at Steve's bag.

'What about you? Doesn't look like you took much.'

Steve took a box from the bag and flipped its lid – inside was the rusted compass Granton had given him.

'No, nothing much. Did you get to see anyone? Family? Friends?'

Roberts shrugged.

'My family was The Church. You?

'My mother.'

'Will she be all right?'

'They took her house.'

'Why?'

'Because I paid for it.'

'Where will she live?'

'The place I grew up. I think she prefers it there anyway. Besides, it's not the first time this has happened.'

'Who else?'

'My father, when I was a boy.'

'Do you think he's still out there? I mean, I didn't…I'm sorry.'

'That's all right. I guess we'll find out.'

'Hey, I'll look after you. I mean – ' he plucked at his pendant. 'As much as this allows me to. We'll stick together, OK?'

'Sure.'

There was another roar from above.

'Can't be long now,' said Roberts.

There were footsteps on the concrete corridor — heels advancing. Steve jumped up, smelling Faith's perfume before he saw her.

'What are you doing?' he whispered, looking up and down the corridor. 'How did you get down here?'

'I'm the president's PA. I have perks.'

She checked back the way she came.

'But I don't have much time. Take this.'

She pushed a long, heavy package through the bars.

'What is it?'

'The gun from your office. I thought it might come in useful.'

'I'm not allowed to take a gun.'

'So hide it.'

'This thing's centuries old. I don't even know if it fires. It doesn't have ammunition.'

'You'll find some. That whole place is built from the past.'

'It's too long, they'll see.'

'They won't.'

She stepped forwards and held the bars.

'Nobody cares, Steve.'

'Nobody?' said Steve.

'Almost nobody.'

She twisted her head and kissed him through the bars.

'I'm going to help you,' she said, and left.

Another roar. The clang of cell doors opening nearby.

Roberts scrabbled to his feet.

'Here we go.'

In the president's box, Priscilla stood tall in her crimson, leather dress. Daniel stood at the railing, looking out at the proceedings.

'They're cheering for you, you know?' she said.

'Do you think?' replied Daniel.

'They love you.'

'How much?'

'Your Like count doubled overnight. You've more Agrees after this morning's address than any other president this century…'

'More than my old man?'

'Easily. And your reviews have shot up. 67% four and five star.'

'What about the rest?'

'Mostly 2s and 3s. Some 1s.'

'Anonymous?'

'Yes.'

'Did you trace them?'

'Of course.'

'Good.'

'As far as they're concerned, you stood up to Soor, Daniel. You're a hero.'

She threaded her fingertips between his as they watched the long line of fired employees traipse across the great plain of the stadium towards the gate.

'Can you see Sumar?' she said.

'He's at the end,' said Daniel. He pointed at a stumbling

figure on his own near the back. 'There.'

'He looks lost, poor thing,' said Priscilla.

Daniel turned his face up to her.

'Priss,' he said. 'You little pussycat. Are you feeling sorry for him?'

Priscilla smiled. Then she laughed. And she didn't stop laughing for a very long time.

Somewhere in the middle of the line, Steve and Father Roberts stumbled, cuffed, towards the gate. A full crowd cheered around them, their taunts as sharp as the heat from the blazing midday sun.

A deep siren blared and the line stopped. The great gate began to open.

Roberts' knees buckled.

'What do we do?' he said.

Steve helped him up.

'Like you said, we stick together. We stick together.'

seventy-seven

the market

AS ALWAYS, the Sweep came the day after The Firing. Most of the population didn't feel like a party — not after what had happened — so they went home, put up the protective panels and bunkered down to celebrate with whatever traditions they had. Couples ate by candlelight, bachelors and bachelorettes gathered together and drank through the night, families sat in the dark by fires and told made-up stories about monkeys, wars and the Underfolk who lived in a far-away sewer.

The next day Daniel Leafen stood in the board room and looked out at the bright, sunlit view of his world. It was a very different view from the one he had had the day before. He turned from the window and watched Ely Loome, who was beside the redwood table, head bowed solemnly and hands together as his Fronds glowed.

'What happened to your face?' said Daniel. He punched the air twice and winked. 'You been doing a spot of boxing?'

Loome looked up, touching a finger to his bruised nose.

'Nothing,' he said, smiling sweetly. 'It matters not. Sir, we have attained a connection. Are you ready to proceed?'

Daniel dropped his smile.

'Yes,' he said. 'I'm ready.'

'Very well,' said Loome. 'You are online with The Market in 5 – 4 – 3 – 2 – '

'Daniel!' boomed a cheery voice over the board room speakers. 'Daniel, Daniel, Daniel, Danny, Danny, Danny, *Dan.* So good to speak to you. So good, so good.'

Daniel swallowed.

'Your Excellency,' he said. 'Thank you for speaking with me. I trust you are – er – well?'

There was a pause, a digital crackle and beep, before the voice erupted into a high, fruity laugh.

'Ha ha ha ha! Oh, very good, Danny, very good. Yes, I am, I suppose, er "well" as you put it. At least as "well" as something like me could be said to be, you understand?'

'Yes, I was just, you know, trying to be friendly.'

'*Friendly*,' repeated the voice, as if it was the first time it had heard the word. 'Friendly, yes. We must always be *friendly*, as you say.'

'Yes, Your Excellency.'

The voice tittered.

'*Your Excellency*, get you, tosh, tosh. Now listen, Daniel, you know what I am, don't you?'

'Yes,' said Daniel. 'At least I think – '

'You know I'm not *actually* The Market, don't you? At least, not fully.'

'I think so,' said Daniel.

'Think so, yes, very good, but just to be sure, I'll tell you. I'm a conduit, a stand-in, a voice, a *proxy* if you will, I speak on behalf of The Market. I am not really The Market. I am the Archetype.'

'Yes, I – '

'I am an extremely powerful artificial intelligence system that has been improved and built over many centuries.'

'I under – '

'I am not a human being.'

'Yes, I gathered – '

'I am a – program, I suppose.'

'I – '

'But then, aren't we all, Danny? Aren't we, in fact, all?'

'I suppose – '

'Now — and this is interesting, Danny — having said what I have just said, I *do* know all that The Market knows and I *do* know all that The Market expects, and I also know all that The

Market demands. So in many ways, to you, Daniel Leafen, *Danny, Dan* – I am, indeed, The Market. The Market which is all around us, which is much bigger than everything you see, much more powerful, much more knowing, much more understanding, much more – *caring*. The force which drives the planet, the species, perhaps even the universe itself. A divine thing. A deep thing. A holy thing. Yes?'

Daniel tapped his feet.

'Truth be told, Your Excellency, I'm not very religious.'

Daniel heard Loome inhale sharply behind him.

'Yes,' said the voice. 'Yes, well, there's a lot of that about at the moment, I hear. Still, not to worry, whether you believe in it or not, The Market will always, always believe in you. And Daniel?'

'Yes, Your Excellency?'

'Please don't be curt. Now, tell me, what's going on with you? How are you? The Firing go all right, hmm?'

'Yes, thank you. Quite a large one this year. A few miscreants and that.'

'Yeees, yeees, I can well imagine, after what happened and all. Terrible business.'

'It was, Your Excellency.'

'Still, these things have a habit of sorting out the wheat from the chaff, eh?'

'They do, Your Excellency.'

'The men from the boys.'

'Yes.'

'The meat from the fat.'

'Aha.'

'The cream from the milk.'

'– '

'And the Sweep, Danny, how was that? Everything to your liking? Did my little Mites do a good job for Leafen this year?'

'Well,' sighed Daniel. 'That's what I wanted to speak with you about.'

'Oh?'

'Yes. Things seem a little – different.'

'Yes. Yes, well they would, wouldn't they?'

'We appear to be more — how can I put this — *fortified*.'

'Fortified, yes, yes.' The voice sounded as if it belonged to somebody leafing idly through papers on their desk.

'There are guns on our buildings.'

'Guns, yes.'

'Lots. And on our perimeter.'

'Perimeter, indeed.'

'And surrounding our airports.'

'Yeeeesss.'

'And our Fabrik is now military grade.'

'Mmhmm, mmhmm.'

There was silence. Daniel tapped his foot.

'Why?'

'Why?' said the voice. 'I'm sorry, I don't understand.'

'Why? Why do we look like we've been armed for war?'

'Well, because *war* is what you are about to undertake.'

Daniel's chest tightened.

'What?' he said, teeth gritted.

'*War*, Danny. Dan.'

'Look, I know the deal with Soor turned sour, but that doesn't mean we can't rebuild things with them. You must know, it was down to a stupid mistake, a rogue executive with mental health issues who is now, thankfully, being *fucked* somewhere deep in the Hordes.'

There was a pause. Daniel thought he heard a tut.

'Daniel, really,' said the voice. 'There's no need for that. Now come on, you mustn't be upset and you have to understand. That deal with Soor, it was never really – well – ' the voice tailed off.

'Never really what?' said Daniel.

'It was never going to *stack up*, I'm afraid. The union between the two corporations. It wouldn't have been good for the economy. Not good for The Market. Not good for poor old me.'

'Why not?' snapped Daniel.

'Now, now, Daniel, you're getting upset again, calm down.'

'I'm sorry,' said Daniel. His jaw shook as he tried to gain some composure. 'Please explain why not.'

The voice cleared a throat that did not exist. There was a pause.

'I wouldn't expect you to understand,' it said.

'Try me,' said Daniel.

'No. It's far too complicated. What's not complicated is that war is always, always, *always* good for the economy.'

Daniel breathed out and closed his eyes. He let his brow fall against the window.

'Daniel? Are you there?'

'Yes,' he said. He rolled his head so that his cheek pressed against the glass and he met Loome's terrified eyes. 'Tell me what happens next.'

'Good. I shall. You shall keep the teleportation technology that was promised to Soor.'

The air from Daniel's nose clouded the glass in front of him.

'Project Spoke. Yes, Your Excellency.'

'You shall not enter into any more negotiations with them.'

'Yes, Your Excellency.'

'And then, you shall prepare to be attacked.'

Daniel closed his eyes.

'Yes, Your Excellency.'

'Good. Oh, and Daniel?'

'Yes, Your Excellency?'

'Please, do call me Robert.'

FROM THE AUTHOR

THANKS FOR reading *Colours,* I really hope you enjoyed it. If you could spare the time, I'd be very grateful if you could post a review on Amazon or Goodreads. And feel free to let me know what you think in person by dropping me an email at adrian@adrianjwalker.com - I'd be happy to hear from you.

You can also sign up for my newsletter here:

http://www.adrianjwalker.com/colours

I'll send you exclusive short stories, some of which feature characters from this book. You'll also find out the *second* a new book is published, including part two of *Earth Incorporated.*

Thanks again for reading.

Adrian

THE END OF THE WORLD RUNNING CLUB

THE ULTIMATE RACE AGAINST TIME THRILLER

When the world ends and you find yourself stranded on the wrong side of the country, every second counts.

No one knows this more than Edgar Hill. 550 miles away from his family, he must push himself to the very limit to get back to them, or risk losing them forever...

His best option is to run.

But what if your best isn't good enough?

Praise for *The End of the World Running Club*:

"Ridiculously gripping straight from the start" (Jenny Colgan)

"Will thrill and delight ... a terrifically well-observed, haunting and occasionally harrowing read" (*Starburst*)

"A page-turning thriller with a pace as relentless as the characters' feet hitting the pavement. A deft look into the mind of a man who needs the near-destruction of the world to show him what truly matters" (Laura Lam *author of False Hearts*)

"A really fun, engaging, exciting, and compassionate take on a familiar scenario: the apocalypse ... Highly recommended" (David Owen *Carnegie longlisted author of Panther*)

"Brilliant ... superb to the end" (Lucy Mangan)

Out now on Del Rey.

ACKNOWLEDGEMENTS

ALL CHARACTERS appearing in this work are fictitious. Any resemblance to real persons, living or dead, is purely coincidental.

ISBN-10: 1533536813

ISBN-13: 978-1533536815

38191017R00292

Printed in Great Britain
by Amazon